WORLD IN A GLASS

WORLD
IN A GLASS

a view of our century
selected from the novels
of

JOHN DOS PASSOS

with an introductory essay
by
KENNETH S. LYNN

HOUGHTON MIFFLIN COMPANY BOSTON
THE RIVERSIDE PRESS CAMBRIDGE

Second Printing R

Introduction

LIKE Thorstein Veblen, "Fighting Bob" La Follette, and the
other lonely men whom he honors in *U.S.A.* for their "constitutional inability to say yes" to the dominant doctrines of
the American mind, John Dos Passos has never been afraid
to be different. In the era of laissez-faire capitalism his fic-
tional spokesmen drank champagne toasts to "Revolution,
to Anarchy, to the Socialist State"; with the dawn of the
welfare economy they switched to the individualistic insist-
ence that "if we want to straighten the people out we've got
to start with number one"; future social changes will doubt-
less engender further disagreements between Mr. Dos Passos's voices and the *vox populi.* Yet to illustrate the intran-
sigence of this Ishmaelite by examples of his political
waywardness is merely to scratch the surface of his prickly
genius. At heart, his formidable independence is a literary
matter, and always has been. Alone of all our modern novelists, and in the face of a critical wisdom which has endlessly reiterated that American writers should stick to telling us about the particular cornpatch in which they were
raised, Dos Passos has persisted for almost fifty years in his
determination to catch both a continent and a century in the
camera eye of his fiction — to project upon a panoramic
screen so many varieties of American experience that they
would constitute, when taken together, a comprehensive record of life in the United States since 1900. Like Whitman,
whose *Leaves* he read and loved "as a kid," Dos Passos has
endeavored to enfold an entire democracy within his vision
— sailors and salesmen, bums and bankers, mechanics and
mannequins, prostitutes and poets; and like Gibbon, whose
Decline and Fall he came to admire in his college days, he
has tried to trace Time's corruption of the world's most

powerful empire. He has wished, in sum, to "tell all." If he has not quite succeeded in doing so (one finds, for example, next to nothing about Negro life in Dos Passos), his failures merely point up the unprecedented magnitude of the task he long ago set himself — and the unclassifiable grandeur of what he has now achieved.

The first real evidence of the largeness of Dos Passos's vision was *Three Soldiers* (1921). In a brilliant act of synthesis, he combined the Stephen Crane kind of war story, in which the horrors of the battlefield are set in ironic contrast against the manufactured romanticism of patriotic slogans, with the Jamesian story of young Americans abroad whose New World innocence is tested and shaken by the confrontation with Old World sophistication — and thereby established the form that the American war novel has followed ever since. Not only Faulkner's apprentice novel, *Soldier's Pay* (1926), which was written in naked imitation, and Hemingway's *A Farewell to Arms* (1929), whose account of how Frederic Henry makes his separate peace was obviously indebted to Dos Passos's story of John Andrews's disastrous defection, but all the World War II novels which show American soldiers emerging from their baptism in fire to encounter further initiations in the arms of Neapolitan street girls and Japanese geishas hark back to *Three Soldiers*. Dos Passos's pioneering book was also the first to emphasize the polyglot make-up of the modern American army and the first to acknowledge the intramural tensions between the conscripted sons of the old and new immigrations (an acknowledgment which Dos Passos was peculiarly fitted to make, for his mother was the descendant of a distinguished Maryland family and his father the offspring of a Portuguese immigrant), while the technical device he employed to accomplish these things — i.e., dividing the narrative focus among three soldiers of widely differing geographical and social backgrounds — has not merely received the flattery of frequent imitation, it has become one of the most resounding clichés of contemporary fiction.

The imaginative freshness and trail-blazing originality of *Three Soldiers* have been manifested again and again in the course of Dos Passos's career. For in addition to goading him into a ceaseless productivity, his ambition to tell the entire story of twentieth-century America has inspired him to remain a continuously inventive author, forever anxious to extend the lines of literary inquiry into new areas of the national experience. In *Number One* (1943), for example, he portrayed a demagogue who was not only a savage reincarnation of the late Huey Long, but a symbol, of the widest general significance, of the suspicions and the resentments which have always smoldered at the secret heart of the populist personality. No serious American writer had previously had the wit — or the courage — to depict the irrational behavior to which such feelings could lead (except Frank Norris, and Norris had reveled in the xenophobia he uncovered), and when Robert Penn Warren took up the "case" of the Louisiana Kingfish a few years after Dos Passos, he was more interested in its metaphysical than its political implications. Finally, in the 1950's, a number of historians and sociologists undertook to study the psychology of populism as a means of explaining McCarthyism; but while these left-liberal social scientists never suggested that they were indebted to a Taft-Republican novelist, the fact remains that their analyses did little more than retrace the behavioral pattern Dos Passos had delineated a decade before. (The only original element in the social scientists' argument was their apparent belief that city folk never hate as vehemently as their country cousins; further study of Dos Passos could have taught them differently.)

By the time other students of the American scene were concerning themselves with the dynamics of American Fascism, Dos Passos had moved on to the even more tricky and painful subject of home-grown Communism. *Most Likely to Succeed* (1954) is probably the bitterest book Dos Passos ever wrote, but it is as illuminating as it is excoriating. Whereas other writers with left-wing memories have spent most of their energies on summoning up remembrances of the 1930's, Dos Passos's novel shows that the Depression years tell only half the story. With his characteristically wide-angled perspective on the past, Dos Passos conceived of the whole interwar period as a continuity, and *Most Likely to Succeed* is a devastating demonstration of how the ferocious leftist infighting in the off-Broadway theatrical world of the 1920's was the perfect sort of training for later survival in the lawless jungle of the Hollywood studios; of how the irresponsible bohemianism of private lives in

Greenwich Village easily led to the deer-park ambiance of the Pacific Slopes; of how Communism could initially appeal to a conceited young man as the political expression of his contemptuously anti-bourgeois aesthetic — and then become a desperate guarantee against guilt feelings after artistic honor has been sold for a mess of movie dollars. By connecting the sickness of the thirties with the infections of the twenties, by understanding the inhumanities of Communism as the consequence of the decay of traditional American values, Dos Passos's bitter book opens up the meaning of a dark and baffling period in American history as no other novel, historical analysis, or ex-radical "confessional" has ever done.

Impressive, however, as such special studies as *Number One* and *Most Likely to Succeed* may be, and as poignant as are the autobiographical recollections in *Chosen Country* (1951) and *The Great Days* (1958), the core of the Dos Passos canon, and the basis of his claim to greatness, consists of the five books which move across the entire range of the American social spectrum, the generous, inclusive books which recall Whitman's relish of variety and Gibbon's sensitivity to social change: *Manhattan Transfer* (1925), the three volumes of *U.S.A.* (1930–1936), and *Midcentury* (1960).

Thematically, *Manhattan Transfer* falls squarely in the center of an important literary succession: on the one hand, it looks back to William Dean Howells's panoramic survey of the New York scene in *A Hazard of New Fortunes* (1890); on the other hand, it anticipates Thomas Wolfe's gargantuan evocations of Brooklyn and Manhattan in *Of Time and the River* (1935) and *You Can't Go Home Again* (1940). But stylistically *Manhattan Transfer* is utterly unlike these novels. Dos Passos's prose lacks the density, the marvelous piling-up of detail, that makes the reader of Howells and Wolfe feel that his senses are all but directly in contact with the sights, sounds, and smells of the metropolis. The style of *Manhattan Transfer* has altogether different qualities, which are as special with Dos Passos as his signature, and which lend to the book an excitement equaled by no other New York novel ever written. With a jagged, broken rhythm that Dos Passos apparently absorbed from his fascination with the movies, the camera eye of the novel ranges restlessly across the city, swooping in for a "shot" and then moving out again, cutting abruptly from the barge captain who is exasperated at having to fish Bud Korpenning's lifeless body out of the river, to the bizarre inhabitants of the theatrical boardinghouse where the unhappy young actress Ellen Thatcher lives, to the ruined "Wizard of Wall Street" cadging whiskey money on the Bowery; from the sound of a newborn baby squalling in a hospital, to the unctuous patter of a real estate agent, to a quarrel between an overwrought Jewish girl and her immigrant mother ("But Rosie, married life ain't all beer and skittles. A vife must submit and work for her husband." ". . . But I ain't a Jew no more," screeched the young girl. "This aint Russia; it's little old New York."). In these strange, hurried scenarios there are no portraits-in-depth, no leisurely evocations of atmosphere, only a split-second responsiveness to the sensuous details of a fleeting image, a beautiful alertness to the nuances of all voices, whether heard or overheard ("the mind of a generation," Dos Passos once wrote, "is its speech"), and an instinct for the jugular in every human situation, no matter how briefly described — while over all the fragments of frenzied lives of which the novel is composed there presides a historical consciousness of a more haunting, more implacable movement: the blind tumbling-forward of everyone and everything down the stream of Time. Thus Dos Passos's camera eye is not only constantly switching focus in any given day, it is also forever scanning forward from today to tomorrow — from the era when there were still empty lots on Broadway ("where tin cans glittered among grass and sumach bushes and ragweed, between ranks of billboards and Bull Durham signs") to the time when a line of cheap hotels has filled up the street (such as the tawdry place where Anna the dressmaker gives the out-of-town buyer "a good time"); from the period when George Baldwin was an ambulance-chasing lawyer to his emergence as a "reform" politician; from Congo Jake the hard-up sailor to Congo Jake the affluent bootlegger. The fire engines that are recurrently heard or seen racing through the crowded streets were intended by Dos Passos to be his leading symbol of the fast-moving, exhilaratingly beautiful, and stupefyingly frightening city that owns them, but in fact the most meaningful emblem of Manhattan in *Manhattan Transfer*, and the quality that makes the book the most original work of American fiction of the 1920's, is the darting, hectic, haunted mode of the narration. The style of the novel is New York — or as close to it, at any rate, as any writer has ever come.

In *U.S.A.* Dos Passos raised his sights from a city to a nation, and much later in *Midcentury* he repeated the effort. Unlike *Manhattan Transfer*, these books cannot be compared to any purpose with the work of other writers. Novelistically, they are *sui generis*; indeed, in their dazzling mixture of biography and fiction, of poetry and social documentary, of autobiographical reminiscence and mass-cult pastiche, they at least partially transcend the novel-form, creating a kind of literature so radically new that it is still unnamed, and that may very well have had more of a technical influence on the way American history is now written (Oscar Handlin's *The Americans* is a recent example of the Dos Passos methodology) than it has on the literary practice of even the most experimental of younger novelists. But if it is difficult to pin an appropriate label on these incomparable books — to decide, once and for all, whether we should call them epics or novels or "contemporary chronicles" — there is no doubt that they cover the ground of our twentieth-century experience as more orthodox storytelling could never have done.

The first and foremost purpose of Dos Passos's experimentation in *U.S.A.* was to record a language. As the author observes at the very outset of the trilogy, "mostly U.S.A. is the speech of the people." The literary ambition implicit in that statement represents the ultimate extension of the prefatory note to *Huckleberry Finn*, wherein Mark Twain lays claim to the linguistic accuracy of the various dialects employed in the book, and of all subsequent attempts by Hamlin Garland, Mary Wilkins Freeman, Stephen Crane, Ernest Hemingway, Sinclair Lewis, and a host of other writers to make American literary expression a registration of the American language. While not blessed with as perfect pitch as some of his colleagues (one recalls, for example, Ring Lardner's unbeatable renditions of "Midwestern Mastoid"), Dos Passos has been willing to listen in more places than they have. *U.S.A.* is, consequently, a veritable anthology of the American idiom — of Texas drawl, Harvard broad "a," and immigrant pidgin; of middle-class female twaddle and proletarian male coarseness; of popular songs, advertising slogans, and fragments from the yellow press. Furthermore, the time-span of the trilogy covers the thirty years from Admiral Dewey's invasion of the Philippines to the stock-market crash of 1929, and the texture of Dos Passos's prose continually adapts to the thousands of alterations, some of them subtle, some of them blatant, which American expression underwent during this period. When we meet Doc Bingham at the beginning of the first volume, the extraordinarily versatile and florid lingo which he brings to his salesmanship of dirty books and religious tracts makes him sound like the last of the old-time confidence men — like the younger brother, perhaps, of the fraudulent King who made life hell for Huck Finn and Nigger Jim; but when we encounter Bingham again, toward the end of the third volume, he is pushing a health-fad "philosophy" which sounds remarkably like the pseudo-scientific nutritional pitch that lifted Bernarr Macfadden to fame and wealth in the 1920's. The permutations in political oratory, from the grandiloquent imperialism of Albert J. Beveridge to the highfalutin idealism of Woodrow Wilson to the crassly provincial realism of Calvin Coolidge, offer equally rich contrasts, as do the changing manners of sexual invitation — especially as exemplified by the disingenuous chatter of Annabelle Marie Strang in the summer of 1909 and the flippancies favored by Margo Dowling twenty years later. Out of his sensitivity to linguistic changes, Dos Passos created in U.S.A. not only an anthology, but a morphology of modern American speech. Out of his awareness that such changes were the sounds made by a culture in the process of a profound upheaval, he wrote an anatomy of money, of power, and of sex — of the great American themes which Henry Adams found so fascinating and wished someone would write about (characteristically, Adams was doomed to disappointment, for he died just as Dos Passos's career was getting underway). If, in Dos Passos's own words, the writer who gets "the words and phrases . . . straight . . . is the architect of history," then the author of U.S.A. is the grand designer of our twentieth-century past.

Midcentury is in its own right a fascinating book. By a similar diversification of narrative techniques, it evokes the period 1945–1960 as effectively as *U.S.A.* summons forth an earlier era. But *Midcentury* becomes even more fascinating when it is read in conjunction with the trilogy it so closely resembles — when it is listened to as if it were the coda to a great American symphony. For in doing so we gain a unique understanding of what has happened to us as a people in the course of a fantastic century. *U.S.A.*, for example, unfolds saga after saga of how poor boys made their way from rags to riches:

> Samuel Insull landed in America on a raw March day in eightyone. Immediately he was taken out to Menlo Park, shown about the little group of laboratories, saw the strings of electriclightbulbs shining at intervals across the snowy lots, all lit from the world's first central electric station. Edison put him right to work and he wasn't through till midnight. Next morning at six he was on the job; Edison had no use for any nonsense about hours or vacations. Insull worked from that time on until he was seventy without a break; no nonsense about hours or vacations. Electric power turned the ladder into an elevator.

But *Midcentury* introduces us to a new kind of American success story, in which self-indulgence has replaced ruthlessness as the golden key:

> In the drab summer desert of New York, James Dean lacked friends; he lacked girls, he lacked dough;
> but when the chance came he knew how to grab it: a young director took an interest, invited him out sailing on a sloop on the Sound — farmboy turned deckhand — gave him a part in a show which immediately flopped;
> but he'd been seen on the stage. Next he played the blackmailing Arab in a dramatization of André Gide's *The Immoraliste*. He walked out on the part, the play closed, but he'd been seen by people who knew show business: rave writeups: he was an actor.
> They took him on to study at the Actor's Studio. The Actor's Studio was celebrity's lobby in those days. That year Marlon Brando was the artistic idol of the screen.

Directors saw a young Brando in Dean (the hepcat school, sideburns and a rat's nest for hair, leather jackets, jackboots and a motorcycle at the curb. These are tough guys, delinquents; but sensitive: Great God how they're sensitive). Elia Kazan hired him to play a sinister adolescent: "Live the part," Stanislavski told his actors.

Dean did just that. He was obstreperous as hell. "I can't divert into being a social human being," he snarled at the reporters through the butt that dangled from his lip, "when I'm working on a hero who's essentially demonic."

Demonic, but lovable under it all.

The sinister adolescent was box office. Long before the picture was released he was besieged by Hollywood agents, promoters, feature writers, photographers.

As late as the 1920's, the world of science had been comprehensible to the mind of the layman:

NEWLY DESIGNED GEARS AFFORDING NOT
ONLY GREATER STRENGTH AND LONGER
LIFE BUT INCREASED SMOOTHNESS

NEW CLUTCH — AN ENGINEERING
ACHIEVEMENT THAT ADDS WONDERFUL
POSITIVENESS TO POWER TRANSMISSION
THAT MAKES GEARSHIFTING EASY AND
NOISELESS

But by the end of the Second World War, scientific talk had become disturbingly, even frighteningly, strange:

*at a few degrees above absolute zero the application
even of a small electric field to a sample of germanium
will grossly affect equilibrium of the conduction of elec-
trons and increase their average energy by a factor of
twenty five or more*

The lines of connection (and contrast) can be endlessly projected: from the Cape Cod cottage to the split-level ranch; from the anodyne of bootleg booze to the tranquilization of the Miltown; from the naïve enthusiasms of advertising's infancy ("WE FEEL VERY FRIENDLY TOWARDS THE TYPEWRITER USERS OF NEW YORK CITY") to the hidden-persuader techniques of Madison Avenue ("IF YOU KNOW THE WOMAN WHO SHOULD HAVE THIS CAR . . . you must admire her very much. She never tries to impress . . . it isn't necessary. She never 'makes an entrance,' yet, somehow, people turn when she comes into a room. If she's impatient, it's only with pretension. If she's proud, it's mostly of being a woman. She's gentle, durable . . . and intensely feminine . . ."); from a solitary, penniless young man named Vag, walking down a road in quest of the just America of his dreams, to that merciless parody of Holden Caulfield named Stan Goodspeed, who loads up with his uncle's credit cards and takes off in search of kicks and chicks. Time, in Dos Passos, is a tissue of ironies.

The ironies are by no means restricted to what the observer has observed, these many years, for Time has also had its effect upon Dos Passos — thereby lending a further fascination to his best books. *U.S.A.* was informed by the idea that Big Business was the chief threat to individual freedom in America, whereas *Midcentury* insists that Big Labor is the power which threatens our liberties. (For all his admiration of Veblen, it took Dos Passos many years to learn the master's bitter lesson that the workers, too, are corruptible.) Yet for all the anti-union indignation that *Midcentury* generates, the book is not nearly as dogmatic in its conservatism as the trilogy was in its radicalism, because Dos Passos is today a humbler and a more troubled man than he was thirty years ago. In the early novels, Dos Passos's typical hero was a young man full of passionate intensities — like Martin Howe in *One Man's Initiation* (1920), or the Harvardman, Wendell, in *Streets of Night* — a young man who was avant-garde in his art and radical in his politics, and who believed that if we could but escape from the past, wipe the slate clean, we could build a better world. This burning belief, which is significantly protected against the acid of the author's otherwise pervasive scorn, towers into a pillar of fire in the three volumes of *U.S.A.* Evil institutions, these books proclaim, must be brought to judgment; Walt Whitman's "storybook democracy" will arise again only by a total reconstitution of society; history, in a word, must go. Thus Dos Passos entered the labyrinth of our twentieth-century past in order to prepare the way for the demolition teams. But the act of recapturing Time had an unexpected effect upon him. Critics who have written about Dos Passos's journey to Spain during the Civil War, and who point to his shocking discovery while there of how ruthlessly the Communists were undercutting their supposed allies within the Popular Front as the operative cause of his disillusionment with radicalism, miss the point; the central experience in Dos Passos's political education in the early 1930's was the titanic labor of creating *U.S.A.* The trilogy changed the man who wrote it, inducing in him a new respect for "the ground we stand on," a new awareness of historical continuity, a new appreciation of the complexities of human motivation. History was not escapable, after all, nor was it as simple as it had seemed.

In the novels after *U.S.A.* we no longer look at American life through the eyes of a fervent and iconoclastic young man; we view men and events through the bloodshot vision of Tyler Spotswood in *Number One* or Ro Lancaster in *The Great Days.* There are no passionate intensities in these men's lives, unless it be the nauseating memory of earlier mistakes: last night's drunk is over, and now the morning after is full upon them, with all its physical and mental punishments. Their hangovers are the symbols of Dos Passos's troubled consciousness, his anguished appreciation of how difficult it is to understand the times we live in. The battle-cry of *U.S.A.* — "all right we are two nations" — evokes the certainty of the younger author's mind, while the title Dos Passos gives to his *Midcentury* sketch of J. Robert Oppenheimer — "The Uncertainty Principle" — indicates the older writer's state of mind. Dos Passos in the 1960's is less sure about everything in his "chosen country," but his power to communicate his doubts is the source of our undiminished interest in an amazing career.

KENNETH S. LYNN

Contents

The Young Man Walks Fast
by Himself

THE YOUNG MAN walks fast by himself through the crowd that thins into the night streets; feet are tired from hours of walking; eyes greedy for warm curve of faces, answering flicker of eyes, the set of a head, the lift of a shoulder, the way hands spread and clench; blood tingles with wants; mind is a beehive of hopes buzzing and stinging; muscles ache for the knowledge of jobs, for the roadmender's pick and shovel work, the fisherman's knack with a hook when he hauls on the slithery net from the rail of the lurching trawler, the swing of the bridgeman's arm as he slings down the whitehot rivet, the engineer's slow grip wise on the throttle, the dirtfarmer's use of his whole body when, whoa-ing the mules, he yanks the plow from the furrow. The young man walks by himself searching through the crowd with greedy eyes, greedy ears taut to hear, by himself, alone.

The streets are empty. People have packed into subways, climbed into streetcars and buses; in the stations they've scampered for suburban trains; they've filtered into lodgings and tenements, gone up in elevators into apartmenthouses. In a showwindow two sallow windowdressers in their shirt-sleeves are bringing out a dummy girl in a red evening dress, at a corner welders in masks lean into sheets of blue flame repairing a cartrack, a few drunk bums shamble along, a sad streetwalker fidgets under an arclight. From the river comes the deep rumbling whistle of a steamboat leaving dock. A tug hoots far away.

The young man walks by himself, fast but not fast enough, far but not far enough (faces slide out of sight, talk trails into tattered scraps, footsteps tap fainter in alleys); he must catch the last subway, the streetcar, the bus, run up the gangplanks of all the steamboats, register at all the hotels,

work in the cities, answer the wantads, learn the trades, take
up the jobs, live in all the boardinghouses, sleep in all the
beds. One bed is not enough, one job is not enough, one
life is not enough. At night, head swimming with wants, he
walks by himself alone.

No job, no woman, no house, no city.

Only the ears busy to catch the speech are not alone; the
ears are caught tight, linked tight by the tendrils of phrased
words, the turn of a joke, the singsong fade of a story, the
gruff fall of a sentence; linking tendrils of speech twine
through the city blocks, spread over pavements, grow out
along broad parked avenues, speed with the trucks leaving
on their long night runs over roaring highways, whisper
down sandy byroads past wornout farms, joining up cities
and fillingstations, roundhouses, steamboats, planes groping
along airways; words call out on mountain pastures, drift
slow down rivers widening to the sea and the hushed
beaches.

It was not in the long walks through jostling crowds at
night that he was less alone, or in the training camp at
Allentown, or in the day on the docks at Seattle, or in the
empty reek of Washington City hot boyhood summer nights,
or in the meal on Market Street, or in the swim off the red
rocks at San Diego, or in the bed full of fleas in New
Orleans, or in the cold razorwind off the lake, or in the
gray faces trembling in the grind of gears in the street
under Michigan Avenue, or in the smokers of limited ex-
presstrains, or walking across country, or riding up the dry
mountain canyons, or the night without a sleepingbag
among frozen beartracks in the Yellowstone, or canoeing
Sundays on the Quinnipiac;

but in his mother's words telling about longago, in his
father's telling about when I was a boy, in the kidding
stories of uncles, in the lies the kids told at school, the
hired man's yarns, the tall tales the doughboys told after
taps;

it was the speech that clung to the ears, the link that
tingled in the blood; U.S.A.

U.S.A. is the slice of a continent. U.S.A. is a group of
holding companies, some aggregations of trade unions, a set
of laws bound in calf, a radio network, a chain of moving
picture theatres, a column of stockquotations rubbed out

and written in by a Western Union boy on a blackboard, a publiclibrary full of old newspapers and dogeared historybooks with protests scrawled on the margins in pencil. U.S.A. is the world's greatest rivervalley fringed with mountains and hills. U.S.A. is a set of bigmouthed officials with too many bankaccounts. U.S.A. is a lot of men buried in their uniforms in Arlington Cemetery. U.S.A. is the letters at the end of an address when you are away from home. But mostly U.S.A. is the speech of the people.

GROUP I

From the Morning
of the Century

Newsreel

It was that emancipated race
That was chargin' up the hill
Up to where them insurrectos
Was afightin' fit to kill

CAPITAL CITY'S CENTURY CLOSED

General Miles with his gaudy uniform and spirited charger was the center for all eyes, especially as his steed was extremely restless. Just as the band passed the Commanding General, his horse stood upon his hind legs and was almost erect. General Miles instantly reined in the frightened animal and dug in his spurs in an endeavor to control the horse which, to the horror of the spectators, fell over backwards and landed squarely on the Commanding General. Much to the gratification of the people, General Miles was not injured, but considerable skin was scraped off the flank of his horse. Almost every inch of General Miles's overcoat was covered with the dust of the street and between the shoulders a hole about an inch in diameter was punctured. Without waiting for anyone to brush the dust from his garments, General Miles remounted his horse and reviewed the parade as if it were an everyday occurrence.

The incident naturally attracted the attention of the crowd, and this brought to notice the fact that the Commanding General never permits a flag to be carried past him without uncovering and remaining so until the colors have passed

And the Captain bold of Company B
Was afightin' in the lead

Just like a trueborn soldier he
Of them bullets took no heed

OFFICIALS KNOW NOTHING OF VICE

Sanitary trustees turn water of Chicago River into drainage canal LAKE MICHIGAN SHAKES HANDS WITH THE FATHER OF THE WATERS German zuchterverein singing contest for canary-birds opens the fight for bimetallism at the ratio of 16 to 1 has not been lost, says Bryan

BRITISH BEATEN AT MAFEKING

For there's many a man been murdered in Luzon

CLAIMS ISLANDS FOR ALL TIME

Hamilton Club listens to Oratory by ex-Congressman Posey of Indiana

NOISE GREETS NEW CENTURY

LABOR GREETS NEW CENTURY

CHURCHES GREET NEW CENTURY

Mr. McKinley is hard at work in his office when the new year begins.

NATION GREETS CENTURY'S DAWN

Responding to a toast, Hail Columbia! at the Columbia Club banquet in Indianapolis, Indiana, ex-President Benjamin Harrison said in part: I have no argument to make here or anywhere against territorial expansion; but I do not, as some do, look upon territorial expansion as the safest and most attractive avenue of national development. By the advantages of abundant and cheap coal and iron, of an enormous overproduction of food products and of invention and economy in production, we are now leading by the nose the original and the greatest of the colonizing nations.

Society Girls Shocked: Danced with Detectives

For there's many a man been murdered
in Luzon and Mindanao

GAIETY GIRLS MOBBED IN NEW JERSEY

One of the lithographs of the leading lady represented her in less than Atlantic City bathing costume, sitting on a red-hot stove; in one hand she held a brimming glass of wine, in the other ribbons drawn over a pair of rampant lobsters.

For there's many a man been murdered in

Luzon and Mindanao
and in Samar

In responding to the toast, "The Twentieth Century," Senator Albert J. Beveridge said in part: *The twentieth century will be American. American thought will dominate it. American progress will give it color and direction. American deeds will make it illustrious.*

Civilization will never lose its hold on Shanghai. Civilization will never depart from Hongkong. The gates of Peking will never again be closed to the methods of modern man. The regeneration of the world, physical as well as moral, has begun, and revolutions never move backwards.

There's been many a good man murdered in the
Philippines
Lies sleeping in some lonesome grave.

The Boy Orator of the Platte

It was in the Chicago Convention in '96 that the prize-winning boy orator, the minister's son whose lips had never touched liquor, let out his silver voice so that it filled the gigantic hall, filled the ears of the plain people:

Mr. Chairman and gentlemen of the convention:
I would be presumptuous indeed
                          to present myself against
the distinguished gentleman to whom you have listened,
if this were a mere measuring of abilities;
                but this is not a contest between persons.
        The humblest citizen in all the land,
    when clad in the armor of a righteous cause,
        is stronger than all the hosts of error.
I come to speak to you in defense of a cause as holy as the
    cause of Liberty . . .

a youngish bigmouthed man in a white tie
barnstormer, exhorter, evangelist,
his voice charmed the mortgageridden farmers of the great plains, rang through weatherboarded schoolhouses in the Missouri Valley, was sweet in the ears of small storekeepers hungry for easy credit, melted men's innards like the song of a thrush or a mockin' in the gray quiet before sunup, or a sudden soar in winter wheat or a bugler playing taps and the flag flying;

silver tongue of the plain people:

    . . . the man who is employed for wages is as much a
businessman as his employer;

the attorney in a country town is as much a businessman as the corporation counsel in a giant metropolis;

the merchant in a crossroads store is as much a business-man as the merchant of New York;

the farmer who goes forth in the morning and toils all day, who begins in the spring and toils all summer, and who by the application of brain and muscle to the natural resources of the country creates wealth, is as much a businessman as the man who goes upon the board of trade and bets upon the price of grain;

the miners who go down a thousand feet in the earth
or climb two thousand feet upon the cliffs
and bring forth from their hidingplaces °
the precious metals
to be poured in the channels of trade,
are as much businessmen
as the few financial magnates
who
in a back room
corner the money of the world.

The hired man and the country attorney sat up and listened,

this was big talk for the farmer who'd mortgaged his crop to buy fertilizer, big talk for the smalltown hardware man, groceryman, feed and corn merchant, undertaker, truckgardener . . .

Having behind us
the producing masses
of this nation and the world,
supported by the commerical interests, the laboring interests,
and the toilers everywhere,
we will answer
their demand
for a gold standard
by saying to them:
You shall not press down upon the brow of labor this crown of thorns,
you shall not crucify mankind upon a cross of gold.

They roared their lungs out (*crown of thorns and cross of gold*)

carried him round the hall on their shoulders, hugged him, loved him, named their children after him, nominated him for President,

boy orator of the Platte,

silver tongue of the plain people.

But McArthur and Forrest, two Scotchmen in the Rand, had invented the cyanide process for extracting gold from ore, South Africa flooded the gold market; there was no need for a prophet of silver.

The silver tongue chanted on out of the big mouth, chanting Pacifism, Prohibition, Fundamentalism,

nibbling radishes on the lecture platform,

drinking grapejuice and water,

gorging big cornbelt meals;

Bryan grew gray in the hot air of Chautauqua tents, in the applause, the handshakes, the backpattings, the cigarsmoky air of committeerooms at Democratic conventions, a silver tongue in a big mouth.

In Dayton he dreamed of turning the trick again, of setting back the clocks for the plain people, branding, flaying making a big joke

of Darwinism and the unbelieving outlook of city folks, scientists, foreigners with beards and monkey morals.

In Florida he'd spoken every day at noon on a float under an awning selling lots for Coral Gables . . . he had to speak, to feel the drawling voices hush, feel the tense approving ears, the gust of handclaps.

Why not campaign again through the length and breadth to set up again the tottering word for the plain people who wanted the plain word of God?

(*crown of thorns and cross of gold*)

the plain prosperous comfortable word of God for plain prosperous comfortable midamerican folks?

He was a big eater. It was hot. A stroke killed him.

Three days later down in Florida the company delivered

the electric horse he'd ordered to exercise on when he'd seen the electric horse the President exercised on in the White House.

Mac

FAINY stood near the door in the crowded elevated train; against the back of the fat man who held on to the strap in front of him, he kept rereading a letter on crisp watermarked stationery:

The Truthseeker Literary Distributing Co., Inc.
General Offices 1104 S. Hamlin Avenue
Chicago, Ill. April 14, 1904

Fenian O'H. McCreary
456 N. Wood Street
Chicago, Ill.
DEAR SIR:

We take the pleasure to acknowledge yours of the 10th inst.

In reference to the matter in hand we feel that much could be gained by a personal interview. If you will be so good as to step around to the above address on Monday April 16th at nine o'clock, we feel that the matter of your adaptability for the position for which you have applied can be thoroughly thrashed out.

Yours in search for Truth,

EMMANUEL R. BINGHAM, D.D.

Fainy was scared. The train got to his station too soon. He had fifteen minutes to walk two blocks in. He loafed along the street, looking in store windows. There was a golden pheasant, stuffed, in a taxidermist's; above it hung a big flat greenish fish with a sawtoothed bill from which dangled a label:

SAWFISH (pristis perrotetti)
Habitat Gulf and Florida waters. Frequents shallow bays
and inlets.

Maybe he wouldn't go at all. In the back of the window was a lynx and on the other side a bobtailed cat, each on its limb of a tree. Suddenly he caught his breath. He'd be late. He went tearing off down the block.

He was breathless and his heart was pounding to beat the cars when he reached the top of the fourth flight of stairs. He studied the groundglass doors on the landing;

THE UNIVERSAL CONTACT COMPANY
F. W. Perkins

Assurance

THE WINDY CITY MAGIC AND NOVELTY
COMPANY

Dr. Noble
Hospital and Sickroom Supplies

The last one was a grimy door in the back beside the toilet. The goldleaf had come off the letters, but he was able to spell out from the outlines:

THE GENERAL OUTFITTING AND MERCHAN-
DISING CORPORATION

Then he saw a card on the wall beside the door with a hand holding a torch drawn out on it and under it the words "Truthseeker Inc." He tapped gingerly on the glass. No answer. He tapped again.

"Come in . . . Don't knock," called out a deep voice. Fainy found himself stuttering as he opened the door and stepped into a dark, narrow room completely filled up by two huge rolltop desks:

"Please, I called to see Mr. Bingham, sir."

At the further desk, in front of the single window sat a big man with a big drooping jaw that gave him a little of the expression of a setter dog. His black hair was long and curled a little over each ear, on the back of his head was a broad black felt hat. He leaned back in his chair and looked Fainy up and down.

"How do you do, young man? What kind of books are you inclined to purchase this morning? What can I do for you this morning?" he boomed.

"Are you Mr. Bingham, sir, please?"

"This is Doc Bingham right here before you."

"Please, sir, I . . . I came about that job."

Doc Bingham's expression changed. He twisted his mouth as if he'd just tasted something sour. He spun around in his swivelchair and spat into a brass spittoon in the corner of the room. Then he turned to Fainy again and leveled a fat finger at him, "Young man, how do you spell experience?"

"E . . . x . . . p . . . er . . . er . . . i . . . a . . . n . . ."

"That'll do . . . No education . . . I thought as much . . . No culture, none of those finer feelings that distinguish the civilized man from the savage aborigines of the wilds . . . No enthusiasm for truth, for bringing light into dark places . . . Do you realize, young man, that it is not a job I'm offering you, it is a great opportunity . . . a splendid opportunity for service and self-improvement. I'm offering you an education gratis."

Fainy shuffled his feet. He had a husk in his throat.

"If it's in the printin' line I guess I could do it."

"Well, young man, during the brief interrogatory through which I'm going to put you, remember that you stand on the threshold of opportunity."

Doc Bingham ferreted in the pigeonholes of his desk for a long time, found himself a cigar, bit off the end, lit it, and then turned again to Fainy, who was standing first on one foot and then on the other.

"Well, if you'll tell me your name."

"Fenian O'Hara McCreary . . ."

"Hum . . . Scotch and Irish . . . that's pretty good stock . . . that's the stock I come from."

"Religion?"

Fainy squirmed. "Pop was a Catholic but . . ." He turned red.

Dr. Bingham laughed, and rubbed his hands.

"Oh, religion, what crimes are committed in thy name. I'm an agnostic myself . . . caring nothing for class or creed when among friends; though sometimes, my boy, you have to bow with the wind . . . No, sir, my God is the truth, that rising ever higher in the hands of honest men will dispel the mists of ignorance and greed, and bring freedom and knowledge to mankind . . . Do you agree with me?"

"I've been working for my uncle. He's a socialdemocrat."

"Ah, hotheaded youth . . . Can you drive a horse?"

"Why, yessir, I guess I could."

"Well, I don't see why I shouldn't hire you."

"The advertisement in the *Tribune* said fifteen dollars a week."

Doc Bingham's voice assumed a particularly velvety tone.

"Why, Fenian, my boy, fifteen dollars a week will be the minimum you will make . . . Have you ever heard of the cooperative system? that is how I'm going to hire you . . . As sole owner and representative of the Truthseeker Corporation, I have here a magnificent line of small books and pamphlets covering every phase of human knowledge and endeavor . . . I am embarking immediately on a sales campaign to cover the whole country. You will be one of my distributors. The books sell at from ten to fifty cents. On each ten cent book you make a cent, on the fifty cent books you make five cents . . ."

"And don't I get anything every week?" stammered Fainy.

"Would you be pennywise and poundfoolish? Throwing away the most magnificent opportunity of a lifetime for the assurance of a paltry pittance. No, I can see by your flaming eye, by your rebellious name out of old Ireland's history, that you are a young man of spirit and determination . . . Are we on? Shake hands on it then and by gad, Fenian, you shall never regret it."

Doc Bingham jumped to his feet and seized Fainy's hand and shook it.

"Now, Fenian, come with me; we have an important preliminary errand to perform." Doc Bingham pulled his hat forward on his head and they walked down the stairs to the front door; he was a big man and the fat hung loosely on him as he walked. Anyway, it's a job, Fainy told himself.

First they went to a tailorshop where a longnosed yellow man whom Doc Bingham addressed as Lee shuffled out to meet them. The tailorshop smelt of steamed cloth and cleansing fluid. Lee talked as if he had no palate to his mouth.

" 'M pretty sick man," he said. "Spen mor'n thou'an dollarm on doctor, no get well."

"Well, I'll stand by you; you know that, Lee."

"Hure, Mannie, hure, only you owe me too much money."

Doctor Emmanuel Bingham glanced at Fainy out of the corner of his eye.

"I can assure you that the entire financial situation will be clarified within sixty days . . . But what I want you to do now is to lend me two of your big cartons, those cardboard boxes you send suits home in."

"What you wan to do?"

"My young friend and I have a little project."

"Don't you do nothin crooked with them cartons; my name's on them."

Doc Bingham laughed heartily as they walked out the door, carrying under each arm one of the big flat cartons that had LEVY AND GOLDSTEIN, RELIABLE TAILORING, written on them in florid lettering.

"He's a great joker, Fenian," he said. "But let that man's lamentable condition be a lesson to you . . . The poor unfortunate is suffering from the consequences of a horrible social disease, contracted through some youthful folly."

They were passing the taxidermist's store again. There were the wildcats and the golden pheasant and the big sawfish . . . *Frequents shallow bays and inlets.* Fainy had a temptation to drop the tailor's cartons and run for it. But anyhow, it was a job.

"Fenian," said Doc Bingham confidentially, "do you know the Mohawk House?"

"Yessir, we used to do their printing for them."

"They don't know you there, do they?"

"Naw, they wouldn't know me from Adam . . . I just delivered some writin paper there once."

"That's superb . . . Now get this right; my room is 303. You wait and come in about five minutes. You're the boy from the tailor's, see, getting some suits to be cleaned. Then you come up to my room and get the suits and take 'em

round to my office. If anybody asks you where you're goin
with 'em, you're goin to Levy and Goldstein, see?"

Fainy drew a deep breath.

"Sure, I get you."

When he reached the small room in the top of the
Mohawk House, Doc Bingham was pacing the floor.

"Levy and Goldstein, sir," said Fainy, keeping his face
straight.

"My boy," said Doc Bingham, "you'll be an able assistant; I'm glad I picked you out. I'll give you a dollar in
advance on your wages." While he talked he was taking
clothes, papers, old books, out of a big trunk that stood in
the middle of the floor. He packed them carefully in one
of the cartons. In the other he put a furlined overcoat.
"That coat cost two hundred dollars, Fenian, a remnant of
former splendors . . . Ah, the autumn leaves at Vallom-
brosa . . . Et tu in Arcadia vixisti . . . That's Latin, a
language of scholars."

"My Uncle Tim who ran the printing shop where I
worked knew Latin fine."

"Do you think you can carry these, Fenian . . . they're
not too heavy?"

"Sure I can carry 'em." Fainy wanted to ask about the
dollar.

"All right, you'd better run along . . . Wait for me at
the office."

In the office Fainy found a man sitting at the second rolltop desk. "Vell, what's your business?" he yelled out in a
rasping voice. He was a sharpnosed waxyskinned young
man with straight black hair standing straight up. Fainy
was winded from running up the stairs. His arms were stiff
from carrying the heavy cartons. "I suppose this is some
more of Mannie's tomfoolishness. Tell him he's got to clear
out of here; I've rented the other desk."

"But Doctor Bingham has just hired me to work for the
Truthseeker Literary Distributing Company."

"The hell he has."

"He'll be here in a minute."

"Well, sit down and shut up; can't you see I'm busy?"

Fainy sat down glumly in the swivelchair by the window,
the only chair in the office not piled high with small paper-
covered books. Outside the window he could see a few

dusty roofs and fire escapes. Through grimy windows he could see other offices, other rolltop desks. On the desk in front of him were paperwrapped packages of books. Between them were masses of loose booklets. His eye caught a title:

THE QUEEN OF THE WHITE SLAVES
Scandalous revelations of Milly Meecham stolen from her parents at the age of sixteen, tricked by her vile seducer into a life of infamy and shame.

He started reading the book. His tongue got dry and he felt sticky all over.

"Nobody said anything to you, eh?" Doc Bingham's booming voice broke in on his reading.

Before he could answer, the voice of the man at the other desk snarled out: "Look here, Mannie, you've got to clear out of here . . . I've rented the desk."

"Shake not thy gory locks at me, Samuel Epstein. My young friend and I are just preparing an expedition among the aborigines of darkest Michigan. We are leaving for Saginaw tonight. Within sixty days I'll come back and take the office off your hands. This young man is coming with me to learn the business."

"Business, hell," growled the other man, and shoved his face back down among his papers again.

"Procrastination, Fenian, is the thief of time," said Doc Bingham, putting one fat hand Napoleonfashion into his doublebreasted vest. "There is a tide in the affairs of men that taken at its full . . ." And for two hours Fainy sweated under his direction, packing booklets into brown paper packages, tying them and addressing them to Truthseeker Inc., Saginaw, Mich.

He begged off for an hour to go home to see his folks. Milly kissed him on the forehead with thin tight lips. Then she burst out crying. "You're lucky; oh, I wish I was a boy," she spluttered and ran upstairs. Mrs. O'Hara said to be a good boy and always live at the Y.M.C.A. — that kept a boy out of temptation, and to let his Uncle Tim be a lesson to him, with his boozin ways.

His throat was pretty tight when he went to look for his Uncle Tim. He found him in the back room at O'Grady's.

His eyes were a flat bright blue and his lower lip trembled when he spoke, "Have one drink with me, son, you're on your own now." Fainy drank down a beer without tasting it.

"Fainy, you're a bright boy . . . I wish I could have helped you more; you're an O'Hara every inch of you. You read Marx . . . study all you can, remember that you're a rebel by birth and blood . . . Don't blame people for things . . . Look at that terrible forktongued virago I'm married to; do I blame her? No, I blame the system. And don't ever sell out to the sonsofbitches, son; it's women'll make you sell out every time. You know what I mean. All right, go on . . . better cut along or you'll miss your train."

"I'll write you from Saginaw, Uncle Tim, honest I will."

Uncle Tim's lanky red face in the empty cigarsmoky room, the bar and its glint of brass and the pinkarmed barkeep leaning across it, the bottles and the mirrors and the portrait of Lincoln gave a misty half turn in his head and he was out in the shiny rainy street under the shiny clouds, hurrying for the Elevated station with his suitcase in his hand.

At the Illinois Central station he found Doc Bingham waiting for him, in the middle of a ring of brown paper parcels. Fen felt a little funny inside when he saw him, the greasy sallow jowls, the doublebreasted vest, the baggy black ministerial coat, the dusty black felt hat that made the hair stick out in a sudden fuzzycurl over the beefy ears. Anyway, it was a job.

"It must be admitted, Fenian," began Doc Bingham as soon as Fainy had come up to him, "that confident as I am of my knowledge of human nature I was a little afraid you wouldn't turn up. Where is it that the poet says that difficult is the first fluttering course of the fledgeling from the nest. Put these packages on the train while I go purchase tickets, and be sure it's a smoker."

After the train had started and the conductor had punched the tickets, Doc Bingham leaned over and tapped Fainy on the knee with a chubby forefinger. "I'm glad you're a neat dresser, my boy; you must never forget the importance of putting up a fine front to the world. Though the heart be as dust and ashes, yet must the outer man be sprightly and of good cheer. We will go sit for a while in the Pullman smoker up ahead to get away from the yokels."

It was raining hard and the windows of the train were striped with transverse beaded streaks against the darkness. Fainy felt uneasy as he followed Doc Bingham lurching through the greenplush parlor car to the small leather upholstered smokingcompartment at the end. There Doc Bingham drew a large cigar from his pocket and began blowing a magnificent series of smoke rings. Fainy sat beside him with his feet under the seat trying to take up as little room as possible.

Gradually the compartment filled up with silent men and crinkly spiraling cigarsmoke. Outside the rain beat against the windows with a gravelly sound. For a long time nobody said anything. Occasionally a man cleared his throat and let fly towards the cuspidor with a big gob of phlegm or a jet of tobaccojuice.

"Well, sir," a voice began, coming from nowhere in particular, addressed to nowhere in particular, "it was a great old inauguration even if we did freeze to death."

"Were you in Washington?"

"Yessir, I was in Washington."

"Most of the trains didn't get in till the next day."

"I know it; I was lucky, there was some of them snowed up for fortyeight hours."

"Some blizzard all right."

> *All day the gusty northwind bore*
> *The lessening drift its breath before*
> *Low circling through its southern zone*
> *The sun through dazzling snowmist shone,*

recited Doc Bingham coyly, with downcast eyes.

"You must have a good memory to be able to recite verses right off the reel like that."

"Yessir, I have a memory that may I think, without undue violation of modesty, be called compendious. Were it a natural gift I should be forced to blush and remain silent, but since it is the result of forty years of study of what is best in the world's epic lyric and dramatic literatures, I feel that to call attention to it may sometimes encourage some other whose feet are also bound on the paths of enlightenment and selfeducation." He turned suddenly to Fainy.

"Young man, would you like to hear Othello's address to the Venetian Senate?"

"Sure I would," said Fainy, blushing.

"Well, at last Teddy has a chance to carry out his word about fighting the trusts." "I'm telling you the insurgent farmer vote of the great Northwest . . ." "Terrible thing the wreck of those inauguration specials."

But Doc Bingham was off:

> *Most potent grave and reverend signiors,*
> *My very noble and approved good masters,*
> *That I have ta'en away this old man's daughter*
> *It is most true; true I have married her . . .*

"They won't get away with those antitrust laws, believe me they won't. You can't curtail the liberty of the individual liberty in that way." "It's the liberty of the individual business man that the progressive wing of the Republican party is trying to protect."

But Doc Bingham was on his feet, one hand was tucked into his doublebreasted vest, with the other he was making broad circular gestures:

> *Rude am I in speech*
> *And little blessed with the soft phrase of peace,*
> *For since these arms of mine had seven years' pith*
> *Till now some nine moons wasted they have used*
> *Their dearest action in the tented field.*

"The farmer vote," the other man began shrilly, but nobody was listening. Doc Bingham had the floor.

> *And little of the great world can I speak*
> *More than pertains to broils and battle*
> *And therefore little shall I grace my cause*
> *In speaking for myself.*

The train began to slacken speed. Doc Bingham's voice sounded oddly loud in the lessened noise. Fainy felt his back pushing into the back of the seat and then suddenly there was stillness and the sound of an engine bell in the distance and Doc Bingham's voice in a queasy whisper:

"Gentlemen, I have here in pamphlet form a complete and unexpurgated edition of one of the world's classics, the famous *Decameron* of Boccaccio, that for four centuries has been a byword for spicy wit and ribald humor . . ." He took a bundle of little books out of one of his sagging pockets and began dandling them in his hand. "Just as an act of friendship I would be willing to part with some if any of you gentlemen care for them . . . Here, Fenian, take these and see if anybody wants one; they're two dollars apiece. My young friend here will attend to distribution . . . Goodnight, gentlemen." And he went off and the train had started again and Fainy found himself standing with the little books in his hand in the middle of the lurching car with the suspicious eyes of all the smokers boring into him like so many gimlets.

"Let's see one," said a little man with protruding ears who sat in the corner. He opened the book and started reading greedily. Fainy stood in the center of the car, feeling pins and needles all over. He caught a white glint in the corner of an eyeball as the little man looked down the line of cigars through the crinkly smoke. A touch of pink came into the protruding ears.

"Hot stuff," said the little man, "but two dollars is too much."

Fainy found himself stuttering: "They're nnnot mmmine, sir; I don't know . . ."

"Oh, well, what the hell . . ." The little man dropped two dollar bills in Fainy's hand and went back to his reading. Fainy had six dollars in his pocket and two books left when he started back to the daycoach. Halfway down the car he met the conductor. His heart almost stopped beating. The conductor looked at him sharply but said nothing.

Doc Bingham was sitting in his seat with his head in his hand and his eyes closed as if he were dozing. Fainy slipped into the seat beside him.

"How many did they take?" asked Doc Bingham, talking out of the corner of his mouth without opening his eyes.

"I got six bucks . . . Golly, the conductor scared me, the way he looked at me."

"You leave the conductor to me, and remember that it's never a crime in the face of humanity and enlightenment to distribute the works of the great humanists among the

merchants and moneychangers of this godforsaken country
. . . You better slip me the dough."

Fainy wanted to ask about the dollar he'd been promised,
but Doc Bingham was off on Othello again.

> *If after every tempest there come such calms as this*
> *Then may the laboring bark climb hills of seas*
> *Olympus high.*

They slept late at the Commercial House in Saginaw, and
ate a large breakfast, during which Doc Bingham discoursed
on the theory and practice of book salesmanship. "I am
very much afraid that through the hinterland to which we
are about to penetrate," he said as he cut up three fried eggs
and stuffed his mouth with bakingpowder biscuit, "that we
will find the yokels still hankering after Maria Monk."

Fainy didn't know who Maria Monk was, but he didn't
like to ask. He went with Doc Bingham round to Hummer's
livery stable to hire a horse and wagon. There followed a
long wrangle between the firm of Truthseeker Inc., and the
management of Hummer's Livery Stable as to the rent of a
springwagon and an elderly piebald horse with cruppers
you could hang a hat on, so that it was late afternoon before
they drove out of Saginaw with their packages of books
piled behind them, bound for the road.

It was a chilly spring day. Sagging clouds moved in a
gray blur over a bluish silvery sky. The piebald kept slacken-
ing to a walk; Fainy clacked the reins continually on his
caving rump and clucked with his tongue until his mouth
was dry. At the first whack the piebald would go into a
lope that would immediately degenerate into an irregular
jogtrot and then into a walk. Fainy cursed and clucked,
but he couldn't get the horse to stay in the lope or the jogtrot. Meanwhile Doc Bingham sat beside him with his broad
hat on the back of his head, smoking a cigar and discours-
ing: "Let me say right now, Fenian, that the attitude of a
man of enlightened ideas, is *A plague on both your houses*
. . . I myself am a pantheist . . . but even a pantheist
. . . must eat, hence Maria Monk." A few drops of rain,
icy and stinging as hail, had begun to drive in their faces.
"I'll get pneumonia at this rate, and it'll be your fault, too;
I thought you said you could drive a horse . . . Here, drive

into that farmhouse on the left. Maybe they'll let us put the horse and wagon in their barn."

As they drove up the lane towards the gray house and the big gray barn that stood under a clump of pines a little off from the road, the piebald slowed to a walk and began reaching for the bright green clumps of grass at the edge of the ditch. Fainy beat at him with the ends of the reins, and even stuck his foot over the dashboard and kicked him, but he wouldn't budge.

"Goddam it, give me the reins."

Doc Bingham gave the horse's head a terrible yank, but all that happened was that he turned his head and looked at them, a green foam of partly chewed grass between his long yellow teeth. To Fainy it looked as if he were laughing. The rain had come on hard. They put their coat collars up. Fainy soon had a little icy trickle down the back of his neck.

"Get out and walk; goddam it to hell, lead it if you can't drive it," sputtered Doc Bingham. Fainy jumped out and led the horse up to the back door of the farmhouse; the rain ran down his sleeve from the hand he held the horse by.

"Good afternoon, ma'am." Doc Bingham was on his feet bowing to a little old woman who had come out of the door. He stood beside her on the stoop out of the rain. "Do you mind if I put my horse and wagon in your barn for a few moments? I have valuable perishable materials in the wagon and no waterproof covering . . ." The old woman nodded a stringy white head. "Well, that's very kind of you, I must say . . . All right, Fenian, put the horse in the barn and come here and bring in that little package under the seat . . . I was just saying to my young friend here that I was sure that some good samaritan lived in this house who would take in two weary wayfarers." "Come inside, mister . . . maybe you'd like to set beside the stove and dry yourself. Come inside, mister — er?" "Doc Bingham's the name . . . the Reverend Doctor Bingham," Fainy heard him say as he went in the house.

He was soaked and shivering when he went into the house himself, carrying a package of books under his arm. Doc Bingham was sitting large as life in a rocking chair in front of the kitchen stove. Beside him on the wellscrubbed deal table was a piece of pie and a cup of coffee. The kitchen had a warm cosy small of apples and bacon grease and lamps. The old woman was leaning over the kitchen table listening intently to what Doc Bingham was saying. Another woman, a big scrawny woman with her scant sandy hair done up in a screw on top of her head, stood in the background with her redknuckled hands on her hips. A black and white cat, back arched and tail in the air, was rubbing against Doc Bingham's legs.

"Ah, Fenian, just in time," he began in a voice that purred like the cat, "I was just telling . . . relating to your kind hostesses the contents of our very interesting and educational library, the prime of the world's devotional and inspirational literature. They have been so kind to us during our little misfortune with the weather that I thought it would be only fair to let them see a few of our titles."

The big woman was twisting her apron. "I like a mite o' readin fine," she said, shyly, "but I don't git much chanct for it, not till wintertime."

Benignly smiling, Doc Bingham untied the string and pulled the package open on his knees. A booklet dropped to the floor. Fainy saw that it was *The Queen of the White Slaves.* A shade of sourness went over Doc Bingham's face. He put his foot on the dropped book. "These are Gospel Talks, my boy," he said. "I wanted *Doctor Spikenard's Short Sermons for All Occasions.*" He handed the halfopen package to Fainy, who snatched it to him. Then he stooped and picked the book up from under his foot with a slow sweeping gesture of the hand and slipped it in his pocket. "I suppose I'll have to go and find them myself," he went on in his purringest voice. When the kitchen door closed behind them he snarled in Fainy's ear, "Under the seat, you little rat . . . If you play a trick like that again I'll break every goddam bone in your body." And he brought his knee up so hard into the seat of Fainy's pants that his teeth clacked together and he shot out into the rain towards the barn. "Honest, I didn't do it on purpose," Fainy whined. But Doc Bingham was already back in the house and his voice was burbling comfortably out into the rainy dusk with the first streak of lamplight.

This time Fainy was careful to open the package before he brought it in. Doc Bingham took the books out of his hand without looking at him and Fainy went round behind the stovepipe. He stood there in the soggy steam of his clothes listening to Doc Bingham boom. He was hungry, but nobody seemed to think of offering him a piece of pie.

"Ah, my dear friends, how can I tell you with what gratitude to the Great Giver a lonely minister of the gospel of light, wandering among the tares and troubles of this world, finds ready listeners. I'm sure that these little books will be consoling, interesting and inspirational to all that undertake the slight effort of perusal. I feel this so strongly that I always carry a few extra copies with me to dispose of for a moderate sum. It breaks my heart that I can't yet give them away free gratis."

"How much are they?" asked the old woman, a sudden sharpness coming over her features. The scrawny woman let her arms drop to her side and shook her head.

"Do you remember, Fenian," asked Doc Bingham, leaning genially back in his chair, "what the cost price of these little booklets was?" Fainy was sore. He didn't answer. "Come here, Fenian," said Doc Bingham in honeyed tones, "allow me to remind you of the words of the immortal bard:

> Lowliness is your ambition's ladder
> Whereto the climber upward turns his face
> But when he once attains the topmost round
> He then unto the ladder turns his back

"You must be hungry. You can eat my pie."

"I reckon we can find the boy a piece of pie," said the old woman.

"Ain't they ten cents?" said Fainy, coming forward.

"Oh, if they're only ten cents I think I'd like one," said the old woman quickly. The scrawny woman started to say something, but it was too late.

The pie had hardly disappeared into Fainy's gullet and the bright dime out of the old tobaccobox in the cupboard into Doc Bingham's vest pocket when there was a sound of clinking harness and the glint of a buggylamp through the rainy dark outside the window. The old woman got to her feet and looked nervously at the door, which immediately opened. A heavyset grayhaired man with a small goatee sprouting out of a round red face came in, shaking the rain off the flaps of his coat. After him came a skinny lad about Fainy's age.

"How do you do, sir; how do you do, son?" boomed Doc Bingham through the last of his pie and coffee.

"They asked if they could put their horse in the barn until it should stop rainin. It's all right, ain't it, James?" asked the old woman nervously. "I reckon so," said the older man, sitting down heavily in the free chair. The old woman had hidden the pamphlet in the drawer of the kitchen table. "Travelin in books, I gather." He stared hard at the open package of pamphlets. "Well, we don't need any of that trash here, but you're welcome to stay the night in the barn. This is no night to throw a human being out inter."

So they unhitched the horse and made beds for themselves in the hay over the cowstable. Before they left the house the older man made them give up their matches. "Where there's matches there's danger of fire," he said. Doc Bingham's face was black as thunder as he wrapped himself in a horseblanket, muttering about "indignity to a wearer of the cloth." Fainy was excited and happy. He lay on his back listening to the beat of the rain on the roof and its gurgle in the gutters, and the muffled stirring and champing of the cattle and horse, under them; his nose was full of the smell of the hay and the warm meadowsweetness of the cows. He wasn't sleepy. He wished he had someone his own age to talk to. Anyway, it was a job and he was on the road.

He had barely got to sleep when a light woke him. The boy he'd seen in the kitchen was standing over him with a lantern. His shadow hovered over them enormous against the rafters.

"Say, I wanner buy a book."

"What kind of a book?" Fainy yawned and sat up.

"You know . . . one o' them books about chorusgirls an white slaves an stuff like that."

"How much do you want to pay, son?" came Doc Bingham's voice from under the horseblanket. "We have a number of very interesting books stating the facts of life frankly and freely, describing the deplorable licentiousness of life in the big cities, ranging from a dollar to five dollars. *The Complete Sexology of Doctor Burnside,* is six-fifty."

"I couldn't go higher'n a dollar . . . Say, you won't tell the ole man on me?" the young man said, turning from one to another. "Seth Hardwick, he lives down the road, he went into Saginaw onct an got a book from a man at the hotel. Gosh, it was a pippin." He tittered uneasily.

"Fenian, go down and get him *The Queen of the White Slaves* for a dollar," said Doc Bingham, and settled back to sleep.

Fainy and the farmer's boy went down the rickety ladder.

"Say, is she pretty spicy? . . . Gosh, if pop finds it he'll give me a whalin . . . Gosh, I bet you've read all them books."

"Me?" said Fainy haughtily. "I don't need to read books. I kin see life if I wanter. Here it is . . . it's about fallen women."

"Ain't that pretty short for a dollar? I thought you could get a big book for a dollar."

"This one's pretty spicy."

"Well, I guess I'll take it before dad ketches me snoopin around . . . Goodnight." Fainy went back to his bed in the hay and fell fast asleep. He was dreaming that he was going up a rickety stair in a barn with his sister Milly who kept getting all the time bigger and white and fatter, and had on a big hat with ostrich plumes all round it and her dress began to split from the neck and lower and lower and Doc Bingham's voice was saying She's Maria Monk, the queen of the white slaves, and just as he was going to grab her, sunlight opened his eyes. Doc Bingham stood in front of him, his feet wide apart, combing his hair with a pocket-comb and reciting:

> Let us depart, the universal sun
> Confines not to one land his blessed beams
> Nor is man rooted like a tree . . .

"Come, Fenian," he boomed, when he saw that Fainy was awake, "let us shake the dust of this inhospitable farm, latcheting our shoes with a curse like philosophers of old . . . Hitch up the horse; we'll get breakfast down the road."

This went on for several weeks until one evening they found themselves driving up to a neat yellow house in a grove of feathery dark tamaracks. Fainy waited in the wagon while Doc Bingham interviewed the people in the house. After a while Doc Bingham appeared in the door, a broad smile creasing his cheeks. "We're going to be very handsomely treated, Fenian, as benfits a wearer of the cloth and all that . . . You be careful how you talk, will you? Take the horse to the barn and unhitch."

"Say, Mr. Bingham, how about my money? It's three weeks, now." Fainy jumped down and went to the horse's head.

An expression of gloom passed over Doc Bingham's face. "Oh, lucre, lucre . . .

> *Examine well*
> *His milkwhite hand, the palm is hardly clean*
> *But here and there an ugly smutch appears,*
> *Foh, 'twas a bribe that left it . . .*

"I had great plans for a cooperative enterprise that you are spoiling by your youthful haste and greed . . . but if you must I'll hand over to you this very night everything due you and more. All right, unhitch the horse and bring me that little package with *Maria Monk*, and *The Popish Plot*."

It was a warm day. There were robins singing round the barn. Everything smelt of sweetgrass and flowers. The barn was red and the yard was full of white leghorns. After he had unhitched the spring wagon and put the horse in a stall, Fainy sat on a rail of the fence looking out over the silvergreen field of oats out back, and smoked a cigarette. He wished there was a girl there he could put his arm round or a fellow to talk to.

A hand dropped onto his shoulder. Doc Bingham was standing beside him.

"Fenian, my young friend, we are in clover," he said. "She is alone in the house, and her husband has gone to town for two days with the hired man. There'll be nobody there but her two little children, sweet bairns. Perhaps I shall play Romeo. You've never seen me in love. It's my noblest role. Ah, some day I'll tell you about my headstrong youth. Come and meet the sweet charmer."

When they went in the kitchen door a dimplefaced pudgy woman in a lavender housecap greeted them coyly.

"This is my young assistant, ma'am," said Doc Bingham, with a noble gesture. "Fenian, this is Mrs. Kovach."

"You must be hungry. We're having supper right away."

The last of the sun lit up a kitchen range that was crowded with saucepans and stewpots. Fragrant steam rose in little jets from round wellpolished lids. As she spoke Mrs. Kovach leaned over so that her big blue behind with starched apronstrings tied in a bow above it stood up straight in the air, opened the oven door and pulled out a great pan of cornmuffins that she dumped into a dish on the dining table already set next the window. Their warm toasted smoke filled the kitchen. Fainy felt his mouth watering. Doc Bingham was rubbing his hands and rolling his eyes. They sat down, and the two blue-eyed smearyfaced children were sat down and started gobbling silently, and Mrs. Kovach heaped their plates with stewed tomatoes, mashed potatoes, beef stew and limabeans with pork. She poured them out coffee and then said with moist eyes, as she sat down herself:

"I love to see men eat."

Her face took on a crushed-pansy look that made Fainy turn away his eyes when he found himself looking at it. After supper she sat listening with a pleased, frightened expression while Doc Bingham talked and talked, now and then stopping to lean back and blow a smoke ring at the lamp.

"While not myself a Lutheran as you might say, ma'am, I myself have always admired, nay, revered, the great figure of Martin Luther as one of the lightbringers of mankind. Were it not for him we would be still groveling under the dread domination of the Pope of Rome."

"They'll never get into this country; land sakes, it gives me the creeps to think of it."

"Not while there's a drop of red blood in the veins of freeborn Protestants . . . but the way to fight darkness, ma'am, is with light. Light comes from education, reading of books and studies . . ."

"Land sakes, it gives me a headache to read most books, an I don't get much time, to tell the truth. My husband, he reads books he gets from the Department of Agriculture. He tried to make me read one once, on raisin poultry, but I couldn't make much sense out of it. His folks they come from the old country . . . I guess people feels different over there."

"It must be difficult being married to a foreigner like that."

"Sometimes I don't know how I stand it; 'course he was awful goodlookin when I married him . . . I never could resist a goodlookin man."

Doc Bingham leaned further across the table. His eyes rolled as if they were going to drop out.

"I never could resist a goodlooking lady."

Mrs. Kovach sighed deeply.

Fainy got up and went out. He'd been trying to get in a word about getting paid, but what was the use? Outside it was chilly; the stars were bright above the roofs of the barns and outhouses. From the chickencoop came an occasional sleepy cluck or the rustle of feathers as a hen lost her balance on her perch. He walked up and down the barnyard cursing Doc Bingham and kicking at an occasional clod of manure.

Later he looked into the lamplit kitchen. Doc Bingham had his arm around Mrs. Kovach's waist and was declaiming verses, making big gestures with his free hand:

> . . . These things to hear
> Would Desdemona seriously incline
> But still the house affairs would draw her hence
> Which ever as she could with haste dispatch
> She'd come again and with a greedy ear . . .

Fainy shook his fist at the window. "Goddam your hide, I want my money," he said aloud. Then he went for a walk down the road. When he came back he was sleepy and chilly. The kitchen was empty and the lamp was turned down low. He didn't know where to go to sleep, so he settled down to warm himself in a chair beside the fire. His head began to nod and he fell asleep.

A tremendous thump on the floor above and a woman's shrieks woke him. His first thought was that Doc Bingham was robbing and murdering the woman. But immediately he heard another voice cursing and shouting in broken English. He had half gotten up from the chair, when Doc

Bingham dashed past him. He had on only his flannel unionsuit. In one hand were his shoes, in the other his clothes. His trousers floated after him at the end of his suspenders like the tail of a kite.

"Hey, what are we going to do?" Fainy called after him, but got no answer. Instead he found himself face to face with a tall dark man with a scraggly black beard who was coolly fitting shells into a doublebarreled shotgun.

"Buckshot. I shoot the sonabitch."

"Hey, you can't do that," began Fainy. He got the butt of the shotgun in the chest and went crashing down into the chair again. The man strode out the door with a long elastic stride, and there followed two shots that went rattling among the farm buildings. Then the woman's shrieks started up again, punctuating a longdrawnout hysterical tittering and sobbing.

Fainy sat in the chair by the stove as if glued to it.

He noticed a fiftycent piece on the kitchen floor that must have dropped out of Doc Bingham's pants as he ran. He grabbed it and had just gotten it in his pocket when the tall man with the shotgun came back.

"No more shells," he said thickly. Then he sat down on the kitchen table among the uncleared supper dishes and began to cry like a child, the tears trickling through the knobbed fingers of his big dark hands. Fainy stole out of the door and went to the barn. "Doc Bingham," he called gently. The harness lay in a heap between the shafts of the wagon, but there was no trace of Doc Bingham or of the piebald horse. The frightened clucking of the hens disturbed in the hencoop mixed with the woman's shrieks that still came from upstairs in the farmhouse. "What the hell shall I do?" Fainy was asking himself when he caught sight of a tall figure outlined in the bright kitchen door and pointing the shotgun at him. Just as the shotgun blazed away he ducked into the barn and out through the back door. Buckshot whined over his head. "Gosh, he found shells." Fainy was off as fast as his legs could carry him across the oatfield. At last, without any breath in his body, he scrambled over a railfence full of briars that tore his face and hands and lay flat in a dry ditch to rest. There was nobody following him.

Steamroller

Bud sat on the edge of his cot and stretched out his arms and yawned. From all round through a smell of sweat and sour breath and wet clothes came snores, the sound of men stirring in their sleep, creaking of bedsprings. Far away through the murk burned a single electric light. Bud closed his eyes and let his head fall over on his shoulder. O God I want to go to sleep. Sweet Jesus I want to go to sleep. He pressed his knees together against his clasped hands to keep them from trembling. Our father which art in Heaven I want to go to sleep.

"Wassa matter pardner can't ye sleep?" came a quiet whisper from the next cot.

"Hell, no." "Me neither."

Bud looked at the big head of curly hair held up on an elbow turned towards him.

"This is a hell of a lousy stinking flop," went on the voice evenly. "I'll tell the world . . . Forty cents too! They can take their Hotel Plaza an . . ."

"Been long in the city?"

"Ten years come August."

"Great snakes!"

A voice rasped down the line of cots, "Cut de comedy yous guys, what do you tink dis is, a Jewish picnic?"

Bud lowered his voice: "Funny, it's years I been thinkin an wantin to come to the city. . . . I was born an raised on a farm upstate."

"Why don't ye go back?"

"I can't go back." Bud was cold; he wanted to stop trembling. He pulled the blanket up to his chin and rolled over facing the man who was talking. "Every spring I says to myself I'll hit the road again, go out an plant myself among the weeds an the grass an the cows comin home milkin time, but I don't; I juss kinder hangs on."

"What d'ye do all this time in the city?"

"I dunno . . . I used to set in Union Square most of the time, then I set in Madison Square. I been up in Hoboken an Joisey and Flatbush an now I'm a Bowery bum."

"God I swear I'm goin to git outa here tomorrow. I git sceered here. Too many bulls an detectives in this town."

"You could make a livin in handouts . . . But take it from me kid you go back to the farm and the ole folks while the goin's good."

Bud jumped out of bed and yanked roughly at the man's shoulder. "Come over here to the light, I want to show ye sumpen." Bud's own voice crinkled queerly in his ears. He strode along the snoring lane of cots. The bum, a shambling man with curly weatherbleached hair and beard and eyes as if hammered into his head, climbed fully dressed out from the blankets and followed him. Under the light Bud unbuttoned the front of his unionsuit and pulled it off his knottymuscled gaunt arms and shoulders. "Look at my back."

"Christ Jesus," whispered the man running a grimy hand with long yellow nails over the mass of white and red deepgouged scars. "I ain't never seen nothin like it."

"That's what the ole man done to me. For twelve years he licked me when he had a mind to. Used to strip me and take a piece of light chain to my back. They said he was my dad but I know he ain't. I run away when I was thirteen. That was when he ketched me and began to lick me. I'm twentyfive now."

They went back without speaking to their cots and lay down.

Bud lay staring at the ceiling with the blanket up to his eyes. When he looked down towards the door at the end of the room, he saw standing there a man in a derby hat with a cigar in his mouth. He crushed his lower lip between his teeth to keep from crying out. When he looked again the man was gone. "Say are you awake yet?" he whispered.

The bum grunted. "I was goin to tell yer. I mashed his head in with the grubbinhoe, mashed it in like when you kick a rotten punkin. I told him to lay offn me an he wouldn't . . . He was a hard godfearin man an he wanted you to be sceered of him. We was grubbin the sumach outa the old pasture to plant pertoters there . . . I let him lay till night with his head mashed in like a rotten punkin. A bit of scrub along the fence hid him from the road. Then I buried him an went up to the house an made me a pot of coffee. He hadn't never let me drink no coffee. Before light I got up an walked down the road. I was tellin myself in a big city it'd be like lookin for a needle in a haystack to find yer. I knowed where the ole man kep his money; he had a roll as big as your head but I was sceered to take more'en ten dollars . . . You awake yet?"

The bum grunted. "When I was a kid I kep company with ole man Sackett's girl. Her and me used to keep company in the ole icehouse down in Sackett's woods an we used to talk about how we'd come to New York City an git rich and now I'm here I can't git work an I can't git over bein sceered. There's detectives follow me all round, men in derbyhats with badges under their coats. Last night I wanted to go with a hooker an she saw it in my eyes an throwed me out . . . She could see it in my eyes." He was sitting on the edge of the cot, leaning over, talking into the other man's face in a hissing whisper. The bum suddenly grabbed him by the wrists.

"Look here kid, you're goin blooy if you keep up like this . . . Got any mazuma?" Bud nodded. "You better give it to me to keep. I'm an old timer an I'll git yez outa this. You put yer clothes on an take a walk round the block to a hash joint an eat up strong. How much you got?"

"Change from a dollar."

"You give me a quarter an eat all the stuff you kin git offn the rest." Bud pulled on his trousers and handed the man a quarter. "Then you come back here an you'll sleep good an tomorrer me'n you'll go upstate an git that roll of bills. Did ye say it was as big as yer head? Then we'll beat it where they can't ketch us. We'll split fifty fifty. Are you on?"

Bud shook his hand with a wooden jerk, then with the laces flickering round his shoes he shuffled to the door and down the spitmarked stairs.

The rain had stopped, a cool wind that smelled of woods and grass was ruffling the puddles in the cleanwashed streets. In the lunchroom in Chatham Square three men sat asleep with their hats over their eyes. The man behind the counter was reading a pink sportingsheet. Bud waited long for his order. He felt cool, unthinking, happy. When it came he ate the browned corned beef hash, deliberately enjoying every mouthful, mashing the crisp bits of potato against his teeth with his tongue, between sips of heavily sugared coffee. After polishing the plate with a crust of bread he took a toothpick and went out.

Picking his teeth he walked through the grimydark entrance to Brooklyn Bridge. A man in a derby hat was smoking a cigar in the middle of the broad tunnel. Bud brushed past him walking with a tough swagger. I don't care about him; let him follow me. The arching footwalk was empty except for a single policeman who stood yawning, looking up at the sky. It was like walking among the stars. Below in either direction streets tapered into dotted lines of lights between square blackwindowed buildings. The river glimmered underneath like the Milky Way above. Silently smoothly the bunch of lights of a tug slipped through the moist darkness. A car whirred across the bridge making the girders rattle and the spiderwork of cables thrum like a shaken banjo.

When he got to the tangle of girders of the elevated railroads of the Brooklyn side, he turned back along the southern driveway. Don't matter where I go, can't go nowhere now. An edge of the blue night had started to glow behind him the way iron starts to glow in a forge. Beyond black chimneys and lines of roofs faint rosy contours of the downtown buildings were brightening. All the darkness was growing pearly, warming. They're all of em detectives chasin me, all of em, men in derbies, bums on the Bowery, old women in kitchens, barkeeps, streetcar conductors, bulls, hookers, sailors, longshoremen, stiffs in employment agencies . . . He thought I'd tell him where the ole man's roll was, the lousy bum . . . One on him. One on all them goddam detectives. The river was smooth, sleek as a bluesteel gunbarrel. Don't matter where I go; can't go nowhere now. The shadows between the wharves and the buildings were powdery like washingblue. Masts fringed the river; smoke, purple chocolatecolor fleshpink climbed into light. Can't go nowhere now.

In a swallowtail suit with a gold watchchain and a red seal

ring riding to his wedding beside Maria Sackett, riding in a
carriage to City Hall with four white horses to be made an
alderman by the mayor; and the light grows brighter behind them
brighter brighter, riding in satins and silks to his wedding,
riding in pinkplush in a white carriage with Maria Sackett
by his side through rows of men waving cigars, bowing,
doffing brown derbies, Alderman Bud riding in a carriage
full of diamonds with his milliondollar bride . . . Bud is
sitting on the rail of the bridge. The sun has risen behind
Brooklyn. The windows of Manhattan have caught fire.
He jerks himself forward, slips, dangles by a hand with the
sun in his eyes. The yell strangles in his throat as he drops.

Captain McAvoy of the tugboat *Prudence* stood in the
pilothouse with one hand on the wheel. In the other he held
a piece of biscuit he had just dipped into a cup of coffee that
stood on the shelf beside the binnacle. He was a wellset man
with bushy eyebrows and a bushy black mustache waxed at
the tips. He was about to put the piece of coffeesoaked
biscuit into his mouth when something black dropped and
hit the water with a thudding splash a few yards off the bow.
At the same moment a man leaning out of the engineroom
door shouted, "A guy juss jumped offn de bridge."

"God damn it to hell," said Captain McAvoy dropping his
piece of biscuit and spinning the wheel. The strong ebbtide
whisked the boat round like a straw. Three bells jangled in
the engineroom. A Negro ran forward to the bow with a
boathook.

"Give a hand there Red," shouted Captain McAvoy.

After a tussle they landed a long black limp thing on the
deck. One bell. Two bells, Captain McAvoy frowning and
haggard spun the tug's nose into the current again.

"Any life in him Red?" he asked hoarsely. The Negro's
face was green, his teeth were chattering.

"Naw sir," said the redhaired man slowly. "His neck's
broke clear off."

Captain McAvoy sucked a good half of his mustache into
his mouth. "God damn it to hell," he groaned. "A pretty
thing to happen on a man's wedding day."

Newsreel

Come on and hear
Come on and hear
Come on and hear

In his address to the Michigan State Legislature the re-tiring governor, Hazen S. Pingree, said in part: I make the prediction that unless those in charge and in whose hands legislation is reposed do not change the present system of in-equality, there will be a bloody revolution in less than a quarter of a century in this great country of ours.

CARNEGIE TALKS OF HIS EPITAPH

Alexander's Ragtime Band
It is the best
It is the best

the luncheon which was served in the physical labora-tory was replete with novel features. A miniature blastfur-nace four feet high was on the banquet table and a narrow-gauge railroad forty feet long ran round the edge of the table. Instead of molten metal the blastfurnace poured hot punch into small cars on the railroad. Icecream was served in the shape of railroad ties and bread took the shape of lo-comotives.

Mr. Carnegie, while extolling the advantages of higher education in every branch of learning, came at last to this conclusion: Manual labor has been found to be the best foundation for the greatest work of the brain.

VICE-PRESIDENT EMPTIES A BANK

> *Come on and hear*
> *Alexander's Ragtime Band*
> *It is the best*
> *It is the best*

brother of Jesse James declares play picturing him as bandit trainrobber and outlaw is demoralizing district battle ends with polygamy, according to an investigation by Salt Lake ministers, still practiced by Mormons clubwomen gasp

> *It is the best band in the land*

say circus animals only eat Chicago horsemeat Taxsale of Indiana marks finale of World's Fair boom uses flag as ragbag killed on cannibal isle keeper falls into water and sealions attack him.

The launch than came alongside the halfdeflated balloon of the aerostat which threatened at any moment to smother Santos Dumont. The latter was half pulled and half clambered over the gunwale into the boat.

The Prince of Monaco urged him to allow himself to be taken on board the yacht to dry himself and change his clothes. Santos Dumont would not leave the launch until everything that could be saved had been taken ashore, then, wet but smiling and unconcerned, he landed amid the frenzied cheers of the crowd.

The American Plan

Frederick Winslow Taylor (they called him Speedy Taylor in the shop) was born in Germantown, Pennsylvania, the year of Buchanan's election. His father was a lawyer, his mother came from a family of New Bedford whalers; she was a great reader of Emerson, belonged to the Unitarian Church and the Browning Society. She was a fervent abolitionist and believed in democratic manners; she was a housekeeper of the old school, kept everybody busy from dawn till dark. She laid down the rules of conduct:

selfrespect, selfreliance, selfcontrol

and a cold long head for figures.

But she wanted her children to appreciate the finer things, so she took them abroad for three years on the Continent, showed them cathedrals, grand opera, Roman pediments, the old masters under their brown varnish in their great frames of tarnished gilt.

Later Fred Taylor was impatient of these wasted years, stamped out of the room when people talked about the finer things; he was a testy youngster, fond of practical jokes, and a great hand at rigging up contraptions and devices.

At Exeter he was head of his class and captain of the ballteam, the first man to pitch overhand. (When umpires complained that overhand pitching wasn't in the rules of the game, he answered that it got results.)

As a boy he had nightmares; going to bed was horrible for him; he thought they came from sleeping on his back. He made himself a leather harness with wooden pegs that stuck into his flesh when he turned over. When he was grown he slept in a chair or in bed in a sitting position propped up with pillows. All his life he suffered from sleeplessness.

He was a crackerjack tennisplayer. In 1881, with his friend Clark, he won the National Doubles Championship. (He used a spoonshaped racket of his own design.)

At school he broke down from overwork, his eyes went back on him. The doctor suggested manual labor. So instead of going to Harvard he went into the machineshop of a small pumpmanufacturing concern, owned by a friend of the family's, to learn the trade of patternmaker and machinist. He learned to handle a lathe and to dress and cuss like a workingman.

Fred Taylor never smoked tobacco or drank liquor or used tea or coffee; he couldn't understand why his fellow-mechanics wanted to go on sprees and get drunk and raise cain Saturday nights. He lived at home; when he wasn't reading technical books he'd play parts in amateur theatricals or step up to the piano in the evening and sing a good tenor of *A Warrior Bold* or *A Spanish Cavalier*.

He served his first year's apprenticeship in the machineshop without pay; the next two years he made a dollar and a half a week, the last year two dollars.

Pennsylvania was getting rich off iron and coal. When he was twentytwo, Fred Taylor went to work at the Midvale Iron Works. At first he had to take a clerical job, but he hated that and went to work with a shovel. At last he got them to put him on a lathe. He was a good machinist, he worked ten hours a day and in the evenings followed an engineering course at Stevens. In six years he rose from machinist's helper to keeper of toolcribs to gangboss to foreman to mastermechanic in charge of repairs to chief draftsman and director of research to chief engineer of the Midvale Plant.

The early years he was a machinist with the other machinists in the shop, cussed and joked and worked with the rest of them, soldiered on the job when they did. Mustn't give the boss more than his money's worth. But when he got to be foreman, he was on the management's side of the fence, *gathering in on the part of those on the management's side all the great mass of traditional knowledge which in the past has been in the heads of the workmen and in the physical skill and knack of the workman.* He couldn't stand to see an idle lathe or an idle man.

Production went to his head and thrilled his sleepless nerves like liquor or women on a Saturday night. He never loafed and he'd be damned if anybody else would. Production was an itch under his skin.

He lost his friends in the shop; they called him niggerdriver. He was a stockily built man with a temper and a short tongue.

. *I was a young man in years, but I give you my word I was a great deal older than I am now, what with the worry, meanness, and contemptibleness of the whole damn thing. It's a horrid life for any man to live, not being able to look any workman in the face without seeing hostility there, and a feeling that every man around you is your virtual enemy.*

That was the beginning of the Taylor System of Scientific Management.

He was impatient of explanations, he didn't care whose hide he took off in enforcing the laws he believed inherent in the industrial process.

When starting an experiment in any field, question everything, question the very foundations upon which the art rests, question the simplest, the most selfevident, the most universally accepted facts; prove everything,

except the dominant Quaker Yankee (the New Bedford skippers were the greatest niggerdrivers on the whaling seas) rules of conduct. He boasted he'd never ask a workman to do anything he couldn't do.

He devised an improved steamhammer; he standarized tools and equipment, he filled the shop with college students with stopwatches and diagrams, tabulating, standardizing. *There's the right way of doing a thing and the wrong way of doing it; the right way means increased production, lower costs, higher wages, bigger profits:* the American plan.

He broke up the foreman's job into separate functions, speedbosses, gangbosses, timestudy men, order-of-work men.

The skilled mechanics were too stubborn for him; what he wanted was a plain handyman who'd do what he was told. If he was a firstclass man and did firstclass work, Taylor was willing to let him have firstclass pay; that's where he began to get into trouble with the owners.

At thirtyfour he married and left Midvale and took a flyer for the big money in connection with a pulpmill started in Maine by some admirals and political friends of Grover Cleveland's;

the panic of '93 made hash of that enterprise,

so Taylor invented for himself the job of Consulting Engineer in Management and began to build up a fortune by careful investments.

The first paper he read before the American Society of Mechanical Engineers was anything but a success; they said he was crazy. *I have found,* he wrote in 1909, *that any improvement is not only opposed but aggressively and bitterly opposed by the majority of men.*

He was called in by Bethlehem Steel. It was in Bethlehem he made his famous experiments with handling pigiron; he taught a Dutchman named Schmidt to handle fortyseven tons instead of twelve and a half tons of pigiron a day and got Schmidt to admit he was as good as ever at the end of the day.

He was a crank about shovels, every job had to have a shovel of the right weight and size for that job alone; every job had to have a man of the right weight and size for that job alone; but when he began to pay his men in proportion to the increased efficiency of their work,

the owners, who were a lot of greedy smalleyed Dutchmen, began to raise Hail Columbia; when Schwab bought Bethlehem Steel in 1901

Fred Taylor

inventor of efficiency

who had doubled the production of the stampingmill by speeding up the main lines of shafting from ninetysix to twohundred and twentyfive revolutions a minute

was unceremoniously fired.

After that Fred Taylor always said he couldn't afford to work for money.

He took to playing golf (using golfclubs of his own design), doping out methods for transplanting huge boxtrees into the garden of his home.

At Boxly in Germantown he kept open house for engineers, factorymanagers, industrialists;

he wrote papers,

lectured in colleges,

appeared before a congressional committee,

everywhere preached the virtues of scientific management and the Barth slide rule, the cutting-down of waste and idleness, the substitution for skilled mechanics of the plain handyman (like Schmidt the pigiron handler) who'd move as he was told

and work by the piece:

production;

more steel rails more bicycles more spools of thread more armorplate for battleships more bedpans more barbedwire more needles more lightningrods more ballbearings more dollarbills;

(the old Quaker families of Germantown were growing rich, the Pennsylvania millionaires were breeding billionaires out of iron and coal)

production would make every firstclass American rich who was willing to work at piecework and not drink or raise cain or think or stand mooning at his lathe.

Thrifty Schmidt the pigiron handler can invest his money and get to be an owner like Schwab and the rest of the greedy smalleyed Dutchmen and cultivate a taste for Bach and have hundredyearold boxtrees in his garden at Bethlehem or Germantown or Chestnut Hill,

and lay down the rules of conduct;

the American plan

But Fred Taylor never saw the working of the American plan;

in 1915 he went to the hospital in Philadelphia suffering from a breakdown.

Pneumonia developed; the nightnurse heard him winding his watch;

on the morning of his fiftyninth birthday, when the nurse went into his room to look at him at fourthirty,

he was dead with his watch in his hand.

Tin Lizzie

"Mr. Ford the automobileer," the featurewriter wrote in 1900,

"Mr. Ford the automobileer began by giving his steed three or four sharp jerks with the lever at the righthand side of the seat; that is, he pulled the lever up and down sharply in order, as he said, to mix air with gasoline and drive the charge into the exploding cylinder . . . Mr. Ford slipped a small electric switch handle and there followed a puff, puff, puff . . . The puffing of the machine assumed a higher key

. . . She was flying along about eight miles an hour. The ruts in the road were deep, but the machine certainly went with a dreamlike smoothness. There was none of the bumping common even to a steamer . . . By this time the boulevard had been reached, and the automobileer, letting a lever fall a little, let her out. Whiz! She picked up speed with infinite rapidity. As she ran on there was a clattering behind, the new noise of the automobile."

For twenty years or more,

ever since he'd left his father's farm when he was sixteen to get a job in a Detroit machineshop, Henry Ford had been nuts about machinery. First it was watches, then he designed a steamtractor, then he built a horseless carriage with an engine adapted from the Otto gasengine he'd read about in *The World of Science,* then a mechanical buggy with a onecylinder fourcycle motor, that would run forward but not back;

at last, in ninetyeight, he felt he was far enough along to risk throwing up his job with the Detroit Edison Company, where he'd worked his way up from night fireman to chief engineer, to put all his time into working on a new gasoline engine,

(in the late eighties he'd met Edison at a meeting of electriclight employees in Atlantic City. He'd gone up to Edison after Edison had delivered an address and asked him if he thought gasoline was practical as a motor fuel. Edison had said yes. If Edison said it, it was true. Edison was the great admiration of Henry Ford's life);

and in driving his mechanical buggy, sitting there at the lever jauntily dressed in a tightbuttoned jacket and a high collar and a derby hat, back and forth over the level illpaved streets of Detroit,

scaring the big brewery horses and the skinny trotting horses and the sleekrumped pacers with the motor's loud explosions,

looking for men scatterbrained enough to invest money in a factory for building automobiles.

He was the eldest son of an Irish immigrant who during the Civil War had married the daughter of a prosperous Pennsylvania Dutch farmer and settled down to farming near Dearborn in Wayne County, Michigan;

like plenty of other Americans, young Henry grew up

hating the endless sogging through the mud about the chores, the hauling and pitching manure, the kerosene lamps to clean, the irk and sweat and solitude of the farm.

He was a slender, active youngster, a good skater, clever with his hands; what he liked was to tend the machinery and let the others do the heavy work. His mother had told him not to drink, smoke, gamble, or go into debt, and he never did.

When he was in his early twenties his father tried to get him back from Detroit, where he was working as mechanic and repairman for the Drydock Engine Company that built engines for steamboats, by giving him forty acres of land.

Young Henry built himself an uptodate square white dwellinghouse with a false mansard roof and married and settled down on the farm.

but he let the hired men do the farming;

he bought himself a buzzsaw and rented a stationary engine and cut the timber off the woodlots.

He was a thrifty young man who never drank or smoked or gambled or coveted his neighbor's wife, but he couldn't stand living on the farm.

He moved to Detroit, and in the brick barn behind his house tinkered for years in his spare time with a mechanical buggy that would be light enough to run over the clayey wagonroads of Wayne County, Michigan.

By 1900 he had a practicable car to promote.

He was forty years old before the Ford Motor Company was started and production began to move.

Speed was the first thing the early automobile manufacturers went after. Races advertised the makes of cars.

Henry Ford himself hung up several records at the track at Grosse Pointe and on the ice on Lake St. Clair. In his .999 he did the mile in thirtynine and fourfifths seconds.

But it had always been his custom to hire others to do the heavy work. The speed he was busy with was speed in production, the records, records in efficient output. He hired Barney Oldfield, a stunt bicyclerider from Salt Lake City, to do the racing for him.

Henry Ford had ideas about other things than the designing of motors, carburetors, magnetos, jigs and fixtures, punches and dies; he had ideas about sales;

that the big money was in economical quantity production, quick turnover, cheap interchangeable easilyreplaced standardized parts;

it wasn't until 1909, after years of arguing with his partners, that Ford put out the first Model T.

Henry Ford was right.

That season he sold more than ten thousand tin lizzies, ten years later he was selling almost a million a year.

In these years the Taylor Plan was stirring up plantmanagers and manufacturers all over the country. Efficiency was the word. The same ingenuity that went into improving the performance of a machine could go into improving the performance of the workmen producing the machine.

In 1913 they established the assemblyline at Ford's. That season the profits were something like twentyfive million dollars, but they had trouble in keeping the men on the job, machinists didn't seem to like it at Ford's.

Henry Ford had ideas about other things than production.

He was the largest automobile manufacturer in the world; he paid high wages; maybe if the steady workers thought they were getting a cut (a very small cut) in the profits, it would give trained men an inducement to stick to their jobs,

wellpaid workers might save enough money to buy a tin lizzie; the first day Ford's announced that cleancut properlymarried American workers who wanted jobs had a chance to make five bucks a day (of course it turned out that there were strings to it; always there were strings to it)

such an enormous crowd waited outside the Highland Park plant

all through the zero January night

that there was a riot when the gates were opened; cops broke heads, jobhunters threw bricks; property, Henry Ford's own property, was destroyed. The company dicks had to turn on the firehose to beat back the crowd.

The American Plan; automotive prosperity seeping down from above; it turned out there were strings to it.

But that five dollars a day

    paid to good, clean American workmen
    who didn't drink or smoke cigarettes or read or think,
    and who didn't commit adultery
    and whose wives didn't take in boarders,
made America once more the Yukon of the sweated workers of the world;
    made all the tin lizzies and the automotive age, and incidentally,
    made Henry Ford the automobileer, the admirer of Edison, the birdlover,
    the great American of his time.

But Henry Ford had ideas about other things besides assemblylines and the livinghabits of his employees. He was full of ideas. Instead of going to the city to make his fortune, here was a country boy who'd made his fortune by bringing the city out to the farm. The precepts he'd learned out of McGuffey's Reader, his mother's prejudices and preconceptions, he had preserved clean and unworn as freshprinted bills in the safe in a bank.

He wanted people to know about his ideas, so he bought the *Dearborn Independent* and started a campaign against cigarettesmoking.

When war broke out in Europe, he had ideas about that too. (Suspicion of armymen and soldiering were part of the Midwest farm tradition, like thrift, stickativeness, temperance, and sharp practice in money matters.) Any intelligent American mechanic could see that if the Europeans hadn't been a lot of ignorant underpaid foreigners who drank, smoked, were loose about women, and wasteful in their methods of production, the war could never have happened.

When Rosika Schwimmer broke through the stockade of secretaries and servicemen who surrounded Henry Ford and suggested to him that he could stop the war,

he said sure they'd hire a ship and go over and get the boys out of the trenches by Christmas.

He hired a steamboat, the *Oscar II*, and filled it up with pacifists and socialworkers,

    to go over to explain to the princelings of Europe
    that what they were doing was vicious and silly.

It wasn't his fault that Poor Richard's commonsense no longer rules the world and that most of the pacifists were nuts,

goofy with headlines.

When William Jennings Bryan went over to Hoboken to see him off, somebody handed William Jennings Bryan a squirrel in a cage; William Jennings Bryan made a speech with the squirrel under his arm. Henry Ford threw American Beauty roses to the crowd. The band played *I Didn't Raise My Boy to Be a Soldier*. Practical jokers let loose more squirrels. An eloping couple was married by a platoon of ministers in the saloon, and Mr. Zero, the flophouse humanitarian, who reached the dock too late to sail,

dove into the North River and swam after the boat.

The *Oscar II* was described as a floating Chautauqua; Henry Ford said it felt like a Middle-Western village, but by the time they reached Christiansand in Norway, the reporters had kidded him so that he had gotten cold feet and gone to bed. The world was too crazy outside of Wayne County, Michigan. Mrs. Ford and the management sent an Episcopal dean after him who brought him home under wraps,

and the pacifists had to speechify without him.

Two years later Ford's was manufacturing munitions, Eagle boats; Henry Ford was planning oneman tanks, and oneman submarines like the one tried out in the Revolutionary War. He announced to the press that he'd turn over his war profits to the government,

but there's no record that he ever did.

One thing he brought back from his trip

was the Protocols of the Elders of Zion.

He started a campaign to enlighten the world in the *Dearborn Independent*; the Jews were why the world wasn't like Wayne County, Michigan, in the old horse-and-buggy days;

the Jews had started the war, Bolshevism, Darwinism, Marxism, Nietzsche, short skirts and lipstick. They were behind Wall Street and the international bankers, and the whiteslave traffic and the movies and the Supreme Court and ragtime and the illegal liquor business.

Henry Ford denounced the Jews and ran for Senator and sued the *Chicago Tribune* for libel,

and was the laughingstock of the kept metropolitan press;

but when the metropolitan bankers tried to horn in on
his business

he thoroughly outsmarted them.

In 1918 he had borrowed on notes to buy out his minor-
ity stockholders for the picayune sum of seventyfive million
dollars.

In February, 1920, he needed cash to pay off some of
these notes that were coming due. A banker is supposed to
have called on him and offered him every facility if the
banker's representative could be made a member of the
board of directors. Henry Ford handed the banker his hat,

and went about raising the money in his own way:

he shipped every car and part he had in his plant to his
dealers and demanded immediate cash payment. Let the
other fellow do the borrowing had always been a cardinal
principle. He shut down production and canceled all orders
from the supplyfirms. Many dealers were ruined, many supplyfirms failed, but when he reopened his plant,

he owned it absolutely,

the way a man owns an unmortgaged farm with the
taxes paid up.

In 1922 there started the Ford boom for President (high
wages, waterpower, industry scattered to the small towns)
that was skillfully pricked behind the scenes

by another crackerbarrel philosopher,

Calvin Coolidge;

but in 1922 Henry Ford sold one million three hundred
and thirtytwo thousand two hundred and nine tin lizzies;
he was the richest man in the world.

Good roads had followed the narrow ruts made in the
mud by the Model T. The great automotive boom was on.
At Ford's production was improving all the time; less waste,
more spotters, strawbosses, stoolpigeons (fifteen minutes for
lunch, three minutes to go to the toilet, the Taylorized
speedup everywhere, reachunder, adjustwasher, screwdown
bolt, shove in cotterpin, reachunder, adjustwasher, screwdown bolt, reachunderadjustscrewdownreachunderadjust,
until every ounce of life was sucked off into production and
at night the workmen went home gray shaking husks).

Ford owned every detail of the process from the ore in
the hills until the car rolled off the end of the assemblyline
under its own power; the plants were rationalized to the last

tenthousandth of an inch as measured by the Johansen scale;

in 1926 the production cycle was reduced to eightyone
hours from the ore in the mine to the finished salable car
proceeding under its own power,

but the Model T was obsolete.

New Era prosperity and the American Plan
(there were strings to it, always there were strings to it)
had killed Tin Lizzie.
Ford's was just one of many automobile plants.
When the stockmarket bubble burst,
Mr. Ford the crackerbarrel philosopher said jubilantly,
"I told you so.
Serves you right for gambling and getting in debt.
The country is sound."
But when the country on cracked shoes, in frayed trou-
sers, belts tightened over hollow bellies,
idle hands cracked and chapped with the cold of that
coldest March day of 1932,
started marching from Detroit to Dearborn, asking for
work and the American Plan, all they could think of at
Ford's was machineguns.
The country was sound, but they mowed the marchers
down.
They shot four of them dead.

Henry Ford as an old man
is a passionate antiquarian
(lives besieged on his father's farm embedded in an estate of thousands of millionaire acres, protected by an army
of servicemen, secretaries, secret agents, dicks under orders
of an English exprizefighter,
always afraid of the feet in broken shoes on the roads,
afraid the gangs will kidnap his grandchildren,
that a crank will shoot him,
that Change and the idle hands out of work will break
through the gates and the high fences;
protected by a private army against
the new America of starved children and hollow bellies
and cracked shoes stamping on souplines,
that has swallowed up the old thrifty farmlands
of Wayne County, Michigan,

as if they had never been).
Henry Ford as an old man
is a passionate antiquarian.

He rebuilt his father's farmhouse and put it back exactly in the state he remembered it in as a boy. He built a village of museums for buggies, sleighs, coaches, old plows, waterwheels, obsolete models of motorcars. He scoured the country for fiddlers to play oldfashioned squaredances.

Even old taverns he bought and put back into their original shape, as well as Thomas Edison's early laboratories.

When he bought the Wayside Inn near Sudbury, Massachusetts, he had the new highway where the newmodel cars roared and slithered and hissed oilily past (*the new noise of the automobile*)

moved away from the door,
put back the old bad road,
so that everything might be
the way it used to be,
in the days of horses and buggies.

Blackie Bowman Speaking

(*Scene: a bed in a Veterans' Hospital*)

THEY'VE BROUGHT IN a new doctor. The trouble they go to to keep this old cracked carcass alive. Sometimes they give me a whiff of oxygen. I get a sort of a jag out of it. I haven't the heart to tell them what's the use? It don't mean that much to me any more. What's the use of being alive if you can't act like a living man? But then I keep thinking, when I die for sure will all that life I keep remembering die too? Somehow it seems to be still living in my head. It was years ago and it's still living, so much vivider than the ward and the nurse and the sick guys gasping at night and the doctor's treatments that don't do any good. It seems to go on existing outside of this paining carcass that has nothing left for lungs but an old pair of leather bellows.

Take the day I ran away from home.

Maybe it's because I've thought about it so often and told the tale drunk or sober in a hundred different shapes to fellows I was exchanging confidences with or girls I was making up to that it all seems so clear. You don't suppose I made it up do you? You would think I'd have talked it away by this time but it is still one of the vividest things in my life. I can even remember thoughts I had about things that were happening to me. I know, a fifteenyearold kid all steaming inside, with two fresh eyes and strong anxious muscles and blood at the boil, is a very different creature than a sixtysevenyearold wreck trussed up and helpless on a hospital cot like the sea turtles I've seen trussed up in rows on the decks of fishing smacks off Honduras, but that kid is me just as much as this old wreck is me.

I was the youngest of the boys but I was the first to leave home. All through grammar school and the first year high I did all right. I was the pet of the family on account of being a pretty fair pitcher on a ball team we had that played kids from other neighborhoods in Patterson Park. Sundays Dad brought his cronies to watch me pitch.

Dad was a stubby shortnecked man with curly red hair all over him. It was very thick on his chest. His tread was heavy on the stairs. It was a relief to us kids when he left the house early to go to work. He was a foreman at a Sparrows Point shipyard. He kept us all scared with his temper and the unreasonable way he'd act after even a bottle of beer, but I worshiped him from a distance when I was little, because he seemed so strong and tough, and had such a joshing confident way of making friends with other men. Nobody ever seemed to be able to put over anything on Dad.

We lived in a narrow new brick row house that everybody said was very well built, in East Baltimore, with white marble steps that my mother used to scrub every morning and a bead curtain that made a picture of Niagara Falls across the entrance hall. Outside it looked like all the other houses on the block, but we thought it had something special about it. Everything about the Bowmans was special.

Mother brought us up to think that the Bowmans and her

people the McMahons were the grandest people in the world. The fact that we weren't as rich as some people didn't count; it was what we were inside that counted. Though the girls were younger than me I was younger than my two brothers. I didn't remember the times when we lived in a tenement downtown and were what Mother called dirt poor.

During the years I remember Dad was always coming home all puffed up from getting a raise or from being elected to something in the local Democratic club or the Masonic lodge or one of the societies he belonged to. He always seemed to have something to be puffed up about. Maybe that was why I began to hate him.

Or maybe it was on account of the split in our family that I didn't really understand till years after I'd left home. It never came out in the open but it was there just the same. Mother was a Catholic but Dad wasn't. Mother did needlework so that the girls could go to parochial school but us boys went to public school, except for my oldest brother Joe who had a scholarship at Notre Dame and was planning to study for the priesthood. He was Mother's favorite. She was all wrapped up in him and us younger kids felt it.

I must have grown five or six inches the year I was fourteen. That was the year the whole world changed on me. All of a sudden everything I did was wrong. The house began to feel like a jail. Dad became a mean old tyrant with a beery breath. My brothers were dumb clucks. They didn't understand me. All my little sisters were good for was to snitch on me.

Sure I loved my mother but she threw me off by always telling me to be a good boy like Joe. I hated the sanctimonious bastard. Ed was the worst. For as long as I could remember I'd slept in the same room with Ed, but now we were always stepping on each others' toes. Ed was two years older than me but he wasn't growing so fast. The minute I was big enough I socked him in the jaw. Ed never forgave me for that. He just wouldn't speak to me. That was where all the trouble began.

Up to the time I had that fight with Ed I'd been near the top of my class at school. The teachers used to write nice little messages on my report cards. All Dad cared about was getting his own way but Mother was ambitious for her children. She used to tell me that because I liked to study and was good at science and arithmetic and stuff like that I ought to go to college and learn to be a civil engineer. It was an awful shock to her when the truant officer came around to ask where Francis Xavier was.

I know I didn't exactly plan to stay away from school so many days, but I was mad at the folks and other things seemed so much more important, particularly loafing around with a bunch of kids my own age who used to gather to smoke cigarettes and cuss and tell dirty stories behind the piles of teakwood and mahogany logs in Higgins' Lumber Yard down on the harbor. The good opinion of my folks and the schoolteachers and of Father Carroll, Joe's friend whom Mother made a great fuss over when he came to dinner on Sundays, suddenly didn't mean a damn thing to me any more. What I wanted was the good opinion of Bug Evans, a gawky towheaded guy with a mean pair of fists who talked big about getting drunk Saturday nights and going down to the Block to pick up a hooker. Even when I did go to school I couldn't think about anything but girls.

There was a family that had come to Baltimore out of some West Virginia mining town to work at the shipyards that lived in a shack on the alley back of our house. My mother and sisters had their noses in the air about them. Mother said they lived more like niggers than white people.

There was a gang of children, all barefoot. Two of the girls, Lou and Dovie, were about my age. I don't know that I really liked them. They were damp smelly little girls with stringy hair but they were mighty curious to learn all about what it was little boys had behind the front of their pants.

We used to sneak up into the loft of a stable down at the end of the street. Right now I can smell the sweated harness and the horse manure and the sweet hay. Hosea, the old colored man who took care of the two white delivery horses they kept there, thought it was a great joke. He used to give me pointers about how to handle the girls.

Hosea was proud of his big white mustaches. He had seen better days as a coachman with a family that lived on Mt. Vernon Place. Drink had been his undoing. He never tired of telling me about the patent leather hat and the livery and his wives and children and the high yallers he'd had when he was a young buck. He never did tell on us. Hosea and me were real friends. Now and then when I could snake a bottle of Dad's beer out of the pantry back of the kitchen, I'd run down the street with it under my shirt for Hosea.

Now when Bug Evans carried on about how hot the floosies were down on Baltimore Street I could come back big about how I had all the girls I wanted without paying them a cent.

Bug said I was a goddam liar and that led to a fight. I didn't exactly lick him but I held my end up pretty good. We each had a bloody nose and a black eye when Bug suddenly said "Let's shake." A couple of the other guys who were standing around watching the fight grumbled that we were a pair of sissies and ought to fight to a finish; then Bug and me, we joined forces and ran 'em out of the lumber yard. Then we went to the nearest pump and washed our faces. The two of us were friends after that.

It was trying to tap a keg of beer Dad had keeping cool in the basement one Saturday afternoon to give Bug a drink that I had my run in with the old man. Of course I did it all wrong and the beer spurted out all over the place and Dad, who was shaving in the kitchen before going out to some kind of political oyster roast, heard us giggling and came running down the steps with his chin full of lather.

When he saw the beer foaming on the basement floor his face got red as a beet and he grabbed me by the shoulder and started to beat me with the razorstrop he had in his hand. I couldn't stand there and let Dad give me a licking right in front of Bug so I ducked and slid out from under his hand and Dad tripped over the beer keg trying to catch me and measured his length in all that foam on the floor. Bug and I didn't stop running till we slid through a hole in the fence into Higgins' Lumber Yard.

I said honest I dassent go home. Bug said he'd be damned if he'd go home either. His dad was an awful religious man. He had taken to beating him with a blacksnake whip, not to hurt Bug, so he said, but to beat the devil inside him. Bug showed me the great red welts he had on his back. "I'll tell you what let's do," Bug said, "let's run away to sea."

There wasn't all this business about work permits and union hiring halls in those days. Bug and I just went around to every old freighter we saw tied up to a dock and asked if they were signing on hands. Most of 'em ran us out when they saw how young we were, but at last we caught up with a Captain Connor in a saloon on East Pratt Street who was in trouble because he had to sail Monday for New Orleans with a cargo of steel plates and would be clearing shorthanded. Three of his crew had gotten into a fight in a joint on the Block and landed in jail for thirty days. He signed us on as boys at fifteen dollars a month which sounded like a fortune to Bug and me. No he wouldn't advance us a cent. He was afraid we'd give him the slip.

It was Saturday night and suppertime and our pockets were inside out. Bug's old man made a practice of taking charge of all the money he brought home but I had twelve dollars saved up from a paper route I'd been running. It was in a castiron bank shaped like a windmill I had in my room. The hardest thing I ever did was go back to the house to tell Mother what we'd done.

Afterwards I was glad because it was the last time I ever saw her in my life. Her eyes were red from crying. Dad had stormed out of the house in a pet. When I told her I was going to sea she didn't protest a bit. Making my own living was the best thing I could do. She packed up my clothes in an old suitcase and put in a prayer book and hung a scapular round my neck and made me swear I'd wear it always.

My brothers and sisters had eaten and gone out. Mother fried up a steak specially for Bug and me. It sure smelt good sizzling in the pan but when I got it on my plate I just couldn't eat. Bug ate his share and mine too and then we went to hunt up Hosea to see if he'd let us sleep in his loft. He was a good old thing. He cooked us up our breakfast next morning. There were tears in his bulging old bloodshot white eyes when he said goodbye.

I had to share my twelve dollars with Bug to get him outfitted a little in the jewstores. They were open Sundays on the waterfront in those days. He was going to pay me back when we got paid but as it turned out we never did get paid.

The SS *Ossining* was quite a ship. Bedbugs in the bunks. Cockroaches everywhere. Weevils in the bread. Coffee that tasted of bilge. We hadn't cleared the harbor before a surly Scot everybody called Mr. Mack put us to work chipping rust. It wasn't so bad going down the Bay, sprinkled with the white sails of oyster boats, but the minute we poked our nose out of the Capes the wind turned cold and the sea got rough. Nobody would lend us any oilskins and we crawled around the deck drenched and shivering chipping and scrubbing at the wet rail. We were seasick and the stuff they gave us to scrub the paint with burned our hands, and every man on the ship seemed to go out of his way to kick us around.

Off Hatteras we shipped so much green water the captain sent us below to keep us from being washed overboard. We neither of us had anything left on our stomachs to puke up, but the stench of stale pipes and wet oilskins and of the stuff the cook spread around under the bunks to kill bedbugs made us start retching all over again. Back home we'd thought we were a pair of pretty tough kids but we didn't feel tough then. I don't know about Bug but I just lay there listening to the seas slamming against the bow and hoping I'd die. In the end I cried myself to sleep like a baby.

Off the Florida coast the weather moderated. The sun came out and the wind smelt of spring. It was March. The days were only twelve hours long, but that Mr. Mack had us chipping and scrubbing from the first dawn till after dark, and the Swede who followed after us with the red lead kept bawling us out for not working fast enough. They kept us at it sixteen hours a day. When they ran out of paint in the locker we thought they'd let us rest, but there was the deck to scrub, and the portholes to clean and the brass to polish.

We'd hardly finished that job when they hung us over the side to chip the plates. We had a smooth sea by that time and were steaming with a balmy following breeze up the Gulf of Mexico. We'd been chipping rust when we got our last sight of Fort McHenry and we still were chipping rust when we passed between McKees Jetties into the smooth earthsmelling swirling Mississippi water.

Our hands were all raw around the nails and our arms felt like they'd fall out of their sockets, but when we smelt the land and saw the palegreen canefields sliding by behind the levees, and plantation houses with columns and the steamboats with iron lace around their twin stacks set way aft over the sternwheel, we were crazy with excitement again. When one of us got close enough to another to nudge him while we worked, we'd give each other sly winks and whisper "New Orleans."

We had dreams of a day off and creole girls in the French

quarter and minstrel shows and I don't know what all but the minute we tied up to the dock we had to work harder than ever handling the heavy tackle on hoists and lugging up sacks of coal for the old donkey engine forward that seemed to be Mr. Mack's particular pet. Unloading those steel plates with the equipment we had was slow as cold molasses.

That night we couldn't sleep. The warm air smelt of sugar. The arclights behind the levee glared into the portholes. At last when everything was quiet Bug shook me by the shoulder. He had that wild look in his eyes. "Let's go," he whispered with his mouth close to my ear.

In the fo'castle everybody was snoring. We went tiptoeing around the decks trying to find some way of getting off the damn boat. The skipper and mate had had the gangway hauled up before they left for the night. The watchman must have strayed away for a drink because nobody saw us when we let ourselves down by a loose end of a hawser. Bug even remembered to bring my suitcase and his little seabag.

Once we had our feet on dry land we ducked into a dark alley behind a warehouse. We knew the cops were tough on seamen jumping ship.

The trouble with New Orleans was everything cost money and money was what we hadn't got. We didn't dare show our faces in any kind of a joint for fear Captain Connor would have us arrested and hauled back on board. We were dead tired. We were hungry and sick of hauling our duffle around the streets. We had only a dollar between us. We just roamed around back alleys between the foreignlooking houses. Every cop we saw threw us into a sweat.

At last Bug got into conversation with a hooker. We caught up with her coming out of the Absinthe House. She'd had a few drinks or maybe she wouldn't have been so kind. Still Bug had quite a way with the women. We walked one on each side of her and told our sad tale. She sized up our situation and said times were bad and she was through for the night and if we gave her our dollar she'd let us sleep at her place. Only no monkey business. She looked us each in the eye one after another just like a schoolteacher. The cop on the beat was her friend and she slept with a police whistle under her pillow. "Savvy?"

Her room was up some iron corkscrew stairs on one of those upper galleries they have in the French quarter. A big meanlooking white cat was waiting outside the door. The cat was mewing his head off. She was crazy about that cat. She had to get him his saucer of food before she'd pay any attention to us.

Her room was neat as a pin. An embroidered cover on the bed. Clean lace curtains in the windows. She laughed at how surprised we were to see things so shipshape. "Ain't you boys ever heard the saying: 'Disorderly life, orderly house'?"

She began to loosen up after she'd fed the cat. Her name was Myrna. She was from Missouri and that went all around the clock. Myrna was a thin skinny palefaced woman with a bony jaw. She looked awful old to us but she sure had a kind heart. She spread out everything to eat she had in the house and a growler half full of stale beer.

Bug began to perk up and get a little fresh when he'd eaten. He was used to getting away with murder with the women on account of his baby blue eyes, but Myrna slapped his face and said she wasn't robbing no cradle. There was only one man living could have her ass for nothing. My that woman had a raucous laugh.

She got out some blankets for us to sleep on and bedded us down in an old closet in the back of the house. She locked the door on us from the outside. She wasn't taking no chances, Myrna said.

Next day round noon she let us out and made us clean up real good at the washstand. She even made us wash our ears. Myrna was a stickler for cleanliness. Then she cooked us up the best breakfast you ever saw and told us twentythree skiddoo, she had her customers to think of. I was hoping she'd give us back our dollar but she never did.

She told us there were no jobs to be had for young punks like us in New Orleans, we'd find a line of buck niggers a mile long at any place they had work. Jump a freight and get out, was her advice. She stood there as we scrambled down the corkscrew stairs, leaning over the rail of the gallery and yelling directions at us about how to reach the yards where they made up the westernbound freights. That cat was arching his back and rubbing against her bare legs that showed through the frilly pink wrapper that kept coming open in front. "You kids head for Texas," she screeched. She was a hardlooking woman but all my life I've remembered how kind she was.

Bug and me we didn't know a damn thing about freights.

We sure would have landed in some chaingang if it hadn't been for Earl Gates. We ran into Earl in some little tank town south of Texarkana. We were hipped on getting to Texas but all the trains seemed to be going the other way.

That day we were standing under the drip from the water tank crouched to make a run for a string of flatcars just gathering speed when a heavy hand came down on each of our shoulders. "Take it easy boys," came a deep voice behind us. We were scared out of our wits. We thought it was a yard dick.

When we turned around we both burst out laughing. It was a runty little guy with a rusty goatee and red hair that stuck straight up in the middle of his head like a rooster's comb. He was small but he was wiry and God he had a grip. He had the pleasantest sounding deep voice you ever heard: "Don't get killed before your time, boys," he was saying.

Earl Gates was one of the really great guys I met up with in my life. It was Earl who first called me Blackie. Right away he started to call me Blackie and Bug Evans Whitie. He made out we were so green that it was the only way he could tell us apart.

Earl must have been twentyfour or twentyfive. He'd been on the bum for five years. The way he liked to put it was that he was carrying on a private scientific investigation of the lower strata of society. Earl sure did love big words. Earl told us his old man had a nice little farm in southern Illinois, but he had left home because he wanted an education. His old man said no amount of booklearning would raise a crop of corn and was dead set against it. He must have been as pigheaded in his way as Earl was in his.

Earl had been beating his way back and forth across the country trying to get a college degree. He'd tried the Cooper Union and nightschool at Northwestern and a whole raft of state colleges, but he never could get credit for his courses because he talked back to his profs. I guess he really wanted to be teaching the courses himself. I never knew a man so crazy about reading. He'd read Marx and Henry George and listened to lectures by Daniel De Leon. When I first met up with him he was a Socialist. Eugene V. Debs was his god. Right away he told Bug and me he was going to educate us if it killed him.

Texas was no place to go, we'd starve to death in Texas.

Earl was headed for the harvest fields. It was only April so we had more than a month to make it out to southern Missouri for the barley and oats. Meanwhile he'd learn us the lore of the road. First lesson: never ride flatcars. A hobo on a flatcar was a sitting duck. Second lesson: never jump a freight on an empty stomach. A man needed all his strength not to make a false step and get killed.

Right away Earl led the two of us down through a gulley back of the water tank to a jungle under some cottonwood trees. Three old tramps were sitting around a little fire. They had a gunny sack full of turnips and beets and cabbage and spuds some farmer had given them because they'd been damaged by frost in his root cellar. The tramps treated Earl with respect. They gave us kids some sidelong looks but they didn't try to molest us.

Bug had been standoffish with Earl at first but those spuds roasted in the ashes convinced him Earl was on the up and up. After that he listened to everything Earl said meek as a lamb. Bug wasn't any reader. He sure was the puzzledest kid in the world when he heard Earl and me, after we'd wrapped ourselves in old newspapers to go to sleep by the fire because the night was cold, go at it hammer and tongs about unearned increment and the labor theory of value.

Somehow I'd just eaten that stuff up since I'd read a copy of *The Appeal to Reason* one of Dad's friends left lying around the house one day, but Earl was the first man who laid socialism on the line so's I could understand it. I was just a highschool kid but I'd heard and seen enough around home to know that, in Baltimore at least, money ruled the roost. The interests did what they pleased and the working man got the short end of the stick.

Dad seemed to go along with that system. He always sided with the strong. He'd tell about the streetcar company buying some city councilman, or the raw deal some poor ignorant bohunk got at the shipyard as if he liked it that way. That was one of the things made me maddest at him. After all poor Mother had tried to bring us up Christians.

Earl was a natural born teacher. Talking to Earl, Christianity and socialism all fell into place. Earl left you thinking that Jesus Christ the carpenter, the first apostle of the working class, and Eugene V. Debs, the railroad leader, had really been out for the same cause. Capitalism was the moneychangers Christ had driven out of the temple. Democracy would be a grand thing if the vested interests weren't in a position to buy all the politicians. Abolish the power of money. All we needed to set things right was for the guys who did the work to take over the running of the industrial system. It wasn't our fault we was starving to death as bums instead of being in school studying, it was the fault of the system.

What convinced Bug and me was that Earl was such a warmhearted guy. That first day we saw him give away his extra shirt to an old stumblebum who'd lost his trying to wash it in the Red River.

Earl watched over Bug and me like a father. When we met Earl we didn't have a plan in the world but Earl always had plans. If we came along with him we'd follow the wheat harvest up from Missouri through Kansas and Nebraska up to the Dakotas. We could go clear to Winnipeg if we wanted to go that far north but this summer he had a notion to beat his way into one of the Colorado mining camps.

He was planning to save himself up a little stake and try mining. Miners were striking it rich. We might try placer mining for gold. He wanted to make enough money quick to go to a first rate college and really get himself an education. I figured I'd try to get me an education too. Plans sounded so easy talking to Earl. I began to see myself walking in on Mother and Dad with a college diploma in my hand. That would show 'em who the smart boy was in the Bowman family.

We had our share of trouble before we got to the wheatfields. We weren't the only ones who had this idea of following the harvest that summer. Business wasn't so good and the freights were crowded. The railroads were putting up No Trespassing signs and hiring fresh dicks to keep migrants off the trains.

Trouble comes up so fast when you are on the bum, always when you don't expect it. The three of us were riding in an empty gondola with a couple of Mexicans we'd met up with, sitting there in the warm sun looking out at the pretty rolling springtime country while Earl talked up socialism and the brotherhood of man in his low even voice that you could hear pretty well under the slambanging of the wheels and the couplings.

The train was slowing down and we were all settling back to listen to Earl talk when we heard yelling and shooting up the line. As the train slowed to a stop a bunch of armed deputies were pulling the boes off the cars and beating them up with their clubs. We jumped and ran for it into a little patch of woods beside the tracks.

At the edge of the wood I turned. Bug wasn't with us. He'd slipped and twisted his ankle maybe jumping. I saw him sprawling on the track. As he struggled to his feet a big plugugly came down on his head with a baseball bat held with both hands. Earl said afterwards he could hear Bug's skull crack right from where he stood. There was nothing we could do because right then a couple of deputies started shooting. They must have been drunk. Their guns were loaded with rock salt. I got a piece in my shoulder and it stung.

On the far side of the wood was an open field and beyond that a dirt road that had a look of leading into a town. Earl and I slackened our pace.

"We got to do something," Earl said as soon as he caught his breath.

The Mexicans never did stop running, but Earl and me, we waited to think what to do. Then we started walking into town. "Our only hope," Earl was saying, "is that the local doctor is an honest man." Already we could see houses through the trees ahead.

We stopped and cleaned ourselves up at a horsetrough on the edge of the village. Earl always carried soap and a razor and a little round mirror in his pocket. He insisted we both of us shave. A mockingbird sang like crazy all the while in the oaktree overhead. It seemed to me desperately long before Earl was satisfied we looked respectable enough. Then Earl asked our way to the local doctor's.

The doctor was a shortnecked grayhaired man with a trimmed beard. He was sitting in his shirtsleeves in his office with his stethoscope hanging over the stiff starched front. Earl talked mighty sweet about how a young boy he knew had been beaten up by the railroad police and he knew he was hurt bad, maybe killed and wouldn't the doctor go with us to try to find him.

The doctor kept saying this was his office hours and he had nobody to leave in charge, but Earl came back about how the boy would die without medical assistance and quoted the Hippocratic oath — now who but Earl would have been able to quote the Hippocratic oath?

The doctor sighed and got to his feet and slipped on his vest and his black coat and made us hitch up his horse and buggy for him and drove us by a crossroad over to the railroad tracks.

We found the place all right on account of the little wood. The train had pulled out. There were dropped bundles and bits of torn shirt and broken bats and other signs of a pitched battle, but not a hobo or a deputy in sight.

In the ditch we found Bug. His head was caked with blood. At first I thought he was dead but there was a bubbling sound from his mouth. His eyes were open but they seemed to have lost all their color. They didn't have any focus. We couldn't tell whether Bug could see us or not.

The doctor wouldn't let us touch him. That sawbones was troubled with shortness of breath but he knew his business all right. He told us he had been a field surgeon in the Philippines. He wouldn't let us move Bug till he drove back to town to get a colored man with a spring wagon and a stretcher. Back at his office he worked over Bug half the night.

We sat on the front porch steps and worried. When the doctor came back he looked haggard. He asked if we knew the address of Bug's parents. For a wonder I did. He said he'd telegraph them, that the boy must stay here but he added that we'd better move on out of town. The sheriff here was mighty tough on vagrants.

"Will he get well?"

The doctor was breathing hard. He shook his head. How did he know? Compound fracture of the skull. It would be months before he could tell how badly the brain was affected.

"This is going to put me to a lot of expense," the doctor complained peevishly after another fit of panting.

We said we didn't have a cent in the world but Earl announced in his deep confident voice that when we made our stake we'd surely pay him for his trouble. Earl made a great show of writing down the sawbones' name and address. He'd convinced the both of us by that time we'd get rich in the goldfields.

We walked out into a drizzly night. We were wretched. We were hungry. We didn't know where we were going but we walked and walked. As we walked we swore to each other that no matter how rich we got in the goldfields we'd never forget Bug. Everything we made, everything we learned we'd dedicate to creating a country where things like that couldn't happen. To tell the truth the world never did seem the same to me after that night.

A day or two later we were so busy we didn't have time to grieve for Bug Evans. We hit a farm where they were harvesting a hundred acres of barley. They needed hands. Right away instead of being kicked around we found ourselves honored guests. The farmer's wife found us clean straw to sleep on in the hayloft over the cowbarn. At meals at a long table set on trestles outside the kitchen door she couldn't feed us enough. Evenings we sat around with the family on the back stoop. One of the young sons had a ukelele and we sang all the songs we knew.

It was hard work but it was cheerful. They had me feeding the shocks off the wagons into the big old steam threshing machine set up behind the barn. On account of his strong hands they had Earl tying the bags. It was heavy work and dusty work and the dust was full of the sharp beards of the barley that got up your sleeves and down your neck and you were soaked with sweat and the chaff stuck to you and you itched, but Earl said you felt what you were doing was of use to the world. He'd been raised on a farm and the work came easy to him.

When we were through at one farm we moved to another. Often we went along with the threshing machine and the reapers and binders or rode in a wagon some farmer who needed hands would send over for us. It was a grand summer.

Earl wouldn't let me spend any money, so I had sixty dollars saved when Earl and I piled off the train in Trinidad, Colorado.

The first thing we saw was a deputy with a gun standing guard at the depot.

I don't know what I'd been expecting but listening to Earl I had gotten to thinking of a mining camp as some wonderful thing. Trinidad was nothing but a mess of rock piles and mineheads and unpainted shacks in a wilderness of bare gray mountains. It was an oriental despotism besides. The coal company owned everything. They paid good wages but they got back every cent through the company stores and the cribhouses and the bars. Half the miners couldn't speak English. Poor dumb oxen right out of Ellis Island, they didn't know how they were being exploited.

Earl and I, we'd been bitter ever since we saw that happen to Bug but now we found ourselves on the firing lines of the class war. There was terror in the air. A man would look behind him before he came out with what he had on his mind. Wherever a few men who talked English could get together out of earshot of the stoolpigeons they talked organization. Bill Haywood, a handsome lion of a man with a fighter look from only having one eye, had been shuttling back and forth through the mining country, always one jump ahead of the bulls, preaching the Western Federation of Miners. The miners had guns, they knew how to use dynamite. Big Bill told them the day would soon come when they would take over the mines for themselves.

Earl Gates ate it up. He had a natural yen to sacrifice himself for a cause. In the WFM he saw the beginning of the revolution that would inaugurate the promised land. Earl forgot all about his plans for college and for making his pile. Before I knew what had happened he was secretary of the miners' secret lodge. Earl's was the spirit that brought forth the Industrial Workers of the World a few years later.

I forgot about my plans too, but the trouble with me was I was just turned sixteen and thought I knew it all. I had money in my pocket and wanted to show those Trinidad floosies how I knew all there was to know about liquor and women. Earl hated drink and loose living. When he found me drunk in a crib one night with a little girl named Suzy Ann he gave me a tonguelashing I'll never forget.

If I hadn't thought so much of the guy I'd have punched him one. I flared right up in his face and asked him who the hell he thought he was, my old man? That was why I'd left home, to do what I goddam pleased. Earl stood there patiently listening with a hurt look on his face. Then he saw it was hopeless and left.

Suzy Ann almost split a gut laughing. She was a dark little rolypoly girl with shoebutton eyes. She claimed to be just my age. She certainly couldn't have been much older.

The tale she was telling me was that she'd been kidnaped over the mountains out of a respectable home in Santa Fe. She begged me to take her back. It sounded like something out of Dick Deadeye. Maybe that was where she read it. Anyway I believed every word of it.

The same night I had my run in with Earl Suzy Ann and I climbed on a couple of saddled horses we found hitched to a rail back of one of the boardinghouses and rode up over Raton Pass in a flurry of snow. Suzy Ann knew the trail. It was a hundred and fifty miles but we made it to Santa Fe. We would never have gotten away with it if the mining camps hadn't been in an uproar. In Trinidad the sheriff and his deputies were too busy trying to round up labor agitators to worry about a stolen cayuse.

Maybe it was being scared to death on account of the ponies — they were still hanging horsethieves in the mountains — or maybe it was just the damn magnificence of the scenery, but I can still see it, like a photograph inside my brain, the way the mountains looked with the dawn at our backs lighting the high snowy peaks and the purple upland country and the broad spread of the pines and the tremblingasps yellow with fall in the valleys. Why we didn't starve to death or freeze to death I'll never know, but somehow we managed to drag those spavined ponies as far as Taos.

There was nothing to Taos but the Indian pueblo in those days. Our mounts were worn out. Mine had gone lame. We sold them for five silver dollars to an old halfbreed sitting on his haunches outside the trading post, and the saddles for another five. That redskin knew what was what. Before we could turn around the ponies had vanished into an arroyo. We rode down to Santa Fe with the mailman on his wagon. Suzy Ann told him she was my sister.

The laugh was on me when we got to Santa Fe. Suzy Ann's folks she talked so big about turned out to be a fat Mexican woman with a mustache who was madam of the local bordello. The old lady greeted me in style and put on the longlost daughter act with Suzy Ann but when she found I'd spent all my money, that is all that Suzy Ann hadn't stowed away in the chamois skin bag she carried inside her corset, she began to talk about how it was time I was moving along. Suzy Ann said be sure and write.

One of their clients was a kind of a padrone who was up

there hiring Mexicans for a construction job in LA. Labor was scarce on the Coast that year. I signed his cutthroat contract and he took me down to the railroad station with the rest of his deluded slaves. All I had to remember Suzy Ann by was a dose of clap that developed while I was working as waterboy on that job in LA.

By the time a Mexican doctor had dried me up at the cost of most of my pay I was a sadder and a wiser boy. I decided the seabreezes would do me good and signed on at San Pedro as deckhand on a tramp bound for Panama with a cargo of steers. Teddy Roosevelt was busy digging his canal through the Isthmus and the merchant marine seemed a fine career for a young fellow to go into. It would have been a fine career for me if I hadn't gotten into the habit of blowing in my pay on liquor and broads every time I hit port. It's not my fault, it's the system, I said to myself. After five years all I had to show for it was a few cuts and bruises and my papers as an ablebodied seaman.

The fall I decided to take a spell on the beach in San Pedro while I looked for better paying work was the fall they blew up the *Los Angeles Times*. To tell the truth I got my first job in structural iron because the cops rounded up so many bridgemen that work was at a standstill on a new downtown hotel. At least in the merchant marine I'd learned how to balance on a scaffolding and paint. The day they arrested the McNamaras, just to prove I wasn't a scab I went around and joined the International Association of Bridgemen and Structural Iron Workers, not that I approved of killing innocent people – that was no way to fight the class war – but I honestly believed the McNamara brothers were being framed.

When McManigel squealed and the McNamaras changed their plea to guilty I felt like I'd had a hodful of bricks dumped down on my head. I wasn't the only one. I understand that Sam Gompers never recovered from the blow. I still think they ought to have kept their mouths shut and taken their medicine like men.

I was never an officer in the union so I didn't get indicted when they railroaded that bunch out of the Indianapolis office. They pinned every dynamiting on those boys that had happened since the Molly Maguires. Still I did enough talking to get my name on the Erectors' Association's blacklist, but particularly as girder construction was on the increase nationwide and qualified men were hard to come by, the bosses found it convenient to have short memories. I don't think I ever lost out on a construction job by being a red, not in those early days. It was later they gave us the works. A bridgeman was the best paid worker in the country.

New York was where the pay was. For a while the Flatiron Building had been a nine days wonder, but now they couldn't build skyscrapers fast enough. It took a lot of structural iron workers to put up that famous skyline. In 1912 I headed for New York. New York's no good without plenty of kale. Soon I was making enough to like it fine.

On my way east I attended an IWW convention in Chicago. It was on Earl Gates's invitation. We kept in touch all those years through a postal card or a letter now and then. He was head over heels in the labor movement. He had a lot to do with getting the miners off who'd been accused of murdering the Governor of Idaho. He'd become Big Bill's right hand man.

At the convention he was so busy I didn't get much chance to talk to him alone. At IWW conventions there used to be as many ideas as there were working stiffs in the hall. Earl had to talk fast to keep even half the boys headed in the same direction.

It was the same old Earl only gaunt and pale. He'd shaved his goatee. His hair wasn't so red as it used to be and was getting thin at the temples. He had a look of strain under the eyes. He was the same smooth talker, but now he was always laying down the law. He never stopped to listen.

The boys had been reading Sorel and were all agog over sabotage. I raised questions about it. I was convinced before I came that solidarity and the one big union and the general strike were the roads to freedom for the working class, but I didn't want any more McNamara cases to set labor back for fifteen years. I never could quite swallow sabotage. I couldn't get Earl to see it my way. We were fighting a class war weren't we, was how he put it to the crowd, well all was fair in love and war. That brought down the house, but I came away uneasy. Too much like the *Los Angeles Times* business to suit me.

I've carried my red card from that day to this, though now it's more of a souvenir than anything else. But those were fiery years just before the first world war.

It was coming back from Mother's funeral on the B & O

Railroad I first read in the paper of the Paterson strike. I hadn't been home when Dad died, I was off at sea somewhere and never got the letter, but now I had the price of the trip and dressed good and all that: I figured it was time to make my peace with the family.

It was heartbreaking how empty the old house was with Mother and Dad gone and just Ed and his frizzlyhaired wife living there. It looked so dark and narrow and small. I had remembered it an enormous place. Joe was a priest all in black with a sleek round face teaching in a Catholic college. Ed worked in a bank and the girls both had prosperous middleclass husbands. Our grief brought us together. I will say this much for the Bowmans; we never thought of quarreling over the will. Mother left nothing but the house, and Joe and I we said leave us out, let Ed and the girls take it on shares and we all shook hands. It made me feel good for Mother's sake. Except for one black sheep they had all come out the way she wanted them. I kept my face buttoned up on the subject of politics and we got along fine.

Now sitting with my necktie loose and my coat off in the daycoach after having gone into the diner for a couple of drinks I could really let myself go reading about that strike. I got so excited with the mass demonstrations and the singing girls I went over to Paterson next time there was a day's layoff to see the fun.

What I saw was a redheaded girl on the picket line. We were marching with red flags and placards on sticks past one of the big silk mills. We were singing the "Marseillaise." I sure forgot my duty as a classconscious worker that day. I couldn't keep my eyes off that girl's face. When the interests staged their daily atrocity trying to break up the demonstration I pulled her out from under a police officer's club and through a back alley out of harm's way.

She fought me as hard as she fought the cops. No use getting unnecessarily arrested I told her. "But I wanted to get arrested," she kept saying with tears of vexation in her eyes. "They are holding my sister in the bastille right now . . . my sister Kate O'Dwyer."

She said it like she expected me to be impressed and of course I was. Kate O'Dwyer's speeches were in all the papers. After Big Bill Haywood and Quinlan and Tresca she was one of the top leaders of the strike. That was great I told her, but she was too young and too pretty to go to jail.

My that made her mad. I had to take her to a lunchroom and feed her a chicken sandwich and a cup of coffee to quiet her down. She wasn't really pacified till I showed her my red card. Then she admitted her name was Eileen and that she was only a junior in highschool. I couldn't stop looking at her as she sat up on that stool nibbling at the sandwich with her even little teeth.

Eileen always did have a good figure, but at seventeen she was the prettiest slenderest creature you ever saw in your life. You could measure her waist with your two hands. She had skin like a lily and eyes that you could never tell whether they were green or blue, and her hair was the color of new copper wire. She moved like a leaf blown by the wind.

Eileen and I we just hit it off from that first minute. We got so busy telling each other about ourselves we forgot all about the strike. We had started squabbling like old friends before we even knew each other's names. When she told me her folks didn't know where she had gone I made her take the first train home to New York.

The O'Dwyers lived in a brick house on Tompkins Square though the saloon Patrick O'Dwyer kept was further uptown on Second Avenue. "The holy saints be praised," cried Mrs. O'Dwyer when she saw me ushering Eileen in through the front door. Mrs. O'Dwyer was a cheerful dumpy dark woman from Enniscorthy with her hair parted in the middle and a brogue you could cut with a knife. The O'Dwyers were all mad she told me but by all that was blessed she thought Eileen was the maddest of the lot. For bringing home strange men she was even worse than her sister Kate. "At least she brings them home Mrs. O'Dwyer," I said.

She looked me up and down and with a sharp kind of a smile that seemed to mean "You'll do young man." Right away she asked me to stay and eat with them. She was just about to put a bit of supper on the table.

The O'Dwyers became a second family to me from the moment I brought Eileen home safe that night. Mrs. O'Dwyer sat us down at the oval table set at the end of the oldfashioned kitchen that occupied the whole back of the house. While she was piling our plates with stewed steak and potatoes, the rest of the family came straggling in. The older boys Pat and Jim were redheaded with big opinionated mouths. Little Benedict was quiet and darkhaired and looked like his mother. They called me Blackie and seemed to take me for granted as Eileen's young man right from the first.

The O'Dwyers ate and drank and slept politics. It was all freedom for Ireland and stand up for the poor Boers. England was the root of all evil.

They went at it hammer and tongs about which was more on the side of the common people, William Jennings Bryan or T.R.'s Bull Moose. A proof that T.R. was an honest man was that the capitalist press was trying to frame him on a charge of drunkenness. They thought Debs was a great orator but they said Gompers as a practical man was doing more for the working people. They were all for woman's suffrage and the referedum and recall and the popular election of senators and the eight hour day. They wouldn't even listen when I said politics was a stageplay arranged to delude the working stiffs.

At that they favored the Paterson strikers against the millowners though Mrs. O'Dwyer cried out to the saints to blast the godless anarchists who were leading her daughter Kate astray. That was hitting me where I lived. I didn't tell the O'Dwyers I carried a red card but I did pipe up to say that there wasn't any conflict between syndicalism and Christianity. We argued and shouted at each other till we must have been heard halfway around the block. I sure felt at home in that house.

In the middle of it, Patrick O'Dwyer, the old man himself, came in. He had a red face and a blue eye and shaggy sandy eyebrows and roared everybody down. His family all called him the Boss. He reminded me a little of my own father except for the glib Irish wit. The difference was that O'Dwyer was a laughing man.

In Paterson he said both sides were wrong. No leadership with a heart. Nothing like that could happen in this great city of New York — he pounded on the table to make us listen — with a great organization like Tammany fostering kindness between rich and poor.

Just about that point Kate O'Dwyer burst into the kitchen. "Tammany," she cried. "That is the rottenest example there is of class collaboration." Kate was a big rawboned girl. Her hair was red but it didn't have the lovely color Eileen's had. She was the eldest and the only one who dared talk back to the Boss. The old man just sat there swallowing air while she went on: "It's collaboration all right. Collaboration to pick the public's pockets."

"And why aren't you in jail with the other agitators?" asked her mother sarcastically.

"Bailed out, my dear, bailed out by a capitalist who believes in fair play."

The Boss shouted that she was an ungrateful hussy, she'd be rotting in a cell right now if he hadn't pulled a few strings over at Tammany Hall. "Tammany watches over even the black sheep that stray from the flock."

Kate didn't listen. She was never one to pay much attention to what other people were saying. She had launched into a speech about how we must all dig into our pockets to support a pageant the strikers were putting on in Madison Square Garden. She'd just come home to change her clothes before going to the house of a wealthy woman who was going to bear part of the cost. A famous young journalist was waiting for her in a car outside. We all must have heard of Freddie Davis.

"Madison Square Garden, that's rich." The Boss laughed with a roar like a bull. "Let the agitators and the millowners step out into the ring. Let 'em put on the gloves and I'll put up a purse to see them fight. Nothing illegal, but a friendly athletic contest. Or make it a battle royal over in Hoboken but leave the poor working people in peace."

Kate went on without paying the slightest attention: the pageant would show the people of this city that it was real flesh and blood struggling and suffering in Paterson and not just foreign names you read about in the newspapers. I could see that the Boss's bark was worse than his bite. He pulled a tenspot off his roll of bills and Kate was gone out the door without so much as a thank you.

That night I went back to my furnished room with my head reeling. I lay down on the bed and smoked a cigarette trying to straighten out my ideas after all that argument, but all I could think of was how crazy I was about Eileen. I could see her every time I closed my eyes.

To tell the truth I'd had my fill of the sailor ashore kind of life, raising hell Saturday nights and getting drunk and whores and waking up with hell in your heart after you've been rolled by some floosy's pimp. No man ever did get much satisfaction out of prostitutes. I was telling myself that that was all over for me now. I was taking a pledge to lay off the liquor. No girl would do any more except Eileen.

One Saturday night in June I took Eileen to the Paterson strikers' pageant. Luckily we arrived at the Garden early because the cops were already trying to keep people out of the hall pretending the place was too full. It was the most exciting meeting either of us had ever been to in our lives. In the gallery people were standing in the aisles. I never saw so many young faces. All the girls wore something red. People waved straw hats and handkerchiefs and cheered and clapped at the slightest thing. That was one show where the audience really did take part.

When we first came in a banner reading No God No Master was stretched across the hall right under the ceiling. I was just telling Eileen that those were my sentiments exactly when some men started climbing up the girders back of the galleries to take it down. It was Big Bill himself who shouted through a megaphone that sentiments like that had nothing to do with the Paterson strike. There were cheers when the crowd recognized him. I guess he knew what he was doing but it left me disappointed.

The band was playing and Eileen and I were standing up on our seats singing the "Marseillaise." A huge stage filled the end of the hall. When the lights went on they lit the backdrop that showed the great square buildings of the Paterson mills and their tiers of windows. Searchlights picked out the action that was all in pantomime. To the music of the band and the singing of strike songs working men and women who had come over from Paterson on a special train acted out the story.

The big moment was the funeral of a worker killed by the deputies. When they took the lid off the coffin and the strikers filed by each dropping in a red carnation they showed such grief on their faces that the enormous audience was silent as the dead. Eileen grabbed my hand and held it tight. Not a sound in Madison Square Garden except now and then a woman's sob.

From where we were sitting – or standing rather – all the people around us were so excited they stood on their seats instead of sitting in them — we couldn't hear too well the speeches the leaders made over the coffin. Only when Big Bill bellowed "We'll fight the strike till hell freezes over and after that we'll fight on the ice" it brought a roar from the crowd. He ended up reminding us that the working class produced all the food people ate and the clothes they wore and the buildings they were housed in and yet it was the working class that suffered hunger and cold and had no place to lay its head. Eileen and I had our arms around each other's shoulders. We looked into each other's faces with wet eyes.

Kate's voice carried well. She looked handsome and dramatic all in black talking about the suffering of the housewives and the mothers with little children. Let the bosses and their wives and daughters go into the silk mills and work and see how they liked the pay and conditions. If the rich wanted to wear silk let them weave it themselves.

The people gave Kate an ovation. Eileen actually hugged me she was so excited at her sister's triumph.

Eight men with bowed heads and dragging steps carried the coffin off to a rolling of drums and the sound of a slow funeral march. There was a touching scene of the mothers waving their children goodbye when they were being sent off to a place of safety and the pageant ended with a victory march across the stage by all those working people singing the "Marseillaise" in all the different languages the strikers used.

Afterwards, Eileen and I, we were walking on air. The streets outside the Garden were full of people humming the "Marseillaise" and waving bits of red bunting. The cops had roped off Madison Square for fear of an outdoor meeting. Mounted police, cossacks we called them, kept the crowds moving. We walked in step, moving slowly with the slow-moving crowd.

Eileen with her arm in mine was steering us down Fifth Avenue, Kate had said to meet her at the Hotel Brevoort. All the strike leaders would be there. Eileen rubbed her face against my arm in that little catlike way she had. "Blackie take me to the Brevoort."

I told her I'd take her any damn place in New York she wanted to go. I'd like to see any goddam copper try to stop us. That pageant had left me full of beans. I felt I could take on any police force in the world singlehanded. The words "No God No Master" kept running through my head.

I tried to explain to Eileen how it made me feel, the general strike rolling up the storefronts and freeing the people imprisoned in the sweatshops in the city slums, the wind of freedom blowing away all the shams and hypocrisies and exploitations of the world. I ended by singing "Solidarity forever" at the top of my lungs. If I'd brayed like a jackass I couldn't have been further from explaining exactly what I meant.

But that night Eileen and I we understood each other without words. She'd nod blinking and smiling at everything I said before I half got it out. By the time we reached Eighth Street she was tired. She said her shoes hurt her. She had a funny little way of lifting up her feet and shaking them, the way a kitten might do.

The Brevoort café was so crowded there was no way of even looking inside. The entrances were packed tight with people trying to get in. When a broadshouldered young man turned to look at Eileen I didn't think much of it, because there was something about Eileen that stopped all sorts of men dead in their tracks. He said "Excuse me, aren't you Kate O'Dwyer's sister?" Eileen nodded excitedly.

He looked me straight in the face out of schoolboyish brown eyes. "My name's Freddie Davis." We shook hands.

"No use trying to get in here. Let's go see if she's at Mabel's," he said. "Kate said to bring you along if I found you." I couldn't help liking the guy but something about the way Eileen looked at him gave me a twinge. I felt better when, rattling along as if he'd known us all our lives, he started to tell us about a beautiful girl he was in love with and how he wanted to spend his life writing poetry about her; but that in spite of that he was leaving for Mexico in the morning to report the revolution for the *Metropolitan Magazine*. Freddie was an attractive young fellow but it sure put me off the way he kept sharing his private life with strangers.

He ushered us into a big fine room in a big fine house, full of the damndest congregation of people you ever saw in your life. There were people in evening dress and Orientals in turbans and working girls from Paterson, strike leaders, and writers and poets, longhaired men and shorthaired women in smocks. This was my first view of Greenwich Village. I wish it had been my last.

It made me feel good that all these different kinds of people were so worked up over the plight of those strikers in Paterson. Made me feel the solidarity of the human race, I said, when Freddie introduced me to a dumpy little woman with cold violet eyes in a white dress with a lot of jewelry hung on it who was the hostess.

What I said pleased her so much she kept repeating it to everybody who came in. She seemed all set up at having a real working man at her party. She kept pointing me out as a structural iron worker to her guests. Looked like some of them had never seen a working stiff before.

We never did find Kate. It wasn't too long before we wearied of the yammer of voices. I'd already worked a ten hour day before I went by to take out Eileen and man I was tired. Evenings seem long when you aren't drinking.

Eileen wasn't half ready to go but I took her on the crosstown car and we sat spooning a few minutes on a bench in the square in front of her house while I tried to bring up the subject of getting married. She kept beating around the bush and never would let me pop the question. She did let me kiss her though and that left my head whirling so I could hardly find my way home to my lodging house after I'd left her at her door. All night that drab old room seemed full of the smell of her hair.

Next time the O'Dwyers asked me to eat at their house I got the Boss in a corner and asked him if he'd have any objection. Why should he have any objection? He clapped me on the shoulder. Didn't I come from a Catholic home and wasn't I in the way of making a good honest living? I stammered something about being a bit of a red but he roared me down. Any boy worth his salt . . . He himself had been the hellroaringest Fenian you ever saw till he was twenty-five. Then he laid down the law. We could be engaged and I could take her out but he didn't want to hear a word about matrimony until the girl had finished school.

Looking forward to it a year seemed a century; but as it turned out I had no choice because that spring Mrs. O'Dwyer noticed I wasn't getting over a cough that had come on with a cold early in the winter. The Boss sent me to their doctor who found I was running a temperature and sent me to another doctor who said I had a spot on my lung. Tuberculosis. The Boss got into a great fright for fear I'd given it to Eileen and arranged overnight for me to go to the state sanatorium at Saranac. To tell the truth I always thought it was me caught it from Eileen because she came down with it soon after.

That was in early July. In those days they made you lie in bed in big open porches for TB. The mania was fresh air. I'd been lying there worrying myself sick over what Eileen might be up to, because I knew she had started to write poetry and had been corresponding with Freddie Davis about it. Then I got this letter from her that made me feel better and worse at the same time. The O'Dwyers' doctor had been checking her over and decided that she had a touch of the white plague too and shipped her to the woman's department of that same huge Saranac hospital. I was scared for her but relieved in my mind in another way. At least it would keep her away from Freddie Davis. It was us both having the same sickness that finally tied the knot on us.

Afterwards Eileen and I used to say that Saranac was where we'd gone to college. We read a lot of the same books and wrote each other notes two or three times a day. I thought Eileen's little poems were the wonderfulest things I'd ever read. She read mostly fiction and plays and verse and I read history and economics. It was the nearest I ever got to an education. We were so busy with our funny little cooped up private lives we hardly noticed the outbreak of the world war in Europe.

Of course it was Earl Gates who directed my reading. We'd kept in touch but now for the first time in my life I got a chance to become a real letter writer. We started up the old argument about sabotage, only this time by mail. Earl was knocking himself out trying to set up a bureau for migratory workers for the IWW. He sent me lists of books on socialism and syndicalism and anarchy he hadn't found time to read himself. I thought Kropotkin was great. I stuffed my head with long words like a regular sea lawyer.

Eileen's health was improving but slower than I was. I'm ashamed to say how relieved I was to have her in the sanatorium. Under wraps. She'd be safe there until the time came for us to get married was how I looked at it. My belief in free love didn't stand up when it came to Eileen. I wanted her all to myself.

For months there was no seeing her, but in the spring we were both on the ambulatory list. They turned us loose on the grounds one day a week. Putting our arms around each other again made us almost crazy with delight.

I'd discovered a hidden nook by the lake in a grove of young balsams. If the crushed sweetfern was any indication, we weren't the only couple who found it. Before I'd been the eager one but now she threw herself against me as if she'd tear me to pieces. She was so passionate I was scared. "Love me, Blackie, love me," she'd whisper in a new deep throaty voice. Her hands would be all over me. When the time came to report back to our various wards we'd tear ourselves apart and hurry off in our separate directions shaking and trembly from the violence of it, without looking back. We were under each other's skins all right.

Earl and I had been making plans to repeat that jaunt we'd made through the harvest fields years ago as soon as I got out of the hospital. The doctors recommended outdoor work for me and Earl wanted to see the harvest stiffs organized at first hand.

I met him at the IWW hall in Kansas City. Earl looked pale and thin from slaving in the office all winter and he had a kind of wild glitter in his eye. The fellow workers looked up to him like a god. The place was full of young kids who expected the revolution to be tomorrow. They just drank up everything he said. Earl always had the gift of gab, but this summer his deep voice seemed richer and his choice of words better than ever before. Those kids made me feel right ashamed of myself. All I'd been thinking about, riding out in a daycoach like a regular scissorbill because I still had a little dough saved up from flush times in New York, was how I could go to work to earn enough to give Eileen a comfortable life once we got married.

That was one of the years when wheat was king of the world. The war in Europe was kicking prices up. The farmers were daffy with the idea of two dollar wheat. They were more worried about hail and thunderheads than they were about chiseling on the wages of the harvest stiffs. Every farmer wanted to beat the other guy to the elevator no matter what it cost.

We wobblies were hitting our peak. It looked to us that the world wide war would do more than all the strikes we could stage to dislodge the capitalist system. With the weight of parasites and moneybags off our shoulders we working people would enjoy the entire product of our labor. When Eileen and I had children they would grow up into a society based on mutual aid.

Earl took charge of me when we joined the harvest crews. I was weak as a kitten after a year lying flat on my bed just reading books and laying up fat, but he managed to steer me into light jobs at first. Earl always was the most considerate fellow in the world. It was several weeks before I really hit my stride. By that time I was lean and sunburned and tough as I'd ever been.

On the very first job we signed up the whole crew. We taught them all the songs out of the little Wobbly songbook. Word had gotten around that a red card was a protection. Fifty cents wasn't much to pay. Brakemen and yard dicks were going easy with boes who waved a red card under their noses. The grain wouldn't get harvested without the harvest stiffs. The railroads weren't worrying about hauling a few free passengers that summer, what they wanted was the profit from hauling the grain.

Once I got my strength back it was a real pleasure, in spite of the heat and the dust, to handle the warm dry grain pouring out into the bags from the threshing machines. It was happy work. Meadow larks rose piping out of the fields of wheat rolling in waves like the ocean under that huge prairie sky scattered full with white blobs of clouds. Locusts and all the little bugs that live in the wheat thudded against your sweaty skin as you toiled to tie the full bags, stripped to the waist under the baking sun. Quail went whirring up from under the horses' feet. There was pleasure in doing it well. In spite of his class war notions Earl worked like ten men. There was still a lot of the farm boy under the skin of the revolutionary agitator. "Wheat is bread," he'd say kind of apologizing for himself. "Bread is the life of mankind."

The first tractors were appearing on the larger farms, big ugly contraptions that looked like the Toonerville trolley. Motor trucks backed up to haul the grain to the elevators. Evenings, sitting around on bales of straw in the cool of the barns, Earl would talk about how once we had production for use instead of a gamble for profit mechanical inventions would take the load of work off working men's shoulders.

The eight hour day was all right as far as it went but maybe the day would come when an eight hour week would accomplish all the work that was needed in the world.

We worked our way clear to Moorehead City on the Red River of the North. There Earl was able to announce to a meeting we held at the stands at the fairgrounds, because there wasn't a hall in town big enough to hold all the working stiffs who wanted to attend, that the number of migratory workers who had signed up with the One Big Union had passed the ten thousand mark.

Wages were going up, working conditions were improving. The day was at hand when the working people of America would take the country over from the moneymasters who lived off other men's sweat and the blood of the poor slaves herded to their deaths on the battlefields of Europe. How those harvest stiffs cheered. Earl Gates was a happy man that day.

At General Delivery at the Fargo post office I found the letter I'd been expecting from Eileen. The doctors had told her she'd be discharged from the hospital September 15. I must come.

Earl gave me a disappointed look when we shook hands at the marshaling yard where they were making up an eastbound freight. "Joining the homeguard, eh Blackie," he said trying to keep the sarcasm out of his voice. "Every man has to live his own life . . . For me," he added bitterly, "it's back to the mines."

It seemed awful slow beating my way East. I was so afraid I'd be late for the day Eileen was to get out of the hospital I paid my fare on the passenger trains to Saranac Lake from Chicago. For the two days I had to wait there I put up at the cheapest flophouse I could find. At that I still had more than a hundred dollars in my jeans when I carried Eileen's wicker suitcase out past the desk in that hospital lobby.

On the way to the train we stopped off at City Hall to get married. All that summer I'd carried the marriage license in my wallet.

Eileen's folks had sent her a money order so we rode to New York in a lower berth on a Pullman. That was the happiest trainride I ever had in my life.

We sat around in the waiting room of the beautiful new Grand Central Station trying to decide whether to go get

ourselves lodgings or to go straight to the O'Dwyers' to face
the music. We knew there would be a row on account of our
not being married in church. While Eileen went to the ladies' room to comb out her hair I sat looking at the morning
paper.

IWW RIOT AT MONTANA MINE
Killed and wounded. Agitator dies in jail.

One of those police lineup snapshots that went with the
article showed Earl Gates. Staring straight at me off the
page. The name was spelled wrong but there was no mistak-
ing the comb of hair and the defiant look about the eyes. I
didn't have time to read the damn lying reporter's preju-
diced story before I saw Eileen coming back. When her eyes
met mine she smiled. I dropped the newspaper in the trash-
can at the end of the bench I was sitting on. I didn't want
anything to upset our happiness that day.

Steamroller

They had to change at Manhattan Transfer. The thumb
of Ellen's new kid glove had split and she kept rubbing it
nervously with her forefinger. John wore a belted raincoat
and a pinkishgray felt hat. When he turned to her and
smiled she couldn't help pulling her eyes away and staring
out at the long rain that shimmered over the tracks.

"Here we are Elaine dear. Oh prince's daughter, you see
we get the train that comes from the Penn station . . . It's
funny this waiting in the wilds of New Jersey this way."
They got into the parlorcar. John made a little clucking
sound in his mouth at the raindrops that made dark dimes
on his pale hat. "Well we're off, little girl . . . Behold
thou art fair my love, thou art fair, thou hast dove's eyes
within thy locks."

Ellen's new tailored suit was tight at the elbows. She wanted to feel very gay and listen to his purring whisper in her ears, but something had set her face in a tight frown; she could only look out at the brown marshes and the million black windows of factories and the puddly streets of towns and a rusty steamboat in a canal and barns and Bull Durham signs and roundfaced Spearmint gnomes all barred and crisscrossed with bright flaws of rain. The jeweled stripes on the window ran straight down when the train stopped and got more and more oblique as it speeded up. The wheels rumbled in her head, saying Man-hattan Tran-sfer. Man-hattan Tran-sfer. Anyway it was a long time before Atlantic City. By the time we get to Atlantic City . . . *Oh it rained forty days* . . . I'll be feeling gay . . . *And it rained forty nights* . . . I've got to be feeling gay.

"Elaine Thatcher Oglethorpe, that's a very fine name, isn't it, darling? Oh stay me with flagons, comfort me with apples for I am sick of love. . ."

It was comfortable in the empty parlorcar in the green velvet chair with John leaning towards her reciting nonsense with the brown marshlands slipping by behind the rain-striped window and a smell like clams seeping into the car. She looked into his face and laughed. A blush ran all over his face to the roots of his redblond hair. He put his hand in its yellow glove over her hand in its white glove. "You're my wife now Elaine."

"You're my husband now John." And laughing they looked at each other in the coziness of the empty parlorcar.

White letters, ATLANTIC CITY, spelled doom over the rainpitted water.

Rain lashed down the glaring boardwalk and crashed in gusts against the window like water thrown out of a bucket. Beyond the rain she could hear the intermittent rumble of the surf along the beach between the illuminated piers. She lay on her back staring at the ceiling. Beside her in the big bed John lay asleep breathing quietly like a child with a pillow doubled up under his head. She was icy cold. She slid out of bed very carefully not to wake him, and stood looking out the window down the very long V of lights of the boardwalk. She pushed up the window. The rain lashed in her face spitefully stinging her flesh, wetting her night-dress. She pushed her forehead against the frame. Oh I want to die. I want to die. All the tight coldness of her body

was clenching in her stomach. Oh I'm going to be sick. She
went into the bathroom and closed the door. When she had
vomited she felt better. Then she climbed into bed again
careful not to touch John. If she touched him she would die.
She lay on her back with her hands tight against her sides
and her feet together. The parlorcar rumbled cosily in her
head; she fell asleep.

Wind rattling the windowframes wakened her. John was
far away, the other side of the big bed. With the wind and
the rain streaming in the window it was as if the room and
the big bed and everything were moving, running forward
like an airship over the sea. *Oh it rained forty days . . .*
Through a crack in the cold stiffness the little tune trickled
warm as blood . . . *And it rained forty nights.* Gingerly
she drew a hand over her husband's hair. He screwed his
face up in his sleep and whined "Don't" in a littleboy's voice
that made her giggle. She lay giggling on the far edge of the
bed, giggling desperately as she used to with girls at school.
And the rain lashed through the window and the song grew
louder until it was a brass band in her ears:

> *Oh it rained forty days*
> *And it rained forty nights*
> *And it didn't stop till Christmas*
> *And the only man that survived the flood*
> *Was longlegged Jack of the Isthmus.*

J. Ward Moorehouse

JOHNNY MOOREHOUSE worked on at Hillyard and Miller's
sitting in the stuffy office, chafing when he had nothing to do
until he thought he'd go mad and run amok and kill somebody, sending songs to the music publishers that they always
sent back, reading the *Success Magazine*, full of sick longing
for the future: to be away from Wilmington and his father's

grumbling and pipesmoking and the racket his little brothers and sisters made and the smell of corned beef and cabbage and his mother's wrinkled crushed figure and her overworked hands.

But one day he was sent down to Ocean City, Maryland, to report on some lots the firm had listed there. Mr. Hillyard would have gone himself only he had a carbuncle on his neck. He gave Johnny the return ticket and ten dollars for the trip.

It was a hot July afternoon. Johnny ran home to get a bag and to change his clothes and got down to the station just in time to make the train. The ride was hot and sticky down through peachorchards and pinebarrens under a blazing slaty sky that flashed back off sandy patches in scraggly cornfields and whitewashed shacks and strips of marshwater. Johnny had taken off the jacket of his gray flannel suit and folded it on the seat beside him to keep it from getting mussed and laid his collar and tie on top of it so that they'd be fresh when he got in, when he noticed a darkeyed girl in a ruffled pink dress and a wide white leghorn hat sitting across the aisle. She was considerably older than he was and looked like the sort of fashionably dressed woman who'd be in a parlorcar rather than in a daycoach. But Johnny reflected that there wasn't any parlorcar on this train. Whenever he wasn't looking at her, he felt that she was looking at him.

The afternoon grew overcast and it came on to rain, big drops spattered against the car windows. The girl in pink ruffles was struggling to put her window down. He jumped over and put it down for her. "Allow me," he said. "Thanks." She looked up and smiled into his eyes. "Oh, it's so filthy on this horrid train." She showed him her white gloves all smudged from the windowfastenings. He sat down again on the inside edge of his seat. She turned her full face to him. It was an irregular brown face with ugly lines from the nose to the ends of the mouth, but her eyes set him tingling. "You won't think it's too unconventional of me if we talk, will you?" she said. "I'm bored to death on this horrid train, and there isn't any parlorcar though the man in New York swore that there was."

"I bet you been traveling all day," said Johnny, looking shy and boyish.

"Worse than that. I came down from Newport on the boat last night."

The casual way she said Newport quite startled him. "I'm going to Ocean City," he said.

"So am I. Isn't it a horrid place? I wouldn't go there for a minute if it weren't for Dad. He pretends to like it."

"They say that Ocean City has a great future . . . I mean in a kind of a realestate way," said Johnny.

There was a pause.

"I got on in Wilmington," said Johnny with a smile.

"A horrid place, Wilmington . . . I can't stand it."

"I was born and raised there . . . I suppose that's why I like it," said Johnny.

"Oh, I didn't mean there weren't awfully nice people in Wilmington . . . lovely old families . . . Do you know the Rawlinses?"

"Oh, thats all right. . . I don't want to spend all my life in Wilmington, anyway . . . Gosh, look at it rain."

It rained so hard that a culvert was washed out and the train was four hours late into Ocean City. By the time they got in they were good friends; it had thundered and lightened and she'd been so nervous and he'd acted very strong and protecting and the car had filled up with mosquitoes and they had both been eaten up and they'd gotten very hungry together. The station was pitchblack and there was no porter and it took him two trips to get her bags out and even then they almost forgot her alligatorskin handbag and he had to go back into the car a third time to get it and his own suitcase. By that time an old darkey with a surrey had appeared who said he was from the Ocean House. "I hope you're going there too," she said. He said he was and they got in, though they had no place to put their feet because she had so many bags. There were no lights in Ocean City on account of the storm. The surreywheels ground through a deep sandbed; now and then that sound and the clucking of the driver at his horse were drowned by the roar on the surf from the beach. The only light was from the moon continually hidden by driving clouds. The rain had stopped, but the tense air felt as if another downpour would come any minute. "I certainly would have perished in the storm if it hadn't been for you," she said; then suddenly she offered him her hand like a man: "My name's Strang . . . Annabelle Marie Strang. . . . Isn't that a funny name?" He took her hand. "John Moorehouse is mine . . . Glad to meet you, Miss Strang." The palm of her hand was hot and dry. It seemed to press into his. When he let go he felt that she had expected him to hold her hand longer. She laughed a husky low laugh. "Now we're introduced, Mr. Moorehouse, and everything's quite all right . . . I certainly shall give Dad a piece of my mind. The idea of his not meeting his only daughter at the station."

In the dark hotel lobby lit by a couple of smoked oillamps he saw her, out of the corner of his eye, throw her arms round a tall whitehaired man, but by the time he had scrawled John W. Moorehouse in his most forceful handwriting in the register and gotten his roomkey from the clerk, they had gone. Up in the little pine bedroom it was very hot. When he pulled up the window, the roar of the surf came in through the rusty screen mingling with the rattle of rain on the roof. He changed his collar and washed in tepid water he poured from the cracked pitcher on the washstand and went down to the diningroom to try to get something to eat. A goat-toothed waitress was just bringing him soup when Miss Strang came in followed by the tall man. As the only lamp was on the table he was sitting at, they came towards it and he got up and smiled. "Here he is, Dad," she said. "And you owe him for the driver that brought us from the station . . . Mr. Morris, you must meet my father, Doctor Strang . . . The name was Morris, wasn't it?" Johnny blushed. "Moorehouse, but it's quite all right. . . . I'm glad to meet you sir."

Next morning Johnny got up early and went round to the office of the Ocean City Improvement and Realty Company that was in a new greenstained shingled bungalow on the freshly laidout street back of the beach. There was no one there yet, so he walked round the town. It was a muggy gray day and the cottages and the frame stores and the unpainted shacks along the railroad track looked pretty desolate. Now and then he slapped a mosquito on his neck. He had on his last clean collar and he was worried for fear it would get wilted. Whenever he stepped off the board sidewalks he got sand in his shoes, and sharp beachburrs stuck to his ankles. At last he found a stout man in a white linen suit sitting on the steps of the realestate office. "Good morning, sir," he said. "Are you Colonel Wedgewood?" The stout man was too out of breath to answer and only nodded. He had one big silk handkerchief stuck into his collar behind and with another was mopping his face. Johnny gave him the letter he had from his firm and stood waiting for him to say something. The fat man read the letter with puckered brows and led the way into the office. "It's this asthma," he gasped between great wheezing breaths. "Cuts ma wind when Ah trah to hurry. Glad to meet you, son."

Johnny hung round old Colonel Wedgewood the rest of the morning, looking blue-eyed and boyish, listening politely to stories of the Civil War and General Lee and his white horse Traveller and junketings befoa de woa on the Easten Shoa, ran down to the store to get a cake of ice for the cooler, made a little speech about the future of Ocean City as a summer resort — "Why, what have they got at Atlantic City or Cape May that we haven't got here?" roared the Colonel — went home with him to his bungalow for lunch, thereby missing the train he ought to have taken back to Wilmington, refused a mint julep — he neither drank nor smoked — but stood admiringly by while the Colonel concocted and drank two good stiff ones, for his asthma, used his smile and his blue eyes and his boyish shamble on the Colonel's colored cook Mamie and by four o'clock he was laughing about the Governor of North Carolina and the Governor of South Carolina and had accepted a job with the Ocean City Improvement and Realty Company at fifteen dollars a week, with a small furnished cottage thrown in. He went back to the hotel and wrote Mr. Hillyard, inclosing the deeds for the lots and his expense account, apologized for leaving the firm at such short notice, but explained that he owed it to his family who were in great need to better himself as much as he could; then he wrote to his mother that he was staying on in Ocean City and please to send him his clothes by express; he wondered whether to write Miss O'Higgins, but decided not to. After all, bygones were bygones.

When he had eaten his supper he went to the desk to ask for his bill, feeling pretty nervous for fear he wouldn't have enough money to pay it, and was just coming out with two quarters in his pocket and his bag in his hand when he met Miss Strang. She was with a short dark man in white flannels whom she introduced as Monsieur de la Rochevillaine. He was a Frenchman but spoke good English. "I hope you're not leaving us," she said. "No, ma'am, I'm just moving down the beach to one of Colonel Wedgewood's cottages." The Frenchman made Johnny uneasy; he stood smiling suave as a barber beside Miss Strang. "Oh, you know our fat friend, do you? He's a great crony of Dad's. I think he's just too boring with his white horse Traveller." Miss Strang and the Frenchman smiled both at once as if they had some secret in common. The Frenchman stood beside her swinging easily on the balls of his feet as if he were standing beside some piece of furniture he owned and was showing off to a friend. Johnny had a notion to paste him one right where the white flannel bulged into a potbelly. "Well, I must go," he said. "Won't you come back later? There's going to be dancing. We'd love to have you." "Yes, come back by all means," said the Frenchman. "I will if I can," said Johnny, and walked off with his suitcase in his hand, feeling sticky under the collar and sore. "Drat that Frenchman," he said aloud. Still, there was something about the way Miss Strang looked at him. He guessed he must be falling in love.

It was a hot August, the mornings still, the afternoons piling up sultry into thundershowers. Except when there were clients to show about the scorched sandlots and pinebarrens laid out into streets, Johnny sat in the office alone under the twoflanged electric fan. He was dressed in white flannels and a pink tennis shirt rolled up to the elbows, drafting the lyrical description of Ocean City (Maryland) that was to preface the advertising booklet that was the Colonel's pet idea: "The lifegiving surges of the broad Atlantic beat on the crystalline beaches of Ocean City (Maryland) . . . the tonic breath of the pines brings relief to the asthmatic and the consumptive . . . nearby the sportsman's paradise of Indian River spreads out its broad estuary teeming with . . ." In the afternoon the Colonel would come in sweating and wheezing and Johnny would read him what he had written and he'd say, "Bully, ma boy, bully," and suggest that it be all done over. And Johnny would look up a new batch of words in a dogeared *Century Dictionary* and start off again.

It would have been a fine life except that he was in love. Evenings he couldn't keep away from the Ocean House.

Each time he walked up the creaking porch steps past the old ladies rocking and fanning with palmleaf fans, and went through the screen doors into the lobby, he felt sure that this time he'd find Annabelle Marie alone, but each time the Frenchman was with her as smiling and cool and potbellied as ever. They both made a fuss over Johnny and petted him like a little dog or a precocious child; she taught him to dance the "Boston," and the Frenchman, who it turned out was a duke or a baron or something, kept offering him drinks and cigars and scented cigarettes. Johnny was shocked to death when he found out that she smoked, but somehow it went with dukes and Newport and foreign travel and that sort of thing. She used some kind of musky perfume and the smell of it and the slight rankness of cigarettesmoke in her hair made him dizzy and feverish when he danced with her. Some nights he tried to tire out the Frenchman playing pool, but then she'd disappear to bed and he'd have to go off home cursing under his breath. While he undressed he could still feel a little tingle of musk in his nostrils. He was trying to make up a song:

> *By the moonlight sea*
> *I pine for thee*
> *Annabelle Marie . . .*

Then it 'ud suddenly sound too damn silly and he'd stride up and down his little porch in his pajamas, with the mosquitoes shrilling about his head and the pound of the sea and the jeer of the dryflies and katydids in his ears, cursing being young and poor and uneducated and planning how he'd make a big enough pile to buy out every damn Frenchman; then he'd be the one she'd love and look up to and he wouldn't care if she did have a few damn Frenchmen for mascots if she wanted them. He'd clench his fists and stride around the porch muttering, "By gum, I can do it."

Then one evening he found Annabelle Marie alone. The Frenchman had gone on the noon train. She seemed glad to see Johnny, but there was obviously something on her mind. She had too much powder on her face and her eyes looked red; perhaps she'd been crying. It was moonlight. She put her hand on his arm, "Moorehouse, walk down the beach with me," she said. "I hate the sight of all these old hens in rockingchairs." On the walk that led across a scraggly lawn down to the beach they met Doctor Strang.

"What's the matter with Rochevillaine, Annie?" he said. He was a tall man with a high forehead. His lips were compressed and he looked worried.

"He got a letter from his mother . . . She won't let him."

"He's of age, isn't he?"

"Dad, you don't understand the French nobility . . . The family council won't let him . . . They could tie up his income."

"You'll have enough for two . . . I told him that."

"Oh, shut up about it, can't you? . . ." She suddenly started to blubber like a child. She ran past Johnny and back to the hotel, leaving Johnny and Doctor Strang facing each other on the narrow boardwalk. Doctor Strang saw Johnny for the first time. "Hm . . . excuse us," he said as he brushed past and walked with long strides up the walk, leaving Johnny to go down to the beach and look at the moon all by himself.

But the nights that followed, Annabelle Marie did walk out along the beach with him and he began to feel that perhaps she hadn't loved the Frenchman so much after all. They would go far beyond the straggling cottages and build a fire and sit side by side looking into the flame. Their hands sometimes brushed against each other as they walked; when she'd want to get to her feet he'd take hold of her two hands and pull her up towards him and he always planned to pull her to him and kiss her, but he hadn't the nerve.

One night was very warm and she suddenly suggested they go in bathing.

"But we haven't our suits."

"Haven't you ever been in without? It's much better . . . Why, you funny boy, I can see you blushing even in the moonlight."

"Do you dare me?"

"I doubledare you."

He ran up the beach a way and pulled off his clothes and went very fast into the water. He didn't dare look and only got a glimpse out of the corner of an eye of white legs and breasts and a wave spuming white at her feet. While he was putting his clothes on again, he was wondering if he wanted to get married to a girl who'd go in swimming with a fellow all naked like that, anyway. He wondered if she'd done it with that damn Frenchman. "You were like a marble faun," she said when he got back beside the fire where she was coiling her black hair round her head. She had hairpins in her mouth and spoke through them. "Like a very nervous marble faun . . . I got my hair wet."

He hadn't intended to, but he suddenly pulled her to him and kissed her. She didn't seem at all put out, but made herself little in his arms and put her face up to be kissed again. "Would you marry a feller like me without any money?"

"I hadn't thought of it, darling, but I might."

"You're pretty wealthy, I guess, and I haven't a cent, and I have to send home money to my folks . . . but I have prospects."

"What kind of prospects?" She pulled his face down and ruffled his hair and kissed him.

"I'll make good in this realestate game. I swear I will."

"Will it make good, poor baby?"

"You're not so much older'n me . . . How old are you, Annabelle?"

"Well, I admit to twentyfour, but you mustn't tell anybody, or about tonight or anything."

"Who would I be telling about it, Annabelle Marie?"

Walking home, something seemed to be on her mind because she paid no attention to anything he said. She kept humming under her breath.

Another evening they were sitting on the porch of his cottage smoking cigarettes — he would occasionally smoke a cigarette now to keep her company — he asked her what it was worrying her. She put her hands on his shoulders and shook him: "Oh, Moorehouse, you're such a fool . . . but I like it."

"But there must be something worrying you, Annabelle . . . You didn't look worried the day we came down on the train together."

"If I told you . . . Gracious, I can imagine your face." She laughed her hard gruff laugh that always made him feel uncomfortable.

"Well, I wish I had the right to make you tell me . . . You ought to forget that damn Frenchman."

"Oh, you're such a little innocent," she said. Then she got up and walked up and down the porch.

"Won't you sit down, Annabelle? Don't you like me even a little bit?"

She rubbed her hand through his hair and down across his face. "Of course I do, you little blue-eyed ninny . . . But can't you see it's everything driving me wild, all those old cats round the hotel talk about me as if I was a scarlet woman because I occasionally smoke a cigarette in my own room . . . Why, in England some of the most aristocratic women smoke right in public without anybody saying 'boo' to them . . . And then I'm worried about Dad; he's sinking too much money in realestate. I think he's losing his mind."

"But there's every indication of a big boom coming down here. It'll be another Atlantic City in time."

"Now look here, 'fess up, how many lots have been sold this month?"

"Well, not so many . . . But there are some important sales pending . . . There's that corporation that's going to build the new hotel."

"Dad'll be lucky if he gets fifty cents out on the dollar . . . and he keeps telling me how rattlebrained I am. He's a physician and not a financial wizard and he ought to realize it. It's all right for somebody like you who has nothing to lose and a way to make in the world to be messing around in realestate . . . As for that fat Colonel I don't know whether he's a fool or a crook."

"What kind of a doctor is your father?"

"Do you mean to say you never heard of Doctor Strang? He's the bestknown nose and throat specialist in Philadelphia . . . Oh, it's so cute . . ." She kissed him on the cheek ". . . and ignorant . . ." she kissed him again . . . "and pure."

"I'm not so pure," he said quickly and looked at her hard in the eyes. Their faces began to blush looking at each other. She let her head sink slowly on his shoulder.

His heart was pounding. He was dizzy with the smell of her hair and the perfume she wore. He pulled her to her feet with his arm round her shoulders. Tottering a little, her leg against his leg, the stiffness of her corset against his ribs, her hair against his face, he pulled her through the little living-room into the bedroom and locked the door behind them.

Then he kissed her as hard as he could on the lips. She sat down on the bed and began to take off her dress, a little coolly he thought, but he'd gone too far to pull back. When she took off her corset, she flung it in the corner of the room. "There," she said. "I hate the beastly things." She got up and walked towards him in her chemise and felt for his face in the dark.

"What's the matter, darling?" she whispered fiercely. "Are you afraid of me?"

Everything was much simpler than Johnny expected. They giggled together while they were dressing. Walking back along the beach to the Ocean House, he kept thinking: "Now she'll have to marry me."

In September a couple of cold northeasters right after Labor Day emptied the Ocean House and the cottages. The Colonel talked bigger about the coming boom and his advertising campaign, and drank more. Johnny took his meals with him now instead of at Mrs. Ames's boardinghouse. The booklet was finished and approved and Johnny had made a couple of trips to Philadelphia with the text and the photographs to get estimates from printers. Running through Wilmington on the train without getting off there gave him a pleasant feeling of independence. Doctor Strang looked more and more worried and talked about protecting his investments. They had not talked of Johnny's engagement to his daughter, but it seemed to be understood. Annabelle's moods were unaccountable. She kept saying she was dying of boredom. She teased and nagged at Johnny continually. One night he woke suddenly to find her standing beside the bed. "Did I scare you?" she said. "I couldn't sleep . . . Listen to the surf." The wind was shrilling round the cottage and a tremendous surf roared on the beach. It was almost daylight before he could get her to get out of bed and go back to the hotel. "Let 'em see me . . . I don't care," she said. Another time when they were walking along the beach she was taken with nausea and he had to stand waiting while she was sick behind a sanddune, then he supported her, white and trembling, back to the Ocean House. He was worried and restless. On one of his trips to Philadelphia he went round to the *Public Ledger* to see if he could get a job as a reporter.

One Saturday afternoon he sat reading the paper in the

lobby of the Ocean House. There was no one else there, most of the guests had left. The hotel would close the fifteenth. Suddenly he found himself listening to a conversation. The two bellhops had come in and were talking in low voices on the bench against the wall.

"Well, I got mahn awright this summer, damned if I didn't, Joe."

"I would of too if I hadn't gotten sick."

"Didn't I tell you not to monkey round with that Lizzie? Man, I b'lieve every sonofabitch in town slep' with that jane, not excludin' niggers."

"Say, did you . . . You know the blackeyed one? You said you would."

Johnny froze. He held the paper rigid in front of him.

The bellhop gave out a low whistle. "Hotstuff," he said. "Jeez, what these society dames gits away with 's got me beat."

"Didye, honest?"

"Well, not exactly . . . 'Fraid I might ketch somethin'. But that Frenchman did . . . Jeez, he was in her room all the time."

"I know he was. I caught him onct." They laughed. "They'd forgot to lock the door."

"Was she all neked?"

"I guess she was . . . under her kimono . . . He's cool as a cucumber and orders icewater."

"Whah didn't ye send up Mr. Greeley?"

"Hell, why should I? Frenchman wasn't a bad scout. He gave me five bucks."

"I guess she can do what she goddam pleases. Her dad about owns this dump, they tell me, him an ole Colonel Wedgewood."

"I guess that young guy in the realestate office is gettin' it now . . . looks like he'd marry her."

"Hell, I'd marry her maself if a girl had that much kale."

Johnny was in a cold sweat. He wanted to get out of the lobby without their seeing him. A bell rang and one of the boys ran off. He heard the other one settling himself on the bench. Maybe he was reading a magazine or something. Johnny folded up the paper quietly and walked out onto the porch. He walked down the street without seeing anything. For a while he thought he'd go down to the station and take the first train out and throw the whole business to ballyhack, but there was the booklet to get out, and there was a chance that if the boom did come he might get in on the ground floor, and this connection with money and the Strangs; opportunity knocks but once at a young man's door. He went back to his cottage and locked himself in his bedroom. He stood a minute looking at himself in the glass of the bureau. The neatly parted light hair, the cleancut nose and chin; the image blurred. He found he was crying. He threw himself face down on the bed and sobbed.

When he went up to Philadelphia the next time to read proof on the booklet:

OCEAN CITY (Maryland)

VACATIONLAND SUPREME

He also took up a draft of the wedding invitations to be engraved:

Doctor Alonso B. Strang
announces the marriage of his daughter
Annabelle Marie
to Mr. J. Ward Moorehouse
at Saint Stephen's Protestant Episcopal Church, Germantown, Pennsylvania, on November fifteenth nineteen hundred and nine at twelve noon

Janey

WHEN JANEY was little she lived in an old flatface brick house a couple of doors up the hill from M Street in Georgetown. The front part of the house was always dark because Mommer kept the heavy lace curtains drawn to and the yellow linen shades with lace inset bands down. Sunday afternoons Janey and Joe and Ellen and Francie had to sit in the front room and look at pictures or read books. Janey and Joe read the funnypaper together because they were the oldest and the other two were just babies and not old enough to know what was funny anyway. They couldn't laugh out loud because Popper sat with the rest of *The Sunday Star* on his lap and usually went to sleep after dinner with the editorial section crumpled in one big blue-veined hand. Tiny curds of sunlight flickering through the lace insets in the windowshade would lie on his bald head and on one big red flange on his nose and on the droop of one mustache and on his speckled Sundayvest and on the white starched shirtsleeves with shiny cuffs, held up above the elbow by a rubber band. Janey and Joe would sit on the same chair feeling each other's ribs jiggle when they laughed about the Katzenjammer kids setting off a cannon-cracker under the captain's stool. The little ones would see them laughing and start laughing too, "Shut up, can't you," Joe would hiss at them out of the corner of his mouth. "You don't know what we're laughing at." Once in a while, if there was no sound from Mommer who was taking her Sunday afternoon nap upstairs stretched out in the back bedroom in a faded lilac sack with frills on it, after they'd listened for a long time to the drawnout snort that ended in a little hiss of Popper's snores, Joe would slip off his chair and Janey would follow him without breathing into the front hall and out the front door. Once they'd closed it very carefully so that the knocker wouldn't bang. Joe would give her a slap, yell "You're it" and run off down the hill towards M Street, and she'd have to run after him, her heart pounding, her hands cold for fear he'd run away and leave her.

Winters the brick sidewalks were icy and there were colored women out spreading cinders outside their doors when the children went to school mornings. Joe never would walk with the rest of them because they were girls, he lagged behind or ran ahead. Janey wished she could walk with him, but she couldn't leave her little sisters who held tight onto her hands. One winter they got in the habit of walking up the hill with a little yaller girl who lived directly across the street and whose name was Pearl. Afternoons Janey and Pearl walked home together. Pearl usually had a couple of pennies to buy bullseyes or candy bananas with at a little store on Wisconsin Avenue, and she always gave Janey half, so Janey was very fond of her. One afternoon she asked Pearl to come in and they played dolls together under the big rose of sharon bush in the back yard. When Pearl had gone Mommer's voice called from the kitchen. Mommer had her sleeves rolled up on her faded pale arms and a checked apron on and was rolling piecrust for supper so that her hands were covered with flour.

"Janey, come here," she said. Janey knew from the cold quaver in her voice that something was wrong.

"Yes, Mommer." Janey stood in front of her mother shaking her head about so that the two stiff sandy pigtails lashed from side to side.

"Stand still, child, for gracious sake . . . Jane, I want to talk to you about something. That little colored girl you brought in this afternoon . . ." Janey's heart was dropping. She had a sick feeling and felt herself blushing, she hardly knew why. "Now, don't misunderstand me; I like and respect the colored people; some of them are fine self-respecting people in their place . . . But you mustn't bring that little colored girl in the house again. Treating colored people kindly and with respect is one of the signs of good breeding . . . You mustn't forget that your mother's people were wellborn every inch of them . . . Georgetown was very different in those days. We lived in a big house with most lovely lawns . . . but you must never associate with colored people on an equal basis. Living in this neighborhood it's all the more important to be careful about those things . . . Neither the whites nor the blacks respect those who do . . . That's all, Janey, you understand; now run out and play, it'll soon be time for your supper."

Janey tried to speak, but she couldn't. She stood stiff in the middle of the yard on the grating that covered the drainpipe, staring at the back fence. "Niggerlover," yelled Joe in her ear. "Niggerlover ump-mya-mya . . . Niggerlover niggerlover ump-mya-mya." Janey began to cry.

Joe was an untalkative sandyhaired boy who could pitch a mean outcurve when he was still little. He learned to swim and dive in Rock Creek and used to say he wanted to be motorman on a streetcar when he grew up. For several years his best friend was Alec McPherson whose father was a locomotive engineer on the B. and O. After that Joe wanted to be a locomotive engineer. Janey used to tag around after the two boys whenever they'd let her, to the carbarns at the head of Pennsylvania Avenue where they made friends with some of the conductors and motormen who used to let them ride on the platform a couple of blocks sometimes if there wasn't any inspector around, down along the canal or up Rock Creek where they caught tadpoles and fell in the water and splashed each other with mud.

Summer evenings when the twilight was long after supper they played lions and tigers with other kids from the neighborhood in the long grass of some empty lots near Oak Hill Cemetery. There were long periods when there was measles or scarlet fever around and Mommer wouldn't let them out. Then Alec would come down and they'd play three-o-cat in the back yard. Those were the times Janey liked best. Then the boys treated her as one of them. Summer dusk would come down on them sultry and full of lightningbugs. If Popper was feeling in a good mood he'd send them up the hill to the drugstore on N Street to buy icecream, there'd be young men in their shirtsleeves and straw hats strolling with girls who wore a stick of punk in their hair to keep off the mosquitoes, a rankness and a smell of cheap perfume from the colored families crowded on their doorsteps, laughing, talking softly with an occasional flash of teeth, rolling of a white eyeball. The dense sweaty night was scary, hummed, rumbled with distant thunder, with junebugs, with the clatter of traffic from M Street, the air of the street dense and breathless under the thick trees; but when she was with Alec and Joe she wasn't scared, not even of drunks or big shamblefooted coloredmen. When they got back Popper would smoke a cigar and they'd sit out in the back yard and the mosquitoes 'ud eat them up and Mommer and Aunt Francine and the kids 'ud eat the icecream and Popper would just smoke a cigar and tell them stories of when he'd been a towboat captain down on the Chesapeake in his younger days and he'd saved the barkentine *Nancy Q* in distress on the Kettlebottoms in a sou'west gale. Then it'd get time to go to bed and Alec 'ud be sent home and Janey'd have to go to bed in the stuffy little back room on the top floor with her two little sisters in their cribs against the opposite wall. Maybe a thunderstorm would come up and she'd lie awake staring up at the ceiling cold with fright, listening to her little sisters whimper as they slept until she heard the reassuring sound of Mommer scurrying about the house closing windows, the slam of a door, the whine of wind and rattle of rain and the thunder rolling terribly loud and near overhead like a thousand beertrucks roaring over the bridge. Times like that she thought of going down to Joe's room and crawling into bed with him, but for some reason she was afraid to, though sometimes she got as far as the landing. He'd laugh at her and call her a softie.

About once a week Joe would get spanked. Popper would come home from the Patent Office where he worked, angry and out of sorts, and the girls would be scared of him and go about the house quiet as mice; but Joe seemed to like to provoke him, he'd run whistling through the back hall or clatter up and down stairs making a tremendous racket with his stubtoed ironplated shoes. Then Popper would start scolding him and Joe would stand in front of him without saying a word glaring at the floor with bitter blue eyes. Janey's insides knotted up and froze when Popper would start up the stairs to the bathroom pushing Joe in front of him. She knew what would happen. He'd take down the razorstrop from behind the door and put the boy's head and shoulders under his arm and beat him. Joe would clench his teeth and flush and not say a word and when Popper was tired of beating him they'd look at each other and Joe would be sent up to his room and Popper would come down stairs trembling all over and pretend nothing had happened, and Janey would slip out into the yard with her fists clenched, whispering to herself, "I hate him . . . I hate him . . . I hate him."

Once a drizzly Saturday night she stood against the fence in the dark looking up at the lighted window. She could hear Popper's voice and Joe's in an argument. She thought maybe she'd fall down dead at the first thwack of the razorstrop. She couldn't hear what they were saying. Then suddenly it came, the leather sound of blows and Joe stifling a gasp. She was eleven years old. Something broke loose. She rushed into the kitchen with her hair all wet from the rain, "Mommer, he's killing Joe. Stop it." Her mother turned up a withered helpless drooping face from a pan she was scouring. "Oh, you can't do anything." Janey ran upstairs and started beating on the bathroom door. "Stop it, stop it," her voice kept yelling. She was scared, but something stronger than she was had hold of her. The door opened; there was Joe looking sheepish and Popper with his face all flushed and the razorstrop in his hand.

"Beat me . . . it's me that's bad . . . I won't have you beating Joe like that." She was scared. She didn't know what to do, tears stung in her eyes.

Popper's voice was unexpectedly kind:

"You go straight up to bed without any supper and remember that you have enough to do to fight your own battles, Janey."

She ran up to her room and lay on the bed shaking. When she'd gone to sleep, Joe's voice woke her up with a start.

He was standing in his nightgown in the door. "Say, Janey," he whispered. "Don't you do that again, see. I can take care of myself, see. A girl can't butt in between men like that. When I get a job and make enough dough I'll get me a gun and if Popper tries to beat me up I'll shoot him dead." Janey began to sniffle. "What you wanna cry for; this ain't no Johnstown flood."

She could hear him tiptoe down the stairs again in his bare feet.

At highschool she took the commercial course and learned stenography and typewriting. She was a plain thinfaced sandyhaired girl, quiet and popular with the teachers. Her fingers were quick and she picked up typing and shorthand easily. She liked to read and used to get books like *The Inside of the Cup, The Battle of the Strong, The Winning of Barbara Worth* out of the library. Her mother kept telling her that she'd spoil her eyes if she read so much. When she read she used to imagine she was the heroine, that the weak brother who went to the bad but was a gentleman at core and capable of every sacrifice, like Sidney Carton in *A Tale of Two Cities*, was Joe and that the hero was Alec.

She thought Alec was the bestlooking boy in Georgetown and the strongest. He had black closecropped hair and a very white skin with a few freckles and a strong squareshouldered way of walking. After him Joe was the bestlooking and strongest and the best baseball player anyway. Everybody said he ought to go on through highschool on account of being such a good baseball player, but at the end of his first year Popper said he had three girls to support and that Joe would have to get to work; so he got a job as a Western Union messenger. Janey was pretty proud of him in his uniform until the girls at highschool kidded her about it. Alec's folks had promised to put him through college if he made good in highschool, so Alec worked hard. He wasn't tough and dirty-talking like most of the boys Joe knew. He was always nice to Janey, though he never seemed to want to be left alone with her. She pretty well admitted to herself that she had a terrible crush on Alec.

The best day of her life was the sweltering summer Sunday they all went canoeing up to Great Falls. She had put up the lunch the night before. In the morning she added a steak she found in the icebox. There was blue haze at the end of every street of brick houses and dark summergreen trees when before anybody else was awake she and Joe crept out of the house round seven that morning.

They met Alec at the corner in front of the depot. He stood waiting for them with his feet wide apart and a skillet in his hand.

They all ran and caught the car that was just leaving for Cabin John's Bridge. They had the car all to themselves like it was a private car. The car hummed over the rails past whitewashed shanties and nigger cabins along the canal, skirting hillsides where the sixfoot tall waving corn marched in ranks like soldiers. The sunlight glanced in bluewhite glare on the wavingdrooping leaves of the tasseling corn; glare, and a whirring and tinkling of grasshoppers and dryflies rose in hot smoke into the pale sky round the clattering shaking electric car. They ate sweet summerapples Joe had bought off a colored woman in the station and chased each other round the car and flopped down on top of each other in the cornerseats; and they laughed and giggled till they were weak. Then the car was running through woods; they could see the trestlework of the rollercoasters of Glen Echo through the trees and they piled off the car at Cabin John's having more fun than a barrel of monkeys.

They ran down to the bridge to look up and down the river brown and dark in the white glary morning between foliagesodden banks; then they found the canoe that belonged to a friend of Alec's and some packages of neccos and started out. Alec and Joe paddled and Janey sat in the bottom with her sweater rolled round a thwart for a pillow. Alec was paddling in the bow. It was sweltering hot. The sweat made the shirt cling to the hollow of his chunky back that curved with every stroke of the paddle. After a while the boys stripped to their bathingsuits that they wore under their clothes. It made Janey's throat tremble to watch Alec's back and the bulging muscles of his arm as he paddled, made her feel happy and scared. She sat there in her white dimity dress, trailing her hand in the weedy browngreen water. They stopped to pick waterlilies and the white flowers of arrowhead that glistened like ice and everything smelt wet rank of the muddy roots of waterlilies. The cream soda got warm and they drank it that way and kidded each other back and forth and Alec caught a crab and covered Janey's dress with greenslimy splashes and Janey didn't care a bit and they called Joe skipper and he loosened up and said he was going to join the navy and Alec said he'd be a civil engineer and build a motorboat and take them all cruising and Janey was happy because they included her when they talked just like she was a boy too. At a place below the Falls where there were locks in the canal they had a long portage down to the river. Janey carried the grub and the paddles and the frying pan and the boys sweated and cussed under the canoe. Then they paddled across to the Virginia side and made a fire in a little hollow among gray rusty bowlders. Joe cooked the steak and Janey unpacked the sandwiches and cookies she'd made and nursed some murphies baking in the ashes. They roasted ears of corn too that they had swiped out of a field beside the canal. Everything turned out fine except that they hadn't brought enough butter. Afterwards they sat eating cookies and drinking rootbeer quietly talking round the embers. Alec and Joe brought out pipes and she felt pretty good sitting there at the Great Falls of the Potomac with two men smoking pipes.

"Geewhiz, Janey, Joe cooked that steak fine."

"When we was kids we used to ketch frogs and broil 'em up in Rock Creek . . . Remember, Alec?"

"Damned if I don't, and Janey she was along once; geewhiz, the fuss you kicked up then, Janey."

"I don't like seeing you skin them."

"We thought we was regular wildwest hunters then. We had packs of fun then."

"I like this better, Alec," said Janey hesitatingly.

"So do I . . ." said Alec. "Dod gast it, I wisht we had a watermelon."

"Maybe we'll see some along the riverbank somewhere goin' home."

"Jiminy crickets, what I couldn't do to a watermelon, Joe."

"Mommer had a watermelon on ice," said Janey; "maybe there'll be some yet when we get home."

"I don't never want to go home," said Joe, suddenly bitter serious.

"Joe, you oughtn't to talk like that." She felt girlish and frightened.

"I'll talk how I goddam please . . . Kerist, I hate the scrimpy dump."

"Joe, you oughtn't to talk like that." Janey felt she was going to cry.

"Dod gast it," said Alec. "It's time we shoved . . . What you say, bo . . . ? We'll take one more dip and then make tracks for home."

When the boys were through swimming they all went up to look at the Falls and then they started off. They went along fast in the swift stream under the steep treehung bank. The afternoon was very sultry, they went through layers of hot steamy air. Big cloudheads were piling up in the north. It wasn't fun any more for Janey. She was afraid her period was coming on. She'd only had the curse a few times yet and the thought of it scared her and took all the strength out of her, made her want to crawl away out of sight like an old sick mangy cat. She didn't want Joe and Alec to notice how she felt. She thought how would it be if she turned the canoe over. The boys could swim ashore all right, and she'd drown and they'd drag the river for her body and everybody'd cry and feel so sorry about it.

Purplegray murk rose steadily and drowned the white summits of the cloudheads. Everything got to be livid white and purple. The boys paddled as hard as they could. They could hear the advancing rumble of thunder. The bridge was well in sight when the wind hit them, a hot stormwind full of dust and dead leaves and bits of chaff and straw, churning the riverwater.

They made the shore just in time. "Dod gast it, this is goin' to be some storm," said Alec; "Janey, get under the boat." They turned the canoe over on the pebbly shore in the lee of a big bowlder and huddled up under it. Janey sat in the middle with the waterlilies they had picked that morning all shriveled and clammy from the heat in her hand. The boys lay in their damp bathingsuits on either side of her. Alec's towsled black hair was against her cheek. The other side of her Joe lay with his head in the end of the canoe and his lean brown feet and legs in their rolledup pants tucked under her dress. The smell of sweat and riverwater and the warm boysmell of Alec's hair and shoulders made her dizzy. When the rain came drumming on the bottom of the canoe curtaining them in with lashing white spray, she slipped her arm round Alec's neck and let her hand rest timidly on his bare shoulder. He didn't move.

The rain passed after a while. "Gee, that wasn't as bad as I thought it would be," said Alec. They were pretty wet and chilly, but they felt good in the fresh rainwashed air. They put the canoe back in the water and went on down as far as the bridge. Then they carried it back to the house they'd gotten it from, and went to the little shelter to wait for the electric car. They were tired and sunburned and sticky. The car was packed with a damp Sunday afternoon crowd, picnickers caught by the shower at Great Falls and Glen Echo. Janey thought she'd never stand it till she got home. Her belly was all knotted up with a cramp. When they got to Georgetown the boys still had fifty cents between them and wanted to go to a movie, but Janey ran off and left them. Her only thought was to get to bed so that she could put her face into the pillow and cry.

After that Janey never cried much; things upset her, but she got a cold hard feeling all over instead. Highschool went by fast, with hot thunderstormy Washington summers in between terms, punctuated by an occasional picnic at Marshall Hall or a party at some house in the neighborhood. Joe got a job at the Adams Express. She didn't see him much, as he didn't eat home any more. Alec had bought a motorcycle and although he was still in highschool Janey heard little about him. Sometimes she sat up to get a word with Joe when he came home at night. He smelt of tobacco and liquor, though he never seemed to be drunk. He went to his job at seven and when he got out in the evenings he went out with the bunch hanging round poolrooms on 4½ Street or playing craps or bowling. Sundays he played baseball in Maryland. Janey would sit up for him, but when he came she'd ask him how things were going where he worked and he'd say "Fine" and he'd ask her how things were going at school and she'd say "Fine" and then they'd both go off to bed. Once in a while she'd ask if he'd seen Alec and he'd say "Yes" with a scrap of a smile and she'd ask how Alec was and he'd say "Fine."

She had one friend, Alice Dick, a dark stubby girl with glasses who took all the same classes with her in highschool. Saturday afternoons they'd dress up in their best and go window-shopping down F Street way. They'd buy a few little things, stop in for a soda and come home on the streetcar feeling they'd had a busy afternoon. Once in a very long while they went to a matinee at Poli's and Janey would take Alice Dick home to supper. Alice Dick liked the Williamses and they liked her. She said it made her feel freer to spend a few hours with broadminded people. Her own folks were Southern Methodists and very narrow. Her father was a clerk in the Government Printing Office and was in daily dread that his job would come under the civil service regulations. He was a stout shortwinded man, fond of playing practical jokes on his wife and daughter, and suffered from chronic dyspepsia.

Alice Dick and Janey planned that as soon as they got through highschool they'd get jobs and leave home. They even picked out the house where they'd board, a greenstone house near Thomas Circle, run by a Mrs. Jenks, widow of a naval officer, who was very refined and had Southern cooking and charged moderately for table board.

One Sunday night during the spring of her last term in highschool Janey was in her room getting undressed. Francie and Ellen were still playing in the backyard. Their voices came in through the open window with a spicy waft of lilacs from the lilacbushes in the next yard. She had just let down her hair and was looking in the mirror imagining how she'd look if she was a peach and had auburn hair, when there was a knock at the door and Joe's voice outside. There was something funny about his voice.

"Come in," she called. "I'm just fixin' my hair."

She first saw his face in the mirror. It was very white and the skin was drawn back tight over the cheekbones and round the mouth.

"Why, what's the matter, Joe?" She jumped up and faced him.

"It's like this, Janey," said Joe, drawling his words out painfully. "Alec was killed. He smashed up on his motorbike. I've just come from the hospital. He's dead, all right."

Janey seemed to be writing the words on a white pad in her mind. She couldn't say anything.

"He smashed up comin' home from Chevy Chase . . . He'd gone out to the ballgame to see me pitch. You oughter seen him all smashed to hell."

Janey kept trying to say something.

"He was your best . . ."

"He was the best guy I'll ever know," Joe went on gently. "Well, that's that, Janey . . . But I wanted to tell you I don't want to hang round this lousy dump now that Alec's gone. I'm goin' to enlist in the navy. You tell the folks, see . . . I don't wanna talk to 'em. That's it; I'll join the navy and see the world."

"But, Joe . . ."

"I'll write you, Janey; honestly, I will . . . I'll write you a hell of a lot. You an' me . . . Well, goodbye, Janey." He grabbed her by the shoulders and kissed her awkwardly on the nose and cheek. All she could do was whisper "Do be careful, Joe," and stand there in front of the bureau in the gust of lilacs and the yelling of the kids that came through the open window. She heard Joe's steps light quick down the stairs and heard the frontdoor shut. She turned out the light, took off her clothes in the dark, and got into bed. She lay there without crying.

The Campers at Kitty Hawk

ON DECEMBER SEVENTEENTH, nineteen hundred and three, Bishop Wright, of the United Brethren, onetime editor of the *Religious Telescope,* received in his frame house on Hawthorn Street in Dayton, Ohio, a telegram from his boys Wilbur and Orville who'd gotten it into their heads to spend their vacations in a little camp out on the dunes of the North Carolina coast tinkering with a homemade glider they'd knocked together themselves. The telegram read:

SUCCESS FOUR FLIGHTS THURSDAY MORNING ALL AGAINST TWENTYONE-MILE WIND STARTED FROM LEVEL WITH EN-GINEPOWER ALONE   AVERAGE SPEED THROUGH AIR THIRTY-ONE MILES   LONGEST FIFTYSEVEN SECONDS   INFORM PRESS HOME CHRISTMAS

The figures were a little wrong because the telegraph operator misread Orville's hasty penciled scrawl.

but the fact remains

that a couple of young bicycle mechanics from Dayton, Ohio,

had designed, constructed, and flown

for the first time ever a practical airplane.

After running the motor a few minutes to heat it up, I released the wire that held the machine to the track and the machine started forward into the wind. Wilbur ran at the side of the machine holding the wing to balance it on the track. Unlike the start on the fourteenth, made in a calm, the machine facing a twentyseven-mile wind started very slowly. . . . Wilbur was able to stay with it until it lifted from the track after a forty-foot run. One of the lifesaving men snapped the camera for us, taking a picture just as it reached the end of the track and the machine had risen to a height of about two feet. . . . The course of the flight up and down was extremely erratic, partly due to the irregularities of the air, partly to lack of experience in handling this machine. A sudden dart when a little over a hundred and twenty feet from the point at which it rose in the air ended the flight. . . . This flight lasted only twelve seconds, but it was nevertheless the first in the history of the world in which a machine carrying a man had raised itself by its own power into the air in full flight, had sailed forward without reduction of speed, and had finally landed at a point as high as that from which it started.

A little later in the day the machine was caught in a gust of wind and turned over and smashed, almost killing the coastguardsman who tried to hold it down;
    it was too bad,
    but the Wright brothers were too happy to care;
    they'd proved that the damn thing flew.

When these points had been definitely established, we at once packed our goods and returned home, knowing that the age of the flyingmachine had come at last.

They were home for Christmas in Dayton, Ohio, where they'd been born in the seventies of a family who had been settled west of the Alleghenies since eighteen-fourteen; in Dayton, Ohio, where they'd been to grammarschool and highschool and joined their father's church and played baseball and hockey and worked out on the parallel bars and the flying swing and sold newspapers and built themselves a printingpress out of odds and ends from the junkheap and flown kites and tinkered with mechanical contraptions and gone around town as boys doing odd jobs to turn an honest penny.

The folks claimed it was the Bishop's bringing home a helicopter, a fiftycent mechanical toy made of two fans worked by elastic bands that was supposed to hover in the air, that had got his two youngest boys hipped on the subject of flight

so that they stayed home instead of marrying the way

the other boys did, and puttered all day about the house picking up a living with jobprinting,

bicyclerepair work,

sitting up late nights reading books on aerodynamics.

Still they were sincere churchmembers, their bicycle business was prosperous, a man could rely on their word. They were popular in Dayton.

In those days flyingmachines were the big laugh of all the crackerbarrel philosophers. Langley's and Chanute's unsuccessful experiments had been jeered down with an I-told-you-so that rang from coast to coast. The Wrights' big problem was to find a place secluded enough to carry on their experiments without being the horselaugh of the countryside. Then they had no money to spend;

they were practical mechanics; when they needed anything they built it themselves.

They hit on Kitty Hawk,

on the great dunes and sandy banks that stretch south towards Hatteras seaward of Albemarle Sound,

a vast stretch of seabeach,

empty except for a coastguard station, a few fishermen's shacks, and the swarms of mosquitoes and the ticks and chiggers in the crabgrass behind the dunes,

and overhead the gulls and swooping terns, in the evening fishhawks and cranes flapping across the saltmarches, occasionally eagles

that the Wright brothers followed soaring with their eyes

as Leonardo watched them centuries before,

straining his sharp eyes to apprehend

the laws of flight.

Four miles across the loose sand from the scattering of shacks, the Wright brothers built themselves a camp and a shed for their gliders. It was a long way to pack their groceries, their tools, anything they happened to need; in summer it was hot as blazes, the mosquitoes were hell;

but they were alone there,

and they'd figured out that the loose sand was as soft as anything they could find to fall in.

There with a glider made of two planes and a tail in

which they lay flat on their bellies and controlled the warp
of the planes by shimmying their hips, taking off again and
again all day from a big dune named Kill Devil Hill,
    they learned to fly.

Once they'd managed to hover for a few seconds
and soar ever so slightly on a rising aircurrent,
they decided the time had come
to put a motor in their biplane.

Back in the shop in Dayton, Ohio, they built an air-
tunnel, which is their first great contribution to the science
of flying, and tried out model planes in it.

They couldn't interest any builders of gasoline engines,
so they had to build their own motor.

It worked; after that Christmas of nineteen-three the
Wright brothers weren't doing it for fun any more; they
gave up their bicycle business, got the use of a big old
cowpasture belonging to the local banker for practice flights,
spent all the time when they weren't working on their
machine in promotion, worrying about patents, infringe-
ments, spies, trying to interest government officials, to make
sense out of the smooth involved heartbreaking remarks of
lawyers.

In two years they had a plane that would cover twentyfour miles at a stretch round and round the cowpasture.

People on the interurban car used to crane their necks
out of the windows when they passed along the edge of the
field, startled by the clattering pop-pop of the old Wright
motor and the sight of the white biplane like a pair of
ironingboards one on top of the other chugging along a
good fifty feet in the air. The cows soon got used to it.

As the flights got longer,
the Wright brothers got backers,
engaged in lawsuits,
lay in their beds at night sleepless with the whine of
phantom millions, worse than the mosquitoes at Kitty Hawk.

In nineteen-seven they went to Paris,
allowed themselves to be togged out in dress suits and
silk hats,

learned to tip waiters,

talked with government experts, got used to gold braid and postponements and Vandyke beards and the outspread palms of politicos. For amusement

they played diabolo in the Tuileries Gardens.

They gave publicized flights at Fort Myers, where they had their first fatal crackup, St. Petersburg, Paris, Berlin; at Pau they were all the rage,

such an attraction that the hotelkeeper

wouldn't charge them for their room.

Alfonso of Spain shook hands with them and was photographed sitting in the machine.

King Edward watched a flight,

the Crown Prince insisted on being taken up,

the rain of medals began.

They were congratulated by the Czar

and the King of Italy and the amateurs of sport, and the society climbers and the papal titles,

and decorated by a society for universal peace.

Aeronautics became the sport of the day.

The Wrights don't seem to have been very much impressed by the upholstery and the braid and the gold medals and the parades of plush horses;

they remained practical mechanics

and insisted on doing all their own work themselves,

even to filling the gasolinetank.

In nineteen-eleven they were back on the dunes

at Kitty Hawk with a new glider.

Orville stayed up in the air for nine and a half minutes, which remained a long time the record for motorless flight.

The same year Wilbur died of typhoidfever in Dayton.

In the rush of new names: Farman, Blériot, Curtiss, Ferber, Esnault-Peltrie, Delagrange;

in the snorting impact of bombs and the whine and rattle of shrapnel and the sudden stutter of machineguns after the motor's been shut off overhead,

and we flatten into the mud

and make ourselves small cowering in the corners of ruined walls,

the Wright brothers passed out of the headlines;
but not even headlines or the bitter smear of newsprint
or the choke of smokescreen and gas or chatter of brokers
on the stockmarket or barking of phantom millions or
oratory of brasshats laying wreaths on new monuments
can blur the memory
of the chilly December day
two shivering bicycle mechanics from Dayton, Ohio,
first felt their homemade contraption,
whittled out of hickory sticks,
gummed together with Arnstein's bicycle cement,
stretched with muslin they'd sewn on their sister's
sewingmachine in their own backyard on Hawthorn Street
in Dayton, Ohio,
soar into the air
above the dunes and the wide beach
at Kitty Hawk.

GROUP II

War's Misadventures

when they return home what will our war veterans think of the American who babbles about some vague new order, while dabbling in the sand of shoal water? From his weak folly they who lived through the spectacle will recall the vast new No Man's Land of Europe reeking with murder and the lust of rapine, aflame with the fires of revolution

Randolph Bourne

Randolph Bourne
came as an inhabitant of this earth
without the pleasure of choosing his dwelling or his career.

He was a hunchback, grandson of a congregational minister, born in 1886 in Bloomfield, New Jersey; there he attended grammarschool and highschool.

At the age of seventeen he went to work as secretary to a Morristown businessman.

He worked his way through Columbia working in a pianola record factory in Newark, working as a proofreader,

pianotuner, accompanist in a vocal studio in Carnegie Hall.
     At Columbia he studied with John Dewey,
     got a traveling fellowship that took him to England
Paris Rome Berlin Copenhagen,
     wrote a book on the Gary schools.
     In Europe he heard music, a great deal of Wagner and
Scriabine
     and bought himself a black cape.

     This little sparrowlike man,
     tiny twisted bit of flesh in a black cape,
     always in pain and ailing,
     put a pebble in his sling
     and hit Goliath in the forehead with it.
     War, he wrote, *is the health of the state.*

     Half musician, half educational theorist (weak health
and being poor and twisted in body and on bad terms with
his people hadn't spoiled the world for Randolph Bourne;
he was a happy man, loved die Meistersinger and playing
Bach with his long hands that stretched so easily over the
keys and pretty girls and good food and evenings of talk.
When he was dying of pneumonia a friend brought him an
eggnog; Look at the yellow, it's beautiful, he kept saying
as his life ebbed into delirium and fever. He was a happy
man.) Bourne seized with feverish intensity on the ideas
then going around at Columbia he picked rosy glasses out
of the turgid ·jumble of John Dewey's teaching through
which he saw clear and sharp
     the shining capitol of reformed democracy,
     Wilson's New Freedom;
     but he was too good a mathematician; he had to work
the equations out;

     with the result
     that in the crazy spring of 1917 he began to get unpop-
ular where his bread was buttered at the *New Republic;*
     for *New Freedom* read *Conscription,* for *Democracy,*
Win the War, for *Reform, Safeguard the Morgan Loans*
     for Progress Civilization Education Service,
     Buy a Liberty Bond,
     Strafe the Hun,

Jail the Objectors.

He resigned from the *New Republic*; only *The Seven Arts* had the nerve to publish his articles against the war. The backers of the *Seven Arts* took their money elsewhere; friends didn't like to be seen with Bourne, his father wrote him begging him not to disgrace the family name. The rainbowtinted future of reformed democracy went pop like a pricked soapbubble.

The liberals scurried to Washington;

some of his friends pled with him to climb up on Schoolmaster Wilson's sharabang; the war was great fought from the swivel chairs of Mr. Creel's bureau in Washington.

He was cartooned, shadowed by the espionage service and the counterespionage service; taking a walk with two girl friends at Wood's Hole he was arrested, a trunk full of manuscript and letters was stolen from him in Connecticut. (Force to the utmost, thundered Schoolmaster Wilson)

He didn't live to see the big circus of the Peace of Versailles or the purplish normalcy of the Ohio Gang.

Six weeks after the armistice he died planning an essay on the foundations of future radicalism in America.

If any man has a ghost
Bourne has a ghost,
a tiny twisted unscared ghost in a black cloak
hopping along the grimy old brick and brownstone streets still left in downtown New York,
crying out in a shrill soundless giggle:
War is the health of the state.

Eleanor Stoddard

Eleanor thought that things were very exciting that winter. She and J. W. went out a great deal together, to all the French operas and to first nights. There was a little French restaurant where they ate hors d'oeuvres way east in Fiftysix Street. They went to see French paintings in the galleries up Madison Avenue. J. W. began to get interested in art, and Eleanor loved going round with him because he had such a romantic manner about everything and he used to tell her she was his inspiration and that he always got good ideas when he'd been talking to her. They often talked about how silly people were who said that a man and a woman couldn't have a platonic friendship. They wrote each other little notes in French every day. Eleanor often thought it was a shame J. W. had such a stupid wife who was an invalid too, but she thought that the children were lovely and it was nice that they both had lovely blue eyes like their father.

She had an office now all by herself and had two girls working with her to learn the business and had quite a lot of work to do. The office was in the first block above Madison Square on Madison Avenue and she had just had her own name on it. Eveline Hutchins didn't have anything to do with it any more as Doctor Hutchins had retired and the Hutchinses had all moved out to Santa Fe. Eveline sent her an occasional box of Indian curios or pottery and the watercolors the Indian children did in the schools, and Eleanor found they sold very well. In the afternoon she'd ride downtown in a taxi and look up at the Metropolitan Life tower and the Flatiron Building and the lights against the steely Manhattan sky and think of crystals and artificial flowers and gilt patterns on indigo and claretcolored brocade.

The maid would have tea ready for her and often there would be friends waiting for her, young architects or painters. There'd always be flowers, calla lilies with the texture of icecream or a bowl of freesias. She'd talk a while before slipping off to dress for dinner. When J. W. phoned that he couldn't come she'd feel very bad. If there was still anybody there who'd come to tea she'd ask him to stay and have potluck with her.

The sight of the French flag excited her always or when a band played *Tipperary*; and one evening when they were going to see *The Yellow Jacket* for the third time, she had on a new furcoat that she was wondering how she was going to pay for, and she thought of all the bills at her office and the house on Sutton Place she was remodeling on a speculation and wanted to ask J. W. about a thousand he'd said he'd invested for her and wondered if there'd been any turnover yet. They'd been talking about the air raids and poison gas and the effect of the war news downtown and the Bowmen of Mons and the Maid of Orleans and she said she believed in the supernatural, and J. W. was hinting something about reverses on the Street and his face looked drawn and worried; but they were crossing Times Square through the eight o'clock crowds and the skysigns flashing on and off. The fine little triangular men were doing exercises on the Wrigley sign and suddenly a grindorgan began to play *The Marseillaise* and it was too beautiful; she burst into tears and they talked about Sacrifice and Dedication and J. W. held her arm tight through the fur coat and gave the organ-grinder man a dollar. When they got to the theater Eleanor hurried down to the ladies' room to see if her eyes had got red. But when she looked in the mirror they weren't red at all and there was a flash of heartfelt feeling in her eyes, so she just freshened up her face and went back up to the lobby, where J. W. was waiting for her with the tickets in his hand; her gray eyes were flashing and had tears in them.

Then one evening J. W. looked very worried indeed and said when he was taking her home from the opera where they'd seen *Manon* that his wife didn't understand their relations and was making scenes and threatening to divorce him. Eleanor was indignant and said she must have a very coarse nature not to understand that their relations were pure as driven snow. J. W. said she had and that he was very worried and he explained that most of the capital invested in his agency was his mother-in-law's and that she could bankrupt him if she wanted to, which was much worse than a divorce. At that Eleanor felt very cold and crisp and said that she would rather go out of his life entirely than break up his home and that he owed something to his lovely children. J. W. said she was his inspiration and he had to have her in his life and when they got back to Eighth Street they walked back and forth in Eleanor's white glittering drawingroom in the heavy smell of lilies wondering what could be done. They smoked many cigarettes, but they couldn't seem to come to any decision. When J. W. left he said with a sigh, "She may have detectives shadowing me this very minute," and he went away very despondent.

After he'd gone, Eleanor walked back and forth in front of the long Venetian mirror between the windows. She didn't know what to do. The decorating business was barely breaking even. She had the amortization to pay off on the house on Sutton Place. The rent of her apartment was two months overdue and there was her fur coat to pay for. She'd counted on the thousand dollars' worth of shares J. W. had said would be hers if he made the killing he expected in that Venezuela Oil stock. Something must have gone wrong or else he would have spoken of it. When Eleanor went to bed she didn't sleep. She felt very miserable and lonely. She'd have to go back to the drudgery of a department store. She was losing her looks and her friends and now if she had to give up J. W. it would be terrible. She thought of her colored maid Augustine with her unfortunate loves that she always told Eleanor about and she wished she'd been like that. Maybe she'd been wrong from the start to want everything so justright and beautiful. She didn't cry, but she lay all night with her eyes wide and smarting staring at the flowered molding round the ceiling that she could see in the light that filtered in from the street through her lavender tulle curtains.

A couple of days later at the office she was looking at some antique Spanish chairs an old furniture dealer was trying to sell her when a telegram came:

DISAGREEABLE DEVELOPMENTS MUST SEE YOU IN-
ADVISABLE USE TELEPHONE MEET ME TEA FIVE
OCLOCK PRINCE GEORGE HOTEL

It wasn't signed. She told the man to leave the chairs and when he'd gone stood a long time looking down at a pot of lavender crocuses with yellow pistils she had on her desk. She was wondering if it would do any good if she went out to Great Neck and talked to Gertrude Moorehouse. She called Miss Lee who was making up some curtains in the other room and asked her to take charge of the office and that she'd phone during the afternoon.

She got into a taxi and went up to the Pennsylvania Station. It was a premature spring day. People were walking along the street with their overcoats unbuttoned. The sky was a soft mauve with frail clouds like milkweed floss. In the smell of furs and overcoats and exhausts and bundledup bodies came an unexpected scent of birchbark. Eleanor sat bolt upright in the back of the taxi driving her sharp nails into the palms of her graygloved hands. She hated these treacherous days when winter felt like spring. They made the lines come out on her face, made everything seem to crumble about her, there seemed to be no firm footing any more. She'd go out and talk to Gertrude Moorehouse as one woman to another. A scandal would ruin everything. If she talked to her awhile she'd make her realize that there had never been anything between her and J. W. A divorce scandal would ruin everything. She'd lose her clients and have to go into bankruptcy and the only thing to do would be to go back to Pullman to live with her uncle and aunt.

She paid the taximan and went down the stairs to the Long Island Railroad. Her knees were shaky and she felt desperately tired as she pushed her way through the crowd to the information desk. No, she couldn't get a train to Great Neck till 2:13. She stood in line a long time for a ticket. A man stepped on her foot. The line of people moved maddeningly slowly past the ticketwindow. When she got to the window it was several seconds before she could remember the name of the place she wanted a ticket for. The man looked at her through the window, with peevish shoebutton eyes. He wore a green eyeshade and his lips were too red for his pale face. The people behind were getting impatient. A man with a tweed coat and a heavy suitcase was already trying to brush past her. "Great Neck and return." As soon as she'd bought the ticket the thought came to her that she wouldn't have time to get out there and back by five o'clock. She put the ticket in her gray silk purse that had a little design in jet on it. She thought of killing herself. She would take the subway downtown and go up in the elevator to the top of the Woolworth Building and throw herself off.

Instead she went out to the taxistation. Russet sunlight was pouring through the gray colonnade, the blue smoke of exhausts rose into it crinkled like watered silk. She got into a taxi and told the driver to take her round Central Park. Some of the twigs were red and there was a glint on the long buds of beeches, but the grass was still brown and there were piles of dirty snow in the gutters. A shivery raw wind blew across the ponds. The taximan kept talking to her. She couldn't catch what he said and got tired of making random answers and told him to leave her at the Metropolitan Art Museum. While she was paying him a newsboy ran by crying "Extra!" Eleanor bought a paper for a nickel and the taximan bought a paper. "I'll be a sonova . . ." she heard the taximan exclaim, but she ran up the steps fast for fear she'd have to talk to him. When she got in the quiet silvery light of the museum she opened up the paper. A rancid smell of printer's ink came from it; the ink was still sticky and came off on her gloves.

DECLARATION OF WAR

A matter of hours now Washington observers declare.
Germans' note thoroughly unsatisfactory.

She left the newspaper on a bench and went to look at the Rodins. After she'd looked at the Rodins she went to the Chinese wing. By the time she was ready to go down Fifth Avenue in the bus — she felt she'd been spending too much on taxis — she felt elated. All the way downtown she kept remembering the Age of Bronze. When she made out J. W. in the stuffy pinkish light of the hotel lobby she went towards him with a springy step. His jaw was set and his blue eyes were on fire. He looked younger than last time she'd seen him. "Well, it's come at last," he said. "I just wired Washington offering my services to the government. I'd like to see 'em try and pull a railroad strike now." "It's wonderful and terrible," said Eleanor. "I'm trembling like a leaf."

They went to a little table in the corner behind some heavy draperies to have tea. They had hardly sat down before the orchestra started playing *The Star-Spangled Banner*, and they had to get to their feet. There was great bustle in the hotel. People kept running about with fresh editions of the papers, laughing and talking loud. Perfect strangers borrowed each other's newspapers, chatted about the war, lit cigarettes for each other.

"I have an idea, J. W.," Eleanor was saying, holding a piece of cinnamontoast poised in her pointed fingers, "that if I went out and talked to your wife as one woman to another, she'd understand the situation better. When I was decorating the house she was so kind and we got along famously."

"I have offered my services to Washington," said Ward. "There may be a telegram at the office now. I'm sure that Gertrude will see that it is her simple duty."

"I want to go, J. W.," said Eleanor. "I feel I must go."

"Where?"

"To France."

"Don't do anything hasty, Eleanor."

"No, I feel I must . . . I could be a very good nurse . . . I'm not afraid of anything; you ought to know that, J. W."

The orchestra played *The Star-Spangled Banner* again; Eleanor sang some of the chorus in a shrill little treble voice. They were too excited to sit still long and went over to J. W.'s office in a taxi. The office was in great excitement. Miss Williams had had a flagpole put up in the center window and was just raising the flag on it. Eleanor went over to her and they shook hands warmly. The cold wind was rustling the papers on the desk and typewritten pages were sailing across the room, but nobody paid any attention. Down Fifth Avenue a band was coming near playing *Hail, Hail, the Gang's All Here*. All along office windows were brightly lit, flags were slapping against their poles in the cold wind, clerks and stenographers were leaning out and cheering, dropping out papers that sailed and whirled in the bitter eddying wind.

"It's the Seventh Regiment," somebody said and they all clapped and yelled. The band was clanging loud under the window. They could hear the tramp of the militiamen's feet. All the automobiles in the stalled traffic tooted their horns. People on the tops of the busses were waving small flags. Miss Williams leaned over and kissed Eleanor on the cheek. J. W. stood by looking out over their heads with a proud smile on his face.

After the band had gone and traffic was running again they put the window down and Miss Williams went around picking up and arranging loose papers. J. W. had a telegram from Washington accepting his services on the Public Information Committee that Mr. Wilson was gathering about him and said he'd leave in the morning. He called up Great Neck and asked Gertrude if he could come out to dinner and bring a friend. Gertrude said he might and that she hoped she'd be able to stay up to see them. She was excited by the warnews, but she said the thought of all that misery and slaughter gave her horrible pains in the back of the head.

"I have a hunch that if I take you out to dinner at Gertrude's, everything will be all right," he said to Eleanor. "I'm rarely wrong in my hunches."

"Oh, I know she'll understand," said Eleanor.

As they were leaving the office they met Mr. Robbins in the hall. He didn't take his hat off or the cigar out of his mouth. He looked drunk. "What the hell is this, Ward?" he said. "Are we at war or not?"

"If we're not we will be before morning," said J. W.

"It's the goddamnedest treason in history," said Mr. Robbins. "What did we elect Wilson for instead of Old Fuzzywhiskers except to keep us out of the goddam mess?"

"Robbins, I don't agree with you for a minute,' said J. W. "I think it's our duty to save . . ." But Mr. Robbins had disappeared through the office door leaving a strong reek of whiskey behind him.

"I'd have given him a piece of my mind," said Eleanor, "if I hadn't seen that he was in no condition."

Driving out to Great Neck in the Pierce Arrow it was thrilling. A long red afterglow lingered in the sky. Crossing the Queensboro Bridge with the cold wind back of them was like flying above lights and blocks of houses and the purple bulk of Blackwell's Island and the steamboats and the tall chimneys and the blue light of powerplants. They talked of Edith Cavell and airraids and flags and searchlights and the rumble of armies advancing and Joan of Arc. Eleanor drew the fur robe up to her chin and thought about what she'd say to Gertrude Moorehouse.

When they got to the house she felt a little afraid of a scene. She stopped in the hall to do up her face with a pocketmirror she had in her bag.

Gertrude Moorehouse was sitting in a long chair beside a crackling fire. Eleanor glanced around the room and was pleased at how lovely it looked. Gertrude Moorehouse went very pale when she saw her. "I wanted to talk to you," said Eleanor.

Gertrude Moorehouse held out her hand without getting up. "Excuse me for not getting up, Miss Stoddard," she said, "but I'm absolutely prostrated by the terrible news."

"Civilization demands a sacrifice . . . from all of us," said Eleanor.

"Of course it is terrible what the Huns have done, cutting the hands off Belgian children and all that," said Gertrude Moorehouse.

"Mrs. Moorehouse," said Eleanor. "I want to speak to you about this unfortunate misunderstanding of my relations with your husband . . . Do you think I am the sort of woman who could come out here and face you if there was anything in these horrible rumors? Our relations are pure as driven snow."

"Please don't speak of it, Miss Stoddard. I believe you."

When J. W. came in they were sitting on either side of the fire talking about Gertrude's operation.

Eleanor got to her feet. "Oh, I think it's wonderful of you, J. W.

J. W. cleared his throat and looked from one to the other. "It's little less than my duty," he said.

"What is it?" asked Gertrude.

"I have offered my services to the government to serve in whatever capacity they see fit for the duration of the war."

"Not at the front," said Gertrude with a startled look.

"I'm leaving for Washington tomorrow . . . Of course I shall serve without pay."

"Ward, that's noble of you," said Gertrude. He walked over slowly until he stood beside her chair, then he leaned over and kissed her on the forehead. "We must all make our sacrifices . . . My dear, I shall trust you and your mother . . ."

"Of course, Ward, of course . . . It's all been a silly misunderstanding." Gertrude flushed red. She got to her feet. "I've been a damn suspicious fool . . . but you mustn't go to the front, Ward. I'll talk mother around" . . . She went up to him and put her hands on his shoulders. Eleanor stood back against the wall looking at them. He wore a smoothfitting tuxedo. Gertrude's salmoncolored teagown stood out against the black. His light hair was ashgray in the light from the crystal chandelier against the tall ivorygray walls of the room. His face was in shadow and looked very sad. Eleanor thought how little people understood a man like that, how beautiful the room was, like a play, like a

Whistler, like Sarah Bernhardt. Emotion misted her eyes.

"I'll join the Red Cross," she said. "I can't wait to get to France."

The Camera Eye

eleven thousand registered harlots said the Red Cross Publicity Man infest the streets of Marseilles

the Ford stalled three times in the Rue de Rivoli in Fontainebleau we had our café au lait in bed the Forest was so achingly red yellow novemberbrown under the tiny lavender rain beyond the road climbed through dovecolored hills the air smelt of apples

Nevers (Dumas nom de dieu) Athos Porthos and d'Artagnan had ordered a bisque at the inn we wound down slowly into red Mâcon that smelt of winelees and the vintage fais ce que voudras sautes Bourgignon in the Rhone valley the first strawcolored sunlight streaked the white road with shadows of skeletal poplars at every stop we drank wine strong as beefsteaks rich as the palace of François Premier bouquet of the last sleetlashed roses we didn't cross the river to Lyon where Jean-Jacques suffered from greensickness as a youngster the landscapes of Provence were all out of the Gallic Wars the towns were dictionaries of Latin roots Orange Tarascon Arles where Van Gogh cut off his ear the convoy became less of a conducted tour we stopped to play craps in the estaminets boys we're going south to drink the red wine the popes loved best to eat fat meals in oliveoil and garlic bound south cèpes provençale the north wind was shrilling over the plains of the Camargue hustling us into Marseilles where the eleven thousand were dandling themselves in the fogged mirrors of the promenoir at the Apollo

oysters and vin de Cassis petite fille tellement brune tête

de lune qui aimait les veentair sports in the end they were all slot machines undressed as Phocean figurines posted with their legs apart around the scummy edges of the oldest port

the Riviera was a letdown, but there was a candycolored church with a pointed steeple on every hill beyond San Remo Porto Maurizio blue seltzerbottles standing in the cinzanocolored sunlight beside a glass of VERMOUTH TORINO Savona was set for the Merchant of Venice painted by Veronese Ponte Decimo in Ponte Decimo ambulances were parked in a moonlit square of bleak stone workingpeople's houses hoarfrost covered everything in the little bar the Successful Story Writer taught us to drink cognac and maraschino half and half

havanuzzerone

it turned out he was not writing what he felt he wanted to be writing What can you tell them at home about the war? it turned out he was not wanting what he wrote he wanted to be feeling cognac and maraschino was no longer young (It made us damn sore we greedy for what we felt we wanted tell 'em all they lied see new towns go to Genoa) havanuzzerone? it turned out that he wished he was a naked brown shepherd boy sitting on a hillside playing a flute in the sunlight

going to Genoa was easy enough the streetcar went there Genoa the new town we'd never seen full of marble doges and breakneck stairs marble lions in the moonlight Genoa was the ancient ducal city burning? all the marble palaces and the square stone houses and the campaniles topping hills had one marble wall on fire

bonfire under the moon

the bars were full of Britishers overdressed civilians strolling under porticoes outside the harbor under the Genoa moon the sea was on fire the member of His Majesty's Intelligence Service said it was a Yankee tanker had struck a mine? been torpedoed? why don't they scuttle her?

Genoa eyes flared with the light of the burning tanker Genoa what are you looking for? the flare in the blood under the moon down the midnight streets in boys' and girls' faces Genoa eyes the question in their eyes

through the crumbling stone courts under the Genoa moon up and down the breakneck stairs eyes on fire under the moon round the next corner full in your face the flare of the bonfire on the sea eleven thousand registered harlots said the Red Cross Publicity Man infest the streets of Marseilles

The Camera Eye

the raindrops fall one by one out of the horsechestnut tree over the arbor onto the table in the abandoned beergarden and the puddly gravel and my clipped skull where my fingers move gently forward and back over the fuzzy knobs and hollows

spring and we've just been swimming in the Marne way off somewhere beyond the fat clouds on the horizon they are hammering on a tin roof in the rain in the spring after a swim in the Marne with that hammering to the north pounding the thought of death into our ears

the winy thought of death stings in the spring blood that throbs in the sunburned neck up and down the belly under the tight belt hurries like cognac into the tips of my toes and the lobes of my ears and my fingers stroking the fuzzy closecropped skull

shyly tingling fingers feel out the limits of the hard immortal skull under the flesh a deathshead and skeleton sits wearing glasses in the arbor under the lucid occasional raindrops inside the new khaki uniform inside my twenty-oneyearold body that's been swimming in the Marne in red and whitestriped trunks in Châlons in the spring

Machines

THE FIELDS and the misty bluegreen woods slipped by slowly as the boxcar rumbled and jolted over the rails, now stopping for hours on sidings amid meadows, where it was quiet and where above the babel of voices of the regiment you could hear the skylarks, now clattering fast over bridges and along the banks of jadegreen rivers where the slim poplars were just coming into leaf and where now and then a fish jumped. The men crowded in the door, grimy and tired, leaning on each other's shoulders and watching the plowed lands slip by and the meadows where the golden-green grass was dappled with buttercups, and the villages of huddled red roofs lost among pale budding trees and masses of peach blossom. Through the smells of steam and coal smoke and of unwashed bodies in uniforms came smells of moist fields and of manure from freshsowed patches and of cows and pasturelands just coming into flower.

"Must be right smart o' craps in this country . . . Ain't like that damn Polignac, Andy?" said Chrisfield.

"Well, they made us drill so hard there wasn't any time for the grass to grow."

"You're damn right there warn't."

"Ah'd lak te live in this country a while," said Chrisfield.

"We might ask 'em to let us off right here."

"Can't be that the front's like this," said Judkins, poking his head out between Andrews's and Chrisfield's heads so that the bristles of his unshaven chin rubbed against Chrisfield's cheek. It was a large square head with closely cropped light hair and porcelainblue eyes under lids that showed white in the red sunburned bace, and a square jaw made a little gray by the sprouting beard.

"Say, Andy, how the hell long have we all been in this

goddam train? . . . Ah've done lost track o' the time . . ."

"What's the matter; are you gettin old, Chris?" asked Judkins laughing.

Chrisfield had slipped out of the place he held and began poking himself in between Andrews and Judkins.

"We've been on this train four days and five nights, an' we've got half a day's rations left, so we must be getting somewhere," said Andrews.

"It can't be like this at the front."

"It must be spring there as well as here," said Andrews.

It was a day of fluffy mauvetinted clouds that moved across the sky, sometimes darkening to deep blue where a small rainstorm trailed across the hills, sometimes brightening to moments of clear sunlight that gave blue shadows to the poplars and shone yellow on the smoke of the engine that puffed on painfully at the head of the long train.

"Funny, ain't it? How lil everythin is," said Chrisfield. "Out Indiana way we wouldn't look at a cornfield that size. But it sort o' reminds me the way it used to be out home in the spring o' the year."

"I'd like to see Indiana in the springtime," said Andrews.

"Well you'll come out when the wa's over and us guys is all home . . . won't you, Andy?"

"You bet I will."

They were going into the suburbs of a town. Rows and clusters of little brick and stucco houses were appearing along the roads. It began to rain from a sky full of lights of amber and lilac color. The slate roofs and the pinkish-gray streets of the town shone cheerfully in the rain. The little patches of garden were all vivid emerald green. Then they were looking at rows and rows of red chimneypots over wet slate roofs that reflected the bright sky. In the distance rose the purplegray spire of a church and the irregular forms of old buildings. They passed through a station.

"Dijon," read Andrews. On the platform were French soldiers in their blue coats and a good sprinkling of civilians.

"Gee, those are about the first real civvies I've seen since I came overseas," said Judkins. "Those goddam country people down at Polignac didn't look like real civilians. There's folks dressed like it was New York."

They had left the station and were rumbling slowly past interminable freight trains. At last the train came to a dead stop.

A whistle sounded.

"Don't nobody get out," shouted the sergeant from the car ahead.

"Hell! They keep you in this goddam car like you was a convict," muttered Chrisfield.

"I'd like to get out and walk around Dijon."

"Oh boy!"

"I swear I'd make a beeline for a dairy lunch," said Judkins.

"Hell of a fine dairy lunch you'll find among those goddam frogs. No, vin blank is all you'd get in that goddam town."

"Ah'm goin to sleep," said Chrisfield. He stretched himself out on the pile of equipment at the end of the car. Andrews sat down near him and stared at his mudcaked boots, running one of his long hands, as brown as Chrisfield's now, through his light shortcut hair.

Chrisfield lay looking at the gaunt outline of Andrews's face against the light through halfclosed eyes. And he felt a warm sort of smile inside him as he said to himself: "He's a damn good kid." Then he thought of the spring in the hills of southern Indiana and the mockingbird singing in the moonlight among the flowering locust trees behind the house. He could almost smell the heavy sweetness of the locust blooms, as he used to smell them sitting on the steps after supper, tired from a day's heavy plowing, while the clatter of his mother's housework came from the kitchen. He didn't wish he was back there, but it was pleasant to think of it now and then, and how the yellow farmhouse looked and the red barn where his father never had been able to find time to paint the door, and the tumbledown cowshed where the shingles were always coming off. He wondered dully what it would be like out there at the front. It couldn't be green and pleasant, the way the country was here. Fellows always said it was hell out there. Well, he didn't give a damn. He went to sleep.

He woke up gradually, the warm comfort of sleep giving place slowly to the stiffness of his uncomfortable position with the hobnails of a boot from the back of a pack sticking into his shoulder. Andrews was sitting in the same position, lost in thought. The rest of the men sat at the open doors or sprawled over the equipment.

Chrisfield got up, stretched himself, yawned, and went to the door to look out. There was a heavy important step on the gravel outside. A large man with black eyebrows that met over his nose and a very black stubbly beard passed the car. There were a sergeant's stripes on his arm.

"Say, Andy," cried Chrisfield, "that bastard is a sergeant."

"Who's that?" asked Andrews getting up with a smile, his blue eyes looking mildly into Chrisfield's black ones.

"You know who Ah mean."

Under their heavy tan Chrisfield's rounded cheeks were flushed. His eyes snapped under their long black lashes. His fists were clutched.

"Oh, I know, Chris. I didn't know he was in this regiment."

"God damn him!" muttered Chrisfield in a low voice, throwing himself down on his packs again.

"Hold your horses, Chris," said Andrews. "We may all cash in our checks before long . . . no use letting things worry us."

"I don't give a damn if we do."

"Nor do I, now." Andrews sat down beside Chrisfield again.

After a while the train got jerkily into motion. The wheels rumbled and clattered over the rails and the clots of mud bounced up and down on the splintered boards of the floor. Chrisfield pillowed his head on his arm and went to sleep again, still smarting from the flush of his anger.

Andrews looked out through his fingers at the swaying black boxcar, at the men sprawled about on the floor, their heads nodding with each jolt, and at the mauvegray clouds and bits of sparkling blue sky that he could see behind the silhouettes of the heads and shoulders of the men who stood in the doors. The wheels ground on endlessly.

The car stopped with a jerk that woke up all the sleepers and threw one man off his feet. A whistle blew shrilly outside.

"All right, out of the cars! Snap it up; snap it up!" yelled the sergeant.

The men piled out stiffly, handing the equipment out from hand to hand till it formed a confused heap of packs and rifles outside. All down the train at each door there was a confused pile of equipment and struggling men.

"Snap it up . . . Full equipment . . . Line up!" the sergeant yelled.

The men fell into line slowly, with their packs and rifles. Lieutenants hovered about the edges of the forming lines, tightly belted into their stiff trenchcoats, scrambling up and down the coal piles of the siding. The men were given "at ease" and stood leaning on their rifles staring at the green watertank on three wooden legs, over the top of which had been thrown a huge piece of torn gray cheesecloth. When the confused sound of tramping feet subsided, they could hear a noise in the distance, like someone lazily shaking a piece of heavy sheetiron. The sky was full of little dabs of red, purple and yellow and the purplish sunset light was over everything.

The order came to march. They marched down a rutted road where the puddles were so deep they had continually to break ranks to avoid them. In a little pinewood on one side were rows of heavy motor trucks and ammunition caissons; supper was cooking in a field kitchen about which clustered the truck drivers in their wide visored caps. Beyond the wood the column turned off into a field behind a little group of stone and stucco houses that had lost their roofs. In the field they halted. The grass was brilliant emerald and the wood and the distant hills were shades of clear deep blue. Wisps of paleblue mist lay across the field. In the turf here and there were small clean bites, that might have been made by some strange animal. The men looked at them curiously.

"No lights, remember we're in sight of the enemy. A match might annihilate the detachment," announced the lieutenant dramatically after having given the orders for the pup tents to be set up.

When the tents were ready, the men stood about in the chilly white mist that kept growing denser, eating their cold rations. Everywhere were grumbling snorting voices.

"God, let's turn in, Chris, before our bones are frozen," said Andrews.

Guards had been posted and walked up and down with

a businesslike stride, peering now and then suspiciously into
the little wood where the truckdrivers were.

Chrisfield and Andrews crawled into their little tent and
rolled up together in their blankets, getting as close to each
other as they could. At first it was very cold and hard, and
they squirmed about restlessly, but gradually the warmth
from their bodies filled their thin blankets and their muscles
began to relax. Andrews went to sleep first and Chrisfield
lay listening to his deep breathing. There was a frown on
his face. He was thinking of the man who had walked past
the train at Dijon. The last time he had seen that man
Anderson was at training camp. He had only been a corporal then. He remembered the day the man had been made
corporal. It had not been long before that that Chrisfield
had drawn his knife on him, one night in the barracks. A
fellow had caught his hand just in time. Anderson had
looked a bit pale that time and had walked away. But he'd
never spoken a word to Chrisfield since. As he lay with his
eyes closed, pressed close against Andrew's limp sleeping
body, Chrisfield could see the man's face, the eyebrows that
joined across the nose and the jaw, always blackish from
the heavy beard, that looked blue when he had just shaved.
At last the tenseness of his mind slackened; he thought of
women for a moment, of a fairhaired girl he'd seen from
the train, and then suddenly crushing sleepiness closed down
on him and everything went softly warmly black, as he
drifted off to sleep with no sense but the coldness of one
side and the warmth of his bunkie's body on the other.

In the middle of the night he awoke and crawled out of
the tent. Andrews followed him. Their teeth chattered a
little, and they stretched their legs stiffly. It was cold but
the mist had vanished. The stars shone brilliantly. They
walked out a little way into the field away from the bunch
of tents to make water.

A faint rustling and breathing noise, as of animals herded
together, came from the sleeping regiment. Somewhere a
brook made a shrill gurgling. They strained their ears, but
they could hear no guns. They stood side by side looking
up at the multitude of stars.

"That's Orion," said Andrews.

"What?"

"That bunch of stars there is called Orion. D'you see 'em.

It's supposed to look like a man with a bow, but he always looks to me like a fellow striding across the sky."

"Some stars tonight, ain't there? Gee, what's that?"

Behind the dark hills a glow rose and fell like the glow in a forge.

"The front must be that way," said Andrews, shivering.

"I guess we'll know tomorrow."

"Yes; tomorrow night we'll know more about it," said Andrews.

They stood silent a moment listening to the noise the brook made.

"God, it's quiet, ain't it? This can't be the front. Smell that?"

"What is it?"

"Smells like an apple tree in bloom somewhere . . . Hell, let's git in, before our blankets git cold."

Andrews was still staring at the group of stars he had said was Orion.

Chrisfield pulled him by the arm. They crawled into their tent again, rolled up together and immediately were crushed under an exhausted sleep.

As far ahead of him as Chrisfield could see were packs and heads with caps at a variety of angles, all bobbing up and down with the swing of the brisk marching time. A fine warm rain was falling, mingling with the sweat that ran down his face. The column had been marching a long time along a straight road that was worn and scarred with heavy traffic. Fields and hedges where clusters of yellow flowers were in bloom had given place to an avenue of poplars. The light wet trunks and the stiff branches hazy with green filed by, interminable, as interminable as the confused tramp of feet and jingle of equipment that sounded in his ears.

"Say, are we goin towards the front?"

"Goddamned if I know."

"Ain't no front within miles."

Men's sentences came shortly through their heavy breathing.

The column shifted over to the side of the road to avoid a train of motor trucks going the other way. Chrisfield felt the heavy mud spurt up over him as truck after truck rumbled by. With the wet back of one hand he tried to wipe it off his face, but the grit, when he rubbed it, hurt his skin, made tender by the rain. He swore long and whiningly, half aloud. His rifle felt as heavy as an iron girder.

They entered a village of plaster and timber houses. Through open doors they could see into comfortable kitchens where copper pots gleamed and where the floors were of clean red tiles. In front of some of the houses were little gardens full of crocuses and hyacinths where boxbushes shone a very dark green in the rain. They marched through the square with its pavement of little yellow rounded cobbles, its gray church with a pointed arch in the door, its cafés with names painted over them. Men and women looked out of doors and windows. The column perceptibly slackened its speed, but kept on, as the houses dwindled and became farther apart along the road the men's hope of stopping vanished. Ears were deafened by the confused tramp of feet on the macadam road. Men's feet seemed as lead, as if all the weight of the pack hung on them. Shoulders worn callous, began to grow tender and sore under the constant sweating. Heads drooped. Each man's eyes were on the heels of the man ahead of him that rose and fell, rose and fell endlessly. Marching became for each man a personal struggle with his pack, that seemed to have come alive, that seemed something malicious and overpowering, wrestling to throw him.

The rain stopped and the sky brightened a little, taking on pale yellowish lights as if the clouds that hid the sun were growing thin.

The column halted at the edge of a group of farms and barns that scattered along the road. The men sprawled in all directions along the roadside hiding the bright green grass with the mudcolor of their uniforms.

Chrisfield lay in the field beside the road, pressing his hot face into the wet sprouting clover. The blood throbbed through his ears. His arms and legs seemed to cleave to the ground, as if he would never be able to move them again. He closed his eyes. Gradually a cold chill began stealing through his body. He sat up and slipped his arms out of the harness of his pack. Someone was handing him a cigarette, and he sniffed a little acrid sweet smoke.

Andrews was lying beside him, his head propped against his pack, smoking, and poking a cigarette towards his friend with a muddy hand. His blue eyes looked strangely from out the flaming red of his mudsplotched face.

Chrisfield took the cigarette, and fumbled in his pocket for a match.

"That nearly did it for me," said Andrews.

Chrisfield grunted. He pulled greedily on the cigarette. A whistle blew.

Slowly the men dragged themselves off the ground and fell into line, drooping under the weight of their equipment.

The companies marched off separately.

Chrisfield overheard the lieutenant saying to a sergeant: "Damn fool business that. Why the hell couldn't they have sent us here in the first place?"

"So we ain't goin to the front after all?" said the sergeant.

"Front, hell!" said the lieutenant. The lieutenant was a small man who looked like a jockey with a coarse red face, which, now that he was angry, was almost purple.

"I guess they're going to quarter us here," said somebody. Immediately everybody began saying: "We're going to be quartered here."

They stood waiting in formation a long while, the packs cutting into their backs and shoulders.

At last the sergeant shouted out: "All right, take yer stuff upstairs." Stumbling on each others' heels they climbed up into a dark loft, where the air was heavy with the smell of hay and with an acridity of cow manure from the stables below. There was a little straw in the corners, on which those who got there first spread their blankets.

Chrisfield and Andrews tucked themselves in a corner from which through a hole where the tiles had fallen off the roof, they could see down into the barnyard, where white and speckled chickens pecked about with jerky movements. A middle-aged woman stood in the doorway of the house looking suspiciously at the files of khaki-clad soldiers that shuffled slowly into the barns by every door.

An officer went up to her, a little red book in his hand. A conversation about some matter proceeded painfully. The officer grew very red. Andrews threw back his head and laughed, luxuriously rolling from side to side in the straw.

Chrisfield laughed too, he hardly knew why. Over their heads they could hear the feet of pigeons on the roof, and a constant drowsy roucoucoucou.

Through the barnyard smells began to drift the greasiness of food cooking in the field kitchen.

"Ah hope they give us somethin good to eat," said Chrisfield. "Ah'm hongry as a thrasher."

"So am I," said Andrews.

"Say, Andy, you kin talk their language a lil, can't ye?"

Andrews nodded his head vaguely.

"Well, maybe we kin git some aigs or somethin out of the lady down there. Will ye try after mess?"

"All right."

They both lay back in the straw and closed their eyes. Their cheeks still burned from the rain. Everything seemed very peaceful; the men sprawled about talking in low drowsy voices. Outside, another shower had come up and beat softly on the tiles of the roof. Chrisfield thought he had never been so comfortable in his life, although his soaked shoes pinched his cold feet and his knees were wet and cold. But in the drowsiness of the rain and of voices talking quietly about him, he fell asleep.

He dreamed he was home in Indiana, but instead of his mother cooking at the stove in the kitchen, there was the Frenchwoman who had stood in the farmhouse door, and near her stood a lieutenant with a little red book in his hand. He was eating cornbread and syrup off a broken plate. It was fine cornbread with a great deal of crust on it, crisp and hot, on which the butter was cold and sweet to his tongue. Suddenly he stopped eating and started swearing, shouting at the top of his lungs: "You goddam . . ." he started, but he couldn't seem to think of anything more to say. "You goddam . . ." he started again. The lieutenant looked towards him, wrinkling his black eyebrows that met across his nose. He was Sergeant Anderson. Chris drew his knife and ran at him, but it was Andy his bunkie he had run his knife into. He threw his arms round Andy's body, crying hot tears . . . He woke up. Mess kits were clinking all about the dark crowded loft. The men had already started piling down the stairs.

The larks filled the winetinged air with a constant chiming of little bells. Chrisfield and Andrews were strolling across a field of white clover that covered the brow of a hill. Below in the valley they could see a cluster of red roofs of farms and the white ribbon of the road where long trains of motor trucks crawled like beetles. The sun had just set behind the blue hills the other side of the shallow valley. The air was full of the smell of clover and of hawthorn from the hedgerows. They took deep breaths as they crossed the field.

"It's great to get away from that crowd," Andrews was saying.

Chrisfield walked on silently, dragging his feet through the matted clover. A leaden dullness weighed like some sort of warm choking coverlet on his limbs, so that it seemed an effort to walk, an effort to speak. Yet under it his muscles were taut and trembling as he had known them to be before when he was about to get into a fight or to make love to a girl.

"Why the hell don't they let us git into it?" he said suddenly.

"Yes, anything'd be better than this . . . wait, wait, wait."

They walked on, hearing the constant chirrup of the larks, the brush of their feet through the clover, the faint jingle of some coins in Chrisfield's pocket, and in the distance the irregular snoring of an airplane motor. As they walked Andrews leaned over from time to time and picked a couple of the white clover flowers.

The airplane came suddenly nearer and swooped in a wide curve above the field, drowning every sound in the roar of its exhaust. They made out the figures of the pilot and the observer before the plane rose again and vanished against the ragged purple clouds of the sky. The observer had waved a hand at them as he passed. They stood still in the darkening field, staring up at the sky, where a few larks still hung chirruping.

"Ah'd lahk to be one o' them guys," said Chrisfield.

"You would?"

"God damn it, Ahd do anything to git out o' this hellish infantry. This ain't no sort o' life for a man to be treated lahk he was a nigger."

"No, it's no sort of life for a man."

"If they'd let us git to the front an do some fightin an be done with it. . . . But all we do is drill and have grenade practice an drill again and then have bayonet practice an drill again. Nough to drive a feller crazy."

"What the hell's the use of talking about it, Chris? We can't-be any lower than we are, can we?" Andrews laughed.

"There's that plane again."

"Where?"

"There, just goin down behind the piece o' woods."

"That's where their field is."

"Ah bet them guys has a good time. Ah put in an application back in trainin camp for Aviation. Ain't never heard nothing from it though. If Ah had, Ah wouldn't be lower than dirt in this hawgpen."

"It's wonderful up here on the hill this evening," said Andrews, looking dreamily at the pale orange band of light where the sun had set. "Let's go down and get a bottle of wine."

"Now yo're talkin'. Ah wonder if that girl's down there tonight."

"Antoinette?"

"Umhum . . . Boy, Ah'd lahk to have her all by maself some night."

Their steps grew brisker as they strode along a grass-grown road that led through high hedgerows to a village under the brow of the hill. It was almost dark under the shadow of the bushes on either side. Overhead the purple clouds were washed over by a pale yellow light that gradually faded to gray. Birds chirped and rustled among the young leaves.

Andrews put his hand on Chrisfield's shoulder.

"Let's walk slow," he said, "we don't want to get out of here too soon." He grabbed carelessly at little clusters of hawthorn flowers as he passed them, and seemed reluctant to untangle the thorny branches that caught in his coat and on his loosely wound puttees.

"Hell, man," said Chrisfield, "we won't have time to get a bellyful. It must be gettin late already."

They hastened their steps again and came in a moment to the first tightly shuttered houses of the village.

In the middle of the road was an M.P., who stood with his legs wide apart, waving his "billy" languidly. He had a red face, his eyes were fixed on the shuttered upper window of a house, through the chinks of which came a few streaks of yellow light. His lips were puckered up as if to whistle, but no sound came. He swayed back and forth indecisively. An officer came suddenly out of the little green door of the house in front of the M.P., who brought his heels together with a jump and saluted, holding his hand a long while to his cap. The officer flicked a hand up hastily to his hat, snatching his cigar out of his mouth for an instant. As the officer's steps grew fainter down the road, the M.P. gradually returned to his former position.

Chrisfield and Andrews had slipped by on the other side and gone in at the door of a small ramshackle house of which the windows were closed by heavy wooden shutters.

"I bet there ain't many of them bastards at the front," said Chris.

"Not many of either kind of bastards," said Andrews laughing, as he closed the door behind them. They were in a room that had once been the parlor of a farmhouse. The chandelier with its bits of crystal and the orangeblossoms on a piece of dusty red velvet under a bell glass on the mantelpiece denoted that. The furniture had been taken out, and four square oak tables crowded in. At one of the tables sat three Americans and at another a very young olive-skinned French soldier, who sat hunched over his table looking moodily down into his glass of wine.

A girl in a faded frock of some purplish material that showed the strong curves of her shoulders and breasts slouched into the room, her hands in the pocket of a dark blue apron against which her rounded forearms showed golden brown. Her face had the same golden tan under a mass of dark blond hair. She smiled when she saw the two soldiers, drawing her thin lips away from her ugly yellow teeth.

"Ça va bien, Antoinette?" asked Andrews.

"Oui," she said, looking beyond their heads at the French soldier who sat at the other side of the little room.

"A bottle of vin rouge, vite," said Chrisfield.

"Ye needn't be so damn vite about it tonight, Chris," said one of the men at the other table.

"Why?"

"Ain't agoin to be no roll call. Corporal tole me hisself.

Sarge's gone out to git stewed, an the Loot's away."

"Sure," said another man, "we kin stay out as late's we goddam please tonight."

"There's a new M.P. in town," said Chrisfield . . . "Ah saw him maself . . . You did, too, didn't you, Andy?"

Andrews nodded. He was looking at the Frenchman, who sat with his face in shadow and his black lashes covering his eyes. A purplish flash had suffused the olive skin at his cheekbones.

"Oh, boy," said Chrisfield. "That ole wine sure do go down fast . . . Say, Antoinette, got any cognac?"

"I'm going to have some more wine," said Andrews.

"Go ahead, Andy; have all ye want. Ah want somethin to warm ma guts."

Antoinette brought a bottle of cognac and two small glasses and sat down in an empty chair with her red hands crossed on her apron. Her eyes moved from Chrisfield to the Frenchman and back again.

Chrisfield turned a little round in his chair and looked at the Frenchman, feeling in his eyes for a moment a glance of the man's yellowishbrown eyes.

Andrews leaned back against the wall sipping his dark-colored wine, his eyes contracted dreamily, fixed on the shadow of the chandelier, which the cheap oil lamp with its tin reflector cast on the peeling plaster of the wall opposite.

Chrisfield punched him.

"Wake up, Andy, are you asleep?"

"No," said Andy smiling.

"Have a lil mo' cognac."

Chrisfield poured out two more glasses unsteadily. His eyes were on Antoinette again. The faded purple frock was hooked at the neck. The first three hooks were undone revealing a V-shape of golden brown skin and a bit of whitish underwear.

"Say, Andy," he said, putting his arm round his friend's neck and talking into his ear, "talk up to her for me, will yer, Andy? . . . Ah won't let that goddam frog get her, no, I won't, by Gawd. Talk up to her for me, Andy."

Andrews laughed.

"I'll try," he said. "But there's always the Queen of Sheba, Chris."

"Antoinette, J'ai un ami," started Andrews, making a gesture with a long dirty hand towards Chris.

Antoinette showed her bad teeth in a smile.

"Joli garçon," said Andrews.

Antoinette's face became impassive and beautiful again. Chrisfield leaned back in his chair with an empty glass in his hand and watched his friend admiringly.

"Antoinette, mon ami vous . . . vous admire," said Andrews in a courtly voice.

A woman put her head in the door. It was the same face and hair as Antoinette's, ten years older, only the skin, instead of being golden brown, was sallow and wrinkled.

"Viens," said the woman in a shrill voice.

Antoinette got up, brushed heavily against Chrisfield's leg as she passed him and disappeared. The Frenchman walked across the room from his corner, saluted gravely and went out.

Chrisfield jumped to his feet. The room was like a white box reeling about him.

"That frog's gone after her," he shouted.

"No, he ain't, Chris," cried someone from the next table. "Sit tight, ole boy. Were bettin on yer."

"Yes, sit down and have a drink, Chris," said Andy. "I've got to have somethin more to drink. I haven't had a thing to drink all the evening." He pulled him back into his chair. Chrisfield tried to get up again. Andrews hung on him so that the chair upset. Then both sprawled on the red tiles of the floor.

"The house is pinched!" said a voice.

Chrisfield saw Judkins standing over him, a grin on his large red face. He got to his feet and sat sulkily in his chair again. Andrews was already sitting opposite him, looking impassive as ever.

The tables were full now. Someone was singing in a droning voice.

> O the oak and the ash and the weeping willow tree,
> O green grows the grass in God's countree!

"Ole Indiana," shouted Chris. "That's the only God's country I know." He suddenly felt that he could tell Andy all about his home and the wide cornfields shimmering and rustling under the July sun, and the creek with red clay banks where he used to go in swimming. He seemed to see it all before him, to smell the winy smell of the silo, to see the cattle, with their chewing mouths always stained a little with green, waiting to get through the gate to the water trough, and the yellow dust and roar of wheatthrashing, and the quiet evening breeze cooling his throat and neck when he lay out on a shuck of hay that he had been tossing all day long under the tingling sun. But all he managed to say was: "Indiana's God's country, ain't it, Andy?"

"Oh, he has so many," muttered Andrews.

"Ah've seen a hailstone measured nine inches around out home, honest to Gawd, Ah have."

"Must be as good as a barrage."

"Ah'd like to see any goddam barrage do the damage one of our thunder an lightnin storms'll do," shouted Chris.

"I guess all the barrage we're going to see's grenade practice."

"Don't you worry, buddy," said somebody across the room. "You'll see enough of it. This war's going to last damn long . . ."

"Ah'd lak to get in some licks at those Huns tonight, honest to Gawd Ah would, Andy," muttered Chris in a low voice. He felt his muscles contract with a furious irritation. He looked through halfclosed eyes at the men in the room, seeing them in distorted white lights and reddish shadows. He thought of himself throwing a grenade among a crowd of men. Then he saw the face of Anderson, a ponderous white face with eyebrows that met across his nose and a bluish, shaved chin.

"Where does he stay at, Andy? I'm going to git him."

Andrews guessed what he meant.

"Sit down and have a drink, Chris," he said, "Remember you're going to sleep with the Queen of Sheba tonight."

"Not if I can't git them goddam . . ." his voice trailed off into an inaudible muttering of oaths.

O the oak and the ash and the weeping willow tree,
O green grows the grass in God's countree!

somebody sang again.

Chrisfield saw a woman standing beside the table with her back to him, collecting the bottles. Andy was paying her.

"Antoinette," he said. He got to his feet and put his

arms round her shoulders. With a quick movement of the elbows she pushed him back into his chair. She turned round. He saw the sallow face and thin breasts of the older sister. She looked in his eyes with surprise. He was grinning drunkenly. As she left the room she made a sign to him with her head to follow her. He got up and staggered out the door, pulling Andrews after him.

In the inner room was a big bed with curtains where the women slept, and the fireplace where they did their cooking. It was dark except for the corner where he and Andrews stood blinking in the glare of a candle on the table. Beyond they could only see ruddy shadows and the huge curtained bed with its red coverlet.

The Frenchman, somewhere in the dark of the room, said something several times.

"Avions boches . . . ss-t!"

They were quiet.

Above them they heard the snoring of airplane motors, rising and falling like the buzzing of a fly against a window-pane.

They all looked at each other curiously. Antoinette was leaning against the bed, her face expressionless. Her heavy hair had come undone and fell in smoky gold waves about her shoulders. The older woman was giggling.

"Come on, let's see what's doing, Chris," said Andrews.

They went out into the dark village street.

"To hell with women, Chris, this is the war!" cried Andrews in a loud drunken voice as they reeled arm in arm up the street.

"You bet it's the war. . . . Ah'm agoin to beat up . . ." Chrisfield felt his friend's hand clapped over his mouth. He let himself go limply, feeling himself pushed to the side of the road.

Somewhere in the dark he heard an officer's voice say: "Bring those men to me."

"Yes, sir," came another voice.

Slow heavy footsteps came up the road in their direction. Andrews kept pushing him back along the side of a house, until suddenly they both fell sprawling in a manure pit.

"Lie still for God's sake," muttered Andrews, throwing an arm over Chrisfield's chest. A thick odor of dry manure filled their nostrils.

They heard the steps come nearer, wander about irresolutely and then go off in the direction from which they had come. Meanwhile the throb of motors overhead grew louder and louder.

"Well?" came the officer's voice.

"Couldn't find them, sir," mumbled the other voice.

"Nonsense. Those men were drunk," came the officer's voice.

"Yes, sir," came the other voice humbly.

Chrisfield started to giggle. He felt he must yell aloud with laughter.

The nearest motor stopped its singsong roar, making the night seem deathly silent.

Andrews jumped to his feet.

The air was split by a shriek followed by a racking snorting explosion. They saw the wall above their pit light up with a red momentary glare.

Chrisfield got to his feet, expecting to see flaming ruins. The village street was the same as ever. There was a little light from the glow the moon, still under the horizon, gave to the sky. A window in the house opposite showed yellow. In it was a blue silhouette of an officer's cap and uniform.

A little group stood in the street below.

"What was that?" the form in the window was shouting in a peremptory voice.

"German plane just dropped a bomb, Major," came a breathless voice in reply.

"Why the devil don't he close that window?" a voice was muttering all the while. "Juss a target for 'em to aim at . . . a target to aim at."

"Any damage done?" asked the major.

Through the silence the snoring of the motors singsonged ominously overhead, like giant mosquitoes.

"I seem to hear more," said the major, in his drawling voice.

"O yes sir, yes sir, lots," answered an eager voice.

"For God's sake tell him to close the window, Lieutenant," muttered another voice.

"How the hell can I tell him? You tell him."

"We'll all be killed, that's all there is about it."

"There are no shelters or dugouts," drawled the major from the window. "That's Headquarters' fault."

"There's the cellar!" cried the eager voice, again.

"Oh," said the major.

Three snorting explosions in quick succession drowned everything in a red glare. The street was suddenly filled with a scuttle of villagers running to shelter.

"Say, Andy, they may have a rollcall," said Chrisfield.

"We'd better cut for home across country," said Andrews.

They climbed cautiously out of their manure pit. Chrisfield was surprised to find that he was trembling. His hands were cold. It was with difficulty he kept his teeth from chattering.

"God, we'll stink for a week."

"Let's git out," muttered Chrisfield, "o' this goddam village."

They ran out through an orchard, broke through a hedge and climbed up the hill across the open fields.

Down the main road an anti-aircraft gun had started barking and the sky sparkled with exploding shrapnel. The put-put-put of a machine gun had begun somewhere.

Chrisfield strode up the hill in step with his friend. Behind them bomb followed bomb, and above them the air seemed full of exploding shrapnel and droning planes. The cognac still throbbed a little in their blood. They stumbled against each other now and then as they walked. From the top of the hill they turned and looked back. Chrisfield felt a tremendous elation thumping stonger than the cognac through his veins. Unconsciously he put his arm round his friend's shoulders. They seemed the only live things in a reeling world.

Below in the valley a house was burning brightly. From all directions came the yelp of anti-aircraft guns, and overhead unperturbed continued the leisurely singsong of the motors.

Suddenly Chrisfield burst out laughing.

"By God, Ah always have fun when Ah'm out with you, Andy," he said.

They turned and hurried down the other slope of the hill towards the farms where they were quartered.

❋

As far as he could see in every direction were the gray trunks of beeches bright green with moss on one side. The ground was thick with last year's leaves that rustled maddeningly with every step. In front of him his eyes followed other patches of olivedrab moving among the treetrunks. Overhead, through the mottled light and dark green of the leaves he could see now and then a patch of heavy gray sky, grayer than the silvery trunks that moved about him in every direction as he walked. He strained his eyes down each alley until they were dazzled by the reiteration of mottled gray and green. Now and then the rustling stopped ahead of him, and the olivedrab patches were still. Then, above the clamor of the blood in his ears, he could hear batteries pong-pong-pong in the distance, and the woods ringing with a sound like hail as a heavy shell hurtled above the treetops to end in a dull rumble miles away.

Chrisfield was soaked with sweat, but he could not feel his arms or legs. Every sense was concentrated in eyes and ears, and in the consciousness of his gun. Time and again he pictured himself taking sight at something gray that moved, and firing. His forefinger itched to press the trigger. He would take aim very carefully, he told himself; he pictured a dab of gray starting up from behind a gray treetrunk, and the sharp detonation of his rifle, and the dab of gray rolling among the last year's leaves.

A branch carried his helmet off his head so that it rolled at his feet and bounced with a faint metallic sound against the root of a tree.

He was blinded by the sudden terror that seized him. His heart seemed to roll from side to side in his chest. He stood stiff, as if paralyzed for a moment before he could stoop and pick the helmet up. There was a curious taste of blood in his mouth.

"Ah'll pay 'em fer that," he muttered between clenched teeth.

His fingers were still trembling when he stooped to pick up the helmet, which he put on again very carefully, fastening it with the strap under his chin.

Furious anger had taken hold of him.

The olivedrab patches ahead had moved forward again. He followed, looking eagerly to the right and the left, praying he might see something. In every direction were the silvery trunks of the beeches, each with a vivid green streak on one side. With every step the last year's russet leaves rustled underfoot, maddeningly loud.

Almost out of sight among the moving treetrunks was a log. It was not a log; it was a bunch of graygreen cloth. Without thinking Chrisfield strode towards it. The silver trunks of the beeches circled about him, waving jagged arms. It was a German lying full length among the leaves.

Chrisfield was furiously happy in the angry pumping of blood through his veins.

He could see the buttons on the back of the long coat of the German, and the red band on his cap.

He kicked the German. He could feel the ribs against his toes through the leather of his boot. He kicked again and again with all his might. The German rolled over heavily. He had no face. Chrisfield felt the hatred suddenly ebb out of him. Where the face had been was a spongy mass of purple and yellow and red, half of which stuck to the russet leaves when the body rolled over. Large flies with bright shiny green bodies circled about it. In a brown clay-grimed hand was a revolver.

Chrisfield felt his spine go cold; the German had shot himself.

He ran off suddenly, breathlessly, to join the rest of the reconnoitering squad. The silent beeches whirled about him, waving gnarled boughs above his head. The German had shot himself. That was why he had no face.

Chrisfield fell into line behind the other men. The corporal waited for him.

"See anything?" he asked.

"Not a goddam thing," muttered Chrisfield almost inaudibly.

The corporal went off to the head of the line.

Chrisfield was alone again. The leaves rustled maddeningly loud underfoot.

❉

At the brow of the hill they rested. Chrisfield sat on the red claybank and looked about him, his rifle between his knees. In front of him on the side of the road was a French burying ground, where the little wooden crosses, tilting in every direction, stood up against the sky, and the bead wreaths glistened in the warm sunlight. All down the road as far as he could see was a long drab worm, broken in places by strings of motor trucks, a drab worm that wriggled down the slope, through the roofless shell of the village and up into the shattered woods on the crest of the next hills. Chrisfield strained his eyes to see the hills beyond. They lay blue and very peaceful in the moon mist. The river glittered about the piers of the wrecked stone bridge, and disappeared between rows of yellow poplars. Somewhere in the valley a big gun fired. The shell shrieked into the distance, towards the blue, peaceful hills.

Chrisfield's regiment was moving again. The men, their feet slipping in the clayey mud, went downhill with long strides, the straps of their packs tugging at their shoulders.

"Isn't this great country?" said Andrews, who marched beside him.

"Ah'd liever be at an O.T.C. like that bastard Anderson."

"Oh, to hell with that," said Andrews. He still had a big faded orange marigold in one of the buttonholes of his soiled tunic. He walked with his nose in the air and his nostrils dilated, enjoying the tang of the autumnal sunlight.

Chrisfield took the cigarette, that had gone out half-smoked, from his mouth and spat savagely at the heels of the man in front of him.

"This ain't no life for a white man," he said.

"I'd rather be this than . . . than that," said Andrews bitterly. He tossed his head in the direction of a staff car full of officers that was stalled at the side of the road. They were drinking something out of a thermos bottle that they passed round with the air of Sunday excursionists. They waved, with a conscious relaxation of discipline, at the men as they passed. One, a little lieutenant with a black mustache with pointed ends, kept crying: "They're running like rabbits, fellers; they're running like rabbits." A wavering half cheer would come from the column now and then where it was passing the staff car.

The big gun fired again. Chrisfield was near it this time and felt the concussion like a blow in the head.

"Some baby," said the man behind him.

Someone was singing:

Good morning, mister Zip Zip Zip,
With your hair cut just as short as,
With your hair cut just as short as,
With your hair cut just as short as mi-ine.

Everybody took it up. Their steps rang in rhythm in the paved street that zigzagged among the smashed houses of the village. Ambulances passed them, big trucks full of huddled men with gray faces, from which came a smell of sweat and blood and carbolic.

Somebody went on:

> *O ashes to ashes*
> *An dust to dust . . .*

"Can that," cried Judkins, "it ain't lucky."

But everybody had taken up the song. Chrisfield noticed that Andrew's eyes were sparkling. "If he ain't the damnedest," he thought to himself. But he shouted at the top of his lungs with the rest:

> *O ashes to ashes*
> *An dust to dust;*
> *If the gasbombs don't get yer*
> *The eightyeights must.*

They were climbing the hill again. The road was worn into deep ruts and there were many shell holes, full of muddy water, into which their feet slipped. The woods began, a shattered skeleton of woods, full of old artillery emplacements and dugouts, where torn camouflage fluttered from splintered trees. The ground and the road were littered with tin cans and brass shellcases. Along both sides of the road the trees were festooned, as with creepers, with strand upon strand of telephone wire.

When next they stopped Chrisfield was on the crest of the hill beside a battery of French seventyfives. He looked curiously at the Frenchmen, who sat about on logs in their pink and blue shirtsleeves playing cards and smoking. Their gestures irritated him.

"Say, tell 'em we're advancin," he said to Andrews.

"Are we?" said Andrews. "All right . . . Dites-donc, les Boches courent-ils comme des lapins?" he shouted.

One of the men turned his head and laughed.

"He says they've been running that way for four years," said Andrews. He slipped his pack off, sat down on it, and fished for a cigarette. Chrisfield took off his helmet and rubbed a muddy hand through his hair. He took a bite of chewing tobacco and sat with his hands clasped over his knees.

"How the hell long are we going to wait this time?" he muttered. The shadows of the tangled and splintered trees crept slowly across the road. The French artillerymen were eating their supper. A long train of motor trucks growled past, splashing mud over the men crowded along the sides of the road. The sun set, and a lot of batteries down in the valley began firing, making it impossible to talk. The air was full of a shrieking and droning of shells overhead. The Frenchmen stretched and yawned and went down into their dugout. Chrisfield watched them enviously. The stars were beginning to come out in the green sky behind the tall lacerated trees. Chrisfield's legs ached with cold. He began to get crazily anxious for something to happen, for something to happen, but the column waited, without moving, through the gathering darkness. Chrisfield chewed steadily, trying to think of nothing but the taste of the tobacco in his mouth.

The column was moving again; as they reached the brow of another hill Chrisfield felt a curious sweetish smell that made his nostrils smart. "Gas," he thought, full of panic, and put his hand to the mask that hung round his neck. But he did not want to be the first to put it on. No order came. He marched on, cursing the sergeant and the lieutenant. But maybe they'd been killed by it. He had a vision of the whole regiment sinking down in the road suddenly, overcome by the gas.

"Smell anythin', Andy?" he whispered cautiously.

"I can smell a combination of dead horses and tuberoses and banana oil and the icecream we used to have at college and dead rats in the garret, but what the hell do we care now?" said Andrews, giggling. "This is the damnedest fool business ever . . ."

"He's crazy," muttered Chrisfield to himself. He looked

at the stars in the black sky that seemed to be going along with the column on its march. Or was it that they and the stars were standing still while the trees moved away from them, waving their skinny shattered arms? He could hardly hear the tramp of feet on the road, so loud was the pandemonium of the guns ahead and behind. Every now and then a rocket would burst in front of them and its red and green lights would mingle for a moment with the stars. But it was only overhead he could see the stars. Everywhere else white and red glows rose and fell as if the horizon were on fire.

As they started down the slope, the trees suddenly broke away and they saw the valley between them full of the glare of guns and the white light of star shells. It was like looking into a stove full of glowing embers. The hillside that sloped away from them was full of crashing detonations and yellow tongues of flame. In a battery near the road, that seemed to crush their skulls each time a gun fired, they could see the dark forms of the artillerymen silhouetted in fantastic attitudes against the intermittent red glare. Stunned and blinded, they kept on marching down the road. It seemed to Chrisfield that they were going to step any minute into the flaring muzzle of a gun.

At the foot of the hill, beside a little grove of uninjured trees, they stopped again. A new train of trucks was crawling past them, huge blots in the darkness. There were no batteries near, so they could hear the grinding roar of the gears as the trucks went along the uneven road, plunging in and out of shellholes.

Chrisfield lay down in the dry ditch, full of bracken, and dozed with his head on his pack. All about him were stretched other men. Someone was resting his head on Chrisfield's thigh. The noise had subsided a little. Through his doze he could hear men's voices talking in low crushed tones, as if they were afraid of speaking aloud. On the road the truckdrivers kept calling out to each other shrilly, raspingly. The motors stopped running one after another, making almost a silence, during which Chrisfield fell asleep.

Something woke him. He was stiff with cold and terrified. For a moment he thought he had been left alone, that the company had gone on, for there was no one touching him.

Overhead was a droning as of gigantic mosquitoes, growing fast to a loud throbbing. He heard the lieutenant's voice calling shrilly: "Sergeant Higgins, Sargeant Higgins!"

The lieutenant stood out suddenly black against a sheet of flame. Chrisfield could see his fatigue cap a little on one side and his trench coat, drawn in tight at the waist and sticking out stiffly at the knees. He was shaken by the explosion. Everything was black again. Chrisfield got to his feet, his ears ringing. The column was moving on. He heard moaning near him in the darkness. The tramp of feet and jingle of equipment drowned all other sound. He could feel his shoulders becoming raw under the tugging of the pack. Now and then the flare from airplane bombs behind him showed up wrecked trucks on the side of the road. Somewhere a machine gun spluttered. But the column tramped on, weighed down by the packs, by the deadening exhaustion.

The turbulent flaring darkness was calming to the gray of dawn when Chrisfield stopped marching. His eyelids stung as if his eyeballs were flaming hot. He could not feel his feet and legs. The guns continued incessantly like a hammer beating on his head. He was walking very slowly in a single file, now and then stumbling against the man ahead of him. There was earth on both sides of him, clay walls that dripped moisture. All at once he stumbled down some steps into a dugout, where it was pitchblack. An unfamiliar smell struck him, made him uneasy; but his thoughts seemed to reach him from out of a great distance. He groped to the wall. His knees struck against a bunk with blankets in it. In another second he was sunk fathoms deep in sleep.

When he woke up his mind was very clear. The roof of the dugout was of logs. A bright spot far away was the door. He hoped desperately that he wasn't on duty. He wondered where Andy was; then he remembered that Andy was crazy — "a yeller dawg," Judkins had called him. Sitting up with difficulty he undid his shoes and puttees, wrapped himself in his blanket. All round him were snores and the deep breathing of exhausted sleep. He closed his eyes.

He was being courtmartialed. He stood with his hands at his sides before three officers at a table. All three had the same white faces with heavy blue jaws and eyebrows that met above the nose. They were reading things out of papers aloud, but, although he strained his ears, he couldn't make out what they were saying. All he could hear was a faint moaning. Something had a curious unfamiliar smell that troubled him. He could not stand still at attention, although the angry eyes of officers stared at him from all round. "Anderson, Sergeant Anderson, what's that smell?" he kept asking in a small whining voice. "Please tell a feller what that smell is." But the three officers at the table kept reading from their papers, and the moaning grew louder and louder in his ears until he shrieked aloud. There was a grenade in his hand. He pulled the string out and threw it, and he saw the lieutenant's trenchcoat stand out against a sheet of flame. Someone sprang at him. He was wrestling for his life with Anderson, who turned into a woman with huge flabby breasts. He crushed her to him and turned to defend himself against three officers who came at him, their trench coats drawn in tightly at the waist until they looked like wasps. Everything faded, he woke up.

His nostrils were still full of the strange troubling smell. He sat on the edge of the bunk, wriggling in his clothes, for his body crawled with lice.

"Gee, it's funny to be in where the Fritzies were not long ago," he heard a voice say.

"Kiddo! we're advancin," came another voice.

"But, hell, this ain't no kind of an advance. I ain't seen a German yet."

"Ah kin smell 'em though," said Chrisfield, getting suddenly to his feet.

Sergeant Higgins's head appeared in the door. "Fall in," he shouted. Then he added in his normal voice, "It's up and at 'em, fellers."

Chrisfield caught his puttee on a clump of briars at the edge of the clearing and stood kicking his leg back and forth to get it free. At last he broke away, the torn puttee dragging behind him. Out in the sunlight in the middle of the clearing he saw a man in olivedrab kneeling beside something on the ground. A German lay face down with a red hole in his back. The man was going through his pockets. He looked up into Chrisfield's face.

"Souvenirs," he said.

"What outfit are you in buddy?"

"143rd," said the man, getting to his feet slowly.

"Where the hell are we?"

"Damned if I know."

The clearing was empty, except for the two Americans and the German with the hole in his back. In the distance they heard a sound of artillery and nearer the "put, put, put" of isolated machine guns. The leaves of the trees about them, all shades of brown and crimson and yellow, danced in the sunlight.

"Say, that damn money ain't no good, is it?" asked Chrisfield.

"German money? Hell, no . . . I got a watch that's a peach though." The man held out a gold watch, looking suspiciously at Chrisfield all the while through halfclosed eyes.

"Ah saw a feller had a goldhandled sword," said Chrisfield.

"Where's that?"

"Back there in the wood"; he waved his hand vaguely. "Ah've got to find ma outfit; comin along?" Chrisfield started towards the other edge of the clearing.

"Looks to me all right here," said the other man, lying down on the grass in the sun.

The leaves rustled underfoot as Chrisfield strode through the wood. He was frightened by being alone. He walked ahead as fast as he could, his puttee still dragging behind him. He came to a barbedwire entanglement half embedded in fallen beech leaves. It had been partly cut in one place, but in crossing he tore his thigh on a barb. Taking off the torn puttee, he wrapped it round the outside of his trousers and kept on walking, feeling a little blood trickle down his leg.

Later he came to a lane that cut straight through the wood where there were many ruts through the puttycoloured mud puddles. Down the lane in a patch of sunlight he saw a figure, towards which he hurried. It was a young man with red hair and a pink and white face. By a gold bar on the collar of his shirt Chrisfield saw that he was a lieutenant. He had no coat or hat and there was greenish slime all over the front of his clothes as if he had lain on his belly in a mud puddle.

"Where you going?"

"Dunno, sir."

"All right, come along." The lieutenant started walking as fast as he could up the lane, swinging his arms wildly.

"Seen any machine gun nests?"

"Not a one."

"Hum."

He followed the lieutenant, who walked so fast he had difficulty keeping up, splashing recklessly through the puddles.

"Where's the artillery? That's what I want to know," cried the lieutenant, suddenly stopping in his tracks and running a hand through his red hair. "Where the hell's the artillery?" He looked at Chrisfield savagely out of green eyes. "No use advancing without artillery." He started walking faster than ever.

All at once they saw sunlight ahead of them and olive-drab uniforms. Machine guns started firing all around them in a sudden gust. Chrisfield found himself running forward across a field full of stubble and sprouting clover among a group of men he did not know. The whiplike sound of rifles had chimed in with the stuttering of the machine guns. Little white clouds sailed above him in a blue sky, and in front of him was a group of houses that had the same color, white with lavendergray shadows, as the clouds.

He was in a house, with a grenade like a tin pineapple in each hand. The sudden loneliness frightened him again. Outside the house was a sound of machine gun firing, broken by the occasional bursting of a shell. He looked at the redtiled roof and at a chromo of a woman nursing a child that hung on the whitewashed wall opposite him. He was in a small kitchen. There was a fire in the hearth where something boiled in a black pot. Chrisfield tiptoed over and looked in. At the bottom of the bubbling water he saw five potatoes. At the other end of the kitchen, beyond two broken chairs, was a door. Chrisfield crept over to it, the tiles seeming to sway under foot. He put his finger to the latch and took it off again suddenly. Holding in his breath he stood a long time looking at the door. Then he pulled it open recklessly. A young man with fair hair was sitting at a table, his head resting on his hands. Chrisfield felt a spurt of joy when he saw that the man's

uniform was green. Very coolly he pressed the spring, held
the grenade a second and then threw it, throwing himself
backwards into the middle of the kitchen. The lighthaired
man had not moved; his blue eyes still stared straight
before him.

In the street Chrisfield ran into a tall man who was running. The man clutched him by the arm and said: "The
barrage is moving up."

"What barrage?"

"Our barrage; we've got to run, we're ahead of it." His
voice came in wheezy pants. There were red splotches on
his face. They ran together down the empty village street.
As they ran they passed the little redhaired lieutenant, who
leaned against a whitewashed wall, his legs a mass of blood
and torn cloth. He was shouting in a shrill delirious voice
that followed them out along the open road.

"Where's the artillery? That's what I want to know;
where's the artillery?"

The woods were gray and dripping with dawn. Chrisfield got stiffly to his feet from the pile of leaves where he
had slept. He felt numb with cold and hunger, lonely and
lost away from his outfit. All about him were men of another division. A captain with a sandy mustache was striding up and down with a blanket about him, on the road
just behind a clump of beech trees. Chrisfield had watched
him passing back and forth, back and forth, behind the
wet clustered trunks of the trees, ever since it had been
light. Stamping his feet among the damp leaves, Chrisfield
strolled away from the group of men. No one seemed to
notice him. The trees closed about him. He could see nothing but moist trees, graygreen and black, and the yellow
leaves of saplings that cut off the view in every direction.
He was wondering dully why he was walking off that way.
Somewhere in the back of his mind there was a vague idea
of finding his outfit. Sergeant Higgins and Andy and Judkins and Small—he wondered what had become of them.
He thought of the company lined up for mess, and the
smell of greasy food that came from the field kitchen. He
was desperately hungry. He stopped and leaned against
the mosscovered trunk of a tree. The deep scratch in his
leg was throbbing as if all the blood in his body beat

through it. Now that his rustling footsteps had ceased, the woods were absolutely silent, except for the dripping of dew from the leaves and branches. He strained his ears to hear some other sound. Then he noticed that he was staring at a tree full of small red crab apples. He picked a handful greedily, but they were hard and sour and seemed to make him hungrier. The sour flavour in his mouth made him furiously angry. He kicked at the thin trunk of the tree while tears smarted in his eyes. Swearing aloud in a whining singsong voice, he strode off through the woods with his eyes on the ground. Twigs snapped viciously in his face, crooked branches caught at him, but he plunged on. All at once he stumbled against something hard that bounced among the leaves.

He stopped still, looking about him, terrified. Two grenades lay just under his foot, a little further on a man was propped against a tree with his mouth open. Chrisfield thought at first he was asleep, as his eyes were closed. He looked at the grenades carefully. The fuses had not been sprung. He put one in each pocket, gave a glance at the man who seemed to be asleep, and strode off again, striking another alley in the woods, at the end of which he could see sunlight. The sky overhead was full of heavy purple clouds, tinged here and there with yellow. As he walked towards the patch of sunlight, the thought came to him that he ought to have looked in the pockets of the man he had just passed to see if he had any hard bread. He stood still a moment in hesitation, but started walking again doggedly towards the patch of sunlight.

Something glittered in the irregular fringe of sun and shadow. A man was sitting hunched up on the ground with his fatigue cap pulled over his eyes so that the little gold bar just caught the horizontal sunlight. Chrisfield's first thought was that he might have food on him.

"Say, Lootenant," he shouted, "d'you know where a fellow can get somethin to eat."

The man lifted his head slowly. Chrisfield turned cold all over when he saw the white heavy face of Anderson; an unshaven beard was very black on his square chin; there was a long scratch clotted with dried blood from the heavy eyebrow across the left cheek to the corner of the mouth.

"Give me some water, buddy" said Anderson in a weak voice.

Chrisfield handed him his canteen roughly in silence. He noticed that Anderson's arm was in a sling, and that he drank greedily, spilling the water over his chin and his wounded arm.

"Where's Colonel Evans?" asked Anderson in a thin petulant voice.

Chrisfield did not reply but stared at him sullenly. The canteen had dropped from his hand and lay on the ground in front of him. The water gleamed in the sunlight as it ran out among the russet leaves. A wind had come up, making the woods resound. A shower of yellow leaves dropped about them.

"First you was a corporal, then you was a sergeant, and now you're a lootenant," said Chrisfield slowly.

"You'd better tell me where Colonel Evans is . . . You must know . . . He's up that road somewhere," said Anderson, struggling to get to his feet.

Chrisfield walked away without answering. A cold hand was round the grenade in his pocket. He walked away slowly, looking at his feet.

Suddenly he found he had pressed the spring of the grenade. He struggled to pull it out of his pocket. It stuck in the narrow pocket. His arm and his cold fingers that clutched the grenade seemed paralyzed. Then a warm joy went through him. He had thrown it.

Anderson was standing up, swaying backward and forward. The explosion made the woods quake. A thick rain of yellow leaves came down. Anderson was flat on the ground. He was so flat he seemed to have sunk into the ground.

Chrisfield pressed the spring of the other grenade and threw it with his eyes closed. It burst among the thick newfallen leaves.

A few drops of rain were falling. Chrisfield kept on along the lane, walking fast, feeling full of warmth and strength. The rain beat hard and cold against his back.

He walked with his eyes to the ground. A voice in a strange language stopped him. A ragged man in green with a beard that was clotted with mud stood in front of him with his hands up. Chrisfield burst out laughing.

"Come along," he said, "quick!"

The man shambled in front of him; he was trembling so hard he nearly fell with each step.

Chrisfield kicked him.

The man shambled on without turning round. Chrisfield kicked him again, feeling the point of the man's spine and the soft flesh of his rump against his toes with each kick, laughing so hard all the while that he could hardly see where he was going.

"Halt!" came a voice.

"Ah've got a prisoner," shouted Chrisfield still laughing.

"He ain't much of a prisoner," said the man, pointing his bayonet at the German. "He's gone crazy, I guess. I'll take keer o' him . . . ain't no use sendin him back."

"All right," said Chrisfield still laughing. "Say, buddy, where can Ah' git somethin to eat? Ah ain't had nothin fur a day an a half."

"There's a reconnoiterin squad up the line; they'll give you somethin . . . How's things goin up that way?" The man pointed up the road.

"Gawd, Ah doan know. Ah ain't had nothin to eat fur a day and a half."

The warm smell of a stew rose to his nostrils from the messkit. Chrisfield stood, feeling warm and important, filling his mouth with soft greasy potatoes and gravy, while men about him asked him questions. Gradually he began to feel full and content, and a desire to sleep came over him. But he was given a gun, and had to start advancing again with the reconnoitering squad. The squad went cautiously up the same lane through the woods.

"Here's an officer done for," said the captain, who walked ahead. He made a little clucking noise of distress with his tongue. "Two of you fellows go back and git a blanket and take him back to the cross-roads. Poor fellow." The captain walked on again, still making little clucking noises with his tongue.

Chrisfield looked straight ahead of him. He did not feel lonely any more now that he was marching in ranks again. His feet beat the ground in time with the other feet. He would not have to think whether to go to the right or to the left. He would do as the others did.

The Camera Eye

alphabetically according to rank tapped out with two cold index fingers on the company Corona *Allots Class A & B Ins prem C & D*

Atten — SHUN snap to the hooks and eyes at my throat constricting the adamsapple bringing together the U.S. and the Caduceus

At Ease

outside they're drilling in the purple drizzle of a winter afternoon in Ferrières en Gatinais, Abbaye founded by Clovis over the skeletons of three disciples of notre seigneur Jésus-Christ *3rd Lib Loan Sec of Treas* Altian Politian and Hermatian *4th Lib Loan Sec of Treas must be on CL E or other form Q.M.C. 38* now it's raining hard and the gutters gurgle there's tinkling from all the little glassgreen streams Alcuin was prior once and millwheels grind behind the mossed stone walls and Clodhilde and Clodomir were buried here

promotions only marked under gains drowsily clacked out on the rusteaten Corona in the cantonment of O'Rielly's Traveling Circus alone except for the undertaker soldiering in his bunk and the dry hack of the guy that has TB that the MO was never sober enough to examine

> *Iodine will make you happy*
> *Iodine will make you well*

fourthirty the pass comes alive among the CC pills in my pocket

the acting QM Sarge and the Topkicker go out through the gate of USAAS base camp in their slickers in the lamplit rain and make their way without a cent in their OD to the

Cheval Blanc where by chevrons and parleyvooing they bum drinks and omelettes avec pommes frites and kid apple-cheeked Madeleine may wee

in the dark hallway to the back room the boys were lined up waiting to get in to the girl in black from out of town to drop ten francs and hurry to the propho station *sol viol sk not L D viol Go 41/14 rd. sent S C M*

outside it's raining on the cobbled town inside we drink vin rouge parlezvous froglegs may wee couchez avec and the old territorial at the next table drinks illegal pernod and remarks Tout est bien fait dans la nature à la votre aux Américains

> *Après la guerre finee*
> *Back to the States for me*

Dans la mort il n'y a rien de terrible Quand on va mourir on pense à tout mais vite

the first day in the year dismissed after rollcall I went walking with a fellow from Philadelphia along the purple wintryrutted roads under the purple embroidery of the pleached trees full of rooks cackling overhead over the ruddier hills to a village we're going to walk a long way get good wine full of Merovingian names millwheels glassgreen streams where the water gurgles out of old stone gargoyles Madeleine's red apples the smell of beech leaves we're going to drink wine the boy from Philadelphia's got beaucoup jack wintry purpler wine the sun breaks out through the clouds on the first day in the year

in the first village

we stop in our tracks

to look at a waxwork

the old man has shot the pretty peasant girl who looks like Madeleine but younger she lies there shot in the left breast in the blood in the ruts of the road pretty and plump as a little quail

The old man then took off one shoe and put the shotgun under his chin pulled the trigger with his toe and blew the top of his head off we stand looking at the bare foot and the shoe and the foot in the shoe and the shot girl and the old man with a gunnysack over his head and the dirty bare

toe he pulled the trigger with Faut pas toucher until the
commissaire comes procès verbale

> on this first day
> of the year the sun
> is shining

Joe Williams

JOE HAD BEEN hanging around New York and Brooklyn for
a while, borrowing money from Mrs. Olsen and getting
tanked up all the time. One day she went to work and threw
him out. It was damned cold and he had to go to a mission a
couple of nights. He was afraid of getting arrested for the
draft and he was fedup with every goddam thing; it ended
by his going out as ordinary seaman on the *Appalachian*, a
big new freighter bound for Bordeaux and Genoa. It kinder
went with the way he felt being treated like a jailbird again
and swobbing decks and chipping paint. In the fo'c'stle
there was mostly country kids who'd never seen the sea and
a few old bums who weren't good for anything. They got
into a dirty blow four days out and shipped a small tidal
wave that stove in two of the starboard lifeboats and the
convoy got scattered and they found that the deck hadn't
been properly caulked and the water kept coming down into
the fo'c'stle. It turned out that Joe was the only man they
had on board the mate could trust at the wheel, so they took
him off scrubbing paint and in his four-hour tricks he had
plenty of time to think about how lousy everything was. In
Bordeaux he'd have liked to look up Marceline, but none of
the crew got to go ashore.

The bosun went and got cockeyed with a couple of doughboys and came back with a bottle of cognac for Joe, whom
he'd taken a shine to, and a lot of latrine talk about how the
frogs were licked and the limeys and the wops were licked

something terrible and how if it hadn't been for us the Kaiser 'ud be riding into gay Paree any day and as it was it was nip and tuck. It was cold as hell. Joe and the bosun went and drank the cognac in the galley with the cook who was an oldtimer who'd been in the Klondike gold rush. They had the ship to themselves because the officers were all ashore taking a look at the mademosels and everybody else was asleep. The bosun said it was the end of civilization and the cook said he didn't give a fuck and Joe said he didn't give a fuck and the bosun said they were a couple of goddam Bolshevikis and passed out cold.

It was a funny trip round Spain and through the Straits and up the French coast to Genoa. All the way there was a single file of camouflaged freighters, Greeks and Britishers and Norwegians and Americans, all hugging the coast and creeping along with lifepreservers piled on deck and boats swung out on the davits. Passing 'em was another line coming back light, transports and colliers from Italy and Saloniki, white hospital ships, every kind of old tub out of the seven seas, rusty freighters with their screws so far out of the water you could hear 'em thrashing a couple of hours after they were hull down and out of sight. Once they got into the Mediterranean there were French and British battleships to seaward all the time and sillylooking destroyers with their long smokesmudges that would hail you and come aboard to see the ship's papers. Ashore it didn't look like the war a bit. The weather was sunny after they passed Gibraltar. The Spanish coast was green with bare pink and yellow mountains back of the shore and all scattered with little white houses like lumps of sugar that bunched up here and there into towns. Crossing the Gulf of Lyons in a drizzling rain and driving fog and nasty choppy sea, they came within an ace of running down a big felucca loaded with barrels of wine. Then they were bowling along the French Riviera in a howling northwest wind, with the redroofed towns all bright and shiny and the dry hills rising rocky behind them, and snowmountains standing out clear up above. After they passed Monte Carlo it was a circus, the houses were all pink and blue and yellow and there were tall poplars and tall pointed churchsteeples in all the valleys.

That night they were on the lookout for the big light marked on the chart for Genoa when they saw a red glare

ahead. Rumor went around that the Heinies had captured
the town and were burning it. The second mate put up to
the skipper right on the bridge that they'd all be captured if
they went any further and they'd better go back and put into
Marseilles, but the skipper told him it was none of his goddam business and to keep his mouth shut till his opinion was
asked. The glare got brighter as they got nearer. It turned
out to be a tanker on fire outside the breakwater. She was a
big new Standard Oil tanker, settled a little in the bows with
fire pouring out of her and spreading out over the water.
You could see the breakwater and the lighthouses and the
town piling up the hills behind with red glitter in all the
windows and the crowded ships in the harbor all lit up with
red flare.

After they'd anchored, the bosun took Joe and a couple of
the youngsters in the dinghy, and they went over to see what
they could do aboard the tanker. The stern was way up out
of water. So far as they could see there was no one on the
ship. Some wops in a motorboat came up and jabbered at
them, but they pretended not to understand what they
meant. There was a fireboat standing by, too, but there
wasn't anything they could do. "Why the hell don't they
scuttle her?" the bosun kept saying.

Joe caught sight of a ropeladder hanging into the water
and pulled the dinghy over to it. Before the others had
started yelling at him to come back, he was halfway up it.
When he jumped down onto the deck from the rail he wondered what the hell he was doing up there. God damn it, I
hope she does blow up, he said aloud to himself. It was
bright as day up there. The forward part of the ship and the
sea around it was burning like a lamp. He reckoned the boat
had hit a mine or been torpedoed. The crew had evidently
left in a hurry, as there were all sorts of bits of clothing and
a couple of seabags by the davits aft where the lifeboats had
been. Joe picked himself out a nice new sweater and then
went down into the cabin. On a table he found a box of Havana cigars. He took out a cigar and lit one. It made him
feel good to stand there and light a cigar with the goddam
tanks ready to blow him to Halifax any minute. It was a
good cigar, too. In a tissuepaper package on the table were
seven pairs of ladies' silk stockings. Swell to take home to
Del was his first thought. But then he remembered that he

was through with all that. He stuffed the silk stockings into his pants pockets anyway, and went back on deck.

The bosun was yelling at him from the boat for chrissake to come along or he'd get left. He just had time to pick up a wallet on the companionway. "It ain't gasoline, it's crude oil. She might burn for a week," he yelled at the guys in the boat as he came slowly down the ladder pulling at the cigar as he came and looking out over the harbor, packed with masts and stacks and derricks, at the big marble houses and the old towers and porticoes and the hills behind all lit up in red. "Where the hell's the crew?"

"Probably all cockeyed ashore by this time, where I'd like to be," said the bosun. Joe divvied up the cigars, but he kept the silk stockings for himself. There wasn't anything in the wallet. "Hellova note," grumbled the bosun, "haven't they got any chemicals?"

"These goddam wops wouldn't know what to do with 'em if they did have," said one of the youngsters.

They rowed back to the *Appalachian* and reported to the skipper that the tanker had been abandoned and it was up to the port authorities to get rid of her.

All next day the tanker burned outside the breakwater. About nightfall another of her tanks went off like a roman candle and the fire began spreading more and more over the water. The *Appalachian* heaved her anchor and went up to the wharf.

That night Joe and the bosun went out to look at the town. The streets were narrow and had steps in them leading up the hill to broad avenues, with cafés and little tables out under the colonnades, where the pavements were all polished marble set in patterns. It was pretty chilly and they went into a bar and drank pink hot drinks with rum in them.

There they ran into a wop named Charley who'd been twelve years in Brooklyn and he took them to a dump where they ate a lot of spaghetti and fried veal and drank white wine. Charley told about how they treated you like a dog in the Eyetalian army and the pay was five cents a day and you didn't even get that, and Charley was all for il Presidente Veelson and the Fourteen Points and said soon they'd make peace without victory and bigga revoluzione in Italia and make bigga war on the Francese and the Inglese treata Eyetalian lika dirt. Charley brought in two girls he said were his cousins, Nedda and Dora, and one of 'em sat on Joe's knees and, boy, how she could eat spaghetti, and they all drank wine. It cost 'em all the money Joe had to pay for supper.

When he was taking Nedda up to bed up an outside staircase in the courtyard, he could see the flare of the tanker burning outside the harbor on the blank walls and tiled roofs of the houses.

Nedda wouldn't get undressed, but wanted to see Joe's money. Joe didn't have any money, so he brought out the silk stockings. She looked worried and shook her head, but she was darn pretty and had big black eyes and Joe wanted it bad and yelled for Charley and Charley came up the stairs and talked wop to the girl and said sure she'd take the silk stockings and wasn't America the greatest country in the world and tutti alleati and Presidente Veelson big man for Italia. But the girl wouldn't go ahead until they'd gotten hold of an old woman who was in the kitchen, who came wheezing up the stairs and felt the stockings, and musta said they were real silk and worth money, because the girl put her arm around Joe's neck and Charley said, "Sure, pard, she sleepa with you all night, maka love good."

But about midnight when the girl had gone to sleep, Joe got tired of lying there. He could smell the closets down in the court and a rooster kept crowing loud as the dickens like it was right under his ear. He got up and put on his clothes, and tiptoed out. The silk stockings were hanging on a chair. He picked 'em up and shoved them in his pockets again. His shoes creaked like hell. The street door was all bolted and barred and he had a devil of a time getting it open. Just as he got out in the street, a dog began to bark somewhere and he ran for it. He got lost in a million little narrow stone streets, but he figured that if he kept on going downhill he'd get to the harbor sometime. Then he began to see the pink glow from the burning tanker again on some of the housewalls and steered by that.

On some steep steps he ran into a couple of Americans in khaki uniforms and asked them the way and they gave him a drink out of a bottle of cognac and said they were on their way to the Eyetalian front and that there'd been a big retreat and that everything was cockeyed and they didn't know where the cockeyed front was and they were going to wait right there till the cockeyed front came right to them. He told 'em about the silk stockings and they thought it was goddam funny, and showed him the way to the wharf where the *Appalachian* was and they shook hands a great many times when they said goodnight and they said the wops were swine and he said they were princes to have shown him the way and they said he was a prince and they finished up the cognac and he went on board and tumbled into his bunk.

When the *Appalachian* cleared for home, the tanker was still burning outside the harbor. Joe came down with a dose on the trip home and he couldn't drink anything for several months and kinda steadied down when he got to Brooklyn. He went to the shoreschool run by the Shipping Board in Platt Institute and got his second mate's license and made trips back and forth between New York and St. Nazaire all through that year on a new wooden boat built in Seattle called the *Owanda*, and a lot of trouble they had with her.

He and Janey wrote each other often. She was overseas with the Red Cross and very patriotic. Joe began to think that maybe she was right. Anyway, if you believed the papers the Heinies were getting licked, and it was a big opportunity for a young guy if you didn't get in wrong by being taken for a pro-German or a Bolshevik or some goddam thing. After all, as Janey kept writing, civilization had to be saved and it was up to us to do it. Joe started a savings account and bought him a Liberty bond.

Armistice night Joe was in St. Nazaire. The town was wild. Everybody ashore, all the doughboys out of their camps, all the frog soldiers out of their barracks, everybody clapping everybody else on the back, pulling corks, giving each other drinks, popping champagne bottles, kissing every pretty girl, being kissed by old women, kissed on both cheeks by French veterans with whiskers. The mates and the skipper and the chief and a couple of naval officers they'd never seen before all started to have a big feed in a café, but they never got further than soup because everybody was dancing in the kitchen and they poured the cook so many drinks he passed out cold, and they all sat there singing and drinking champagne out of tumblers and cheering the Allied flags that girls kept carrying through.

Joe went cruising looking for Jeanette, who was a girl he'd kinder taken up with whenever he was in St. Nazaire.

He wanted to find her before he got too zigzag. She'd promised to couchay with him that night before it turned out to be Armistice Day. She said she never couchayed with anybody else all the time the *Owanda* was in port and he treated her right and brought her beaucoup presents from L'Amérique, and du sucer and du cafay. Joe felt good, he had quite a wad in his pocket and, goddam it, American money was worth something these days; and a couple of pounds of sugar he'd brought in the pockets of his raincoat was better than money with the mademosels.

He went in back where there was a cabaret all red plush with mirrors and the music was playing "The Star-Spangled Banner" and everybody cried Vive L'Amérique and pushed drinks in his face as he came in and then he was dancing with a fat girl and the music was playing some damn foxtrot or other. He pulled away from the fat girl because he'd seen Jeanette. She had an American flag draped over her dress. She was dancing with a big sixfoot black Senegalese. Joe saw red. He pulled her away from the nigger who was a frog officer all full of gold braid and she said, "Wazamatta chérie," and Joe hauled off and hit the damn nigger as hard as he could right on the button, but the nigger didn't budge. The nigger's face had a black puzzled smiling look like he was just going to ask a question. A waiter and a coupla frog soldiers came up and tried to pull Joe away. Everybody was yelling and jabbering. Jeanette was trying to get between Joe and the waiter and got a sock in the jaw that knocked her flat. Joe laid out a couple of frogs and was backing off towards the door, when he saw in the mirror that a big guy in a blouse was bringing down a bottle on his head held with both hands. He tried to swing around, but he didn't have time. The bottle crashed his skull and he was out.

The Body of an American

Whereasthe Congressoftheunitedstates byaconcurrent-resolutionadoptedon the4thdayofmarch lastauthorizedthe Secretaryofwar to cause to be brought to theunitedstates-the body of an American whowasamemberoftheamerican-expeditionaryforceineuropewholosthislifeduringtheworld-warandwhoseidentityhasnotbeenestablished for burial inthememorialamphitheatreofthenationalcemeteryatarling-tonvirginia

In the tarpaper morgue at Châlons-sur-Marne in the reek of chloride of lime and the dead, they picked out the pine box that held all that was left of

ennie meenie minie moe . . . plenty of other pine boxes stacked up there containing what they'd scraped up of Richard Roe

and other person or persons unknown. Only one can go. How did they pick John Doe?

Make sure he ain't a dinge, boys.

make sure he ain't a guinea or a kike,

how can you tell a guy's a hunredpercent when all you've got's a gunnysack full of bones, bronze buttons stamped with the screaming eagle and a pair of roll puttees?

. . . and the gagging chloride and the puky dirtstench of the yearold dead . . .

The day withal was too meaningful and tragic for applause. Silence, tears, songs and prayer, muffled drums and soft music were the instrumentalities today of national approbation.

John Doe was born (thudding din of blood in love into

the shuddering soar of a man and a woman alone indeed
together lurching into

and ninemonths sick drowse waking into scared agony
and the pain and blood and mess of birth). John Doe was
born

and raised in Brooklyn, in Memphis, near the lake-
front in Cleveland, Ohio, in the stench of the stockyards in
Chi, on Beacon Hill, in an old brick house in Alexandria,
Virginia, on Telegraph Hill, in a halftimbered Tudor cottage in Portland, the city of roses,

in the Lying-In Hospital old Morgan endowed on
Stuyvesant Square,

across the railroad tracks, out near the country club,
in a shack cabin tenement apartmenthouse exclusive resi-
dential suburb;

scion of one of the best families in the social register,
won first prize in the baby parade at Coronado Beach, was
marbles champion of the Little Rock grammarschools, crack
basketballplayer at the Booneville High, quarterback at the
State Reformatory, having saved the sheriff's kid from
drowning in the Little Missouri River was invited to Washington to be photographed shaking hands with the President on the White House steps —

though this was a time of mourning, such an assem-
blage necessarily has about it a touch of color. In the
boxes are seen the court uniforms of foreign diplomats,
the gold braid of our own and foreign fleets and armies,
the black of the conventional morning dress of American
statesmen, the varicolored furs and outdoor wrapping
garments of mothers and sisters come to mourn, the
drab and blue of soldiers and sailors, the glitter of musical instruments and the white and black of a vested
choir

— busboy harveststiff hogcaller boyscout champeen
cornshucker of Western Kansas bellhop at the United States
Hotel at Saratoga Springs officeboy callboy fruiter tele-
phonelineman longshoreman lumberjack plumber's helper,

worked for an exterminating company in Union City,
filled pipes in an opium joint in Trenton, New Jersey.

Y.M.C.A. secretary, express agent, truckdriver, ford-mechanic, sold books in Denver, Colorado: Madam would you be willing to help a young man work his way through college?

President Harding, with a reverence seemingly more significant because of his high temporal station, concluded his speech:

We are met today to pay the impersonal tribute;
the name of him whose body lies before us took flight
with his imperishable soul . . .
as a typical soldier of this representative democracy he
fought and died believing in the indisputable justice of
his country's cause . . .

by raising his right hand and asking the thousands within the sound of his voice to join in the prayer:

Our Father which art in heaven hallowed be thy
name . . .

Naked he went into the army;
they weighed you, measured you, looked for flat feet, squeezed your penis to see if you had clap, looked up your anus to see if you had piles, counted your teeth, made you cough, listened to your heart and lungs, made you read the letters on the card, charted your urine and your intelligence,
gave you a service record for a future (imperishable soul)
and an identification tag stamped with your serial number to hang around your neck, issued O.D. regulation equipment, a condiment can and a copy of the articles of war.
Atten'SHUN suck in your gut you c——r wipe that smile off your face eyes right wattja tink dis is a choirch social? For-war-D'ARCH.
John Doe
and Richard Roe and other person or persons unknown
drilled, hiked, manual of arms, ate slum, learned to salute, to soldier, to loaf in the latrines, forbidden to smoke on deck, overseas guard duty, forty men and eight horses, shortarm inspection and the ping of shrapnel and the shrill bullets combing the air and the sorehead woodpeckers the

machineguns mud cooties gasmasks and the itch.

Say feller tell me how I can get back to my outfit.

John Doe had a head
for twentyodd years intensely the nerves of the eyes the
ears the palate the tongue the fingers the toes the armpits,
the nerves warmfeeling under the skin charged the coiled
brain with hurt sweet warm cold mine must don't sayings
print headlines:

Thou shalt not the multiplication table long division,
Now is the time for all good men knocks but once at a
young man's door, It's a great life if Ish gebibbel, The first
five years'll be the Safety First, Suppose a Hun tried to
rape your my country right or wrong, Catch 'em young
What he don't know won't treat 'em rough, Tell 'em nothin',
He got what was coming to him he got his, This is a white
man's country, Kick the bucket, Gone west, If you don't
like it you can croaked him

*Say buddy can't you tell me how I can get back to my
outfit?*

Can't help jumpin' when them things go off, give me
the trots them things do. I lost my identification tag swim-
min' in the Marne, roughhousin' with a guy while we was
waitin' to be deloused, in bed with a girl named Jeanne
(Love moving picture wet French postcard dream began
with saltpeter in the coffee and ended at the propho station) —

*Say soldier for chrissake can't you tell me how I can
get back to my outfit?*

John Doe
heart pumped blood:
alive thudding silence of blood in your ears

down in the clearing in the Oregon forest where the
punkins were punkincolor pouring into the blood through
the eyes and the fallcolored trees and the bronze hoopers
were hopping through the dry grass, where tiny striped
snails hung on the underside of the blades and the flies
hummed, wasps droned, bumblebees buzzed, and the woods

smelt of wine and mushrooms and apples, homey smell of fall pouring into the blood,

and I dropped the tin hat and the sweaty pack and lay flat with the dogday sun licking my throat and adamsapple and the tight skin over the breastbone.

The shell had his number on it.

The blood ran into the ground.

The service record dropped out of the filing cabinet when the quartermaster sergeant got blotto that time they had to pack up and leave the billets in a hurry.

The identification tag was in the bottom of the Marne.

The blood ran into the ground, the brains oozed out of the cracked skull and were licked up by the trenchrats, the belly swelled and raised a generation of bluebottle flies,

and the incorruptible skeleton,

and the scraps of dried viscera and skin bundled in khaki

they took to Châlons-sur-Marne

and laid it out neat in a pine coffin

and took it home to God's Country on a battleship

and buried it in a sarcophagus in the Memorial Amphitheater in the Arlington National Cemetery

and draped the Old Glory over it

and the bugler played taps

and Mr. Harding prayed to God and the diplomats and the generals and the admirals and the brasshats and the politicians and the handsomely dressed ladies out of the society column of the *Washington Post* stood up solemn

and thought how beautiful sad Old Glory God's Country it was to have the bugler play taps and the three volleys made their ears ring.

Where his chest ought to have been they pinned the Congressional Medal, the D.S.C., the Médaille Militaire, the Belgian Croix de Guerre, the Italian gold medal, the Vitutea Militara sent by Queen Marie of Rumania, the Czechoslovak War Cross, the Virtuti Militari of the Poles, a wreath sent by Hamilton Fish, Jr., of New York, and a little wampum presented by a deputation of Arizona redskins in warpaint and feathers. All the Washingtonians brought flowers.

Woodrow Wilson brought a bouquet of poppies.

Meester Veelson

The year that Buchanan was elected President Thomas Woodrow Wilson
was born to a Presbyterian minister's daughter
in the manse at Staunton in the valley of Virginia; it was the old Scotch-Irish stock; the father was a Presbyterian minister, too, and a teacher of rhetoric in theological seminaries; the Wilsons lived in a universe of words linked into an incontrovertible firmament by two centuries of Calvinist divines,

God was the Word
and the Word was God.

Doctor Wilson was a man of standing who loved his home and his children and good books and his wife and correct syntax and talked to God every day at family prayers;

he brought his sons up
between the Bible and the dictionary.

The years of the Civil War
the years of fife and drum and platoonfire and proclamations

the Wilsons lived in Augusta, Georgia; Tommy was a backward child, didn't learn his letters till he was nine, but when he learned to read, his favorite reading was Parson Weems's

Life of Washington

In 1870 Doctor Wilson was called to the Theological

Seminary at Columbia, South Carolina; Tommy attended Davidson College,

where he developed a good tenor voice;

then he went to Princeton and became a debater and editor of the *Princetonian*. His first published article in the *Nassau Literary Magazine* was an appreciation of Bismarck.

Afterwards he studied law at the University of Virginia; young Wilson wanted to be a Great Man, like Gladstone and the eighteenth-century English Parliamentarians; he wanted to hold the packed benches spellbound in the cause of Truth; but law practice irked him; he was more at home in the booky air of libraries, lecturerooms, college chapel, it was a relief to leave his law practice at Atlanta and take a Historical Fellowship at Johns Hopkins; there he wrote *Congressional Government*.

At twentynine he married a girl with a taste for painting (while he was courting her he coached her in how to use the broad "a") and got a job at Bryn Mawr teaching the girls History and Political Economy. When he got his Ph.D. from Johns Hopkins he moved to a professorship at Wesleyan, wrote articles, started a History of the United States,

spoke out for Truth Reform Responsible Government Democracy from the lecture platform, climbed all the steps of a brilliant university career; in 1901 the trustees of Princeton offered him the presidency;

he plunged into reforming the university, made violent friends and enemies, set the campus by the ears,

and the American people began to find on the front pages

the name of Woodrow Wilson.

In 1909 he made addresses on Lincoln and Robert E. Lee

and in 1910

the Democratic bosses of New Jersey, hardpressed by muckrakers and reformers, got the bright idea of offering the nomination for Governor to the stainless college president who attracted such large audiences

by publicly championing Right.

When Mr. Wilson addressed the Trenton convention that nominated him for Governor he confessed his belief in the common man (the smalltown bosses and the wardheelers looked at each other and scratched their heads); he went on, his voice growing firmer:

that is, the man by whose judgment I for one wish to be guided, so that as the tasks multiply, and as the days come when all will feel confusion and dismay, we may lift up our eyes to the hills out of these dark valleys where the crags of special privilege overshadow and darken our path, to where the sun gleams through the great passage in the broken cliffs, the sun of God,

the sun meant to regenerate men,

the sun meant to liberate them from their passion and despair and lift us to those uplands which are the promised land of every man who desires liberty and achievement.

The smalltown bosses and the wardheelers looked at each other and scratched their heads; then they cheered; Wilson fooled the wiseacres and doublecrossed the bosses, was elected by a huge plurality;

so he left Princeton only halfreformed to be Governor of New Jersey,

and became reconciled with Bryan

at the Jackson Day dinner: when Bryan remarked, "I of course knew that you were not with me in my position on the currency," Mr. Wilson replied, "All I can say, Mr. Bryan, is that you are a great big man."

He was introduced to Colonel House,

that amateur Merlin of politics who was spinning his webs at the Hotel Gotham,

and at the convention in Baltimore the next July the upshot of the puppetshow staged for sweating delegates by Hearst and House behind the scenes, and Bryan booming in the corridors with a handkerchief over his wilted collar, was that Woodrow Wilson was nominated for the presidency.

The bolt of the Progressives in Chicago from Taft to T. R. made his election sure;

so he left the State of New Jersey halfreformed

(pitiless publicity was the slogan of the Shadow Lawn Campaign)

and went to the White House

our twentyeighth President.

While Woodrow Wilson drove up Pennsylvania Avenue beside Taft, the great buttertub, who as President had been genially undoing T.R.'s reactionary efforts to put business under the control of the government,

J. Pierpont Morgan sat playing solitaire in his back office on Wall Street, smoking twenty black cigars a day, cursing the follies of democracy.

Wilson flayed the interests and branded privilege, refused to recognize Huerta and sent the militia to the Rio Grande,

to assume a policy of watchful waiting. He published *The New Freedom* and delivered his messages to Congress in person, like a college president addressing the faculty and students. At Mobile he said:

I wish to take this occasion to say that the United States will never again seek one additional foot of territory by conquest;

and he landed the marines at Vera Cruz.

We are witnessing a renaissance of public spirit, a reawakening of sober public opinion, a revival of the power of the people, the beginning of an age of thoughtful reconstruction . . .

but the World had started spinning round Sarajevo.

First it was *neutrality in thought and deed*, then *too proud to fight* when the *Lusitania* sinking and the danger to the Morgan loans and the stories of the British and French propagandists set all the financial centers in the East bawling for war, but the suction of the drumbeat and the guns was too strong; the best people took their fashions from Paris and their broad "a's" from London, and T. R. and the House of Morgan.

Five months after his re-election on the slogan *He kept us out of war*, Wilson pushed the Armed Ship Bill through Congress and declared that a state of war existed between the United States and the Central Powers:

Force without stint or limit, force to the utmost.

Wilson became the state (war is the health of the state), Washington his Versailles, manned the socialized government with dollar-a-year men out of the great corporations and ran the big parade

of men munitions groceries mules and trucks to France.

Five million men stood at attention outside of their tarpaper barracks every sundown while they played "The Star-Spangled Banner."

War brought the eighthour day, women's votes, prohibition, compulsory arbitration, high wages, high rates of interest, cost plus contracts, and the luxury of being a Gold Star Mother.

If you objected to making the world safe for cost plus democracy you went to jail with Debs.

Almost too soon the show was over, Prince Max of Baden was pleading for the Fourteen Points, Foch was occupying the bridgeheads on the Rhine, and the Kaiser, out of breath, ran for the train down the platform at Potsdam wearing a silk hat and some say false whiskers.

With the help of *Almighty God, Right, Truth, Justice, Freedom, Democracy, the Selfdetermination of Nations, No indemnities no annexations,*

and Cuban sugar and Caucasian manganese and Northwestern wheat and Dixie cotton, the British blockade, General Pershing, the taxicabs of Paris and the seventyfive gun,

we won the war.

On December 4, 1918, Woodrow Wilson, the first President to leave the territory of the United States during his presidency, sailed for France on board the *George Washington,*

the most powerful man in the world.

In Europe they knew what gas smelt like and the sweet sick stench of bodies buried too shallow and the gray look of the skin of starved children; they read in the papers that Meester Veelson was for peace and freedom and canned goods and butter and sugar;

he landed at Brest with his staff of experts and publicists after a rough trip on the *George Washington.*

La France héroique was there with the speeches, the singing schoolchildren, the mayors in their red sashes. (Did Meester Veelson see the gendarmes at Brest beating back the demonstration of dockyard workers who came to meet him with red flags?)

At the station in Paris he stepped from the train onto a wide red carpet that led him, between rows of potted palms, silk hats, legions of honor, decorated busts of uniforms, frockcoats, rosettes, boutonnieres, to a Rolls-Royce. (Did Meester Veelson see the women in black, the cripples in their little carts, the pale anxious faces along the streets; did he hear the terrible anguish of the cheers as they hurried him and his new wife to the Hôtel de Murat, where in rooms full of brocade, gilt clocks, Buhl cabinets, and ormolu cupids the presidential suite had been prepared?)

While the experts were organizing the procedure of the peace conference, spreading green baize on the tables, arranging the protocols,

the Wilsons took a tour to see for themselves: the day after Christmas they were entertained at Buckingham Palace; at Newyear's they called on the Pope and on the microscopic Italian King at the Quirinal. (Did Meester Veelson know that in the peasants' wargrimed houses along the Brenta and the Piave they were burning candles in front of his picture cut out of the illustrated papers?) (Did Meester Veelson know that the people of Europe spelled a challenge to oppression out of the Fourteen Points, as centuries before they had spelled a challenge to oppression out of the ninety-five articles Martin Luther nailed to the churchdoor in Wittenberg?)

January 18, 1919, in the midst of serried uniforms, cocked hats, and gold braid, decorations, epaulettes, orders of merit and knighthood, the High Contracting Parties, the Allied and Associated Powers, met in the Salon de l'Horloge at the Quai d'Orsay to dictate the peace,

but the grand assembly of the peace conference was too public a place to make peace in,

so the High Contracting Parties

formed the Council of Ten, went into the Gobelin Room, and, surrounded by Rubens's History of Marie de Medici,

began to dictate the peace.

But the Council of Ten was too public a place to make peace in, so they formed the Council of Four.

Orlando went home in a huff,

and then there were three:

Clemenceau,

Lloyd George,

Woodrow Wilson.

Three old men shuffling the pack,

dealing out the cards:

the Rhineland, Danzig, the Polish Corridor, the Ruhr, selfdetermination of small nations, the Saar, League of Nations, mandates, the Mespot, Freedom of the Seas, Transjordania, Shantung, Fiume, and the Island of Yap:

machinegun fire and arson
starvation, lice, cholera, typhus;
oil was trumps.

Woodrow Wilson believed in his father's God,

so he told the parishioners in the little Lowther Street Congregational Church where his grandfather had preached in Carlisle in Scotland, a day so chilly that the newspapermen sitting in the old pews all had to keep their overcoats on.

On April 7 he ordered the *George Washington* to be held at Brest with steam up ready to take the American delegation home;

but he didn't go.

On April 19 sharper Clemenceau and sharper Lloyd George got him into their little cosy threecard game they called the Council of Four.

On June 28 the Treaty of Versailles was ready

and Wilson had to go back home to explain to the politicians, who'd been ganging up on him meanwhile in the Senate and House, and to sober public opinion and to his father's God how he'd let himself be trimmed and how far he'd made the world safe

for democracy and the New Freedom.

From the day he landed in Hoboken, he had his back to the wall of the White House, talking to save his faith in words, talking to save his faith in the League of Nations, talking to save his faith in himself, in his father's God.

He strained every nerve of his body and brain, every agency of the government he had under his control (if anybody disagreed he was a crook or a red; no pardon for Debs).

In Seattle the wobblies whose leaders were in jail, in Seattle the wobblies whose leaders had been lynched, who'd been shot down like dogs, in Seattle the wobblies lined four blocks as Wilson passed, stood silent with their arms folded staring at the great liberal as he was hurried past in his car, huddled in his overcoat, haggard with fatigue, one side of his face twitching. Then men in overalls, the workingstiffs let him pass in silence after all the other blocks of handclapping and patriotic cheers.

In Pueblo, Colorado, he was a gray man hardly able to stand, one side of his face twitching:

Now that the mists of this great question have cleared away, I believe that men will see the Truth, eye for eye and face to face. There is one thing the American People always rise to and extend their hand to, that is, the truth of justice and of liberty and of peace. We have accepted that truth and we are going to be led by it, and it is going to lead us, and through us the world, out into pastures of quietness and peace such as the world never dreamed of before.

That was his last speech;

on the train to Wichita he had a stroke. He gave up the speaking tour that was to sweep the country for the League of Nations. After that he was a ruined paralyzed man barely able to speak;

the day he gave up the presidency to Harding the joint committee of the Senate and House appointed Henry Cabot Lodge, his lifelong enemy, to make the formal call at the executive office in the Capitol and ask the formal question whether the President had any message for the Congress assembled in joint session;

Wilson managed to get to his feet, lifting himself painfully by the two arms of the chair. "Senator Lodge, I have no further communication to make, thank you . . . Good morning," he said.

In 1924 on February 3, he died.

GROUP III

Echoes from the New Era

The Camera Eye

throat tightens when the redstacked steamer churning the faintly heaving slate colored swell swerves slicking in a long greenmarbled curve past the red lightship

spine stiffens with the remembered chill of the offshore Atlantic

and the jag of frame houses in the west above the invisible land and spiderweb rollercoasters and the chewinggum towers of Coney and the freighters with their stacks way aft and the blur beyond Sandy Hook

and the smell of saltmarshes warmclammysweet

remembered bays silvery inlets barred with trestles

the put-put before day of a gasolineboat way up the creek

raked masts of bugeyes against straight tall pines on the shellwhite beach

the limeycold reek of an oysterboat in winter

and creak of rockers on the porch of the scrollsaw cottage and uncles' voices pokerface stories told sideways out of the big mouth (from Missouri who took no rubber nickels) the redskin in the buffalorobe selling snakeroot in the flare of oratorical redfire the sulphury choke and the hookandladder clanging down the redbrick street while the clinging firemen with uncles' faces pull on their rubbercoats

and the crunch of whitecorn muffins and coffee with cream gulped in a hurry before traintime and apartment house mornings stifling with newspapers and the smooth powdery feel of new greenbacks and the whack of a cop's billy cracking a citizen's skull and the faces blurred with newsprint of men in jail

the whine and shriek of the buzzsaw and the tipsy smell of raw lumber and straggling through slagheaps through fireweed through wasted woodlands the shantytowns the shantytowns

what good burying those years in the old graveyard by the brokendown brick church that morning in the spring when the sandy lanes were treated with blue puddles and the air was violets and pineneedles

what good burying those hated years in the latrine-stench at Brocourt under the starshells

if today the crookedfaced custominspector with the soft tough talk the burring speech the funnypaper antics of thick hands jerking thumb

(So you brought home French books didjer?)

is my uncle

Art and Isadora

In San Francisco in eighteen-seventyeight Mrs. Isadora O'Gorman Duncan, a highspirited lady with a taste for the piano, set about divorcing her husband, the prominent Mr. Duncan, whose behavior we are led to believe had been grossly indelicate; the whole thing made her so nervous that she declared to her children that she couldn't keep anything on her stomach but a little champagne and oysters; in the middle of the bitterness and recriminations of the family row,

into a world of gaslit boardinghouses kept by ruined Southern belles and railroadmagnates and swinging doors and whiskery men nibbling cloves to hide the whiskey on their breaths and brass spittoons and fourwheel cabs and basques and bustles and long ruffled trailing skirts (in which lecturehall and concertroom, under the domination of ladies of culture, were the centers of aspiring life)

she bore a daughter whom she named after herself Isadora.

The break with Mr. Duncan and the discovery of his duplicity turned Mrs. Duncan into a bigoted feminist and an atheist, a passionate follower of Bob Ingersoll's lectures and writings; for God read Nature; for duty beauty, *and only man is vile*.

Mrs. Duncan had a hard struggle to raise her children in the love of beauty and the hatred of corsets and conventions and manmade laws. She gave pianolessons, she did embroidery and knitted scarves and mittens.

The Duncans were always in debt.

The rent was always due.

Isadora's earliest memories were of wheedling grocers and butchers and landlords and selling little things her mother had made from door to door,

helping hand valises out of back windows when they had to jump their bills at one shabbygenteel boardinghouse after another in the outskirts of Oakland and San Francisco.

The little Duncans and their mother were a clan; it was the Duncans against a rude and sordid world. The Duncans weren't Catholics any more or Presbyterians or Quakers or Baptists; they were Artists.

When the children were quite young they managed to stir up interest among their neighbors by giving theatrical performances in a barn; the older girl Elizabeth gave lessons in society dancing; they were Westerners, the world was a goldrush; they weren't ashamed of being in the public eye. Isadora had green eyes and reddish hair and a beautiful neck and arms. She couldn't afford lessons in conventional dancing, so she made up dances of her own.

They moved to Chicago. Isadora got a job dancing to *The Washington Post* at the Masonic Temple Roof Garden for fifty a week. She danced at clubs. She went to see Augustin Daly and told him she'd discovered

the Dance

and went on in New York as a fairy in cheesecloth in a production of *Midsummer Night's Dream* with Ada Rehan.

The family followed her to New York. They rented a big room in Carnegie Hall, put mattresses in the corners, hung drapes on the wall and invented the first Greenwich Village studio.

They were never more than one jump ahead of the sheriff, they were always wheedling the tradespeople out of bills, standing the landlady up for the rent, coaxing handouts out of rich philistines.

Isadora arranged recitals with Ethelbert Nevin

danced to readings of Omar Khayyám for society women at Newport. When the Hotel Windsor burned they lost all their trunks and the very long bill they owed and sailed for London on a cattleboat

to escape the materialism of their native America.

In London at the British Museum

they discovered the Greeks;

the Dance was Greek.

Under the smoky chimneypots of London, in the soot-coated squares, they danced in muslin tunics, they copied poses from Greek vases, went to lectures, artgalleries, concerts, plays, sopped up in a winter fifty years of Victorian culture.

Back to the Greeks.

Whenever they were put out of their lodgings for nonpayment of rent, Isadora led them to the best hotel and engaged a suite and sent the waiters scurrying for lobster and champagne and fruits outofseason; nothing was too good for Artists, Duncans, Greeks;

and the nineties London liked her gall.

In Kensington and even in Mayfair she danced at parties in private houses,

the Britishers, Prince Edward down,

were carried away by her preraphaelite beauty

her lusty American innocence

her California accent.

After London, Paris during the great exposition of nineteenhundred. She danced with Loïe Fuller. She was still a virgin too shy to return the advances of Rodin the great master, completely baffled by the extraordinary behavior of Loïe Fuller's circle of crackbrained invert beauties. The Duncans were vegetarians, suspicious of vulgarity and men and materialism. Raymond made them all sandals.

Isadora and her mother and her brother Raymond went about Europe in sandals and fillets and Greek tunics staying at the best hotels leading the Greek life of nature in a flutter of unpaid bills.

Isadora's first solo recital was at a theater in Budapest; after that she was the diva, had a loveaffair with a leading actor; in Munich the students took the horses out of her carriage. Everything was flowers and handclapping and champagne suppers. In Berlin she was the rage.

With the money she made on her German tour she took the Duncans all to Greece. They arrived on a fishingboat from Ithaca. They posed in the Parthenon for photographs and danced in the Theater of Dionysus and trained a crowd of urchins to sing the ancient chorus from the *Suppliants* and built a temple to live in on a hill overlooking the ruins of ancient Athens, but there was no water on the hill and their money ran out before the temple was finished

so they had to stay at the Hôtel d'Angleterre and run up a bill there. When credit gave out, they took their chorus back to Berlin and put on the *Suppliants* in ancient Greek. Meeting Isadora in her peplum marching through the Tiergarten at the head of her Greek boys marching in order, all in Greek tunics, the Kaiserin's horse shied,

and Her Highness was thrown.

Isadora was the vogue.

She arrived in St. Petersburg in time to see the night funeral of the marchers shot down in front of the Winter Palace in 1905. It hurt her. She was an American like Walt Whitman; the murdering rulers of the world were not her people; the marchers were her people; artists were not on the side of the machineguns; she was an American in a Greek tunic, she was for the people.

In St. Petersburg, still under the spell of the eighteenth-century ballet of the court of the Sunking,

her dancing was considered dangerous by the authorities.

In Germany she founded a school with the help of her sister Elizabeth who did the organizing, and she had a baby by Gordon Craig.

She went to America in triumph as she'd always planned and harried the home philistines with a tour; her followers were all the time getting pinched for wearing

Greek tunics; she found no freedom for Art in America.

Back in Paris it was the top of the world; Art meant Isadora. At the funeral of the Prince de Polignac she met the mythical millionaire (sewingmachine king) who was to be her backer and to finance her school. She went off with him in his yacht (whatever Isadora did was Art)

to dance in the Temple at Paestum

only for him,

but it rained and the musicians all got drenched. So they all got drunk instead.

Art was the millionaire life. Art was whatever Isadora did. She was carrying the millionaire's child to the great scandal of the oldlady clubwomen and spinster artlovers when she danced on her second American tour;

she took to drinking too much and stepping to the footlights and bawling out the boxholders.

Isadora was at the height of glory and scandal and power and wealth, her school going, her millionaire was about to build her a theater in Paris, the Duncans were the priests of a cult (Art was whatever Isadora did),

when the car that was bringing her two children home from the other side of Paris stalled on a bridge across the Seine. Forgetting that he'd left the car in gear the chauffeur got out to crank the motor. The car started, knocked down the chauffeur, plunged off the bridge into the Seine.

The children and their nurse were drowned.

The rest of her life moved desperately on

in the clatter of scandalized tongues, among the kidding faces of reporters, the threatening of bailiffs, the expostulations of hotelmanagers bringing overdue bills.

Isadora drank too much, she couldn't keep her hands off goodlooking young men, she dyed her hair various shades of brightred, she never took the trouble to make up her face properly, was careless about her dress, couldn't bother to keep her figure in shape, never could keep track of her money

but a great sense of health

filled the hall

when the pearshaped figure with the beautiful great arms tramped forward slowly from the back of the stage.

She was afraid of nothing; she was a great dancer.

In her own city of San Francisco the politicians wouldn't let her dance in the Greek Theater they'd built under her influence. Wherever she went she gave offense to the philistines. When the war broke out she danced the *Marseillaise*, but it didn't seem quite respectable and she gave offense by refusing to give up Wagner or to show the proper respectable feelings
of satisfaction at the butchery.
On her South American tour
she picked up men everywhere,
a Spanish painter, a couple of prizefighters, a stoker on the boat, a Brazilian poet,
brawled in tangohalls, bawled out the Argentines for niggers from the footlights, lushly triumphed in Montevideo and Brazil; but if she had money she couldn't help scandalously spending it on tangodancers, handouts, afterthetheater suppers, the generous gesture, no, all on my bill. The managers gypped her. She was afraid of nothing, never ashamed in the public eye of the clatter of scandalized tongues, the headlines in the afternoon papers.

When October split the husk off the old world, she remembered St. Petersburg, the coffins lurching through the silent streets, the white faces, the clenched fists that night in St. Petersburg, and danced the *Marche Slave*.
and waved red cheesecloth under the noses of the Boston old ladies in Symphony Hall;
but when she went to Russia full of hope of a school and work and a new life in freedom, it was too enormous, it was too difficult: cold, vodka, lice, no service in the hotels, new and old still piled pellmell together, seedbed and scrapheap, she hadn't the patience, her life had been too easy;
she picked up a yellowhaired poet
and brought him back
to Europe and the grand hotels.
Yessenin smashed up a whole floor of the Adlon in Berlin in one drunken party, he ruined a suite at the Continental in Paris. When he went back to Russia he killed himself. It was too enormous, it was too difficult.

*

When it was impossible to raise any more money for Art, for the crowds eating and drinking in the hotel suites and the rent of Rolls-Royces and the board of her pupils and disciples,

Isadora went down to the Riviera to write her memoirs to scrape up some cash out of the American public that had awakened after the war to the crassness of materialism and the Greeks and scandal and Art, and still had dollars to spend.

She hired a studio in Nice, but she could never pay the rent. She'd quarreled with her millionaire. Her jewels, the famous emerald, the ermine cloak, the works of art presented by the artists, had all gone into the pawnshops or been seized by hotelkeepers. All she had was the old blue drapes that had seen her great triumphs, a redleather handbag, and an old furcoat that was split down the back.

She couldn't stop drinking or putting her arms round the neck of the nearest young man; if she got any cash she threw a party or gave it away.

She tried to drown herself, but an English naval officer pulled her out of the moonlit Mediterranean.

One day at a little restaurant at Golfe Juan she picked up a goodlooking young wop who kept a garage and drove a little Bugatti racer.

Saying that she might want to buy the car, she made him go to her studio to take her out for a ride;

her friends didn't want her to go, said he was nothing but a mechanic; she insisted, she'd had a few drinks (there was nothing left she cared for in the world but a few drinks and a goodlooking young man);

she got in beside him and

she threw her heavilyfringed scarf round her neck with a big sweep she had and

turned back and said,

with the strong California accent her French never lost: Adieu, mes amis, je vais à la gloire.

The mechanic put his car in gear and started.

The heavy trailing scarf caught in a wheel, wound tight. Her head was wrenched against the side of the car. The car stopped instantly; her neck was broken, her nose crushed, Isadora was dead.

Newsreel

there was nothing significant about the morning's trading. The first hour consisted of general buying and selling to even up accounts, but soon after eleven o'clock prices did less fluctuating and gradually firmed

TIMES SQUARE PATRONS LEFT HALF-SHAVED

Will Let Crop Rot In Producers' Hands Unless
Prices Drop

RUSSIAN BARONESS SUICIDE AT MIAMI

. . . the kind of a girl that men forget
Just a toy to enjoy for a while

Coolidge Pictures Nation Prosperous Under His Policies

HUNT JERSEY WOODS FOR ROVING LEOPARD

PIGWOMAN SAW SLAYING

It had to be done and I did it, says Miss Ederle

FORTY-TWO INDICTED IN FLORIDA DEALS

Saw a Woman Resembling Mrs. Hall Berating Couple
Near Murder Scene, New Witness Says

several hundred tents and other light shelters put up by campers on a hill south of Front Street, which overlooks Hempstead Harbor, were laid in rows before the tornado as grass falls before a scythe

When they play Here comes the bride
You'll stand outside

THREE THOUSAND AMERICANS FOUND PENNILESS IN
PARIS

I am a poor girl
My fortune's been sad
I always was courted
By the wagoner's lad

NINE DROWNED IN UPSTATE FLOODS

SHEIK SINKING

Rudolph Valentino, noted screen star, collapsed suddenly yesterday in his apartment at the Hotel Ambassador. Several hours later he underwent

Adagio Dancer

The nineteenyearold son of a veterinary in Castellaneta in the south of Italy was shipped off to America like a lot of other unmanageable young Italians when his parents gave up trying to handle him, to sink or swim and maybe send a few lire home by international postal moneyorder. The family was through with him. But Rodolpho d'Antonguolla wanted to make good.

He got a job as assistant gardener in Central Park, but that kind of work was the last thing he wanted to do; he wanted to make good in the brightlights; money burned his pockets.

He hung around cabarets doing odd jobs, sweeping out for the waiters, washing cars; he was lazy handsome well-built slender goodtempered and vain; he was a born tango-dancer.

Lovehungry women thought he was a darling. He began to get engagements dancing the tango in ballrooms and cabarets; he teamed up with a girl named Jean Acker on a vaudeville tour and took the name of Rudolph Valentino.

Stranded on the Coast he headed for Hollywood, worked for a long time as an extra for five dollars a day; directors began to notice he photographed well.

He got his chance in *The Four Horsemen*
and became the gigolo of every woman's dreams.

Valentino spent his life in the colorless glare of kleig lights, in stucco villas obstructed with bricabrac, Oriental rugs, tigerskins, in the bridalsuites of hotels, in silk bathrobes in private cars.

He was always getting into limousines or getting out of limousines,

or patting the necks of fine horses.

Wherever he went the sirens of the motorcyclecops screeched ahead of him.

flashlights flared,

the streets were jumbled with hysterical faces, waving hands, crazy eyes; they stuck out their autographbooks, yanked his buttons off, cut a tail off his admirablytailored dress-suit; they stole his hat and pulled at his necktie; his valets removed young women from under his bed; all night in nightclubs and cabarets actresses leching for stardom made sheepseyes at him under their mascaraed lashes.

He wanted to make good under the glare of the million-dollar searchlights

of El Dorado:

the Sheik, the Son of the Sheik;

personal appearances.

He married his old vaudeville partner, divorced her, married the adopted daughter of a millionaire, went into lawsuits with the producers who were debasing the art of the screen, spent a million dollars on one European trip;

he wanted to make good in the brightlights.

When the Chicago *Tribune* called him a pink powder-puff

and everybody started wagging their heads over a slave-
bracelet he wore that he said his wife had given him and his
taste for mushy verse of which he published a small volume
called *Daydreams* and the whispers grew about the testi-
mony in his divorce case that he and his first wife had never
slept together,

it broke his heart.

He tried to challenge the Chicago *Tribune* to a duel;

he wanted to make good

in heman twofisted broncobusting pokerplaying stock-
juggling America. (He was a fair boxer and had a good
seat on a horse; he loved the desert like the sheik and was
tanned from the sun of Palm Springs.) He broke down in
his suite in the Hotel Ambassador in New York: gastric
ulcer.

When the doctors cut into his elegantlymolded body,
they found that peritonitis had begun; the abdominal cavity
contained a large amount of fluid and food particles; the
viscera were coated with a greenishgray film; a round hole
a centimeter in diameter was seen in the anterior wall of
the stomach; the tissue of the stomach for one and onehalf
centimeters immediately surrounding the perforation was
necrotic. The appendix was inflamed and twisted against
the small intestine.

When he came to from the ether, the first thing he said
was, "Well, did I behave like a pink powderpuff?"

His expensivelymassaged actor's body fought peritonitis
for six days.

The switchboard at the hospital was swamped with
calls, all the corridors were piled with flowers, crowds filled
the street outside, filmstars who claimed they were his
betrothed entrained for New York.

*Late in the afternoon a limousine drew up at the hospi-
tal door* (where the grimyfingered newspapermen and photographers stood around bored tired hoteyed smoking too
many cigarettes making trips to the nearest speak exchanging wisecracks and deep dope waiting for him to die in time
to make the evening papers), *and a woman, who said she
was a maid employed by a dancer who was Valentino's first
wife, alighted. She delivered to an attendant an envelope
addressed to the filmstar and inscribed "From Jean," and a
package. The package contained a white counterpane with*

*lace ruffles and the word "Rudy" embroidered in the four
corners. This was accompanied by a pillowcover to match
over a blue silk scented cushion.*

Rudolph Valentino was only thirtyone when he died.

His managers planned to make a big thing of his
highlypublicized funeral, but the people in the streets were
too crazy.

While he lay in state in a casket covered with a cloth
of gold, tens of thousands of men, women, and children
packed the streets outside. Hundreds were trampled, had
their feet hurt by policehorses. In the muggy rain the cops
lost control. Jammed masses stampeded under the clubs
and the rearing hoofs of the horses. The funeral chapel
was gutted, men and women fought over a flower, a piece
of wallpaper, a piece of the broken plateglass window.
Showwindows were burst in. Parked cars were overturned
and smashed. When finally the mounted police after repeated charges beat the crowd off Broadway, where traffic
was tied up for two hours, they picked up twentyeight
separate shoes, a truckload of umbrellas, papers, hats, torn-
off sleeves. All the ambulances in that part of the city were
busy carting off women who'd fainted, girls who'd been
stepped on. Epileptics threw fits. Cops collected little
groups of abandoned children.

The fascisti sent a guard of honor and the antifascists
drove them off. More rioting, cracked skulls, trampled feet.
When the public was barred from the undertaking parlors,
hundreds of women groggy with headlines got in to view
the poor body,

claiming to be exdancingpartners, old playmates, relatives from the old country, filmstars; every few minutes a
girl fainted in front of the bier and was revived by the
newspapermen who put down her name and address and
claim to notice in the public prints. Frank E. Campbell's
undertakers and pallbearers, dignified wearers of black
broadcloth and tackersup of crape, were on the verge of a
nervous breakdown. Even the boss had his fill of publicity
that time.

It was two days before the cops could clear the streets
enough to let the flowerpieces from Hollywood be brought
in and described in the evening papers.

*

The church service was more of a success. The police commissioner barred the public for four blocks round.

Many notables attended.

America's Sweetheart, sobbing bitterly in a small black straw with a black band and a black bow behind, in black georgette over black with a white lace collar and white lace cuffs, followed the coffin that was

covered by a blanket of pink roses

sent by a filmstar who appeared at the funeral heavily veiled, and swooned and had to be taken back to her suite at the Hotel Ambassador after she had shown the reporters a message allegedly written by one of the doctors alleging that Rudolph Valentino had spoken of her at the end

as his bridetobe.

A young woman committed suicide in London.

Relatives arriving from Europe were met by police reserves and Italian flags draped with crape. Exchamp Jim Jeffries said, "Well, he made good." The champion allowed himself to be quoted that the boy was fond of boxing and a great admirer of the champion.

The funeral train left for Hollywood.

In Chicago a few more people were hurt trying to see the coffin, but only made the inside pages.

The funeral train arrived in Hollywood on page 23 of the *New York Times*.

Margo Dowling

AGNES GOT OFF the sleeper dressed from head to foot in black crape. She had put on weight and her face had a gray rumpled look Margo hadn't noticed on it before. Margo put her head on Agnes's shoulder and burst out crying right there in the sunny crowded Miami station. They got into

the Buick to go out to the beach. Agnes didn't even notice
the car or the uniformed chauffeur or anything. She took
Margo's hand and they sat looking away from each other
out into the sunny streets full of slowlymoving people in
light clothes. Margo was patting her eyes with her lace
handkerchief.

"Oughtn't you to wear black?" Agnes said. "Wouldn't
you feel better if you were wearing black?"

It wasn't until the blue Buick drew up at the door of the
bungalow on the beach and Raymond, the thinfaced mu-
latto chauffeur, hopped out smiling respectfully to take the
bags, that Agnes began to notice anything. She cried out,
"Oh, what a lovely car."

Margo showed her through the house and out on the
screened porch under the palms facing the purpleblue sea
and the green water along the shore and the white breakers.
"Oh, it's too lovely," Agnes said and let herself drop into
a Gloucester hammock, sighing. "Oh, I'm so tired." Then
she began to cry again. Margo went to do her face at the
long mirror in the hall. "Well," she said when she came
back looking freshpowdered and rosy, "how do you like
the house? Some little shack, isn't it?"

"Oh, we won't be able to stay here now . . . What'll we
do now?" Agnes was blubbering. "I know it's all the wicked
unreality of matter . . . Oh, if he'd only had proper
thoughts."

"Anyway, the rent's paid for another month," said Margo.

"Oh, but the expense," sobbed Agnes.

Margo was looking out through the screendoor at a big
black tanker on the horizon. She turned her head and
talked peevishly over her shoulder. "Well, there's nothing
to keep me from turning over a few options, is there? I tell
you what they are having down here's a boom. Maybe we
can make some money. I know everybody who is anybody
in this town. You just wait and see, Agnes."

Eliza, the black maid, brought in a silver coffeeservice and
cups and a plate of toast on a silver tray covered by a lace
doily. Agnes pushed back her veil, drank some coffee in
little gulps and began to nibble at a piece of toast.

"Have some preserves on it," said Margo, lighting herself
a cigarette. "I didn't think you and Frank believed in
mourning."

"I couldn't help it. It made me feel better. Oh, Margo, have you ever thought that if it wasn't for our dreadful unbelief they might be with us this day." She dried her eyes and went back to the coffee and toast. "When's the funeral?"

"It's going to be in Minnesota. His folks have taken charge of everything. They think I'm ratpoison."

"Poor Mr. Anderson . . . You must be prostrated, you poor child."

"You ought to see 'em. His brother Jim would take the pennies off a dead man's eyes. He's threatening to sue to get back some securities he claims were Charley's. Well, let him sue. Homer Cassidy's my lawyer and what he says goes in this town . . . Agnes, you've got to take off those widow's weeds and act human. What would Frank think if he was here?"

"He is here," Agnes shrieked and went all to pieces and started sobbing again. "He's watching over us right now. I know that!" She dried her eyes and sniffed. "Oh, Margie, coming down on the train I'd been thinking that maybe you and Mr. Anderson had been secretly married. He must have left an enormous estate."

"Most of it is tied up . . . But Charley was all right, he fixed me up as we went along."

"But just think of it, two such dreadful things happening in one winter."

"Agnes," said Margo, getting to her feet, "if you talk like that I'm going to send you right back to New York . . . Haven't I been depressed enough? Your nose is all red. It's awful . . . Look, you make yourself at home. I'm going out to attend to some business."

"Oh, I can't stay here. I feel too strange," sobbed Agnes.

"Well, you can come along if you take off that dreadful veil. Hurry up, I've got to meet somebody."

She made Agnes fix her hair and put on a white blouse. The black dress really was quite becoming to her. Margo made her put on a little makeup. "There, dearie. Now you look lovely," she said and kissed her.

"Is this really your car?" sighed Agnes as she sank back on the seat of the blue Buick sedan. "I can't believe it."

"Want to see the registration papers?" said Margo. "All right, Raymond, you know where the broker's office is."

"I sure do, Miss," said Raymound, touching the shiny visor of his cap as the motor started to hum under the unscratched paint of the hood.

At the broker's office there was the usual welldressed elderly crowd in sportclothes filling up the benches, men with panamahats held on knees of palmbeach suits and linen plusfours, women in pinks and greens and light tan and white crisp dresses. It always affected Margo a little like church, the whispers, the deferential manners, the boys quick and attentive at the long blackboards marked with columns of symbols, the click of the telegraph, the firm voice reading the quotations off the ticker at a desk in the back of the room. As they went in, Agnes in an awed voice whispered in Margo's ear hadn't she better go and sit in the car until Margo had finished her business. "No, stick around," said Margo. "You see those boys are chalking up the stockmarket play by play on those blackboards . . . I'm just beginning to get on to this business." Two elderly gentlemen with white hair and broadflanged Jewish noses smilingly made room for them on a bench in the back of the room. Several people turned and stared at Margo. She heard a woman's voice hissing something about Anderson to the man beside her. There was a little stir of whispering and nudging. Margo felt welldressed and didn't care.

"Well, ma dear young lady," Judge Cassidy's voice purred behind her, "buyin' or sellin' today?"

Margo turned her head. There was the glint of a gold tooth in the smile on the broad red face under the thatch of silvery hair the same color as the gray linen suit which was crossed by another glint of gold in the watchchain looped double across the ample bulge of the judge's vest. Margo shook her head. "Nothing much doing today," she said. Judge Cassidy jerked his head and started for the door. Margo got up and followed, pulling Agnes after her. When they got out in the breezy sunshine of the short street that ran to the bathingbeach, Margo introduced Agnes as her guardian angel.

"I hope you won't disappoint us today the way you did yesterday, ma dear young lady," began Judge Cassidy. "Perhaps we can induce Mrs. Mandeville . . ."

"I'm afraid not," broke in Margo. "You see the poor darling's so tired . . . She's just gotten in from New York

. . . You see, Agnes dear, we are going to look at some lots. Raymond will take you home, and lunch is all ordered for you and everything . . . You just take a nice rest."

"Oh, of course I do need a rest," said Agnes, flushing. Margo helped her into the Buick that Raymond had just brought around from the parkingplace, kissed her, and then walked down the block with the judge to where his Pierce Arrow touringcar stood shiny and glittery in the hot noon sunlight.

The judge drove his own car. Margo sat with him in the front seat. As soon as he'd started the car, she said, "Well, what about that check?"

"Why, ma dear young lady, I'm very much afraid that no funds means no funds . . . I presume we can recover from the estate."

"Just in time to make a first payment on a cemetery lot."

"Well, those things do take time . . . the poor boy seems to have left his affairs in considerable confusion."

"Poor guy," said Margo, looking away through the rows of palms at the brown reaches of Biscayne Bay. Here and there on the green islands new stucco construction stuck out raw, like stagescenery out on the sidewalk in the daytime. "Honestly I did the best I could to straighten him out."

"Of course . . . Of course he had very considerable holdings . . . It was that crazy New York life. Down here we take things easily, we know how to let the fruit ripen on the tree."

"Oranges," said Margo, "and lemons." She started to laugh, but the judge didn't join in.

Neither of them said anything for a while. They'd reached the end of the causeway and turned past yellow frame wharfbuildings into the dense traffic of the Miami waterfront. Everywhere new tall buildings iced like layercake were standing up out of scaffolding and builder's rubbish.

Rumbling over the temporary wooden bridge across the Miami River in a roar of concretemixers and a drive of dust from the construction work, Margo said, turning a round-eyed pokerface at the judge, "Well, I guess I'll have to hock the old sparklers."

The judge laughed and said, "I can assure you the bank will afford you every facility . . . Don't bother your pretty little head about it. You hold some very considerable options right now if I'm not mistaken."

"I don't suppose you could lend me a couple of grand to run on on the strength of them, judge."

They were running on a broad new concrete road through dense tropical scrub. "Ma dear young lady," said Judge Cassidy in his genial drawl, "I couldn't do that for your own sake . . . think of the false interpretations . . . the idle gossip. We're a little oldfashioned down here. We're easygoin', but once the breath of scandal . . . Why, even drivin' with such a charmin' passenger through the streets of Miamah is a folly, a very pleasant folly. But you must realize, ma dear young lady . . . A man in ma position can't afford . . . Don't misunderstand ma motive, ma dear young lady. I never turned down a friend in ma life . . . But ma position would unfortunately not be understood that way. Only a husband or a . . ."

"Is this a proposal, judge?" she broke in sharply. Her eyes were stinging. It was hard keeping back the tears.

"Just a little advice to a client . . ." The judge sighed. "Unfortunately I'm a family man."

"How long is this boom going to last?"

"I don't need to remind you what type of animal is born every minute."

"No need at all," said Margo gruffly.

They were driving into the parkinglot behind the great new caramelcolored hotel.

As she got out of the car, Margo said, "Well, I guess some of them can afford to lose their money, but we can't, can we, judge?"

"Ma dear young lady, there's no such word in the bright lexicon of youth." The judge was ushering her into the diningroom in his fatherly way. "Ah, there are the boys now."

At a round table in the center of the crowded diningroom sat two fatfaced young men with big mouths wearing pink-striped shirts and nilegreen wash neckties and white suits. They got up still chewing and pumped Margo's hand when the judge presented them. They were twins. As they sat down again, one of them winked and shook a fat forefinger. "We used to see you at the Palms, girlie, naughty, naughty."

"Well, boys," said the judge, "how's tricks?"

"Couldn't be better," one of them said with his mouth full.

"You see, boys," said the judge, "this young lady wants to make a few small investments with a quick turnover . . ." The twins grunted and went on chewing.

After lunch the judge drove them all down to the Venetian Pool where William Jennings Bryan sitting in an armchair on the float under a striped awning was talking to the crowd. From where they were they couldn't hear what he was saying, only the laughter and handclapping of the crowd in the pauses. "Do you know, judge," said one of the twins, as they worked their way through the fringes of the crowd around the pool, "if the old boy hadn't wasted his time with politics, he'da made a great auctioneer."

Margo began to feel tired and wilted. She followed the twins into the realestateoffice full of perspiring men in shirtsleeves. The judge got her a chair. She sat there tapping with her white kid foot on the tiled floor with her lap full of blueprints. The prices were all so high. She felt out of her depth and missed Mr. A to buy for her, he'd have known what to buy sure. Outside, the benches on the lawn were crowded. Bawling voices came from everywhere. The auction was beginning. The twins on the stand were waving their arms and banging with their hammers. The judge was striding around behind Margo's chair talking boom to anybody who would listen.

When he paused for breath, she looked up at him and said, "Judge Cassidy, could you get me a taxi?"

"Ma dear young lady, I'll drive you home myself. It'll be a pleasure."

"O.K.," said Margo.

"You are very wise," whispered Judge Cassidy in her ear.

As they were walking along the edge of the crowd, one of the twins they'd had lunch with left the auctioneer's stand and dove through the crowd after them. "Miss Dowlin'," he said, "kin me an' Al come to call?"

"Sure," said Margo, smiling. "Name's in the phonebook under Dowling."

"We'll be around." And he ran back to the stand where his brother was pounding with his hammer. She'd been afraid she hadn't made a hit with the twins. Now she felt the tired lines smoothing out of her face.

"Well, what do you think of the great development of Coral Cables?" said the judge as he helped her into the car.

"Somebody must be making money," said Margo dryly.

Once in the house she pulled off her hat and told Raymond, who acted as butler in the afternoons, to make some martini cocktails, found the judge a cigar, and then excused herself for a moment. Upstairs she found Agnes sitting in her room in a lavender négligée manicuring her nails at the dressingtable. Without saying a word Margo dropped on the bed and began to cry.

Agnes got up looking big and flabby and gentle and came over to the bed. "Why, Margie, you never cry . . ."

"I know I don't," sobbed Margo, "but it's all so awful . . . Judge Cassidy's down there, you go and talk to him . . ."

"Poor little girl. Surely I will, but it's you he'll be wanting to see . . . You've been through too much."

"I won't go back to the chorus . . . I won't," Margo sobbed.

"Oh, no, I wouldn't like that . . . But I'll go down now . . . I feel really rested for the first time in months," said Agnes.

When Margo was alone, she stopped bawling at once. "Why, I'm as bad as Agnes," she muttered to herself as she got to her feet. She turned on the water for a bath. It was late by the time she'd gotten into an afternoondress and come downstairs. The judge looked pretty glum. He sat puffing at the butt of a cigar and sipping at a cocktail while Agnes talked to him about Faith.

He perked up when he saw Margo coming down the stairs. She put some dancemusic on the phonograph.

"When I'm in your house I'm like that famed Grecian sage in the house of the sirens . . . I forget hometies, engagements, everything," said the judge, coming toward her onestepping.

They danced. Agnes went upstairs again. Margo could see that the judge was just on the edge of making a pass at her. She was wondering what to do about it when Cliff Wegman was suddenly ushered into the room. The judge gave the young man a scared suspicious look. Margo could see he thought he was going to be framed.

"Why, Mr. Wegman, I didn't know you were in Miami."

She took the needle off the record and stopped the phonograph. "Judge Cassidy, meet Mr. Wegman."

"Glad to meet you, judge. Mr. Anderson used to talk about you. I was his personal secretary." Cliff looked haggard and nervous. "I just pulled into this little old town," he said. "I hope I'm not intruding." He grinned at Margo. "Well, I'm woiking for the Charles Anderson estate now."

"Poor fellow," said Judge Cassidy, getting to his feet. "I had the honor of bein' quite a friend of Lieutenant Anderson's . . ." Shaking his head he walked across the soft plumcolored carpet to Margo. "Well, ma dear young lady, you must excuse me. But duty calls. This was indeed delightful."

Margo went out with him to his car. The rosy evening was fading into dusk. A mockingbird was singing in a peppertree beside the house. "When can I bring the jewelry?" Margo said, leaning toward the judge over the front seat of the car.

"Perhaps you better come to my office tomorrow noon. We'll go over to the bank together. Of course, the appraisal will have to be at the expense of the borrower."

"O.K. and by that time I hope you'll have thought of some way I can turn it over quick. What's the use of having a boom if you don't take advantage of it?" The judge leaned over to kiss her. His wet lips brushed against her ear as she pulled her head away. "Be yourself, judge," she said.

In the livingroom Cliff was striding up and down fit to be tied. He stopped in his tracks and came toward her with his fists clenched as if he were going to hit her. He was chewing gum; the thin jaw moving from side to side gave him a face like a sheep. "Well, the boss soitenly done right by little Orphan Annie."

"Well, if that's all you came down here to tell me you can just get on the train and go back home."

"Look here, Margo, I've come on business."

"On business?" Margo let herself drop into a pink overstuffed chair. "Sit down, Cliff . . . but you didn't need to come barging in here like a process-server. Is it about Charley's estate?"

"Estate, hell . . . I want you to marry me. The pickin's are slim right now, but I've got a big career ahead."

Margo let out a shriek and let her head drop on the back of the chair. She got to laughing and couldn't stop laughing. "No, honestly, Cliff," she spluttered. "But I don't want to marry anybody just now . . . Why, Cliff, you sweet kid. I could kiss you." He came over and tried to hug her. She got to her feet and pushed him away. "I'm not going to let things like that interfere with my career either."

Cliff frowned. "I won't marry an actress . . . You'd have to can that stuff."

Margo got to laughing again. "Not even a movingpicture actress?"

"Aw, hell, all you do is kid and I'm nuts about you." He sat down on the davenport and wrung his head between his hands.

She moved over and sat down beside him. "Forget it, Cliff."

Cliff jumped up again. "I can tell you one thing, you won't get anywheres fooling around with that old buzzard Cassidy. He's a married man and so crooked he has to go through a door edgeways. He gypped hell out of the boss in that airport deal. Hell . . . That's probably no news to you. You probably were in on it and got your cut first thing . . . And then you think it's a whale of a joke when a guy comes all the way down to the jumpingoff place to offer you the protection of his name. All right, I'm through. Good . . . night." He went out slamming the glass doors into the hall so hard that a pane of glass broke and tinkled down to the floor.

Agnes rushed in from the diningroom. "Oh, how dreadful," she said. "I was listening. I thought maybe poor Mr. Anderson had left a trustfund for you."

"That boy's got bats in his belfry," said Margo.

A minute later the phone rang. It was Cliff with tears in his voice, apologizing, asking if he couldn't come back to talk it over. "Not on your tintype," said Margo and hung up. "Well, Agnes," said Margo as she came from the telephone, "that's that . . . We've got to figure these things out . . . Cliff's right about that old fool Cassidy. He never was in the picture anyways."

"Such a dignified man," said Agnes, making clucking noises with her tongue.

Raymond announced dinner. Margo and Agnes ate alone,

each at one end of the long mahogany table covered with doilies and silverware. The soup was cold and too salty. "I've told that damn girl a hundred times not to do anything to the soup but take it out of the can and heat it," Margo said peevishly. "Oh, Agnes, please do the housekeeping . . . I can't get 'em to do anything right."

"Oh, I'd love to," said Agnes. "Of course I've never kept house on a scale like this."

"We're not going to, either," said Margo. "We've got to cut down."

"I guess I'd better write Miss Franklyn to see if she's got another job for me."

"You just wait a little while," said Margo. "We can stay on here for a coupla months. I've got an idea it would do Tony good down here. Suppose we send him his ticket to come down? Do you think he'd sell it on me and hit the dope again?"

"But he's cured. He told me himself he'd straightened out completely." Agnes began to blubber over her plate. "Oh, Margo, what an openhanded girl you are . . . just like your poor mother . . . always thinking of others."

When Tony got to Miami, he looked pale as a mealyworm, but lying on the beach in the sun and dips in the breakers soon got him into fine shape. He was good as gold and seemed very grateful and helped Agnes with the housework, as they'd let the maids go; Agnes declared she couldn't do anything with them and would rather do the work herself. When men Margo knew came around, she introduced him as a Cuban relative. But he and Agnes mostly kept out of sight when she had company. Tony was tickled to death when Margo suggested he learn to drive the car. He drove fine right away, so they could let Raymond go. One day when he was getting ready to drive her over to meet some big realtors at Cocoanut Grove, Margo suggested, just as a joke, that Tony try to see if Raymond's old uniform wouldn't fit him. He looked fine in it. When she suggested he wear it when he drove her, he went into a tantrum, and talked about honor and manhood. She cooled him down saying that the whole thing was a joke and he said, well, if it was a joke, and wore it. Margo could tell he kinder liked the uniform because she saw him looking at himself in it in the pierglass in the hall.

Miami realestate was on the skids, but Margo managed to make a hundred thousand dollars profit on the options she held; on paper. The trouble was that she couldn't get any cash out of her profits.

The twins she'd met at Coral Gables gave her plenty of advice, but she was leery, and advice was all they did give her. They were always around in the evenings and Sundays, eating up everything Agnes had in the icebox and drinking all the liquor and talking big about the good things they were going to put youall onto. Agnes said she never shook the sand out of her beachslippers without expecting to find one of the twins in it. And they never came across with any parties either, didn't even bring around a bottle of Scotch once in a while. Agnes was kinder soft on them because Al made a fuss over her while Ed was trying to make Margo. One Sunday when they'd all been lying in the sun on the beach and sopping up cocktails all afternoon Ed broke into Margo's room when she was dressing after they'd come in to change out of their bathingsuits and started tearing her wrapper off her. She gave him a poke, but he was drunk as a fool and came at her worse than ever. She had to yell for Tony to come in and play the heavy husband. Tony was white as a sheet and trembled all over, but he managed to pick up a chair and was going to crown Ed with it when Al and Agnes came in to see what the racket was about. Al stuck by Ed and gave Tony a poke and yelled that he was a pimp and that they were a couple of goddam whores. Margo was scared. They never would have got them out of the house if Agnes hadn't gone to the phone and threatened to call the police. The twins said nothing doing, the police were there to run women like them out of town, but they got into their clothes and left and that was the last Margo saw of them.

After they'd gone, Tony had a crying fit and said that he wasn't a pimp and that this life was impossible and that he'd kill himself if she didn't give him money to go back to Havana. To get Tony to stay, they had to promise to get out of Miami as soon as they could. "Now, Tony, you know you want to go to California," Agnes kept saying and petting him like a baby. "Sandflies are getting too bad on the beach, anyway," said Margo. She went down in the living room and shook up another cocktail for them all.

"The bottom's dropped out of this dump. Time to pull out," she said. "I'm through."

It was a sizzling hot day when they piled the things in the Buick and drove off up U.S. 1 with Tony, not in his uniform, but in a new waspwaisted white linen suit, at the wheel. The Buick was so piled with bags and household junk there was hardly room for Agnes in the back seat. Tony's guitar was slung from the ceiling. Margo's wardrobetrunk was strapped on behind. "My goodness," said Agnes when she came back from the restroom of the fillingstation in West Palm Beach where they'd stopped for gas, "we look like a traveling tentshow."

Between them they had about a hundred dollars in cash that Margo had turned over to Agnes to keep in her black handbag. The first day Tony would talk about nothing but the hit he'd make in the movies. "If Valentino can do it, it will be easy for me," he'd say, craning his neck to see his clear brown profile in the narrow drivingmirror at the top of the windshield.

At night they stopped in touristcamps, all sleeping in one cabin to save money, and ate out of cans. Agnes loved it. She said it was like the old days when they were on the Keith Circuit and Margo was a child actress. Margo said child actress, hell, it made her feel like an old crone. Toward afternoon Tony would complain of shooting pains in his wrists and Margo would have to drive.

Along the gulf coast of Alabama, Mississippi, and Louisiana the roads were terrible. It was a relief when they got into Texas, though the weather there was showery. They thought they never would get across the State of Texas, though. Agnes said she didn't know there was so much alfalfa in the world. In El Paso they had to buy two new tires and get the brakes fixed. Agnes began to look worried when she counted over the roll of bills in her purse. The last couple of days across the desert to Yuma they had nothing to eat but one can of baked beans and a bunch of frankfurters. It was frightfully hot, but Agnes wouldn't even let them get Coca-Cola at the dustylooking drugstores in the farbetween little towns because she said they had to save every cent if they weren't going to hit Los Angeles deadbroke. As they were wallowing along in the dust of the unfinished highway outside of Yuma, a shinylooking

S.P. expresstrain passed them, big new highshouldered locomotive, Pullmancars, diner, clubcar with girls and men in
light suits lolling around on the observation platform. The
train passed slowly and the colored porters leaning out
from the Pullmans grinned and waved. Margo remembered
her trips to Florida in a drawingroom and sighed.

"Don't worry, Margie," chanted Agnes from the back
seat. "We're almost there."

"But where? Where? That's what I want to know," said
Margo, with tears starting into her eyes. The car went over
a bump that almost broke the springs.

"Never mind," said Tony, "when I make the orientations
I shall be making thousands a week and we shall travel in
a private car."

In Yuma they had to stop in the hotel because the camps
were all full and that set them back plenty. They were all
in, the three of them, and Margo woke up in the night in a
high fever from the heat and dust and fatigue. In the
morning the fever was gone, but her eyes were puffed up
and red and she looked a sight. Her hair needed washing
and was stringy and dry as a handful of tow.

The next day they were too tired to enjoy it when they
went across the high fragrant mountains and came out into
the San Bernardino Valley full of wellkept fruittrees,
orangegroves that still had a few flowers on them, and
coolsmelling irrigation ditches. In San Bernardino Margo
said she'd have to have her hair washed if it was the last
thing she did on this earth. They still had twentyfive dollars that Agnes had saved out of the housekeeping money
in Miami, that she hadn't said anything about. While
Margo and Agnes went to a beautyparlor, they gave Tony
a couple of dollars to go around and get the car washed.
That night they had a regular fiftycent dinner in a restaurant
and went to a movingpicture show. They slept in a nice
roomy cabin on the road to Pasadena in a camp the woman
at the beautyparlor had told them about, and the next
morning they set out early before the white clammy fog
had lifted.

The road was good and went between miles and miles
of orangegroves. By the time they got to Pasadena the sun
had come out and Agnes and Margo declared it was the
loveliest place they'd ever seen in their lives. Whenever

they passed a particularly beautiful residence Tony would point at it with his finger and say that was where they'd live as soon as he had made the orientations.

They saw signs pointing to Hollywood, but somehow they got through the town without noticing it, and drew up in front of a small rentingoffice in Santa Monica. All the furnished bungalows the man had listed were too expensive and the man insisted on a month's rent in advance, so they drove on. They ended up in a dusty stucco bungalow court in the outskirts of Venice where the man seemed impressed by the blue Buick and the wardrobe trunk and let them take a place with only a week paid in advance. Margo thought it was horrid, but Agnes was in the highest spirits. She said Venice reminded her of Holland's in the old days. "That's what gives me the sick," said Margo. Tony went in and collapsed on the couch and Margo had to get the neighbors to help carry in the bags and wardrobetrunk. They lived in that bungalow court for more months than Margo ever liked to admit even at the time.

Margo registered at the agency as Margo de Garrido. She got taken on in society scenes as extra right away on account of her good clothes and a kind of a way of wearing them she had that she'd picked up at old Piquot's. Tony sat in the agency and loafed around outside the gate of any studio where there was a Spanish or South American picture being cast, wearing a broadbrimmed Cordoba hat he'd bought at a costumer's and tightwaisted trousers and sometimes cowboy boots and spurs, but the one thing there always seemed to be enough of was Latin types. He turned morose and peevish and took to driving the car around filled up with simpering young men he'd picked up, until Margo put her foot down and said it was her car and nobody else's, and not to bring his fagots around the house either. He got sore at that and walked out, but Agnes, who did the housekeeping and handled all the money Margo brought home, wouldn't let him have any pocketmoney until he'd apologized. Tony was away two days and came back looking hungry and hangdog.

After that Margo made him wear the old chauffeur's uniform when he drove her to the lot. She knew that if he wore that he wouldn't go anywhere after he'd left her except right home to change and then Agnes could take the car key. Margo would come home tired from a long day on the lot to find that he'd been hanging around the house all day strumming "It Ain't Gonna Rain No More" on his guitar and sleeping and yawning on all the beds and dropping cigaretteashes everywhere. He said Margo had ruined his career. What she hated most about him was the way he yawned.

One Sunday, after they had been three years in the outskirts of L.A., moving from one bungalow to another, Margo getting on the lots fairly consistently as an extra, but never getting noticed by a director, managing to put aside a little money to pay the interest, but never getting together enough in a lump sum to bail out her jewelry at the bank in Miami, they had driven up to Altadena in the afternoon; on the way back they stopped at a garage to get a flat fixed; out in front of the garage there were some secondhand cars for sale. Margo walked up and down looking at them to have something to do while they were waiting.

"You wouldn't like a Rolls-Royce, would you, lady?" said the garage attendant kind of kidding as he pulled the jack out from under the car.

Margo climbed into the big black limousine with a red coatofarms on the door and tried the seat. It certainly was comfortable. She leaned out and said, "How much is it?"

"One thousand dollars . . . it's a gift at the price."

"Cheap at half the price," said Margo.

Agnes had gotten out of the Buick and come over. "Are you crazy, Margie?"

"Maybe," said Margo and asked how much they'd allow her if she traded in the Buick. The attendant called the boss, a toadfaced young man with a monogram on his silk shirt. He and Margo argued back and forth for an hour about the price. Tony tried driving the car and said it ran like a dream. He was all pepped up at the idea of driving a Rolls, even an old one. In the end the man took the Buick and five hundred dollars in tendollar weekly payments. They signed the contract then and there, Margo gave Judge Cassidy's and Tad Whittlesea's names as references; they changed the plates and drove home that night in the Rolls-Royce to Santa Monica where they were living at the time. As they turned into Santa Monica Boulevard at Beverly Hills, Margo said carelessly, "Tony, isn't that mailed hand holding a sword very much like the coatof-arms of the Counts de Garrido?"

"These people out here are so ignorant they wouldn't know the difference," said Tony.

"We'll just leave it there," said Margo.

"Sure," said Tony, "it looks good."

The other extras surely stared when Tony in his trim gray uniform drove her down to the lot next day, but Margo kept her pokerface. "It's just the old family bus," she said when a girl asked her about it. "It's been in hock."

"Is that your mother?" the girl asked again, pointing with her thumb at Agnes who was driving away sitting up dressed in her best black in the back of the huge shiny car with her nose in the air.

"Oh, no," said Margo coldly. "That's my companion."

Plenty of men tried to date Margo up, but they were mostly extras or cameramen or propertymen or carpenters and she and Agnes didn't see that it would do her any good to mix up with them. It was a lonely life after all the friends and the guys crazy about her and the business deals and everything in Miami. Most nights she and Agnes just played Russian bank or threehanded bridge if Tony was in and not too illtempered to accommodate. Sometimes they went to the movies or to the beach if it was warm enough. They drove out through the crowds on Holly-wood Boulevard nights when there was an opening at Grauman's Chinese Theater. The Rolls looked so fancy and Margo still had a good eveningdress not too far out of style so that everybody thought they were filmstars.

One dusty Saturday afternoon in midwinter Margo was feeling particularly desperate because styles had changed so she couldn't wear her old dresses any more and didn't have any money for new; she jumped up from her seat knocking the pack of solitaire cards onto the floor and shouted to Agnes that she had to have a little blowout or she'd go crazy. Agnes said why didn't they drive to Palm Springs to see the new resort hotel. They'd eat dinner there if it wouldn't set them back too much and then spend the night at a touristcamp down near the Salton Sea. Give them a chance to get the chill of the Los Angeles fog out of their bones.

When they got to Palm Springs, Agnes thought everything looked too expensive and wanted to drive right on, but Margo felt in her element right away. Tony was in his uniform and had to wait for them in the car. He looked so black in the face Margo thought he'd burst when she told him to go and get himself some supper at a dogwagon, but he didn't dare answer back because the doorman was right there.

They'd been to the ladies' room to freshen their faces up and were walking up and down under the big datepalms looking at the people to see if they could recognize any movie actors, when Margo heard a voice that was familiar. A dark thinfaced man in white serge who was chatting with an importantlooking baldheaded Jewish gentleman was staring at her. He left his friend and came up. He had a stiff walk like an officer reviewing a company drawn up at attention.

"Miss Dowling," he said, "how very lucky for both of us."

Margo looked smiling into the twitching sallow face with dark puffs under the eyes. "You're the photographer," she said.

He stared at her hard. "Sam Margolies," he said. "Well, I've searched all over America and Europe for you . . . Please be in my office for a screentest at ten o'clock tomorrow . . . Irwin will give you the details." He waved his hand lackadaisically toward the fat man. "Meet Mr. Harris . . . Miss Dowling . . . forgive me, I never take upon myself the responsibility of introducing people . . . But I want Irwin to see you . . . this is one of the most beautiful women in America, Irwin." He drew his hand down in front of Margo a couple of inches from her face working the fingers as if he were modeling something out of clay. "Ordinarily it would be impossible to photograph her. Only I can put that face on the screen . . ."

Margo felt cold all up her spine. She heard Agnes's mouth come open with a gasp behind her. She let a slow kidding smile start in the corners of her mouth.

"Look, Irwin," cried Margolies, grabbing the fat man by the shoulder. "It is the spirit of comedy . . . But why didn't you come to see me?" He spoke a strong foreign accent of some kind. "What have I done that you should neglect me?"

Margo looked bored. "This is Mrs. Mandeville, my . . . companion . . . We are taking a little look at California."

"What's there here except the studios?"

"Perhaps you'd show Mrs. Mandeville around a moving-picture studio. She's so anxious to see one, and I don't know a soul in this part of the world . . . not a soul."

"Of course, I'll have someone take you to all you care to see tomorrow. Nothing to see but dullness and vulgarity . . . Irwin, that's the face I've been looking for for the little blond girl . . . you remember . . . You talk to me of agencies, extras, nonsense, I don't want actors . . . But, Miss Dowling, where have you been? I halfexpected to meet you at Baden-Baden last summer . . . You are the type for Baden-Baden. It's a ridiculous place, but one has to go somewhere . . . Where have you been?"

"Florida . . . Havana . . . that sort of thing." Margo was thinking to herself that the last time she met him he hadn't been using the broad "a."

"And you've given up the stage?"

Margo gave a little shrug. "The family were so horrid about it."

"Oh, I never liked her being on the stage," cried Agnes who'd been waiting for a chance to put a word in.

"You'll like working in pictures," said the fat man soothingly.

"My dear Margo," said Margolies, "it is not a very large part, but you are perfect for it, perfect. I can bring out in you the latent mystery . . . Didn't I tell you, Irwin, that the thing to do was to go out of the studio and see the world . . . open the book of life? . . . In this ridiculous caravanserai we find the face, the spirit of comedy, the smile of the Mona Lisa . . . That's a famous painting in Paris said to be worth five million dollars . . . Don't ask me how I knew she would be here . . . But I knew. Of course we cannot tell definitely until after the screentest . . . I never commit myself . . ."

"But, Mr. Margolies, I don't know if I can do it," Margo said, her heart pounding. "We're in a rush . . . We have important business to attend to in Miami . . . family matters, you understand."

"That's of no importance. I'll find you an agent . . . we'll send somebody . . . Petty details are of no importance to me. Realestate, I suppose."

Margo nodded vaguely.

"A couple of years ago the house where we'd been living, it was so lovely, was washed clear out to sea," said Agnes breathlessly.

"You'll get a better house . . . Malibu Beach, Beverly Hills . . . I hate houses . . . But I have been rude, I have detained you . . . But you will forget Miami. We have everything out here . . . You remember, Margo dearest, I told you that day that pictures had a great future . . . you and . . . you know, the great automobile magnate, I have forgotten his name . . . I told you you would hear of me in the pictures . . . I rarely make predictions, but I am never wrong. They are based on belief in a sixth sense."

"Oh, yes," interrupted Agnes, "it's so true, if you believe you're going to succeed you can't fail, that's what I tell Margie . . ."

"Very beautifully said, dear lady . . . Miss Dowling darling, Continental Attractions at ten . . . I'll have somebody stationed at the gate so that they'll let your chauffeur drive right to my office. It is impossible to reach me by phone. Even Irwin can't get at me when I am working on a picture. It will be an experience for you to see me at work."

"Well, if I can manage it and my chauffeur can find the way."

"You'll come," said Margolies and dragged Irwin Harris away by one short white flannel arm into the diningroom. Welldressed people stared after them as they went. Then they were staring at Margo and Agnes.

"Let's go to the dogwagon and tell Tony. They'll just think we are eccentric," whispered Margo in Agnes's ear. "I declare I never imagined the Margolies was him."

"Oh, isn't it wonderful!" said Agnes.

They were so excited they couldn't eat. They drove back to Santa Monica that night and Margo went straight to bed so as to be rested for the next morning.

Next morning when they got to the lot at a quarter of ten Mr. Margolies hadn't sent word. Nobody had heard of an appointment. They waited half an hour. Agnes was having trouble keeping back the tears. Margo was laughing. "I bet that bozo was full of hop or something and forgot all about it." But she felt sick inside.

Tony had just started the motor and was about to pull

away because Margo didn't like being seen waiting at the gate like that when a white Pierce Arrow custombuilt towncar with Margolies all in white flannel with a white beret sitting alone in the back drove up alongside. He was peering into the Rolls-Royce and she could see him start with surprise when he recognized her. He tapped on the window of his car with a porcelainheaded cane. Then he got out of his car and reached in and took Margo by the hand. "I never apologize . . . It is often necessary for me to keep people waiting. You will come with me. Perhaps your friend will call for you at five o'clock . . . I have much to tell you and to show you."

They went upstairs in the elevator in a long plainfaced building. He ushered her through several offices where young men in their shirtsleeves were working at draftingboards, stenographers were typing, actors were waiting on benches. "Frieda, a screentest for Miss Dowling right away, please," he said, as he passed a secretary at a big desk in the last room. Then he ushered her into his own office hung with Chinese paintings and a single big carved Gothic chair set in the glare of a babyspot opposite a huge carved Gothic desk. "Sit there, please . . . Margo darling, how can I explain to you the pleasure of a face unsmirched by the camera? I can see that there is no strain . . . You do not care. Celtic freshness combined with insouciance of noble Spain . . . I can see that you've never been before a camera before . . . Excuse me." He sank in the deep chair behind his desk and started telephoning. Every now and then a stenographer came and took notes that he recited to her in a low voice. Margo sat and sat. She thought Margolies had forgotten her. The room was warm and stuffy and began to make her feel sleepy. She was fighting to keep her eyes open when Margolies jumped up from his desk and said, "Come, darling, we'll go down now."

Margo stood around for a while in front of some cameras in a plasterysmelling room in the basement and then Margolies took her to lunch at the crowded restaurant on the lot. She could feel that everybody was looking up from their plates to see who the new girl was that Margolies was taking to lunch. While they ate, he asked her questions about her life on a great sugarplantation in Cuba, and her debutante girlhood in New York. Then he talked about

Carlsbad and Baden-Baden and Marienbad and how Southern California was getting over its early ridiculous vulgarity: "We have everything here that you can find anywhere," he said.

After lunch they went to see the rushes in the projection room. Mr. Harris turned up, too, smoking a cigar. Nobody said anything as they looked at Margo's big gray and white face, grinning, turning, smirking, mouth opening and closing, head tossing, eyes rolling. It made Margo feel quite sick looking at it, though she loved still photographs of herself. She couldn't get used to its being so big. Now and then Mr. Harris would grunt and the end of his cigar would glow red. Margo felt relieved when the film was over and they were in the dark again. Then the lights were on and they were filing out of the projectionroom past a redfaced operator in shirtsleeves who had thrown open the door to the little black box where the machine was and gave Margo a look as she passed. Margo couldn't make out whether he thought she was good or not.

On the landing of the outside staircase, Margolies put out his hand coldly and said, "Goodbye, dearest Margo . . . There are a hundred people waiting for me." Margo thought it was all off. Then he went on: "You and Irwin will make the business arrangements . . . I have no understanding of those matters . . . I'm sure you'll have a very pleasant afternoon."

He turned back into the projectionroom swinging his cane as he went. Mr. Harris explained that Mr. Margolies would let her know when he wanted her and that meanwhile they would work out the contract. Did she have an agent? If she didn't he would recommend that they call in his friend Mr. Hardbein to protect her interests.

When she got into the office with Mr. Harris sitting across the desk from her and Mr. Hardbein, a hollowfaced man with a tough kidding manner, sitting beside her, she found herself reading a threeyear contract at three hundred a week. "Oh, dear," she said, "I'm afraid I'd be awfully tired of it after that length of time . . . Do you mind if I ask my companion Mrs. Mandeville to come around? . . . I'm so ignorant about these things." Then she called up Agnes and they fiddled around talking about the weather until Agnes got there.

Agnes was wonderful. She talked about commitments and important business to be transacted and an estate to care for, and said that at that figure it would not be worth Miss Dowling's while to give up her world cruise, would it, darling, if she appeared in the picture, anyway, it was only to accommodate an old friend Mr. Margolies, and of course Miss Dowling had always made sacrifices for her work, and that she herself made sacrifices for it, and if necessary would work her fingers to the bone to give her a chance to have the kind of success she believed in and that she knew she would have because if you believed with an unsullied heart God would bring things about the way they ought to be. Agnes went on to talk about how awful unbelief was and at five o'clock just as the office was closing they went out to the car with a contract for three months at five hundred a week in Agnes's handbag. "I hope the stores are still open," Margo was saying. "I've got to have some clothes."

A toughlooking grayfaced man in ridingclothes with light tow hair was sitting in the front seat beside Tony. Margo and Agnes glared at the flat back of his head as they got into the car.

"Take us down to Tasker and Harding's on Hollywood Boulevard . . . the Paris Gown Shop," Agnes said. "Oh, goody, it'll be lovely to have you have some new clothes," she whispered in Margo's ear.

When Tony let the stranger off at the corner of Hollywood and Sunset, he bowed stiffly and started off up the broad sidewalk. "Tony, I don't know how many times I've told you you couldn't pick up your friends in my car," began Margo.

She and Agnes nagged at him so that when he got home he was in a passion and said that he was moving out next day. "You have done nothing but exploit me and interfere with my career. That was Max Hirsch. He's an Austrian count and a famous poloplayer." Next day, sure enough, Tony packed his things and left the house.

The five hundred a week didn't go as far as Agnes and Margo thought it would. Mr. Hardbein the agent took ten per cent of it first thing, then Agnes insisted on depositing fifty to pay off the loan in Miami so that Margo could get her jewelry back. Then moving into a new house in the nice part of Santa Monica cost a lot. There was a cook and a housemaid's wages to pay and they had to have a chauffeur now that Tony had gone. And there were clothes and a publicityman and all kinds of charities and handouts around the studio that you couldn't refuse. Agnes was wonderful. She attended to everything. Whenever any business matter came up, Margo would press her fingers to the two sides of her forehead and let her eyes close for a minute and groan. "It's too bad, but I just haven't got a head for business."

It was Agnes who picked out the new house, a Puerto Rican cottage with the cutest balconies, jampacked with antique Spanish furniture. In the evening Margo sat in an easychair in the big livingroom in front of an open fire playing Russian bank with Agnes. They got a few invitations from actors and people Margo met on the lot, but Margo said she wasn't going out until she found out what was what in this town.

"First thing you know we'll be going around with a bunch of bums who'll do us more harm than good."

"How true that is," sighed Agnes. "Like those awful twins in Miami."

They didn't see anything of Tony until, one Sunday night that Sam Margolies was coming to the house for the first time, he turned up drunk at about six o'clock and said that he and Max Hirsch wanted to start a polo school and that he had to have a thousand dollars right away.

"But Tony," said Agnes, "where's Margie going to get it? . . . You know just as well as I do how heavy our expenses are."

Tony made a big scene, stormed and cried and said Agnes and Margo had ruined his stage career and that now they were out to ruin his career in pictures. "I have been too patient," he yelled, tapping himself on the chest. "I have let myself be ruined by women."

Margo kept looking at the clock on the mantel. It was nearly seven. She finally shelled out twentyfive bucks and told him to come back during the week. "He's hitting the hop again," she said after he'd gone. "He'll go crazy one of these days."

"Poor boy," sighed Agnes, "he's not a bad boy, only weak."

"What I'm scared of is that that Heinie'll get hold of him and make us a lot of trouble . . . That bird had a face like state's prison . . . guess the best thing to do is get a lawyer and start a divorce."

"But think of the publicity," wailed Agnes.

"Anyway," said Margo, "Tony's got to pass out of the picture. I've taken all I'm going to take from that greaser."

Sam Margolies came an hour late. "How peaceful," he was saying. "How can you do it in delirious Hollywood?"

"Why, Margie's just a quiet little workinggirl," said Agnes, picking up her sewingbasket and starting to sidle out.

He sat down in the easychair without taking off his white beret and stretched out his bowlegs towards the fire. "I hate the artificiality of it."

"Don't you now?" said Agnes from the door.

Margo offered him a cocktail, but he said he didn't drink. When the maid brought out the dinner that Agnes had worked on all day, he wouldn't eat anything but toast and lettuce. "I never eat or drink at mealtimes. I come only to look and to talk."

"That's why you've gotten so thin," kidded Margo.

"Do you remember the way I used to be in those days? My New York period. Let's not talk about it. I have no memory. I live only in the present. Now I am thinking of the picture you are going to star in. I never go to parties, but you must come with me to Irwin Harris's tonight. There will be people there you'll have to know. Let me see your dresses. I'll pick out what you ought to wear. After this you must always let me come when you buy a dress." Following her up the creaking stairs to her bedroom, he said, "We must have a different setting for you. This won't do. This is suburban."

Margo felt funny driving out through the avenues of palms of Beverly Hills sitting beside Sam Margolies. He'd made her put on the old yellow eveningdress she'd bought at Piquot's years ago that Agnes had recently had done over and lengthened by a little French dressmaker she'd found in Los Angeles. Her hands were cold and she was afraid Margolies would hear her heart knocking against her ribs. She tried to think of something funny to say, but what was the use, Margolies never laughed. She wondered what he was thinking. She could see his face, the narrow forehead under his black bang, the pouting lips, the beak-like profile very dark against the streetlights as he sat stiffly beside her with his hands on his knees. He still had on his white flannels and a white stock with a diamond pin in it in the shape of a golfclub. As the car turned into a drive toward a row of bright tall frenchwindows through the trees, he turned to her and said, "You are afraid you will be bored . . . You'll be surprised. You'll find we have something here that matches the foreign and New York society you are accustomed to." As he turned his face toward her the light glinted on the whites of his eyes and sagging pouches under them and the wet broad lips. He went on whispering, squeezing her hand as he helped her out of the car. "You will be the most elegant woman there, but only as one star is brighter than the other stars."

Going into the door past the butler, Margo caught herself starting to giggle. "How you do go on," she said. "You talk like a . . . like a genius."

"That's what they call me," said Margolies in a loud voice, drawing his shoulders back and standing stiffly at attention to let her go past him through the large glass doors into the vestibule.

The worst of it was going into the dressingroom to take off her wraps. The women who were doing their faces and giving a last pat to their hair all turned and gave her a quick onceover that started at her slippers, ran up her stockings, picked out every hook and eye of her dress, ran round her neck to see if it was wrinkled and up into her hair to see if it was dyed. At once she knew that she ought to have an ermine wrap. There was one old dame standing smoking a cigarette by the lavatory door in a dress all made of cracked ice who had X-ray eyes; Margo felt her reading the pricetag on her stepins. The colored maid gave Margo a nice toothy grin as she laid Margo's coat over her arm that made her feel better. When she went out, she felt the stares clash together on her back and hang there like a tin can on a dog's tail. Keep a stiff upper lip, they can't eat you, she was telling herself as the door of the ladies' room closed behind her. She wished Agnes was there to tell her how lovely everybody was.

Margolies was waiting for her in the vestibule full of

sparkly chandeliers. There was an orchestra playing and they were dancing in a big room. He took her to the fireplace at the end. Irwin Harris and Mr. Hardbein, who looked as alike as a pair of eggs in their tight dress suits, came up and said goodevening. Margolies gave them each a hand without looking at them and sat down by the fireplace with his back to the crowd in a big carved chair like the one he had in his office. Mr. Harris asked her to dance with him. After that it was like any other collection of dressedup people. At least until she found herself dancing with Rodney Cathcart.

She recognized him at once from the pictures, but it was a shock to find that his face had color in it, and that there was warm blood and muscle under his rakish eveningdress. He was a tall tanned young man with goldfishyellow hair and an English way of mumbling his words. She'd felt cold and shivery until she started to dance with him. After he'd danced with her once, he asked her to dance with him again. Between dances he led her to the buffet at the end of the room and tried to get her to drink. She held a Scotch and soda in a big blue glass each time and just sipped it while he drank down a couple of Scotches straight and ate a large plate of chicken salad. He seemed a little drunk, but he didn't seem to be getting any drunker. He didn't say anything, so she didn't say anything either. She loved dancing with him.

Every now and then when they danced round the end of the room, she caught sight of the whole room in the huge mirror over the fireplace. Once when she got just the right angle she thought she saw Margolies's face staring at her from out of the carved highbacked chair that faced the burning logs. He seemed to be staring at her attentively. The firelight playing on his face gave it a warm lively look she hadn't noticed on it before. Immediately blond heads, curly heads, bald heads, bare shoulders, black shoulders got in her way and she lost sight of that corner of the room.

It must have been twelve o'clock when she found him standing beside the table where the Scotch was.

"Hello, Sam," said Rodney Cathcart. "How's every little thing?"

"We must go now, the poor child is tired in all this noise . . . Rodney, you must let Miss Dowling go now."

"O.K., pal," said Rodney Cathcart and turned his back to pour himself another glass of Scotch.

When Margo came back from getting her wraps, she found Mr. Hardbein waiting for her in the vestibule. He bowed as he squeezed her hand. "Well, I don't mind telling you, Miss Dowling, that you made a sensation. The girls are all asking what you use to dye your hair with." A laugh rumbled down into his broad vest. "Would you come by my office? We might have a bite of lunch and talk things over a bit."

Margo gave a little shudder. "It's sweet of you, Mr. Hardbein, but I never go to offices . . . I don't understand business . . . You call us up, won't you?"

When she got out to the colonial porch there was Rodney Cathcart sitting beside Margolies in the long white car. Margo grinned and got in between them as cool as if she'd expected to find Rodney Cathcart there all the while. The car drove off. Nobody said anything. She couldn't tell where they were going, the avenues of palms and the strings of streetlamps all looked alike. They stopped at a big restaurant.

"I thought we'd better have a little snack . . . You didn't eat anything all evening," Margolies said, giving her hand a squeeze as he helped her out of the car.

"That's the berries," said Rodney Cathcart who'd hopped out first. "This dawncing makes a guy beastly 'ungry."

The headwaiter bowed almost to the ground and led them through the restaurant full of eyes to a table that had been reserved for them on the edge of the dancefloor. Margolies ate shreddedwheat biscuits and milk, Rodney Cathcart ate a steak, and Margo took on the end of her fork a few pieces of a lobsterpatty.

"A blighter needs a drink after that," grumbled Rodney Cathcart, pushing back his plate after polishing off the last fried potato.

Margolies raised two fingers. "Here it is forbidden . . . How silly we are in this country! . . . How silly they are!" He rolled his eyes toward Margo. She caught a wink in time to make it just a twitch of the eyelid and gave him that slow stopped smile he'd made such a fuss over at Palm Springs.

Margolies got to his feet. "Come, Margo darling . . . I

have something to show you." As she and Rodney Cathcart followed him out across the red carpet, she could feel ripples of excitement go through the people in the restaurant the way she'd felt it when she went places in Miami after Charley Anderson had been killed.

Margolies drove them to a big creamcolored apartmenthouse. They went up in an elevator. He opened a door with a latchkey and ushered them in. "This," he said, "is my little bachelor flat."

It was a big dark room with a balcony at the end hung with embroideries. The walls were covered with all kinds of oil paintings, each lit by a little overhead light of its own. There were Oriental rugs piled one on the other on the floor and couches round the walls covered with zebra and lion skins.

"Oh, what a wonderful place!" said Margo.

Margolies turned to her smiling. "A bit baronial, eh? The sort of thing you're accustomed to see in the castle of a Castilian grandee."

"Absolutely," said Margo.

Rodney Cathcart lay down full length on one of the couches. "Say, Sam, old top," he said, "have you got any of that good Canadian ale? 'Ow about a little Guinness in it?"

Margolies went out into a pantry and the swinging door closed behind him. Margo roamed around looking at the brightcolored pictures and the shelves of wriggling Chinese figures. It made her feel spooky.

"Oh, I say," Rodney Cathcart called from the couch. "Come over here, Margo . . . I like you . . . You've got to call me Si . . . My friends call me that. It's more American."

"All right by me," said Margo, sauntering toward the couch.

Rodney Cathcart put out his hand. "Put it there, pal," he said. When she put her hand in his, he grabbed it and tried to pull her toward him on the couch. "Wouldn't you like to kiss me, Margo?" He had a terrific grip. She could feel how strong he was.

Margolies came back with a tray with bottles and glasses and set it on an ebony stand near the couch. "This is where I do my work," he said. "Genius is helpless without the proper environment . . . Sit there." He pointed to the couch where Cathcart was lying. "I shot that lion myself . . . Excuse me a moment." He went up the stairs to the balcony and a light went on up there. Then a door closed and the light was cut off. The only light in the room was over the pictures.

Rodney Cathcart sat up on the edge of the couch. "For crissake, sister, drink something . . ."

Margo started to titter. "All right, Si, you can give me a spot of gin," she said, and sat down beside him on the couch.

He was attractive. She found herself letting him kiss her, but right away his hand was working up her leg and she had to get up and walk over to the other side of the room to look at the pictures again. "Oh, don't be silly," he sighed, letting himself drop back on the couch.

There was no sound from upstairs. Margo began to get the jeebies wondering what Margolies was doing up there. She went back to the couch to get herself another spot of gin and Rodney Cathcart jumped up all of a sudden and put his arms around her from behind and bit her ear.

"Quit that caveman stuff," she said, standing still. She didn't want to wrestle with him for fear he'd muss her dress.

"That's me," he whispered in her ear. "I find you most exciting."

Margolies was standing in front of them with some papers in his hand. Margo wondered how long he'd been there. Rodney Cathcart let himself drop back on the couch and closed his eyes.

"Now sit down, Margo darling," Margolies was saying in an even voice. "I want to tell you a story. See if it awakens anything in you." Margo felt herself flushing. Behind her Rodney Cathcart was giving long deep breaths as if he were asleep.

"You are tired of the giddy whirl of the European capitals," Margolies was saying. "You are the daughter of an old armyofficer. Your mother is dead. You go everywhere, dances, dinners, affairs. Proposals are made for your hand. Your father is a French or perhaps a Spanish general. His country calls him. He is to be sent to Africa to repel the barbarous Moors. He wants to leave you in a convent, but you insist on going with him. You are following this?"

"Oh, yes," said Margo eagerly. "She'd stow away on the ship to go with him to the war."

"On the same boat there's a young American collegeboy who has run away to join the Foreign Legion. We'll get the reason later. That'll be your friend Si. You meet . . . Everything is lovely between you. Your father is very ill. By this time you are in a mud fort besieged by natives, howling bloodthirsty savages. Si breaks through the blockade to get the medicine necessary to save your father's life . . . On his return he's arrested as a deserter. You rush to Tangier to get the American consul to intervene. Your father's life is saved. You ride back just in time to beat the firingsquad. Si is an American citizen and is decorated. The general kisses him on both cheeks and hands his lovely daughter over into his strong arms . . . I don't want you to talk about this now . . . Let it settle deep into your mind. Of course, it's only a rudimentary sketch. The story is nonsense, but it affords the director certain opportunities. I can see you risking all, reputation, life itself, to save the man you love. Now I'll take you home . . . Look, Si's asleep. He's just an animal, a brute blond beast."

When Margolies put her wrap around her, he let his hands rest for a moment on her shoulders. "There's another thing I want you to let sink into your heart . . . not your intelligence . . . your heart . . . Don't answer me now. Talk it over with your charming companion. A little later, when we have this picture done, I want you to marry me. I am free. Years ago in another world I had a wife as men have wives, but we agreed to misunderstand and went our ways. Now I shall be too busy. You have no conception of the intense detailed work involved. When I am directing a picture, I can think of nothing else, but when the creative labor is over, in three months' time perhaps, I want you to marry me . . . Don't reply now."

They didn't say anything as he sat beside her on the way home to Santa Monica driving slowly through the thick white clammy morning mist. When the car drove up to her door, she leaned over and tapped him on the cheek. "Sam," she said, "you've given me the loveliest evening."

Agnes was all of a twitter about where she'd been so late. She was walking around in her dressinggown and had the lights on all over the house. "I had a vague brood-ing feeling after you'd left, Margie. So I called up Madame Esther to ask her what she thought. She had a message for me from Frank. You know she said last time he was trying to break through unfortunate influences."

"Oh, Agnes, what did it say?"

"It said success is in your grasp, be firm. Oh, Margie, you've just got to marry him . . . That's what Frank's been trying to tell us."

"Jiminy crickets," said Margo, falling on her bed when she got upstairs, "I'm all in. Be a darling and hang up my clothes for me, Agnes."

Margo was too excited to sleep. The room was too light. She kept seeing the light red through her eyelids. She must get her sleep. She'd look a sight if she didn't get her sleep. She called to Agnes to bring her an aspirin.

Agnes propped her up in bed with one hand and gave her the glass of water to wash the aspirin down with the other; it was like when she'd been a little girl and Agnes used to give her medicine when she was sick. Then suddenly she was dreaming that she was just finishing the "Everybody's Doing It" number and the pink cave of faces was roaring with applause and she ran off into the wings where Frank Mandeville was waiting for her in his black cloak with his arms stretched wide open, and she ran into his arms and the cloak closed about her and she was down with the cloak choking her and he was on top of her clawing at her dress and past his shoulder she could see Tony laughing, Tony all in white with a white beret and a diamond golfclub on his stock jumping up and down and clapping. It must have been her yelling that brought Agnes. No, Agnes was tell-ing her something. She sat up in bed shuddering.

Agnes was all in a fluster. "Oh, it's dreadful. Tony's down there. He insists on seeing you, Margie. He's been reading in the papers. You know it's all over the papers about how you are starring with Rodney Cathcart in Mr. Margolies's next picture. Tony's wild. He says he's your husband and he ought to attend to your business for you. He says he's got a legal right."

"The little rat," said Margo. "Bring him up here . . . What time is it?" She jumped out of bed and ran to the dressingtable to fix her face. When she heard them coming up the stairs, she pulled on her pink lace bedjacket and jumped back into bed. She was very sleepy when Tony came in the room. "What's the trouble, Tony?" she said.

"I'm starving and here you are making three thousand a week . . . Yesterday Max and I had no money for dinner. We are going to be put out of our apartment. By rights everything you make is mine . . . I've been too soft . . . I've let myself be cheated."

Margo yawned. "We're not in Cuba, dearie." She sat up in bed. "Look here, Tony, let's part friends. The contract isn't signed yet. Suppose when it is, we fix you up a little so that ou and your friend can go and start your polo school in Havana. The trouble with you is you're home-sick."

"Wouldn't that be wonderful!" chimed in Agnes. "Cuba would be just the place . . . with all the tourists going down there and everything."

Tony drew himself up stiffly. "Margo, we are Christians. We believe. We know that the church forbids divorce . . . Agnes, she doesn't understand."

"I'm a lot better Christian than you are . . . you know that, you . . ." began Agnes shrilly.

"Now, Agnes, we can't argue about religion before break-fast." Margo sat up and drew her knees up to her chin underneath the covers. "Agnes and I believe that Mary Baker Eddy taught the truth, see, Tony. Sit down here, Tony . . . You're getting too fat, Tony, the boys won't like you if you lose your girlish figure . . . Look here, you and me we've seen each other through some tough times." He sat on the bed and lit a cigarette. She stroked the spiky black hair off his forehead. "You're not going to try to gum the game when I've got the biggest break I ever had in my life."

"I been a louse. I'm no good," Tony said. "How about a thousand a week? That's only a third of what you make. You'll just waste it. Women don't need money."

"Like hell they don't. You know it costs money to make money in this business."

"All right . . . make it five hundred. I don't understand the figures, you know that. You know I'm only a child."

"Well, I don't either. You and Agnes go downstairs and talk it over while I get a bath and get dressed. I've got a dressmaker coming and I've got to have my hair done. I've got a hundred appointments this afternoon . . . Good boy, Tony." She patted him on the cheek and he went away with Agnes meek as a lamb.

When Agnes came upstairs again after Margo had had her bath, she said crossly, "Margie, we ought to have divorced Tony long ago. This German who's got hold of him is a bad egg. You know how Mr. Hays feels about scandals."

"I know I've been a damn fool."

"I've got to ask Frank about this. I've got an appointment with Madame Esther this afternoon. Frank might tell us the name of a reliable lawyer."

"We can't go to Vardaman. He's Mr. Hardbein's lawyer and Sam's lawyer too. A girl sure is a fool ever to put anything in writing."

The phone rang. It was Mr. Hardbein calling up about the contract. Margo sent Agnes down to the office to talk to him. All afternoon, standing there in front of the long pierglass while the dressmaker fussed around her with her mouth full of pins, she was worrying about what to do. When Sam came around at five to see the new dresses, her hair was still in the dryer.

"How attractive you look with your head in that thing," Sam said, "and the lacy negligee and the little triangle of Brussels lace between your knees . . . I shall remember it. I have total recall. I never forget anything I've seen. That is the secret of visual imagination."

When Agnes came back for her in the Rolls, she had trouble getting away from Sam. He wanted to take them wherever they were going in his own car. "You must have no secrets from me, Margo darling," he said gently. "You will see I understand everything . . . everything . . . I know you better than you know yourself. That's why I know I can direct you. I have studied every plane of your face and of your beautiful little girlish soul so full of desire . . . Nothing you do can surprise or shock me."

"That's good," said Margo.

He went away sore.

"Oh, Margie, you oughtn't to treat Mr. Margolies like that," whined Agnes.

"I can do without him better than he can do without me," said Margo. "He's got to have a new star. They say he's pretty near on the skids, anyway."

"Mr. Hardbein says that's just because he's fired his publicityman," said Agnes.

It was late when they got started. Madame Esther's house was way downtown in a dilapidated part of Los Angeles. They had the chauffer let them out two blocks from the house and walked to it down an alley between dusty bungalow courts like the places they'd lived in when they first came out to the Coast years ago.

Margo nudged Agnes. "Remind you of anything?"

Agnes turned to her, frowning. "We must only remember the pleasant beautiful things, Margie."

Madame Esther's house was a big old frame house with wide porches and cracked shingle roofs. The blinds were drawn on all the grimy windows. Agnes knocked at a little groundglass door in back. A thin spinsterish woman with gray bobbed hair opened it immediately. "You are late," she whispered. "Madame's in a state. They don't like to be kept waiting. It'll be difficult to break the chain."

"Has she had anything from Frank?" whispered Agnes.

"He's very angry. I'm afraid he won't answer again . . . Give me your hand."

The woman took Agnes's hand and Agnes took Margo's hand and they went in single file down a dark passageway that had only a small red bulb burning in it, and through a door into a completely dark room that was full of people breathing and shuffling.

"I thought it was going to be private," whispered Margo.

"Shush," hissed Agnes in her ear.

When her eyes got accustomed to the darkness she could see Madame Esther's big puffy face swaying across a huge round table and faint blurs of other faces around it. They made way for Agnes and Margo and Margo found herself sitting down with somebody's wet damp hand clasped in hers. On the table in front of Madame Esther were a lot of little pads of white paper. Everything was quiet except for Agnes's heavy breathing next to her.

It seemed hours before anything happened. Then Margo saw that Madame Esther's eyes were open, but all she could see was the whites. A deep baritone voice was coming out of her lips talking a language she didn't understand. Somebody in the ring answered in the same language, evidently putting questions.

"That's Sidi Hassan the Hindu," whispered Agnes. "He's given some splendid tips on the stockmarket."

"Silence!" yelled Madame Esther in a shrill woman's voice that almost scared Margo out of her wits. "Frank is waiting. No, he has been called away. He left a message that all would be well. He left a message that tomorrow he would impart the information the parties desired and that his little girl must on no account take any step without consulting her darling Agnes."

Agnes burst into hysterical sobs and a hand tapped Margo on the shoulder. The same grayhaired woman led them to the back door again. She had some smellingsalts that she made Agnes sniff. Before she opened the ground-glass door she said, "That'll be fifty dollars, please. Twenty-five dollars each . . . And Madame says that the beautiful girl must not come any more, it might be dangerous for her, we are surrounded by hostile influences. But Mrs. Mande-ville must come and get the messages. Nothing can harm her, Madame says, because she has the heart of a child."

As they stepped out into the dark alley to find that it was already night and the lights were on everywhere, Margo pulled her fur up around her face so that nobody could recognize her.

"You see, Margie," Agnes said as they settled back into the deep seat of the old Rolls, "everything is going to be all right, with dear Frank watching over us. He means that you must go ahead and marry Mr. Margolies right away."

"Well, I suppose it's no worse than signing a threeyear contract," said Margo. She told the chauffeur to drive as fast as he could because Sam was taking her to an opening at Grauman's that night.

When they drove up round the drive to the door, the first thing they saw was Tony and Max Hirsch sitting on the marble bench in the garden.

"I'll talk to them," said Agnes.

Margo rushed upstairs and started to dress. She was sitting looking at herself in the glass in her stepins when Tony rushed into the room. When he got into the light over the dressingtable, she noticed that he had a black eye. "Taking up the gentle art, eh, Tony?" she said, without turning around.

Tony talked breathlessly. "Max blacked my eye because

I did not want to come. Margo, he will kill me if you don't give me one thousand dollars. We will not leave the house till you give us a check and we got to have some cash, too, because Max is giving a party tonight and the bootlegger will not deliver the liquor until he's paid cash. Max says you are getting a divorce. How can you? There is no divorce under the church. It's a sin that I will not have on my soul. You cannot get a divorce."

Margo got up and turned around to face him. "Hand me my negligee on the bed there . . . no use catching my death of cold . . . Say, Tony, do you think I'm getting too fat? I gained two pounds last week . . . Look here, Tony, that squarehead's going to be the ruination of you. You better cut him out and go away for another cure somewhere. I'd hate to have the federal dicks get hold of you on a narcotic charge. They made a big raid in San Pedro only yesterday."

Tony burst into tears. "You've got to give it to me. He'll break every bone in my body."

Margo looked at her wristwatch that lay on the dressing-table beside the big powderbox. Eight o'clock. Sam would be coming by any minute now.

"All right," she said, "but next time this house is going to be guarded by detectives . . . Get that," she said. "And any monkeybusiness and you birds land in jail. If you think Sam Margolies can't keep it out of the papers, you've got another think coming. Go downstairs and tell Agnes to make you out a check and give you any cash she has in the house." Margo went back to her dressing.

A few minutes later, Agnes came up crying. "What shall we do? I gave them the check and two hundred dollars . . . Oh, it's awful. Why didn't Frank warn us? I know he's watching over us, but he might have told us what to do about that dreadful man."

Margo went into her dresscloset and slipped into a brand-new eveninggown. "What we'll do is stop that check first thing in the morning. You call up the homeprotection office and get two detectives out here on day and night duty right away. I'm through, that's all."

Margo was mad, she was striding up and down the room in her new white spangly dress with a trimming of ostrich feathers. She caught sight of herself in the big triple mirror standing between the beds. She went over and stood in front of it. She looked at the three views of herself in the white spangly dress. Her eyes were a flashing blue and her cheeks were flushed. Agnes came up behind her bringing her the rhinestone band she was going to wear in her hair. "Oh, Margie," she cried, "you never looked so stunning."

The maid came up to say that Mr. Margolies was waiting. Margo kissed Agnes and said, "You won't be scared with the detectives, will you, dearie?" Margo pulled the ermine wrap that they'd sent up on approval that afternoon round her shoulders and walked out to the car. Rodney Cathcart was there lolling in the back seat in his dress-clothes. A set of perfect teeth shone in his long brown face when he smiled at her.

Sam had got out to help her in. "Margo darling, you take our breaths away, I knew that was the right dress," he said. His eyes were brighter than usual. "Tonight's a very important night. It is the edict of the stars. I'll tell you about it later. I've had our horoscopes cast."

In the crowded throbbing vestibule, Margo and Rodney Cathcart had to stop at the microphone to say a few words about their new picture and their association with Sam Margolies as they went in through the beating glare of lights and eyes to the lobby. When the master of ceremonies tried to get Margolies to speak, he turned his back angrily and walked into the theater as if it was empty, not looking to the right or the left. After the show they went to a restaurant and sat at a table for a while. Rodney Cathcart ordered kidneychops.

"You mustn't eat too much, Si," said Margolies. "The pièce de résistance is at my flat."

Sure enough, there was a big table set out with cold salmon and lobstersalad and a Filipino butler opening champagne for just the three of them when they went back there after the restaurant had started to thin out. This time Margo tore loose and ate and drank all she could hold. Rodney Cathcart put away almost the whole salmon, muttering that it was topping, and even Sam, saying he was sure it would kill him, ate a plate of lobstersalad.

Margo was dizzygiggly drunk when she found that the Filipino and Sam Margolies had disappeared and that she and Si were sitting together on the couch that had the lionskin on it.

"So you're going to marry Sam," said Si, gulping down a

glass of champagne. She nodded. "Good girl," Si took off his coat and vest and hung them carefully on a chair. "Hate clothes," he said. "You must come to my ranch . . . Hot stuff."

"But you wear them so beautifully," said Margo.

"Correct," said Si.

He reached over and lifted her onto his knee.

"But, Si, we oughtn't to, not on Sam's lionskin."

Si put his mouth to hers and kissed her. "You find me exciting? You ought to see me stripped."

"Don't, don't," said Margo. She couldn't help it, he was too strong, his hands were all over her under her dress.

"Oh, hell, I don't give a damn," she said. He went over and got her another glass of champagne. For himself he filled a bowl that had held cracked ice earlier in the evening.

"As for that lion it's bloody rot. Sam shot it, but the blighter shot it in a zoo. They were sellin' off some old ones at one of the bloody lionfarms and they had a shoot. Couldn't miss 'em. It was a bloody crime." He drank down the champagne and suddenly jumped at her. She fell on the couch with his arms crushing her.

She was dizzy. She walked up and down the room trying to catch her breath. "Goodnight, hot sketch," Si said and carefully put on his coat and vest again and was gone out the door. She was dizzy.

Sam was back and was showing her a lot of calculations on a piece of paper. His eyes bulged shiny into her face as she tried to read. His hands were shaking. "It's tonight," he kept saying, "it's tonight that our lifelines cross . . . We are married, whether we wish it or not. I don't believe in free will. Do you, darling Margo?"

Margo was dizzy. She couldn't say anything. "Come, dear child, you are tired." Margolies's voice burned soothingly in her ears. She let him lead her into the bedroom and carefully take her clothes off and lay her between the black silk sheets of the big poster bed.

It was broad daylight when Sam drove her back to the house. The detective outside touched his hat as they turned into the drive. It made her feel good to see the man's big pugface as he stood there guarding her house. Agnes was up and walking up and down in a padded flowered dressing gown in the livingroom with a newspaper in her hand. "Where have you been?" she cried. "Oh, Margie, you'll ruin your looks if you go on like this and you're just getting a start too . . . Look at this . . . now don't be shocked . . . remember it's all for the best."

She handed the *Times* to Margo, pointing out a headline with the sharp pink manicured nail of her forefinger. "Didn't I tell you Frank was watching over us?"

HOLLYWOOD EXTRA SLAIN AT PARTY
NOTED POLO PLAYER DISAPPEARS
SAILORS HELD

Two enlisted men in uniform, George Cook and Fred Costello, from the battleship *Kenesaw* were held for questioning when they were found stupefied with liquor or narcotics in the basement of an apartmenthouse at 2234 Higueras Drive, San Pedro, where residents allege a drunken party had been in progress all night. Near them was found the body of a young man whose skull had been fractured by a blow from a blunt instrument who was identified as a Cuban, Antonio Garrido, erstwhile extra on several prominent studio lots. He was still breathing when the police broke in in response to telephoned complaints from the neighbors. The fourth member of the party, a German citizen named Max Hirsch, supposed by some to be an Austrian nobleman, who shared an apartment at Mimosa in a fashionable bungalow court with the handsome young Cuban, had fled before police reached the scene of the tragedy. At an early hour this morning he had not yet been located by the police.

Margo felt the room swinging in great circles around her head. "Oh, my God!" she said. Going upstairs she had to hold tight to the baluster to keep from falling. She tore off her clothes and ran herself a hot bath and lay back in it with her eyes closed.

"Oh, Margie," wailed Agnes from the other room, "your lovely new gown is a wreck."

Margo and Sam Margolies flew to Tucson to be married. Nobody was present except Agnes and Rodney Cathcart.

After the ceremony Margolies handed the justice of the peace a new hundreddollar bill. The going was pretty bumpy on the way back and the big rattly Ford trimotor gave them quite a shakingup crossing the desert. Margolies's face was all colors under his white beret, but he said it was delightful. Rodney Cathcart and Agnes vomited frankly into their cardboard containers. Margo felt her pretty smile tightening into a desperate grin, but she managed to keep the wedding breakfast down. When the plane came to rest at the airport at last, they kept the cameramen waiting half an hour before they could trust themselves to come down the gangplank flushed and smiling into a rain of streamers and confetti thrown by the attendants and the whir of the motionpicture cameras. Rodney Cathcart had to drink most of a pint of Scotch before he could get his legs not to buckle under him. Margo wore her smile over a mass of yellow orchids that had been waiting for her in the refrigerator at the airport and Agnes looked tickled to death because Sam had bought her orchids too, lavender ones, and insisted that she stride down the gangplank into the cameras with the rest of them.

It was a relief after the glare of the desert and the lurching of the plane in the airpockets to get back to the quiet dressingroom at the lot. By three o'clock they were in their makeup. In a small room in the groundfloor Margolies went right back to work taking closeups of Margo and Rodney Cathcart in a clinch against the background of a corner of a mud fort. Si was stripped to the waist with two cartridgebelts crossed over his chest and a canvas legionnaire's képi on his head and Margo was in a white eveningdress with highheeled satin slippers. They were having trouble with the clinch on account of the cartridgebelts. Margolies with his porcelainhandled cane thrashing in front of him kept strutting back and forth from the little box he stood on behind the camera into the glare of the klieg light where Margo and Si clinched and unclinched a dozen times before they hit a position that suited him.

"My dear Si," he was saying, "you must make them feel it. Every ripple of your muscles must make them feel passion . . . you are stiff like a wooden doll. They all love her, a piece of fragile beautiful palpitant womanhood ready to give all for the man she loves . . . Margo, darling, you faint, you let yourself go in his arms. If his strong arms weren't there to catch you, you would fall to the ground. Si, my dear fellow, you are not an athletic instructor teaching a young lady to swim, you are a desperate lover facing death . . . They all feel they are you, you are loving her for them, the millions who want love and beauty and excitement, but forget them, loosen up, my dear fellow, forget that I'm here and the camera's here, you are alone together snatching a desperate moment, you are alone except for your two beating hearts, you and the most beautiful girl in the world, the nation's newest sweetheart . . . All right . . . hold it . . . Camera."

Newsreel

Don't blame it all on Broadway

with few exceptions the management of our government has been and is in honest and competent hands, that the finances are sound and well managed, and that the business interests of the nation, including the owners, managers, and employee, are representative of honorable and patriotic motives and that the present economic condition warrants a continuation of confidence and prosperity

You have yourself to blame
Don't shame the name of dear old Broadway

GRAND JURY WILL QUIZ BALLPLAYERS

IMPROVED LUBRICATING SYSTEM THAT INSURES
POSITIVE AND CONSTANT OILING OVER THE
ENTIRE BEARING SURFACES

I've got a longin' way down in my heart
For that old gang that has drifted apart

the Dooling Shipbuilding Corporation has not paid or agreed to pay and will not pay, directly or indirectly, any bribe of any sort or description to any employee or representative of the U.S. Shipping Board, the Emergency Fleet Corporation, or any other government agency

SLAIN RICH MAN BURIED IN CELLAR

I can't forget that old quartette
That sang Sweet Adeline
Goodbye forever old fellows and gals
Goodbye forever old sweethearts and pals

NEWLY DESIGNED GEARS AFFORDING NOT
ONLY GREATER STRENGTH AND LONGER
LIFE BUT INCREASED SMOOTHNESS

NEW CLUTCH — AN ENGINEERING ACHIEVEMENT
THAT ADDS WONDERFUL POSITIVENESS TO
POWER TRANSMISSION THAT MAKES
GEARSHIFTING EASY AND NOISELESS

NEW AND LARGER BULLET LAMPS AFFORD THE
MOST PERFECT ILLUMINATION EVER
DEVELOPED FOR MOTOR USE

GARY CALLS ROMANTIC PUBLIC RESPONSIBLE
FOR EIGHTHOUR DAY

the prices obtained for packinghouse products were the results of purely economic laws. Official figures prove that if wheat prices are to respond to the law of supply and demand

PIGIRON OUTPUT SHARPLY CURBED

And if you should be dining with a little stranger
Red lights seem to warn you of a danger
Don't blame it all on Broadway

Theatre

THE NEWSPAPERS next morning were worse than Jed had imagined they could be. None of the critics had ever heard of expressionism. John Taylor Briggs ended his short notice by saying that the kindest thing to do was to treat the whole thing as a boyish prank.

"A boyish prank," the phrase rankled in Jed's head all week. He kept imagining it printed in bold letters across the tiny advertisements of The Craftsman's Theatre that cost so much to run on the theatrical pages. The Sunday theatrical sections were full of it as he thumbed through them sleepily on the stale train out to Ashbury Park Sunday morning. Every critic repeated the phrase in some form or other. Most of them added something about bad taste.

Jed was too tired to care. He and Kenneth Magill had been up with the cast until five in the morning rehearsing changes in the script after the Saturday night performance. Kenneth had talent Jed had to admit, but he'd never liked him. They'd been classmates in college, together in all the local theatricals. Red hair and mushroomwhite skin, something too soft about the touch of his hand. He was quite masculine though when he was directing. And patient, my God. That performance had been a mess. Empty seats. Saturday night of all nights for Sylvia Levy to go up on her lines. Jed had a lousy headache and he felt tireder than he ever had in his life but he just had to go out to see J.E. He'd planned to sleep on the train but he couldn't close his eyes.

As he stepped off the coach into the fuzzy glare and the salt seabreeze, he almost walked past a small man with dark glasses. A hand pulled at his sleeve.

"Emmanuel dear, you didn't recognize me. Can I have

aged so in a few short months?" His father pulled off his dark glasses and was kissing him on the cheek. As he looked into J.E.'s face Jed felt with a pang how much like his own face it was, only so yellow and shriveled. The wrinkled skin round the eyes had a trodden look. The closecropped hair was still as dark as his own. Less wave to it perhaps; after all J.E. was seventyfour. It was like looking at his own face in some stained reducing mirror.

"Your train was late," J.E. was saying querulously. "You know it plays hob with my digestion to be late to my meals. I've ordered a shore dinner for you. You always used to like a shore dinner. Emmanuel, you're looking thin."

"The girls complain that I'm getting a potbelly." Jed broke through the strain of meeting with a burst of laughter. "I can't please everybody, now can I, J.E.?"

"We must hurry or it will all be cold."

They had reached the curb on the street side of the station. J.E. was slipping the dark spectacles back over his eyes. "My eyes can't stand the glare any more, dear. They are not as strong as they were," he explained. "I must save them for my work."

Jed tenderly took his father's arm. As he steered him through the cars and taxicabs backing and filling in front of the station he explained that he would have caught an earlier train only that he'd overslept. In this theatre business a man could never get to bed.

"You mustn't wear yourself out . . . Even as a cub reporter I was careful about my sleep . . . Here it is, the Olympic."

When they ducked in out of the hot September sunlight the shut-in smell of cold grease and laundered napkins almost made Jed retch. If I could only have a drink or a swim, he was thinking. The place was empty and airless. On the back wall the hands of a clock were joined at twelve sharp.

"We're not late after all," said J.E. happily. "There's my table all ready for us."

They settled themselves at a table already set in a dark corner. A pimplyfaced waiter who needed a shave advanced smiling.

"This is my boy, Nick," said J.E. pulling off his glasses and blinking up at the waiter. "Back from across the her-

ring pond . . . We'll start with the steamed clams. Drink
the broth first, dear. Nick you know I only take the broth.
Nothing more settling to the stomach than clam broth.
Sometimes I eat nothing else all day, a cup of clam broth
and a hard biscuit." He sat drinking his broth out of its
thick cup with little noisy sips. "Emmanuel." He looked
hard in Jed's face when he had finished. "How close are
you to Adolph Baum?"

"I only met him once. Everybody else was so busy playing up to him I couldn't get a word in edgewise."

"Did he ask for me?" asked J.E. frowning. Jed shook his
head. "I fear no good will come of your relationship with
that man . . . Eat the clams, dear, they are delicious." He
wiped his mouth with his napkin.

"Emmanuel," he added suddenly, "I'm going to tell you
a story . . . Years ago when I was in my salad days," he
smiled. "Even I had my salad days, dear . . . I wrote a column called 'The Money Market' in the *Financial Times*. It
had a certain fame in its day as any surviving old-timer on
Wall Street will tell you. There are not many left. I have
attended most of their funerals. Well in the course of working up one of my columns, I think I was collecting opinions
on the freesilver fallacy, I had an appointment to interview
old Jerome Samuels in his office. I was a little flustered because he was not an easy man to interview. A great man on
the Street in his day. A proud overbearing man. Suddenly
I became aware that on the edge of his desk sat the most
beautiful creature I had ever seen in my life. It was his
daughter Judith, who became after so much heartbreak and
trouble your darling mother. She had run into the office to
get a check cashed. Someday, dear, I may be able to tell
you about our secret courtship but today it is still too near.
You were six years old and such a pretty little boy when
she passed away. Sometimes it seems as if I had died with
her . . . Only seven short years of happiness. But in those
days I was full of fire . . . not so wild as you've been, dear,
but a gay young blade at that. Until I met your darling
mother . . . From the first she felt about me, as she told
me afterwards, just as I felt about her. Jerome Samuels dis-
inherited her. He never forgave her, or me. He treated her
with heartless brutality. He never relented. Newspapermen were not considered respectable in those days, at least

not respectable enough to marry bankers' daughters. Samuels' junior partner was Jules Baum, Adolph Baum's father. They were both creatures of old J.P.'s. When I incurred their enmity I incurred the enmity of the most powerful men in the world. That enmity pursued me relentlessly throughout my career. The Morgan interests . . ."

Jed had been trying to think of some way of breaking in. The tense glitter in his father's eyes frightened him.

"Then there's a sort of poetic justice," he said laughing, "in Adolph Baum's giving me the break of my life." He threw back his head but his laugh sounded forced to his own ears. "I'll tell him that when I see him."

"Tell him nothing . . . Avoid him, Emmanuel . . . Deal with him through intermediaries."

"But he's such a nice little man."

"As nice as a rattlesnake. When your darling mother lay ill in the hospital he refused to transmit a message to her old father. He may even have helped bring about her death. There have been such torturing suspicions."

"J.E., how could Adolph Baum have had anything to do with it?" Jed found his own voice unnecessarily peevish.

A group of men in their shirtsleeves had lumbered into the restaurant. "Quiet. We may be overhead," said J.E. sharply. He went on silently picking the bones out of a piece of boiled scrod.

Meanwhile Jed chewed desperately on the bluefish and the lobster and the blueberry pie his father had ordered for him. Each bite seemed harder to swallow than the last. He knew J.E. had been planning the meal for days. He had to stuff it down. He could feel the tense dark eyes so full of concern, searching his face for every passing thought.

At last the meal was over and he was walking beside his father along the gray gritty street towards the beach, feeling again the stuffed constraint of all the Sundays when he was a small boy, the tedium of inspirational sermons at the Ethical Culture Society, the dreary dark men in turbans or round black silk caps his father and old Mr. Davidson took him to hear in outoftheway lecture halls, the dreadful slow meals squirming on the hard chairs of restaurants, while his father and godfather talked about the reign of peace and brotherhood that would come to all creeds and conditions when mankind took heed of the words spoken in the East.

As if he had been following Jed's thought his father said, stopping at a corner to look into Jed's face: "Emmanuel I pray for you daily to the allwise Father of all men."

Jed had a tantalizing glimpse of the beach, tanned girls in bathsuits running along the edge of the scalloped spume who brought up a stinging memory of Marlowe's sunbrowned body and of the sweet morocco leather seabeach smell that lingered in Suite A, as, still the little obedient schoolboy who'd won all the prizes, his father's pride, always at the head of his class, he turned his back to the shore drive to follow J.E. into the gloom of the rooming house. It was with the pain remembered from boyhood, the feeling of being cramped into his father's dingy life, that he followed his father up the grimycarpeted stairs of the big old shingled mansion, bristling with turrets and baywindows, built by some rich man in the seventies.

J.E. unlocked his door and flattened himself against the wall, almost as a servant would, to let his son go in first. The smell of bayrum and shavingsoap and newsprint was so familiar Jed almost burst into tears.

"Always lock your door," J.E. was saying as he made sure the latch of the yale lock was set to close. "You never know who may have an interest in ransacking your papers."

"J.E. do you know what I'm going to do?" Jed mumbled through a yawn. "I'm going to lay down on your bed and take a nap."

It made his father happy to have his boy take a nap on his bed; Jed could see that through the blur of drowsiness.

"Meanwhile," J.E. was saying, "I'll sit up in the morrischair and read the Sunday papers. I save every clipping . . . We both, Jed," he added in a voice that quavered with the fear of giving offense, "know too much about how the theatrical page is set up to let ourselves be worried by what the critics say, now don't we? They are ignorant poor devils most of them. We must always remember, dear, there is no evil for those who believe in divine love."

He went on and on, as he'd been going on all these years; Jed didn't listen. He'd heard it before. Still he got a childish pleasure out of his father's soothing voice. He pulled off his jacket and necktie and crawled up on the old brass bed that jingled when he moved. In a moment he was asleep.

When he awoke the sky he saw through the baywindow was full of amberedged afternoon clouds. In a panic he reached for his watch. It was four o'clock. Time to catch the train. He sat up carefully on the edge of the bed so as not to jingle the springs.

His father had fallen into a doze in his morrischair with newspapers piled on his knees. As he sat fastening his shoelaces on the edge of the bed, Jed looked into J.E.'s tired old face with its green waxy skin so dark in the creases. His chin was sunk on his chest. J.E. was snoring very lightly. With his narrow head and lusterless dark hair he looked like a handsome old Indian. Thoughts of the loneliness and womanlessness of old age rushed through Jed's head, thoughts that made him feel ashamed, sinful somehow, like the sons of Noah who looked on their father's nakedness. When he got to his feet a board creaked on the floor and J.E. woke.

With an amused twinkle J.E.'s black eyes were looking into Jed's. "I know what you are going to say. You have to hurry back to the city on the four fortyseven. I was going to wake you because it's the only train. These theatrical managers lead busy lives . . . I'm going back to the city myself next week. I don't like leaving my files alone at the hotel. Of course they are quite reliable at the Great Western. They have known me so long but sometimes — you'll laugh at your poor old father — I think that man's operatives are trailing me. Just a mental aberration, that's what you'll say, the aberrations of old age. God keep you safe, dear."

When Jed found himself alone and out in the Atlantic air walking fast toward the station everything looked amusing again. The people on the street were funnypaper characters. He felt like a funnypaper character himself.

He walked fast with his hat in his hand. The salty seabreeze was cool in his hair. He felt rested from his nap. Having done his duty to J.E. had left a feeling of lightness in him.

Jed loved J.E. better than anybody in the world, he was telling himself, but being with him put him back into the straitjacket of childhood. Thank God he'd gotten over being a child. He was a man, he told himself as he looked out at the graygreen salt marshes sliding past the window

of the train. He was a man grown, with wives and con-
cubines and a little daughter; with his way to make; and
plays to write and a theatre to run.

He must get all that into the play. The bursting of that
straitjacket, the mastery of the environment. The man
who thought the great thoughts imposing them on all the
rest. He got out his notebook and started to cover page
after page with his rapid scrawl. By the time the train had
slid through the tunnel into the Penn Station he had a new
ending for the first act of *The Man Who Was Thursday*.
He rushed into a phone booth in the station and called
the theatre.

Nobody there yet.

He called Kenneth Magill's apartment. A marcelled
dramatic school voice answered. Was Kenneth there? "Oh
dear he's in his bath." It was Hugh Atwood. The broad
"a" irritated Jed so that he almost snapped at the mouth-
piece. "Shall I make him come all wet and drippy?"

"I got to speak to him. I've got a new finale to the first
act."

When Kenneth came to the phone panting and apologetic, Jed talked his ear off about the new finale. At first
Kenneth sounded doubtful. Jed explained it again, in words
of one syllable, he thought to himself; then suddenly Kenneth caught on. "Marvelous," he cried, "marvelous." His
high jaunty voice jangled the receiver. "Shoot it into me,
Jed old top. I'll call a rehearsal. We'll climax it by letting
him drop out of sight through a trapdoor. We must be
visual, you know. We'll make it . . . er . . . vibrate."

Newsreel

Jack o' Diamonds Jack o' Diamonds
You rob my pocket   of silver and gold

WITNESS OF MYSTERY IN SLUSH PROBE

PHILADELPHIAN BEATEN TO DEATH IN HIS ROOM

the men who the workers had been told a short year before were fighting their battle for democracy upon the bloodstained fields of France and whom they had been urged to support by giving the last of their strength to the work of production — these men were coming to teach them democracy and with them came their instruments of murder, their automatic rifles, their machineguns, their cannon that could clear a street two miles long in a few minutes and the helmets that the workers of Gary had produced

Yes we have no bananas
We have no bananas today

TRACTION RING KILLS BUS BILL

DRUNKEN TROOPS IN SKIRTS DANCE AS HOUSES BURN

GIRL SUICIDE WAS FRIEND OF OLIVE THOMAS

KILLS SELF DESPITE WIFE WHO GOES MAD

SEEKS FACTS OF HUNT FOR CASH IN THE EAST

the business consists in large part of financing manufacturers and merchants by purchasing evidences of indebtedness arising from the sale of a large variety of naturally marketed products such as automobiles, electrical appliances, machinery

The Moment of Choice

THE ROAD grew steeper as they wound up the mountain. There were patches of mist and, higher, the rain began to turn to sleet and to freeze on the windshield, so that Glenn had to lean forward over the wheel with his eyes screwed up as he drove, to try to see the curves. Even in low the motor of the old touringcar strained and knocked. Now and then he had to stop dead when his headlights flattened out suddenly in a wall of mist, and it was hard getting started again on account of the thin scrim of ice on the road. All the while he could hear Less Minot's hoarse voice beside him mumbling on and on about how this was a tough proposition they were going into, these here mountaineers would just as soon shoot a man as not. Warn't no more than taking a bite out of an apple. Suppose they missed the comrades who were going to meet them in the gap and rode right on into town and landed in the arms of the deputy sheriffs, that would be the end of the pair of them. At least they'd ought to had a couple drinks before they started. It was all right for the central committee sitting around with a map and a lot of mimeographed statistics in a nice warm office, but not one of those comrades understood what an organizer was up against in a proposition like this. "Sure they do, Less . . . Have a heart," Glenn said, without turning his head. "You're the toughest organizer the American Miners have got. Hell, their deputy sheriffs can't be any more dangerous than their mountain scenery."

Glenn's hands were icy in the wet cotton workgloves he was driving in. On one curve the car took a skid that brought his heart right up into his throat. He kept her in the road but couldn't get her started up the hill again until they had piled out to put stones behind the rear wheels. At last they were grinding along a straight gravelly level. "Less, I bet you we're up in the gap," said Glenn.

"Well, you needn't sound so cocky about it. How do we know some stoolpigeon ain't tipped off the company guards? A night like this you could shove the car and us in it out over the edge of one of them places and nobody'd be the wiser . . . By God, there's a light."

Ahead on the road there was a dim red glow. Glenn put his foot on the brakes and the car slewed around. He pressed on the gas to give headway to the spinning wheels and managed to bring her to a stop sideways across the road with the front fender dug into a glistening claybank.

"Whoa there," came a voice. Somebody was holding up the lantern and peering into the car.

Less Minot was out on his feet in a second and his voice was firm and hearty. "Who are you expectin?"

"Brothers," came the voice.

"I'm Less Minot, are you Joe Kusick?"

"Sure; glad to meet you, brothers. This here's Pearl Napier. He's secretary to the Muddy Fork local . . . Well, you made it right on the dot, boys, we sure didn't expect to see yous this night."

Glenn was leaning out from the car straining his eyes to see. He could make out the red outline of the flame in the lantern and two white faces, one very young and smooth, and one wrinkled and lopsided. "Meet Comrade Crockett, Sandy Crockett," said Less. "He's an eddicated feller but I'd trust him before I'd trust most people."

Glenn wasn't quite used to his Party name yet, so he hesitated a moment before he stuck out his hand. Two hard hands gripped it in turn. "Say, brothers," he said, "give me a hand to push us back on the road, will you?" They jumped at the car and lifted the front axle right off the ground. "Thataboy," said Glenn, laughing. "Gosh, you fellers are hefty." They were all laughing, silly with relief.

"Don't you fellers want to ride?" "No, we'll walk ahead with the lantern to show you the way. Hit's hard to find," said the younger man. "Hit's good you boys came. Half the brothers was sayin you dassent."

"Why?"

"Hit's a rough country acrost this here gap."

"Well, we been in some tough spots before up in the Pittsburgh district, ain't that so, Sandy?" bawled Less in his deep voice.

"Did you bring plenty litrachur?" asked the younger man.

"Sure, the whole car's stacked with it."

"The boys is hongry for it."

Driving slowly in low Glenn followed the swinging lantern down the road. After the first bend the men struck off down a steep deeprutted wagontrail. "Do you think we can make it?" whispered Less nervously. "Sure," said Glenn. "Gee, I like those guys."

At the bottom of the gulch they had to ford a stony creek and almost stuck. The car charged out the other side with the motor sputtering. The headlights cut out a rail fence against the mist and two black figures leaning over to take down the rails to let the car through. Then Glenn was driving over the grassy ridges of what had once been a cornfield, towards the faintly lit blur of a window.

He stopped the car and turned off the switch and the lights and followed the others round the edge of a shack. He could smell woods and there was the warm sweet reek of a cowbarn and the sound of something fourlegged treading on cornstalks.

Then he was stepping through a low doorway into a room full of white faces outlined with coaldust lit by yellow flame from a softcoal fire in a grate under a toppling stone chimney. "Comrades and brothers," said Less in his deep voice. "We bring you the greetings of the American Miners' Union."

"Oh boy," whispered Glenn as he brushed past Less, pulling off his wet gloves, "let me at that fire." Pearl Napier followed him and put his arm round Glenn's shoulders as he stood opening and closing his hands in front of the flames to get the blood back into his fingers. "We was fixin to have somethin hot for you all to eat," he whispered in Glenn's ear in his slow, serious voice, "but we just ain't got nothin, that's all. We been livin on the mercy of the people sence we started this here strike . . . Joe Kusick, he's got a lil store, he'll feed ye up strong when he carries you all down there tomorrow."

Less and Joe Kusick were already getting down to business, sitting on two stools in the middle of the room, while the miners round the walls watched them silently. The black dust in their eyelashes and eyebrows and in the hollows of their cheeks gave them the look of being made up for the stage. Sure, Joe Kusick was explaining, they'd oughta waited till they got their charter to pull out Muddy Fork but the boys was right mad since the company had brought in them gunthugs swaggering around and treating themselves to the best of everything and the boys swore they warn't going to wait for no charter, and now everything was ready to pull out Slade's Knob at the break of day. "Jesus Christ, you don't need no agitators in this neck of the woods," roared out Less. "What you boys need is moderators."

"Our agitators is honger an the flux an High Sheriff Blaine," said a solemnvoiced, bent old man who'd just come in the door of the cabin. "Amen," said the miners along the walls. As the old man turned to bolt the door behind him Glenn saw that he had a gun slung over his back. "Amen to that, Pappy," said Pearl. "But ain't you posted for sentry?"

The old man walked slowly over to the chimney and hung up his gun on a hook. "There won't none of Caleb Blaine's gunthugs dast come out this night," he said. "I want to listen to the meetin."

Less got to his feet and said he had the charters right out in the car and asked Glenn to go out and bring in his satchel. Somewhere in the dark end of the cabin a child had begun to cry.

Outside the night was full of driving sleety rain. Glenn found Less's satchel and grabbed an old piece of canvas out from under the seat to throw over the hood of the car to keep the ignition from getting wet. When he got back in the cabin Pearl was on his feet saying that as elected secretary of this here Muddy Fork local of the American Miners he moved this here assembly be duly constituted a meeting in accordance with the constitution and bylaws and he was going to give the floor to brother Minot, but first he wanted Pappy to say a few words of prayer. "Amen," said the miners round the walls.

The old man straightened up and stood with his back to the fire with his two hands lifted above his head. "O Lawd . . ." he began, his voice a deep rattle in his throat. A barefoot girl in a torn cotton skirt with her hair in a tangle over her face pushed her way out from behind the men. She was carrying a crying baby wrapped in a torn piece of patchwork quilt. She crossed the shaky boards of the floor with two long strides and crouched on her heels in front of the fire. The baby's cries died into a choking whimper. "Can't you make it hush, Wheatly?" whispered the old man, letting his hands with their bent knobbed fingers drop to his sides. "Hit's cold and hongry. Mom said she ain't got no milk for it."

"Hain't you got no sugartit, Wheatly?"

The girl's eyes flashed black under their tangle of hair that the firelight edged with gold fuzz. "Pappy, you know we ain't had no sweetenin in this house since they won't let us go to the store."

"Hush it as well as you can, Wheatly," said the old man wearily. The girl let her head drop and began to rock the child, moving her whole body from her hips. "Oh Lawd," the rumbling voice started again, "bless this here house and this here meetin of the 'Merican Miners like you blessed the Mineworkers in the old days before them organizers got to be traitors an scallywags an sold us out to the opressors . . . O Lawd, we need bread an meat an clothin for our children, that's terrible sick of the flux an can't sleep because they's so cold an hongry, an can't go to school to learn to be good citizens because they's so naked, an they's likely to grow up the worst trash is ever been seen in these mountains. O Lawd, the operators an Miss Nancy Pringle the postmistress, who gits the Red Cross relief an keeps it all to herself, tries to tell us hit's sinful to jine the union an that the 'Merican Miners is the sinfullest antichrists an rednecks in these mountains; but ain't it true, Lawd, that poverty and wrechedness is the highroad to sin and damnation? An in the old days of the Mineworkers we used to make a livin in these mountains an now the coal operators won't let us live and has sent in foreigners and gunthugs to oppress us an Caleb Blaine, that we went down to the polls to elect for sheriff, has hardened his heart against us, an he won't never git another miner's vote in these mountains . . ." "Amen to that," shouted the miners round the walls.

The old man lifted his shaky hand for silence and went on, his voice filling the cabin. "An ain't it gospel true, O Lawd, that if the 'Merican Miners was red Rooshians or the devil hisself, we'd do right to jine with them to git food for our chillun, an stand up agin the oppression of the Law with our guns in our hands, because nobody else in this world's ever come forward to help us . . . An, O Lawd, set thy blessin upon this meetin." As the miners roared "Amen," Glenn untied a bundle of newspapers and handed them around. The miners stood holding the papers reverently in front of them. The thought flashed across the back of Glenn's head somewhere that it was like handing out hymnbooks at a revival meeting.

Less Minot got up and said that the American Miners was affiliated with organizations all over the country that was working to overthrow the rotten capitalistic system that kept the working class down to starvation wages with guns and grafting officers of the law, and that if that was being a red he was glad to be called a red, and as for the Rooshians, he didn't know much about them, but so far as he could hear tell the working class had overthrown its capitalistic oppressors over there under the leadership of the Marxist-Leninist Comunist Party and was running the country in their own interests and was ready to help the workers in other countries to do the same.

Then Glenn told about the soupkitchens the American Miners were going to organize and how the Workers' Defense was already shipping in clothes and flour and groceries with a girl comrade, Jane Sparling, who was a doctor and who'd tend the sick and ailing children as long as the strike lasted.

Then Pearl Napier stepped into the center of the floor and said, "Brothers, I ain't much a one to break down an cry, but I tell you brothers I was all broke up with thanksgivin when I stood up in that gap in the rain an the sleet an saw the lights of that automobile an knowed that these here brothers, or comrades like they say, had come away from their homes an their families an given up their jobs if they had 'em, to come an help us poor people up here in these mountains. Now don't let 'em tell you that these boys is furreners. When you're facin the coal they ain't no furreners in the mine, only your buddy by your side. Now we're facin High Sheriff Blaine an the Slade County Coal Operators' Association an there ain't no furreners 'xcep the gunthugs that wants to kill us. I vote the meetin's adjourned with heartfelt thanks to Comrade Minot and Comrade Crockett. All in favor say Aye."

While the miners were crowding round Glenn and Less to shake hands, Joe Kusick said boys, hadn't they better get a couple of winks of sleep because they was going to march before day while the gunthugs was all asleep drunk in their beds in the Appalachian Hotel down to McCreary. Pearl Napier came back from the dark end of the cabin and whispered in Glenn's ear he'd have to apologize they didn't have no bed to offer them; the old woman was mighty poorly and she and the children was asleeping in the bed, but he reckoned he could scare up a coverlet and they'd be right warm in front of the chimbley.

As the men settled themselves to sleep in a row across the floor, Glenn noticed that some didn't have any shirts on under the old army tunics shiny with grime most of them wore. He and Less wouldn't take the clean patchwork quilt Pearl brought them but said to lay it over the children who must need it.

They took off their shoes and put them on the stone hearth to dry and stretched out side by side in the place the others left for them nearest the fire. When the cabin had quieted down to the heavy breathing and snoring of crowded sleepers Less began to whisper in Glenn's ear that Jesus Christ, if they marched on Slade's Knob it would be a massacre, but they were in for it now, there was no holding them back. For one thing it was up to Glenn to see the miners didn't carry their guns, because there'd be shooting sure as fate, and if the miners shot back the Governor would have in the militia and the strike would turn into a lockout before they could get any locals organized and they might as well have stayed home. Glenn said sure, he'd talk to Pearl about it as soon as he woke up, and lay back with his head on his arm and closed his eyes.

He couldn't sleep. He lay on his back staring at the flicker of the firelight among the cobwebs that hung looped from the rafters overhead. Cold spurts of wind came in through the chinks in the boards under his back. Excitement made his heart thump and made the skin round his eyes feel tight; his face had a scalded feeling from the long drive through the winddriven rain. The baby cried at intervals all night and the girl walked back and forth, stepping across the sleepers with her long barefooted stride, rocking it as she went. Glenn watched her through halfclosed eyes. When she leaned over with the child on one hip, to put a fresh hunk of soft coal on the fire, he could see the points of her firm breasts and the flat curves of her belly and thighs through her skimpy rumpled dress. He had a pitiful tender feeling as he watched her, as if he'd known these people in this shack in these mountains all his life. He thought of the other shacks in these mountains and the crowded rooms in slums, and working people asleep in shacks and crowded barracks all over the world. Now he was one of them for keeps, part of them, like a povertystricken kid asleep in bed with his brothers and sisters.

The noise of men shuffling about and talking hoarsely woke him. The rain and wind had stopped, but mist sagged like a blob of wet cotton in through the door of the shack whenever it was opened. Somebody had brought in a bucket of cold water with a dipper in it; that seemed to be all the breakfast there was.

Glenn was stamping around outside the cabin, tightening his belt after he'd taken a leak, when he bumped into Less Minot. "Say, Less, oughtn't I go on this march?"

"Nuttin doin, Sandy," Less said, "Your business is soup-kitchens. You go down and see what you can do with Mrs. Kusick. We got to have somepin for these guys to eat when they're through marchin. Then we'll have a big organiza-tion meetin down to Bull Crik. Jane's comin up to Kusick's from McCreary today. You got to be there to make contact, see . . . Hell, I wouldn't march myself except the boys ud think I was a yellowbelly if I didn't." Less's voice dropped to a shaky whisper. "If they get me, Sandy, you'll go see the old woman, won't you, Sandy? . . . And git up a fund so's she can buy a little house or somepin."

"Less, there's nothing going to happen."

"Who said there warn't? This here operators' association means business, I tell you . . . What about the guns?"

"Pearl's talking to the boys about 'em now. He's going to make 'em put away every gun they got."

"That's the stuff. I wanted it to come from you and not from me, see. Pearl's a smart kid . . . there's a firstclass workin'class leader in that boy if the bosses don't git him."

"How would they?"

"Jesus Christ, man, they shoot to kill around here, and then there's other ways: jail, money, a woman, a good job, liquor. I seen so many of 'em go to hell. Well, so long, Sandy, it's got to come sometime . . . I'll carry the flag, God damn it." He grabbed Glenn's hand and shook it. Glenn was surprised that Less's hand was cold and sweaty and trembling.

The miners faded off into the mist that was beginning to churn overhead with faint rosy light. Everything was suddenly very quiet. Old Napier had led a skinny swaybacked cow out of the cowshed and was standing in front of the cabin waiting. The cow had a halter around her neck and stood placidly moving her lower jaw from side to side. Old Napier said he was going past Joe Kusick's place and would carry Glenn on down there. First Glenn put the car in the cowbarn that was still sweetly steamy with the cow's warmth, and closed the door on it. He asked old Napier if the kids would keep their mouths shut about its being there. They wouldn't talk to nobody but their own folks, not if they was Napiers, old Napier answered proudly.

They started down the slippery path that zigzagged between brokendown rail fences into the valley. They had to hop from side to side to avoid the little clear stream that ran down the middle of it. Glenn asked old Napier where he was taking the cow and the old man said he reckoned he was going to sell her, she didn't give no milk no more, too bad after they'd fed her corn all winter, but he had to do something to even up his store account.

They came out on a rough macadam road winding up the side of the mountain and turned down it. The mist was beginning to lift from the valley floor. It was almost day. Old Napier pointed with a crooked forefinger to where the railroad curved through the valley in front of the black hunched buildings and inclined trestles of a mine. "Look yonder," he said.

A piece of wet road caught the light where it curved up over a clay hill beside the tipple. Up the road moved a black crawling mass of men marching. At the head of it fluttered a tiny pink and white patch. "Yonder's the flag." Glenn and old Napier stood still in their tracks watching the mass move up the hill, blotting out the wet gleam of the road. Then the flag dipped out of sight over the ridge of the hill.

Glenn's tongue was dry in his mouth. A long freight pulled by two engines slowly puffing white steam was toiling up the line on the valleyfloor. They started walking again with the cow ambling behind them.

At the next curve the mine was hidden by the wooded flank of a hill already sifted over with spring greens. "Hit's been a hongry winter," said old Napier, shaking his head.

Where the road came out onto the highway beside the railroad tracks, there was a small unpainted clapboard store plastered with Moxie and Coca-Cola and Chicken Dinner signs. A stumpy grayhaired woman stood in the door with her hands in the pockets of her apron looking fixedly down the empty highroad towards Slade's Knob. "Ella," said old Napier, "this here's the furrener Joe said to carry down to you all . . . I'll be on my way."

The woman's brown eyes, set in a mass of little wrinkles, searched Glenn's face. "So you've come here to help these poor creatures? I don't know where you've come from or why you done it, but come inside . . . I'm crazy worried about Joe. He told me he wouldn't go with that march, and now he's gone and done it. I thought I heard shootin while ago. Right now I'm goin to show you a place to hide in case the Law comes along because if they find what they call a foreign agitator here, there's goin to be trouble."

Talking his ear off all the time she showed Glenn how to climb on a packingcase in the middle of the little dark storeroom that opened back of the counter and to push up a trapdoor that led up into the loft overhead. Then she asked him if he'd had anything to eat that day. Glenn said he was about starved.

She took him in the kitchen in back, that was hot from the roaring range, and fried him up some fat bacon and brought some hot biscuits out of the oven and some weak coffee off the back of the stove, all the time telling about how there'd been a time when her and Joe lived pretty well, but now nobody could pay their store account, and the companies made the poor creatures trade at the commissaries, charging thirty per cent more than the ordinary store prices, and if her and Joe did scrape up a little something to eat, Joe gave it away to those poor creatures. What folks didn't know outside was that the poor creatures in these mountains was hongry and it was right pitiful the way the little children died with the flux and the lack of proper feeding.

Glenn sat there, eating away on the biscuits and bacon-grease, feeling like a pig to be eating so much. As she talked Mrs. Kusick kept watch down the road out of the back window. Suddenly she said, "You git up there quick, here comes a carful o' Law." With his mouth still full Glenn shot into the storeroom and up through the trapdoor and into the little loft that was piled with woodshavings the carpenters had left. He lay out flat across the rafters and tried not to breathe.

From below he could hear Mrs. Kusick making a great clatter with her dishes in the kitchen sink. Then he heard a car stop with a screech of brakes outside the store, and heavy steps and voices. Somebody was grumbling hoarsely that there'd been trouble up to Slade's Knob and some of those damn hotheads from Sladetown had gotten in the way of some lead slugs. Glenn could hear Mrs. Kusick's voice pipe up shakily to ask if Joe was all right. He was all right now but he sure wouldn't be for long if he didn't keep his nose out of all this sedition and conspiracy, answered the other voice gruffly. Why didn't Joe mind his own business?

Mrs. Kusick quavered that there warn't no business to mind, the poor creatures didn't have no money to spend no more, that was the trouble with this country, Sheriff Blaine. These here Jew agitators from New York must think they got some money yet, roared the sheriff's voice, because they was two of them come over the gap last night. He said he had a mind to search the premises. Mrs. Kusick's voice rose shrill. "Caleb Blaine, you ain't got no warrant . . . you can't search my place without a warrant."

There followed confused angry talking and heavy boots tramping and Mrs. Kusick's voice in a shriek. "The first sonofabitch steps into my kitchen I'll scald him with the teakettle, by God and by Jesus I will."

There was a pause. The sheriff's voice rose in a pacifying tone saying he guessed her and Joe must have liquor stowed away somewhere, and other voices laughed and the car drove off down the road.

Glenn lay there for a while and then he pulled up the trapdoor and peeked down. "You kin come down now, they won't be back," Mrs. Kusick said in a shaky whisper. "They're off for McCreary to the grand jury to swear out warrants hellbent for election." Glenn let himself drop to the floor and stood in the kitchen brushing the dust and shavings off his clothes. "I reckon I kinder forgot to talk like a lady but Caleb Blaine makes me so goddam mad apokin his dirty face into my kitchen. I wisht I'd ascalded it. I'd ascalded it plenty if he'd taken one step further, I wouldn't acared if they'd sent me to the chair. That low-down lowtalkin ole piece of nothin. Warn't so long ago he was hangin around here tryin to git him a job tendin store. That was before he got in with the Operators' Association and messed in county politics. Well, if you heard me not talkin quite ladylike I sure must apologize."

At that moment a truck stopped in front of the door and Glenn, peering nervously out over the counter, saw Jane Sparling jump out from the front seat. She was wearing a print dress like the miners' wives wore, with a motheaten fur coat over it. "Where's the American Miners' soup-kitchen?" she asked. "Hello, Sandy." She strode in the door in her jaunty flatfooted way.

"Mrs. Kusick, this is Dr. Sparling from the workers' relief. She's come up with some food and she's got some funds." Mrs. Kusick looked Jane up and down with her small sharp eyes. Jane walked up to Glenn and asked again, pushing her untidy graying hair back under her hat with her big hand, well, where was the soupkitchen, the truck-driver was in a hurry to unload and get out of here, he seemed scared to death about something, what was the trouble, she couldn't see anything to worry about.

Glenn had a time convincing Mrs. Kusick that Joe had said they could use the brokendown cabin on the lot behind the store for a soupkitchen. They backed the truck up there over the soft grass and unloaded the crates of groceries; as soon as Jane paid the colored man who drove it, he was off in a hurry.

When Glenn could get a word with Jane out of earshot of Mrs. Kusick he said severely, "Jane, please remember Less and I are underground. You don't know us any more than any other union members. There's the worst reign of terror here you ever saw."

"Well, I don't see anything to be scared of," said Jane, lighting a cigarette. "If you can get me a stove you can have about ten gallons of nourishing soup to distribute by noon. That's more useful than conspiratorial monkeyshines."

Joe Kusick came back walking alone down the road from

Slade's Knob with his whole lopsided face wrinkled up in a
frown. Things was bad. They'd shot two boys dead and
wounded some more, but the mine was out all right. Hadn't
nobody gone to work on the morning shift but the superintendent and a half a dozen niggers.

Joe knew where there was an old cookstove and sent a
couple of miners, who were standing around waiting for
something to do, over to get it. They got some boards and
a hammer and nails and by noon they had a counter and
some long tables fixed up and had propped up the walls of
the old shack and were on the roof patching up the gaps
in the curly chestnut shingles. Jane had tied an apron
around her rawboned hips and had a big washboiler of
soup started while daylight was still coming in through the
roof overhead.

Glenn was at work handing up shingles while Joe Kusick
tacked them down, when somebody tapped him on the
back. It was Pearl Napier who made a gesture with his
thumb over his shoulder and walked away fast. Glenn followed him. "Hit's Less," Pearl said as he leaned over to
crank a rusty Model T Ford without any top parked beside
the store. "You an him's got to meet some feller from the
higher degrees . . . Say, how deep are you in this business?"

Glenn grinned and said, all the way, he guessed.

"Me too," said Pearl. "I'm in up to my neck."

As he drove Glenn down the main road towards McCreary
he talked about the union, he said this here shooting this
morning would bring the whole county out, the miners up
in these mountains was sick and tired of being herded like
cattle and shot down like niggers, this would bring them
out all right. Now if they could have the right kind of support from the outside, food to keep the chillun from dying
like they was and litrachur to eddicate the boys up a little,
they'd have the grandest union in Slade County that had
ever been seen in the minefields; but right now there wasn't
a miner's shack in these mountains where they had a cup of
flour from one day to the next, most of them was living
on the mercy of the people. They had to have help from
a national organization.

"Well, that's what Less and Comrade Sparling and I are
here for. We bring you the support not only of a national
but of an international organization." "Hot damn," said

Pearl. "You and me sure is goin to be buddies, Sandy."

They were driving down the valley, crossing and recrossing the great loops of the coffeecolored river, through meadows and patches of red plowedland, past barns and white farmhouses with fruittrees in bloom around them. Then they went under the tipple of another mine and came out among the crowded rows of little unpainted shacks set on stilts of a coaltown. The car rattled over the cobbles past a fillingstation and a couple of brickfront stores and stopped in front of a frame building with staring black windows. Over the door the words ROOMS barely showed through the grime on a cracked electric globe.

They got out of the car, gave a quick look up and down the street, where the wind was blowing little whirlwinds of black dust, already dried out by the hot spring sun, between rows of weatherbeaten parked cars. Nobody seemed to be watching them, so they went in the house. Pearl led the way up a back stairway and knocked on a door with a white enamelled number eight on it. Less Minot's voice said, "Come in," and Pearl slipped away saying he'd be back presently.

Less and Irving Silverstone were sitting on the rickety iron bed with a satchelful of papers between them. A tall welldressed redfaced man in a tweed cap was walking up and down the room. "Comrade Crockett, meet Comrade Stong, he's getting the story for the party press. Also he makes the report," said Irving in a cold voice without getting to his feet.

Irving was stouter than when Glenn had last seen him. He still wore his hair cropped close and his goldrimmed tortoiseshell spectacles. There was more authority in his manner and he had a way of lifting his forefinger when he spoke.

"Well, soupkitchen number one is started," said Glenn, squeezing in beside Less on the bed. "And there won't be a load o' coal goin out of the county by the end of the week," added Less, pushing his thick grizzled hair, that grew low in a thick cowlick on his forehead, back with a stubby hand.

"I'm staying here," Irving said. "Stong's going back tomorrow. Now the first thing I want to bring up is this O.B.U. local. These workers they killed belonged to their bunch."

"Well, they're from Sladetown. The Sladetown local seems to be joiners," drawled Less. "They're an old Mineworkers' outfit. Then they took out an O.B.U. charter and now they've asked us for a charter too . . . Those boys want action."

"Politically immature."

"I guess so . . . I been talkin to 'em about mass pressure and all that all mornin," said Less, "but they're all so mad they can't see straight."

"We've got to put on a meeting to show them what mass pressure looks like," said Glenn.

Irving got to his feet suddenly and walked up and down with pursed lips. "Here we have a chance to organize a group of absolutely untouched militant American workers. It's the start of a series of real revolutionary industrial unions. These miners drink the class struggle with their mother's milk." Irving threw his head back and looked from one face to another.

"That's about all the kids get these days," said Less, looking at his feet. "They are great boys, but it takes a treasury to win a strike . . . What will the Party do to back us up?"

"We organize the whole Appalachian coalfield into one great union. Why not?" Irving let his voice ring out.

"You tell us," said Less sullenly, sitting with his broad shoulders hunched over his chest and his short legs apart. "The O.B.U. boys are militant as hell."

"As district organizer," said Irving, in precise tones, "it's up to you to bring them in."

"Well," said Glenn soothingly, "is it all set about the meeting at Bull Creek Sunday?"

"Suppose they shoot it up?" asked Less.

"We rouse the liberal elements all over the country." Irving lifted his finger to the level of his glasses as he spoke.

"Sure," drawled Glenn. "Free Speech, Freedom of Assembly, the U.S. Constitution suspended in Slade County . . . We ought even get a decent play in the capitalist press."

"The O.B.U. confuses all the issues . . . Outworn opportunism." Irving began to pace up and down the narrow room.

"As a national organization they don't amount to a hill of beans," said Less. "But the boys are all right."

There was a knock on the door. Irving walked over to

the window with his hands in his pockets. "Who is it?" growled Less. "Hit's me," came Pearl Napier's voice. Glenn opened the door.

"Well, comrades," said Pearl as he stepped into the room. "Cornorer's jury asettin on those two boys found person or persons unknown . . . They found they was atrespassin on company property and didn't make no recommendations to the grand jury."

"Gosh, they didn't lose any time about it, did they?"

"Coal Operators' Association don't lose no time."

"Well, we were just talkin about the big protest meetin we're goin to have up to Bull Crik Sunday, they can't stop that without infringin our constitutional rights," said Less.

"They can't stop us from buryin our brothers," said Pearl.

"That's it," said Irving, coming back suddenly from the window. "A mass funeral for the two classwar victims."

"Look, brothers," said Pearl, drawing Less and Glenn over to the window that looked out on a roundhouse and the rows and rows of tracks of the trainyard. "See them coal cars. They're empty. If they was aworkin up the valley, they'd be acomin down full . . . Them empty gondolas says more'n the best kind o' speakin."

Next Sunday turned out to be a sunny spring day. Glenn was so busy fixing in his mind what he was going to say to the miners when his turn came to speak that he hardly knew what was going on all morning. Birds were singing in the red swampmaples back of the Bull Creek Missionary Baptist Church. The Reverend McDonnell, a tall man with sunken eyes under thick black brows, who'd been a miner himself when he was younger, read the service over the two pine coffins in the church. Meanwhile miners kept coming; men and boys in carefully brushed clothes and clean shirts frayed by much scrubbing, and their wives and little girls in starched threadbare cotton dresses, piling out of old crowded Fords and Chevvies or walking in long silent straggles up the road or down the footpath that curved over the brow of the hill past the minetipple. The crowd got so big Less decided they'd have to conduct the speaking outside the church; so Pearl and the boys from the Muddy Fork local, all in their best clothes and wearing red armbands, started to build a speakers' stand on four flourbarrels. Meanwhile people kept coming until the whole grassy space between the ranked parked cars and the little pointed white church, that the paint had almost worn off of, was mottled black and white with a tense closepacked quiet crowd.

Pearl's boys with the armbands kept a lane open to the church porch that had a little crooked steeple over it where swallows had built their nests. All through the services the swallows kept up a great twittering, flying in and out. After the services the boys carried the coffins up into the graveyard that was in a grove of great dead silverybranched trees that had once been chestnuts. The thin voices singing "Nearer, my God, to Thee" as they lowered the coffins into the graves had hardly died away when the first speaker started exhorting from the stand in front of the church. It was old Napier who got up to say he'd been a voter in this country for fifty-seven years and a Republican, but he felt he had to say that these terrible things that was happening in this country and no one putting out a hand to help the poor people of these mountains from the terror of the gunthugs had made a Democrat out of him.

Then a tall man who stamped back and forth so hard he almost brought down the flimsy platform gave a hellroaring talk, making his points by thumping his right fist into his left hand saying he'd been a miner thirtythree years and things had gotten worse instead of better, and now with these here hellbound criminal syndicalist laws a man didn't even have no right to complain of his condition. If things went on the time would come when a man would have to go out with a gun to rob and murder and steal to keep his children from starving. And, if they wanted to know, he loved the flag of the United States of America and he loved our government, if it was handled right, but he loved his children ten thousand times better than he loved the President of the United States or the High Sheriff of Slade County. The coal operators said that was being a Rooshian red; maybe they was right but to his way of thinking a man who wouldn't stand by his children was worse than an infidel.

Pearl, who was chairman, sang out he couldn't imagine why it was they called us poor miners reds and rednecks unless it was because we was so thin living on pinto beans and bulldawg gravy that if you set one of us up against the sun you could see daylight right through him. And as for him and his folks, pappy, grandpap and greatgrandpap, they'd been in these mountains so long, longer than these here coaloperators who was foreigners nobody knowed where they'd come from, that if you went fur enough back you'd mebbe find some Cherokee injun blood, and that was red all right. Then he called on Glenn. "Comrade Sandy Crockett who risked his skin to come up outa Pennsylvania into these mountains and help organize us poor sinners before we starve to death aworkin for coallight and carbide."

Glenn climbed up on the stand and looked around at the closepacked lean gray faces eagerly strained to listen that filled the space in front of the church. At the edge of the crowd he noticed a shiny new touringcar with the top down full of prosperouslooking men in felt hats. Beside it stood a thin man in black with a notebook and pencil taking everything down. Out of the corner of his eye he noticed other burly figures with bulging hips skulking about the outskirts of the crowd. He felt a funny taste like iron in his mouth. He took a deep breath and began to talk.

The one way the working people of this country, he said, could make it so that their friends and brothers who'd been shot down for standing up for their rights as citizens hadn't died in vain was to organize solidly, he didn't mean only coalminers but all the workers . . . He was talking slowly. He could feel the people listening; his voice seemed to fill the quiet sunny afternoon, the little graywhite weathered church and the graveyard with the gaunt branches of the dead tree spreading over it, and to surge over the patch of scraggly woods and beat against the black tipple of the Bull Creek mine and the ruddy mountains patched with sprouting green beyond. His words soared easily and hovered in the sunlight and the quiet over the big listening crowd. His body felt easily balanced on the balls of his feet so that he could hardly feel the shaky boards of the speakers' stand. They were listening to every word. When he paused there was a roar of cheering and clapping. He was through.

Less grabbed him by the arm as he climbed down from the stand and hauled him around the corner of the church. "Sandy, you and Pearl git . . . Carry as many of the Muddy Fork boys as you kin with you . . . There's two carloads of deputies down the road. We got to handle this right or we'll have a fight. The reason you boys got to go is the C. C.

Johnson Company up to Muddy Fork is ready to sign up with the union. You got to be there to see they don't put nothin over on the boys."

"But I don't like to pull out now."

"Ain't no two ways about it." Less climbed on the platform and took over the chair from Pearl and introduced the Reverend James Breckenridge, an Episcopal bishop interested in social conditions and the criminal syndicalism laws. The bishop was a grayhaired man in knickerbockers and golfstockings who started to speak in a smooth easy voice. To hear him carried Glenn back to chapel at college; no, nothing could happen while the bishop was there.

Pearl was puzzled but he said he reckoned old Less knowed what was what. They got together four boys from the local and his sister Wheatly, who looked very pretty in a green wash dress with her reddish brown hair combed back from her forehead and neatly plaited in a pigtail down her back. As they got into the car the boys took off their armbands and tucked them under the seats.

Down the road in front of the mine they passed three carloads of deputies who stared hard in their faces. No guns were showing. The deputies stared and the miners stared back without a word. After they had gotten past them Pearl said he'd regret it till his dying day if it came to a shooting and here he'd run off home.

Glenn said he'd guarantee old Less could handle the situation, he had the coolest head in a pinch of any man he'd ever known, and the most important thing now was for the Muddy Fork local to sign the contract and get to work. That would make it hard for the Operators' Association to keep the small mines in line. That would be the first victory of the American Miners in these mountains. "Anyways," said Pearl, smiling, "you all kin spend the night at my house an Wheatly too. Hit'll be too late for her to go on up to Pappy's."

Halfway up the valley they got a flat and had to pile out on the side of the road to fix the puncture in the inner tube with one of the patches Pearl carried in a little tin box in his back pocket, so it was dark before they got to Muddy Creek village, which was a square of company houses down in the gulch just below old Napier's cabin where Glenn had slept the first night after coming over the gap. They crossed the swollen creek, full of fast brown water from melting snow over the mountains, on a narrow swinging footbridge. In the moist air of the deep gulch the coalsmoke of the fires hung low about the little ramshackle cabins set on stilts.

Pearl's was the first cabin they came to. Glenn noticed as they stepped on the porch that the creaky floor had been repaired with fresh lumber. Two skinny towheaded kids, with puffed bellies sticking out from under their grimy little shirts, ran to meet them in the doorway, and Pearl picked up one in each arm and carried them into the house with him. Glenn and Wheatly and two of the boys who had driven back with them followed him in.

"Jessie," Pearl said to his wife, tall skinny girl with pouches under her blue eyes, who came to meet them wiping her hands on her apron that bulged ahead of her very big with child, "this here's Brother Crockett, or Comrade Crockett like we say now. Sence the way he's acted and the way he talked at Bull Crik this afternoon, he's a big man in these mountains."

"Was there any shootin?" asked the girl in a flat whining voice. The men all shook their heads. The girl turned back to stirring something in a saucepan on the edge of the little grate. "I can't seem to git these beans soft," she said peevishly. "Well, let's eat," said Pearl. "I'm hongry."

The two men who had come in with them said goodnight and went out. Jessie brought out three tin plates and two bent spoons and a fork and Glenn and Pearl and Wheatly sat on a rough bench in front of the fire eating the beans. Pearl and Wheatly had pulled their shoes off, and as they ate were toasting their feet, grimed with coaldust where they were chapped round the ankles, at the fire. Meanwhile Jessie shuffled around the cabin trying to get the children to bed.

Glenn asked her if she'd eaten. She said yes, she'd eat bakersbread and 'vaporated milk with the children, Miss Sparling had brung it around, she sure was a nice lady, she'd brung some to every house and said she was going to organize the women in a ladies' auxiliary to the union, and she thought it was wonderful getting the women together, because they suffered more'n the men did from conditions in these coalcamps, seeing their children blue with cold and without no shoes to go to school in. Wheatly looked up with a black flash of her eyes and said women and children had been a drag on men sence time began, by God she wisht she was a man. "Wait till you git gone on one of these boys around here," said Jessie. "You'll be right glad you're a girl." "Suppose I am. Don't do me no good," said Wheatly, her face turning red in the firelight. "My, you look pretty when you blush like that," said Glenn. Wheatly started to giggle and ran out the door.

Pearl set down his plate and took a dipper of water from the bucket and said well, the first thing he was going to do when they'd signed that contract with Mr. Johnson and was getting some money payday was buy him a shotgun so's he could go hunting. They'd fared right well, hadn't they, Jessie, when he'd had his gun and been able to buy shells and bring home a rabbit or a fat possum sometimes. Even if he could clear a dollar a day it would be something, he knowed conditions was bad all over the country and operators warn't making no prices for their coal, but now that they had the union, they'd see they had to let the miners live. Next thing he'd like to get him some kind of little old car, that old flivver belonged to Joe Kusick who let him run it on account of the union, poor ole Joe, he just had to be interested in the union because the miners owed him so much on their store accounts that they just had to have wages to pay him back. "I been a workin man all my life. I git to feel ornery jus hangin around."

"Hain't it work organizin the union?" asked Wheatly, sticking her head in the cabin door.

"Not like cuttin coal."

"Hit's a blame sight more risky," saia Wheatly.

"How old were you when you first went to work in a mine, Pearl?" Glenn asked.

"Nine years old."

"How old are you now?"

"I'm acomin on twentyone, ain't I, Jessie?"

"That's what they tell me," said Jessie. "Pearl's a year and two months older'n me."

"And you got two kids?"

"An' one acomin," said Pearl.

"Gosh," said Glenn. "I'm twentyeight and I'm not even married yet." "You better git busy," said Pearl, laughing. "Up in these mountains we don't have nothin to do but work and git chillun. Do we, Jessie?" Pearl stretched out his arm to grab Jessie around the waist but she slipped away from him and went into the end of the cabin where the whimpering of the children in the bed had risen to a choking yell.

Pearl stood up in front of the fire and stretched himself and yawned. "Sandy, if you and Wheatly was married, we could let you an her have the other bed, but thisaway she got to sleep with Jessie an the chillun. I guess me an you won't fight if we sleep in the narrow bed. Hit's got clean cornshucks in the tickin'. I fixed it myself for Jessie when she was sick."

Glenn stepped outside. Except for the swashing clatter of the creek the valley was dark and quiet. A little piece of moon was shining over the rim of the steep hill opposite through the stiff bare branches of a thicket of sapling oaks. Glenn found he was shivering.

Pearl was already in bed, lying against the wall. The cornshucks rustled when Glenn sat down on the edge to take off his shoes. "We ain't got much cover but we'll keep each other warm, Sandy," Pearl whispered. "If we sign that contract, tomorrer's goin to be the happiest day the boys in this coalfield has seen for many's the year. I'm askeered somethin's agoin to happen. Hit's so long sence things come our way."

"Nothing's going to happen. I bet you inside of a week all the independent companies'll sign up."

"That's what I'm aprayin for." Glenn suddenly felt warm and secure lying next to Pearl on the narrow mattress that rustled whenever either one of them moved. He fell asleep.

A flashlight shining in his face woke him. Something hard stuck in his ribs. "Put up your hands, the both of you," a voice shouted. Tottering and dazed Glenn and Pearl got to their feet. The cabin was full of men in heavy boots. In the circle of light from another flashlight Glenn caught a glimpse of Wheatly running forward with her hair over her face and Jessie sitting on the edge of the bed trying to hush the children's crying. Glenn and Pearl stood up with their arms over their heads while big hands ran expertly up their sides and felt all their pockets. Meanwhile a man stood in front of each of them poking them in the stomach with an automatic. The other flashlight was travelling over all the corners of the cabin. "What's the trouble, Mr. Blaine?" asked Pearl coolly.

A large man was leaning over the fire warming his hands. Glenn caught sight of his bigjowled blank face in the yellow light of the coal as he turned. "We got a warrant for criminal syndicalism for you boys an it looks now like we'd slap on murder an conspiracy to murder."

"Hain't nobody been murdered around here."

"It's too bad to disturb a pretty lil alibi," the sheriff drawled in his rumbling voice, "but there was two deputies killed in the gunfight after the Bull Crik speakin."

"We ain't been in no gunfight."

"Sure, I know, jus sat around the patch all day and went to bed early and the womenfolks'll swear 'emselves blue in the face hit's the gospel."

"Caleb Blaine," shrieked Wheatly, running out into the circle of firelight, "I never told a lie in my life."

"All right, boys, put your shoes on an come along," said the sheriff. "You'd oughta thank me for takin you to jail. If those there companyguards from Bull Crik git aholt of you I swear they'll tear you to pieces. Hit's my duty to the people of this county to see that everythin's done legal and orderly and so help me God . . ."

"Don't say it," cried Wheatly. "We don't want no false-swearer struck by lightnin in our house."

While Glenn got his clothes on, the deputies were ripping open the two mattresses and turning out the drawers of the dresser. He was handcuffed and led across the swinging bridge over the creek and set in the back of a car between two deputies who kept their pistols poked into his stomach. He heard them putting Pearl in the other car and the sheriff calling back to the men still in the house to be sure to bring along anything that had writing on it. Just before the car drove off a face was pressed into his suddenly. It was Wheatly. She gave him a smacking kiss in the corner of the mouth and was gone. The two deputies laughed. "Don't we get no kiss too?" they yelled back into the darkness as the car drove off.

When they got out on the highway, Glenn asked the younger of them what the devil had happened at Bull Creek. The man in the front seat turned around and said seriously, "Boys, I wouldn't talk to him. Sheriff says how he's a Rooshian red. Hain't our kinder folks."

Down in the rivervalley the heavy mist slowed them up. Glenn's clothes were thin; he couldn't help shivering from the chill. In McCreary the two cars stopped for a while in front of the courthouse while the sheriff and some of the deputies went in. There was a group of men with newlooking sawedoff shotguns on their shoulders standing around under the light at the door of the jail. Two men were opening a packingcase and pulling out black metal objects that Glenn guessed were takendown parts of machineguns.

"How did you like the ride, Sandy?" came Pearl's voice cheerfully from the back of the other car. "Fine," sang out Glenn, trying to keep his teeth from chattering.

While they were waiting they saw miners being herded along out of the darkness and shoved in through the door between the men with shotguns. The deputy who had been in the front seat came back strutting importantly, with a batch of papers in his hand. "Boys," he said, "we're takin these here down to Bluegrass. Sheriff's got the jail so full o' rednecks they're standin up edgewise."

The mist was getting gray with dawn as they drove out of McCreary. It was broad daylight when the car stopped in front of a pretty little redbrick courthouse with white columns set in the middle of a little square lined with old brick houses used for feed and fertilizer and agricultural implement stores, and a few dwellings with whitecolumned porches. They were hurried in through a stone passage under the courthouse and taken into a neat bright greenpainted office.

A whitehaired old man with a big gray felt hat on the back of his head was seated behind the desk smoking a cigar. Glenn felt a pair of steelgray eyes looking him up and down. The deputy pointed at Glenn with his thumb. "This here's the furrener," he said and leaned over the desk to spread his papers out in front of the old man, who sat looking down at them peevishly for a while without a word. Only his mouth moved, chewing thoughtfully on the end of his cigar. "I don't want 'em but I guess I got to take 'em. Blaine called me up," he said. "Look here, son," he looked up in Glenn's face, "I don't know who you are. But in my jail every man who acts right gets a square deal. If he don't it goes hard with him . . . Understand? Turn out your pockets and take off your belt and necktie."

Making out the commitment and fingerprinting him and itemizing his possessions seemed to Glenn to take an endless time. Then he was led up a iron stairway into a small block of cages painted peagreen with a space for exercise in the middle. Sunlight was coming in through dusty windows on the other side of a passage. On the whole the place didn't look as bad as Glenn had expected.

The air was hot from steamheat and dense with the greasy smell of slum cooking somewhere. The fat turnkey, who was wheezing from dragging his lame leg up the steep stairs, showed Glenn into a cell with four iron bunks in it and a gloomylooking toilet seat in back and told him he could walk around in the space between the cells until he got his dinner. He'd get a mattress later.

Glenn took off his coat and laid it on the bunk and sat down on the steel slats. Through the light green bars that looked quite gay where the sunlight struck them, he could see the eyes of the other inmates looking him over. After a while Pearl came in smiling, saying it was right nice they let them bunk together sence they sure was buddies in misfortune now, and sat down beside him and told what one of the deputies had told him about the gunfight.

The guards at Bull Creek had been drinking that afternoon and started driving their car fullspeed up and down the road when the boys was going home from the speaking. They'd run a woman down and somebody had gotten so hellfired mad he'd started shooting, at least that was what the deputy said, and some of our boys had been hurt but nobody knowed how many, and now the county prosecutor claimed that the union boys had made a conspiracy to shoot up the gunthugs and they was agoing to lock up every redneck union agitator in the penitentiary. That was what the deputy said. What about Less, was the first thing Glenn asked. Deputy hadn't knowed nothing about Less.

During the afternoon the little jail began to fill up with miners. Most of the boys who were brought in were from the local at Sladetown. With them came Harve Farrell, who said, hell, he warn't no organizer, One Big Union boys organized themselves, he'd just come on down from Chicago to give the boys a little advice about keeping out of jail, well, he guessed it hadn't taken. Harve was a stocky bull-necked Irishman with a red face and red hair nearly turned white, he said he'd spent eight years in Leavenworth for resisting the draft. The minute the barred door clanged to behind him, he began to pick on Glenn and call him the comical commissar.

That made Pearl sore at first, but after a couple of days Glenn could see that Pearl thought Harve Farrell was all right. From the time they were let out of their cells in the morning until they were locked up again in the afternoon, they were at it hammer and tongs, starting with the row between Marx and Bakunin, through the Knights of Labor and the Western Federation of Miners right down to the Sandhills Convention. The other men played cards and checkers and told stories or passed around the one local newspaper the lame turnkey brought into the cage each day, but Harve and Glenn never seemed to get through arguing. At first Pearl sat listening to them, with his black eyes fixed on one, then the other, but gradually he began to get gloomy. He took to spending most of the time lying flat on his back on his bunk with his hands clasped under his head, and began to say how he wished they'd try him quick and convict him so's he'd be quit of the whole goddam business.

Pearl and Hank Davis, who was the only other miner from the Muddy Fork local in that jail, got to sitting off in a corner by themsleves and talking low with their heads together. The days dragged on into a week and still no word had come to any of them from the outside. Harve and Glenn pestered the turnkey half to death telling him they were going to sue him for false arrest. When the warden, always with his cigar and his broadbrimmed hat, made his daily rounds to inspect the cells they all crowded around him asking when they were going to be brought up in court. "Boys, all I can say is that you're better off here than you would be in the penitentiary," was all he'd answer.

Harve and Glenn got to be good friends finally. Harve said Sandy was the only comical he'd ever met who even looked straight, and they shook hands on the proposition that their job was to organize union locals and let the other guys do the wrangling. A raise looked just as good to a miner if it came wrapped in a syndicalist or Marxist line of talk. The fancy work came in when you had to choose what kind of piecards to pay your union dues to.

That afternoon the turnkey hobbled up the stairway and called Harve out, said they were taking him back to McCreary for trial. Harve went around and shook hands with the boys and said whatever happened to him the defense committee would be working their heads off to get 'em out of jail, if they were bringing him up for trial that meant he could see a lawyer and get in touch with his outfit. Last thing he went up to Glenn and held out his hand and said he hoped he could get his people to cooperate fifty fifty on these cases. Glenn shook his hand and said sure, he'd do everything he could.

Next morning Glenn was standing in line with the other guys waiting to get to the faucet to wash up when somebody called his name. Irving Silverstone was standing in the passage outside the cage with the warden and a tall man with a mane of steelgray hair. Glenn couldn't help running over and grabbing Irv's hand through the bars and pumping it up and down.

Irving was making out not to know him more than anybody else and waited until Pearl and Hank Davis and the rest of them came over, to make a little speech, introducing the tall man as Colonel Ferris, a prominent attorney from McCreary who was going to take the cases for the Workers' Defense. Then Colonel Ferris said he reckoned you all were pretty sick of being cooped up in there but he was going to get every last one of you boys out if he had to take a habeas corpus clear up to the Soupreme Court of the Younited States.

"It's this way, comrades," said Irving, "we have held a conference of the workers' organizations involved in this strike and we have decided that all the cases should be handled together. This way we can pool all our efforts and get the best legal advice available in this state and make the heroic fight of the miners of Slade County tell as part of the class struggle."

Pearl was frowning. "Say, how about these boys from the Sladetown local? There's only Hank an me here from the American Miners."

"All they've got to do is sign a paper retaining Colonel Ferris as their counsel. Of course, we'd like to see their local come into the American Miners." The boys from Sladetown were putting their heads together and whispering. "Can't you see, comrades," said Irving, his voice breaking, "that what we want to do is get you boys out of jail as soon as we can."

"We can't do nothin until we know what the boys at our local wants. Harve Farrell, our secretary, and the Prisoners' Defense up in Chicago is takin care of us," one of the miners answered.

Irving Silverstone's face looked pale and thin through the bars. He was sweating so he took his glasses off to wipe them. Without his glasses his bulging gray eyes with their slight cast had a vague girlish and innocent look they didn't have behind the flashing goldrimmed spectacles. The thin bridge of his nose had red marks on either side and the blond eyelashes grew out sparsely from redrimmed lids. He began to talk fast, whispering with his mouth close to the bars. "Comrades, I don't like to sling mud at anybody who's not present but we have a definite suspicion, backed by confidential reports from our Pittsburgh office and general headquarters in New York, that this man Farrell may be a provocator."

"A what?" asked Pearl, his black brows knitted in a frown as if he were trying to make out a small object very far away.

"Well . . . a stoolpigeon. We can't say for sure of course but anyway the conference of allied and affiliated working-class organizations feels that you comrades will be better defended by the American Workers' Defense that is in a position to use mass pressure and to put this struggle in its true light as part of the international movement of the working class."

A blackjowled husky from Sladetown with long arms and big fists pushed his way through to the bars and said if he wasn't in this here birdcage he'd knock the block off any man who said Harve was a stoolpigeon. The other miners started backing away from the bars and went and sat on the bench scowling at their feet.

"Well, I guess it's only Crockett and Napier and Davis at present, but I'm sure you comrades will accept our defense when you see what a good job we've done raising bail." Hank and Pearl were both looking Glenn hard in the eye. "Sandy . . . What do you think?" they asked in unison.

Glenn felt himself turn red. "Well, I think we'd better all stick together with the American Workers' Defense and the American Miners. That don't mean I don't think Harve

Farrell isn't a perfectly straight guy . . . I just think he's wrong."

"Boys," said Pearl. "I'm stickin together . . . Us miners we don't want no different lawyer from the Sladetown boys. We better stick with our own folks."

"Name callin don't git nobody outa jail," went on Hank Davis. "We've had union officials up here in these mountains git all our dues an then go to Jacksonville an sell us out to the highest bidder. We had plenty piecards up in these mountains. One thing about that Farrell I know, he come down here an gets him a job drivin a coaltruck. He ain't no swivelchair piecard."

"Well, come on, we can't argue all day," said the warden in a cross quaver. "Crockett, you can come along." Pearl and Hank had turned their backs and walked over to join the bunch of miners sitting along the bench. The warden hurried Glenn off so fast that he didn't get a chance to say goodbye, and once he got outside in the car with the deputy and Irving and the lawyer he forgot everything in the sweet taste of the spring morning. The trees, that had been just budding the last time he'd seen the valley road, were almost in full leaf. Three bluebirds flew out of a green appletree that he'd remembered in bloom in front of a brokendown barn where the road curved into McCreary.

Irving didn't say anything on the whole drive, but the lawyer who sat beside Glenn with the deputy in the back seat said Sheriff Blaine was releasing most of the miners under their own bond to keep the peace and only holding a few that County Prosecutor Prout was going to charge with murder. He'd had a talk yesterday afternoon with Herb Prout and he felt that old Herb was beginning to take a more reasonable attitude, he was a ver' reasonable feller; for one thing he was going to nollepros the C.S. cases.

"What's he got me charged with?" asked Glenn. "Well, we're goin to have a lil conference about that, Mr. Crockett, in Mr. Prout's office, as I say he's willin to take a ver' reasonable attitude." Irving hadn't said anything. As they were getting out of the car in front of the courthouse in McCreary Glenn noticed that Irving was holding up in front of him a notebook with a corner of white paper sticking out of it. On it was written, *Terms: low bail leave state: we accept.*

Glenn couldn't help feeling his insides turn over wetly with joy; he'd been trying to accustom himself to the idea of a fiveyear sentence in the pen, that was what the boys in jail at Bluegrass had decided they'd get if they came up before Judge Crawford in Sladetown because Judge Crawford's wife and brotherinlaw owned controlling interests in half the mines in the county. All the time the lawyer was talking to County Prosecutor Prout about the details of posting the bailbond, Glenn couldn't pay much attention to what was going on; all he could think of was that it was a fine spring day and he didn't have to go back to jail.

He and Irving and the lawyer had a good lunch of steak and fried potatoes at the Appalachian Hotel with the Coal Operators' Association guards glaring in at them through the door from the lobby. Then they drove over the gap to Slocum in the adjoining state for a meeting of the Slade County Miner's Defense Committee that was held in a room on the tenth story of a big metropolitanlooking hotel.

The first person Glenn saw when he stepped out of the elevator in the hall was Less Minot. They shook hands and slapped each other on the back in high spirits, old Less saying well, Sandy, he sure hadn't expected him out of that jail for twenty years. Glenn asked how come they hadn't picked Less up. Less said he didn't know; all he did was keep on talking and talking on the principles of unionism, dullest talk he'd ever made in his life, he'd gone rambling on and on with the court stenographer taking down every word of it, and all the time the folks were melting away, lighting out for home, getting their wives and kids out of the way; for some reason he had an idea the gunthugs wouldn't try to start anything while the speaking was still going on and it turned out he'd been right; the trouble had all been down the road. He'd talked and talked till there wasn't nobody left but him and the bishop and the Baptist minister, and the bishop had driven him in his own car down to Joe Kusick's and then out to Slocum; they'd driven right past the deputies about ten times, sure, they'd seen him, but they didn't seem to have the heart to pick him right off the seat next to a bishop. "Oughta seen me stickin to that bishop like I was glued to him."

Still laughing, they knocked on the door of the room where the meeting was. Elmer Weeks himself opened the door for them, smiling at them under his neat mustache. "Comrades, I congratulate you," he said, shaking their hands stiffly with his schoolteacher manner. Then he walked them around the room and introduced them to everybody. The delegates from the liberal organizations made a particular fuss over Glenn because he was the one that was fresh out of jail. That seemed to put old Less's nose out of joint a little. Even Jane Sparling was polite to Glenn; she introduced him to Mark Burgess of the League for Citizens' Rights as one of the nerviest damned organizers we've got.

During the meeting somebody called up Glenn from downstairs. It was Harve Farrell. Harve said he'd just come in on the bus and wanted to come up and put some propositions before the meeting. He'd just had the Sladetown local on the wire; they said the prosecutor had let everybody go except eight miners, and he was holding them for murder, six of 'em were his Sladetown boys and the other two were from Muddy Fork. Glenn couldn't keep the tremble out of his voice when he asked was that Napier and Davis? What was the use of asking; he knew it already.

Glenn put his hand over the receiver and beckoned to Irving Silverstone. Irving went over and whispered to Elmer Weeks and then came tiptoeing back to Glenn and said on no account to let him come up, Comrade Weeks had deputed him and Crockett to talk to him downstairs.

They found Harve walking nervously up and down in the lobby. His short stocky frame looked ready to burst out of his rumpled storesuit that showed a gap of grayish shirt between the vest and pants; his face was gray and he had pockets under his eyes as if he hadn't been sleeping recently. "Got a room? We better go up because the house dick won't take his eyes off me."

"We'll go in the writing room on the mezzanine," said Irving in a cold firm voice. "All right, have it your own way . . . So they turned you loose, Crockett?" Glenn nodded, grinning as he shook Harve's hand. "What charge did they bring against you?" he asked Harve.

"Bandin and confederatin, but they turned me loose on a thousand dollars bail like they did you, Crockett . . . I guess they want us to jump it."

"Who put up your bail?" asked Irving, blinking his colorless eyes behind his glasses. "J. P. Morgan, of course," said

Harve and laughed, as he settled himself on the stained red upholstered sofa in the little stuffy writingroom that was curtained off from the hall where the elevator doors were. He pulled out a package of Luckies and passed them around. Irving shook his head. Glenn took one. "Conolly did."

Irving's thin lips tightened into a line. Glenn cleared his throat and finally broke the silence. "You mean the old Mineworkers' state president?"

Harve nodded. "Seems a damn good thing to me, though he's a parasite from way back, maybe we've made enough stink so that the Consolidated Mineworkers'll come in and help . . . That's what I want to talk to you guys about. I want you to go with me and see Conolly and see if we can't all get together on this."

"That socialfascist," said Irving, getting to his feet. "If you want to help him sell out the workers you can; that's not what we came down here for."

Harve's face was getting red. His big fists clenched the knees of his shiny pantlegs. "Your outfit came down here to raise a big political stink and git yourselves a new crop of martyrs to raise money for . . . for your own mealtickets." Harve got up with his fists tight and ground his cigarette out under his foot on the green carpet. "Well, you can go fuck yourselves." He hitched up his pants that were too short for him and walked out.

Glenn hadn't said a word. When Harve had gone he said suddenly, "How about going to talk to Conolly . . . he's probably got political influence . . . after all, Burgess is a socialfascist too, isn't he, and all the nambypamby liberals, and we're cooperating with them, aren't we? They tell me Conolly and Prout have always been thick. Prout used to be the Consolidated's attorney. We got to get those boys out, Irv . . . particularly Pearl Napier. That boy's got the makings of a real laborleader."

"They're all of them politically undeveloped," said Irving as they were going back up in the elevator.

"I'd rely on Napier anywhere."

"I know," said Irving in a doleful tone. "Real proletarians . . . lovely people . . . but they lack Marxist preparation. There's too much of the artist in you, Sandy. You are sentimental."

When they went back into the room where the meeting was going on, Mark Burgess, who was a middleaged blueeyed man with steelgray hair and a broad freshlooking pink and white face and knowall manner like a country doctor's, came up to Glenn saying, Crockett, the committee had just decided he was taking a speaking tour for them under the auspices of the League for Citizens' Rights to tell the people of this country just to what degree constitutional rights had been suspended in Slade County.

Two weeks later Glenn started his tour; sometimes he had a couple of miners with him in their black caps with little lights on them, or Mary Lou Napier, a cousin of Pearl's who sang mountain songs about the strike, or a liberalminded newspaperman who had a report to make about conditions in the coalfields, or the bishop who had turned up at the speaking at Bull Creek. The first chance he got he wrote Pearl a letter explaining that everything possible was being done to get the boys the best legal talent they could find. After he'd closed the envelope he sat there at the writing desk in the noisy hotel lobby, smelling again the greasy smell of slum and seeing again the greenpainted bars of the little jail at Bluegrass. "Irv's right. I'm too damn sentimental," he said so near aloud that he felt his lips forming the words.

One night after Glenn talked at the Y.M.C.A. in a southern collegetown he was amazed to see Paul Graves in the group of people waiting to speak to him after the lecture. Paul looked older; his skull seemed to have gotten bigger and his eyes to have sunken into it under dense black brows. Paul grabbed Glenn's hand as he hurried out of the hall. "Paul, it can't be you're beginning to get red," Glenn said in a voice that sounded unnecessarily sarcastic in his own ears.

"I always used to be kinder pink, an outdoor pink, didn't I?"

"Gosh, Paul, I wish I had time to chew the rag . . . I've got to go along to a conference about raising some money for the miners."

"I'll go by your hotel afterwards. I saw your picture in the paper and drove all the way over especially to see you."

"All right, it's the Mountain View, room 21, the dump across from the station."

When Glenn got back to the hotel at midnight deadtired

from the speaking and the conferences, there was Paul waiting for him, smoking a pipe in the grimy little lobby with its moosehead over the desk and its old brass spittoons under the tables piled with last week's newspapers.

When they got up to Glenn's airless room, with its gangrenous green wallpaper, Paul pulled a pint of corn out of his back pocket and set it on the nighttable and let himself sink down on the brass bed that jingled with his weight. "First thing, Glenn I want to ask you about this alias . . . I think what you're doing's great, but why can't you do it under your own name?"

"Plenty of reasons, Paul, lots of the time we're underground, particularly in the South."

Paul poured himself a drink in the only glass. Glenn had refused one, saying that his kind of work and drinking didn't mix. "Don't you kind of forget who you are, who your folks were, all that sort of stuff?"

Glenn felt his face getting red. "I believe in it, the lack of a name . . . our folks are the workingclass . . . can't you see?"

"Well, Glenn, I'd rather you'd kept your identity, after all you were quite a friend of mine . . . and don't forget that the cells that make up your carcass contain the same chromosomes whether you go under one name or another."

"Paul, I gotto go to bed, I pull outa here on a bus at six-thirty."

"I just wanted to know if you ever went to the Soviet Union."

"Not yet."

"Well, I'm going this fall taking Peggy and the kids, we got four now, you oughta see 'em. I've got a job running one of their new agricultural experiment stations for a year. I thought it would be a chance to make a little dough and to check up on how the great experiment's going."

"You lucky bastard," said Glenn. "Meanwhile I'll be going back to get my block knocked off in the Slade County minefields."

After Paul had gone Glenn noticed he'd left the pint of corn. First Glenn thought of putting it in the wastebasket but then he decided he'd better take it with him. This was the kind of thing they framed radicals on. Why the hell had Paul brought it? He went to bed feeling vaguely sore at

Paul, though he'd been glad to see him; here he had a nice wife and four nice children and was getting a rep as an agricultural expert and was going to make big money going to the Soviet Union, and Glenn didn't have anything in the world, no wife, no children, he'd even thrown his name overboard. He went to sleep feeling cosily sorry for himself; as sorry for himself as he remembered feeling sometimes as a small boy.

He still had Paul's pint of corn with him the night he met Less in Slocum to go back over the gap to see if they couldn't straighten things out among the locals. Less was full of bad news and even gloomier than usual. About half the locals had gone back to the old Consolidated Mineworkers after the boys at Bluegrass had been convicted for the Bull Creek shooting and sentenced to twenty years. The lawyers were up at the state capital arguing an appeal right now.

Old Less sure was glad to get the corn after the comrades who'd driven them over to the gap had left them halfway up the mountainside. They'd decided to walk over by the old trail for fear the operators might have guards posted on the road. "This time," Less kept saying, "they'll pump us full of lead and ask no questions."

"But they won't dare do anything to us in Colonel Ferris's office at the state capital," said Glenn. Less drank down the corn in about two gulps. "We won't git to no state capital. We got to go around to see the locals first to tell 'em what's what, see? Well, you can't tell me they ain't got some stools in some of them locals."

"Well, it's too late to back out now," said Glenn beginning to get sore.

"That's what I'm tryin to tell you, Sandy," said Less in a hoarse voice, and pitched the bottle away from him down the mountainside.

They both stopped still and listened for its crash on the rocks below. The hillside was absolutely silent and already bluedark, although the sky overhead was still rosy with long streamers of afterglow from the sunset the other side of the range. "Well, we'd better hurry if we're going to make it by dark," said Less in an even kind of tone. They both picked up their grips heavy from being jammed full of copies of party newspapers that told about the campaign for the boys in jail, and started toiling up the steep rocky trail again.

It was pitchblack by the time they reached the gap. They found the highway and walked cautiously down it, stopping every now and then to listen. Once they heard a car coming up and hid flat on their faces in the deep shadow of a culvert until it drove past them. At last they found the wagonroad through the woods that led to old man Napier's cabin, just in time because the moon that was almost full had risen back of the range and all the contours of the mountains began to show up dripping with milky light.

Down below in the valley they began to see the scattering pinpoints of the lights of Muddy Fork, and the strings and tangled rectangles of lights halfhidden in smoke, of Slade-town. They caught a little rough taste of coalsmoke in the air from the cabins down in the gulch.

Less got across the creek all right over the slippery stepping stones but Glenn's foot slipped and he went splashing in, both legs up to his knees in the cold water. The water squudged in his shoes as he walked across the grassy ridges of the old cornfield. When they came up to the cabin they first thought it was empty because no light was showing from the window, but around in front they saw a chink of light from the door and knocked. "Who's that?" came a girl's voice. "I bet that's Wheatly," said Glenn. The door opened a crack at a time.

Wheatly looked more filled out than when Glenn had last seen her. She let him and Less in and closed the door and barred it behind them. For a moment it looked as if she were alone in the cabin. Then a pair of feet in heavy black boots shot down from the rafters above and Joe Kusick was standing in front of them sheepishly wiping the cobwebs off his arms. Meanwhile two of the boys from Muddy Fork were crawling out from under the bed where Wheatly's mother and the little children were fretfully asleep.

They stood around in front of the fire looking at each other and laughing a little in their throats. "Looks like there might be some trouble around here, boys," said Less.

"Trouble," said Joe Kusick. "Just wait. They blowed up the soupkitchen last night . . . Caleb Blaine and Judge Crawford, they say they're out to run every redneck out of this end of the county and it looks like they could do it. He's so afraid of that appeal that he wants to scare any of the miners outa testifyin." Joe stopped and took a long breath and then he grabbed one of their hands in each of his and shook it. "Well, boys, I'm glad you come. They's been a lot of oldtime walkin delegates in here of the old sellout variety tellin the miners if they'll give up this here comyounist business and go back to the old Consolidated Mineworkers everything'll be hunkydory. They all said you two had yellered out on us."

"Jesus Christ, what do you think we been doin, takin the cure at Atlantic City? We been shouting our lungs out raisin money for you bastards," said Less. Wheatly had been looking hard, first in his face, then in Glenn's. She gave her head a toss. "I seen plenty preachers shout and ain't brung no rain . . . I hain't seen Pearl and Hank gettin out jail yet."

"Honest, Wheatly," said Glenn, his voice breaking, "we're doing everything we can. We hope we can get 'em out on this appeal, or at least get new trials."

Wheatly started to laugh. She put her hands on her hips and laughed till her face was red. "Fell in the crik, did yer? Well, you'd better take them pants off and let me dry 'em." "Look out there, Sandy," said Less, giving Glenn a poke in the ribs with his elbow. "When a pretty young girl starts takin a man's pants off first thing . . ." "You shet your dirty ole mouth before I shet it for ye," said Wheatly, still laughing. "Hain't nothin new to me in how God made a man."

While Glenn was blushingly taking off his wet clothes, Joe and Less were deciding what to do. They'd have to move quick, Joe would drive Less down to Sladetown so that he could talk to the boys before they went home after the shift changed, then Joe'd drive him right on through to Bluegrass and he'd be out of the county before them gunthugs was outa bed at the Appalachian Hotel. Then Glenn would be checking on the Muddy Fork and Bull Creek locals and walk over and stay in Joe Kusick's store till the next night when Joe would drive him straight out to the state capital. When Joe gave Glenn the key to the store he had to put it in the pocket of his jacket because he didn't have any pants on to put it in; Wheatly, with her brow furrowed like a little girl doing a difficult piece of schoolwork, was carefully toasting them over the flaring coalgrate.

"Say, Joe, I always meant to ask you," Less was saying in a casual kind of voice. "How come Sheriff Blaine don't never pick on you none?"

Glenn found that both he and Less were staring hard in

Joe Kusick's lined lopsided face. For a second everybody in the cabin was so still they could hear the roar of the draft in the chimney. Joe pointed with a thumb to a masonic emblem he wore in the lapel of his old O.D. coat and said in an easy voice, "Caleb Blaine's been beholden to me for a lot of things. He's a yellow dawg but he ain't so crooked as some . . . If I coulda sworn on their alibi I know Pearl and Hank would be free men this day."

"Why didn't you, ye little old man?" Wheatly strode out from the fireplace waving Glenn's steaming pants under Joe's nose.

"I was down to McCreary all day . . . the old lady wouldn't let me go to the speakin . . . I never saw either one of them from sunup to sundown. Yesterday I carried the old lady down to stay with her sister in Bluegrass. There's nothin those coal operators won't do now. This strike's beginnin to pinch 'em where it does the most good."

"Sure," said Less, "that's why we just had to come in and talk to you boys. If we can hold the union together for another two months they'll be eatin out our hands; if we don't, the miners in this county'll be down on their knees before the operators every time they want a drink of water. You know that . . . Price o' coal's goin up. That's what you want to tell the boys . . . Well, so long, Sandy, have you got the program straight? We'll go along. You better follow along as soon as the lady lets you have your trousers." All their hands shook Glenn's and the door closed behind them.

Glenn and Wheatly stood looking at each other in the flicker of the firelight. From the bed at the end there came heavy snoring and the intermittent sickly whimper of a sleeping child. For a corner of a second Glenn remembered another fire, and Gladys, as if it had been in a different world; then he was thinking of the first time he'd seen Wheatly in that cabin last spring. Wheatly hung his pants over a stool and went to the cabin door and went out. Glenn followed her.

Outside the high moon was brimming the valley with light and shimmered over the flat mist that covered the coal-towns below like over the surface of a lake. The girl was facing him standing right up against him so that her firm breasts touched him. When he grabbed her to him and kissed her upturned mouth she began to sob. The jagged door of the old brokendown cowshed cut off the moonlight with blackness. A pile of dry cornstalks crackled and rasped crazily under them.

He was lying beside her stroking the warm curve of her shoulder that had broken out through her torn dress when suddenly she jumped on him, with her thin knees on his chest, and started to choke him. Her long hands were very strong. He had to use all his strength to tear them away from his throat. "What the . . . ?" He went into a fit of coughing.

"I'm achokin you so you won't forgit me or brother Pearl rottin in that penitentiary. You go git him out, do you hear, if you don't I'll take an axe an split your skull right in half an spill your brains out on the highroad an tromp on 'em . . . No boy kin ever go around asayin he had my ass for nothin." She started to pummel him blindly with her fists.

He broke away from her and ran panting back to the cabin to put on his trousers and shoes and stockings. Then he took the bundle of papers out of his suitcase. She came in and grabbed him by the arm just as he was leaving. "Hain't you goin to sleep none? Hain't no call to be down there before day." Glenn shook his head. "I might forget what I came for . . . Keep the bag and stuff for me, will you, Wheatly?"

His head was spinning as he walked slowly down the rocky path into the valley with the bundle of newspapers on his shoulder. As he walked down the trail the sound of the creek below got louder. He went through streaks of cool and warm air, here and there tinged with the sulphury reek of coalsmoke. In one place there was a strong smell of honeysuckle.

He stepped out on the valley road, white and empty in the moonlight, and walked up it to the footbridge that crossed to the Muddy Fork patch. Opposite the bridge he half caught sight of the glint of metal of a car parked under some trees. Anyway he couldn't go back. He had to get across. As he stepped on the swinging bridge a voice behind him said in a low conversational tone, "Put 'em up, Buddy, let's see who you are."

Glenn dropped his bundle and stood staring into a flashlight. The lights of a car went on full behind him at the same moment. There was nothing to do but stand there dazed.

"Boys," shouted a voice, "we got one of them visitin reds and he's got enough litrachur to set red Rooshia on fire." Glenn's arms were pulled behind his back and handcuffed and he was shoved into the back seat of the car. They didn't take him far, but it must have been to the Bull Creek mine, as he saw the tall shadow of a tipple cut into the moonlight overhead as he was hustled into a building. Down the passage was a little room that had a cot and a barred window. They took the handcuffs off him and slammed the door to. There was nothing left to do but try to get some sleep.

When he woke up he was sitting up on the cot. Daylight was filtering grayly through the bars. Less Minot was standing over him scratching his grayblack head with his stubby hand. "Well, Sandy, I have to hand it to you, there you go sleepin like a baby and these gorillas is plannin to kill the two of us dead." "How do you know?" "I know," Less said in a tired voice and sat down on the bed with his head in his hands.

After an hour or two they began to want to go to the toilet and knocked on the door until a guard came with a big automatic in his hand. As he walked Glenn down the hall to the stinking watercloset Glenn asked him what they were going to do with them. The guard said he could tell them one thing, they was going to be quit of troublemakers round here from now on, they was a pair of thoroughbred reds he could see that and they was going to be quit of them. A little later the same guard brought them in a couple of tin cups of coffee and some stale ham sandwiches wrapped in oiled paper.

That night just when the barred window had gone black, four men with shiny sawedoffshotguns and big pistolholsters came stamping in and told them to get a move on. Glenn could smell whiskey on their breaths. He noticed that they talked loud and wouldn't look him in the eye. He was piled into the back of a car between two of them and they were off at sixty miles an hour.

Instead of going into McCreary they turned off on the road up to the gap. Nobody spoke. Glenn could feel the car laboring on the grade. Now and then the four tall men in the car passed a flask around. As the car zigzagged up the incline to the gap, Glenn could feel the pounding of his heart grow louder and louder until he was scared the gunthugs could hear it. He managed to keep his lips very still, just meeting in front of his clenched teeth.

Overhead was pitchblack under an even blanket of clouds; for some reason Glenn kept wishing the moon would rise. The car rounded the last curve and drew up with a shriek of brakes in the loose gravel of a parkingplace on the highest point of the gap. The men on either side of Glenn started poking him in the ribs with their guns. Their voices were thick. "Redneck, unload."

As Glenn stepped out on the gravel another car drove up facing them and in the place where the headlights crossed he could see a big man sparring at Less who'd just been pushed out from the car. "Any you rednecks want to fight?" the man was yelling as he shadowboxed around in a circle.

Less was about half his size. He put up his fists and stood waiting for him. Glenn saw another guy creep up from behind and land an uppercut on the side of Less's jaw that almost bowled him over, but he managed to keep his feet, spinning around, protecting his head with his short arms.

Just then something hard came down on the back of Glenn's skull and felled him to the ground. He came to with lights flashing around him and heavy boots kicking him. Somehow he managed to wriggle out of the circle of light just as a big stone grazed his shoulder. He felt the rocks at the edge of the parking place and dragged himself over the edge. There was a red flash from a gun and a bullet zinged overhead.

He'd let go and was rolling down the mountainside in a whirl of loose stone and dirt. Now I'm done for, he had time to think. He had caught in a clump of bushes. It wasn't hard to lie still; he was almost out. Overhead he heard yells and curses and shots.

Everything was silvery around him. He was drenched and shaking with cold. When he moved he had a knifelike pain in his ribs. One side of his face throbbed. He managed to get up in a sitting position in the clump of bushes. He spat out a mouthful of blood. The whole hillside was full of bright moonlight; through the forested valley below a stream curved in loops of silver wire. From the bushes he crawled along a ledge out over a turn in the road. It seemed to take him hours to let himself down little by little to the parapet of the road below. He sat there with his head and his whole body throbbing with pain. When his strength seemed to come back a little he got to his feet and called out, "Hey, Less, where are you?" a couple of times, but his voice didn't carry. Didn't seem much use. Then he started thumping down the road in the early dawn still silvery from the selling moon.

For a week Glenn had been flat on his back with his ribs strapped up and his jaw in plaster of Paris and his head swathed in itchy gauze. Through the doze of an aching stiff sickness he remembered stabbing pain and brilliant morning sunlight and two colored men picking him up and putting him in a truck and the agony of the joggling on his broken ribs. They had brought him in and laid him in the carbolic-reeking entry of the hospital, and some nurses and a doctor in a white coat had come out and made a big row and said they wouldn't take him. He must have passed out again because he next remembered ether and the sharp pain when they were setting his jaw, and Jane Sparling being there and quarreling with the orderly who wouldn't let her smoke in the ward. She'd gone off leaving Glenn some Workers Defenders to read, saying that she was late, and had a hundred miles to drive in two hours, to meet a delegation of liberal writers on its way in from Slocum to try to distribute food, because the striking miners were in bad shape now that the second soupkitchen had been blown up; she sure hoped Sheriff Blaine would beat up a couple of the prominent stuffedshirts on their committee because dollars to doughnuts that would get them a senatorial investigation.

The hospital people wouldn't let her leave before she'd paid the hospital bill; he remembered hearing her and the matron rowing about the anesthetist's charge. The ward was seedy and smelled bad; nobody paid any attention to the patients, and a gaunt man in the cot at the end kept Glenn awake all night retching and coughing. Then one morning when the nurse came up to tidy his bed he noticed something different in her manner. She said a lady who was a relative of his was coming in to see him, a Mrs. Gulick, and he must comb his hair. For a minute he couldn't think who it was. It was Marice.

Marice came sailing into the ward with her bracelets jangling, wearing a mink coat and a red hat shaped like the prow of an oldfashioned battleship, spreading a mist of sandalwood perfume, and saying that Glenn was a hero and she'd just found out who he was and she never imagined he had it in him, and she was going to get him out of this filthy hole before he could say Jack Robinson and he wasn't safe from arrest here anyway. She was as good as her word; by afternoon she had him in a drawingroom on the train to New York.

As the train rumbled through the night she sat up beside him, holding on to a jar of roses that kept falling off the little table of the drawingroom onto the floor, telling him how she and Mike had separated, they were still good friends but they couldn't help nagging each other and had decided it was better for the children if they lived their own lives separately. She thought the horrid old capitalist system was on its last legs and she had been so interested in the Slade County miners and when Mike called her up and told her that Sandy Crockett, the heroic leader of the miners, was their old star boarder from Ohio who'd always seemed so quiet and mousy and inhibited, she declared she hadn't been able to believe her ears. She decided one thing she could do to help was to give him the best medical and legal care. The minute she'd laid eyes on him in that hospital she had decided not to leave him there another day but to take him up to New York where she'd put him in the hands of the best specialists Dr. Blumenthal could recommend. The next morning she took him right from the train to the hospital in an ambulance. It made him feel like an ass to have so many doctors and nurses fussing over him. But he was in so much pain he didn't care what happened.

When he was able to walk around, and the knitting bones gave him a stiff ache instead of sharp agony, Marice made him move to her house, saying that she was alone there with the children and it would be good for them to see what a real labor leader looked like, and that she had every intention of spoiling him, because he was still shaky from the concussion, and it was much better for her to spoil him than to spoil the children, and maybe give them complexes.

It was a funny feeling for Glenn, after the rough life he'd been leading, to sleep between fine linen sheets and on box-springs, and to have a bath of his own with plenty of hot water and soap that smelled of almonds and big thick mono-grammed towels, and to feel the rumble of the city coming in to him through the heavy silk draperies of the old brown-stone house, and to have his meals brought to him by a col-ored maid and to have Marice barging into his room at all hours with her silk negligee with blue and red poppies on it floating out behind her. Sleeping with Marice, once he'd gotten rid of his casts and felt like a human being again, seemed so much part of the picture, he hardly knew when it started up. She told him he was a very satisfactory lover.

What did embarrass him was to have Marice tell the twins, who were towheaded nineyearold boys by this time, that their Uncle Sandy was mother's lover; but she said she believed in the most absolute frankness about those things, especially with children. She invited Mike, who was still teaching at Columbia, to come over and have dinner with them, and Glenn certainly felt a fool shaking hands with old Mike, although he was darn glad to see him at that. Marice didn't let them stick for very long to general conversation. She had made very strong cocktails that went to her head, and she started to tease them both for acting humorous and civilized about the situation, until Mike flared up and said the only choice was between being humorous and civilized and beating her face in with the leg of a table; and that he wasn't going to continue humorous and civilized if she made a public scandal of this thing because that would cost him his job and he didn't have the income from Grandpa's nut and bolt factory to live on like she did, and had to make his living, and besides he had his academic career to think of. He was going to get a divorce, that's what he was going to do. Oh, why did we all have to act so conventional, Marice kept whooping.

Once dinner was announced things were better because the soup sobered them and Marice shut up in front of the housemaid. Glenn got to telling Mike about the setup in Slade County and they all talked about what could be done to help the national campaign to free the eight miners who had been framed for the shootings at Bull Creek. As they talked Glenn caught himself wishing that things were the same as they had been the last time he'd had dinner there with the Gulicks, when he was still in college; he couldn't imagine how it had all happened so fast. When Mike left them to go home to his bachelor quarters Glenn and Marice stood at the open door saying goodnight, while he walked down the steps from the stoop. Marice had an arm tight around Glenn's neck.

Glenn didn't know what Elmer Weeks would say about the situation, he knew he and Irving must be wise to it, because Marice was all the time answering the phone for him, and drifting in and out of his room when they came up to the house, while he was still in bed, to confer about what tactics the Party should pursue in the minefields now that the American Miners' locals had all been driven underground in Slade County. He made up his mind to bring it up the first time he went downtown to headquarters and got a chance to talk to Elmer Weeks alone.

It was a fine fall afternoon. Marice called him a taxi and made him take five dollars and told him to be sure to be back in time for dinner. He sat there leaning back in the taxi, wearing the new suit and new tan oxfords and the new light overcoat Marice had had sent up to the house for him, looking out at the hazy glitter of afternoon traffic and wondering what the hell he ought to do next.

Elmer Weeks was waiting for him in his cramped little office, seated at his rolltop desk, smoking a briar pipe in a last ray of sunlight that came in through the dusty windowpane. He pushed back a pile of reports on yellow paper, smiled broadly at Glenn from under his mustache and whispered into the telephone, "Comrade Silverstone, please· . . . Irv, step across the hall, will you?" Then he gave Glenn another broad grin and said, "Glad to see you on your feet . . . hope you're ready for some speaking . . . my, you look the prosperous capitalist."

Glenn felt himself getting red as a beet. "I don't know what to do about it."

"In the first place," said Irving in a brisk tone, who had just stepped in through the glass door behind Glenn, "private morals are no affair of the Party's . . . We're only interested in social morals. In the second place, there is always the danger of being contaminated by the decadence of the liberal bourgeoisie . . . after all, that's probably your sphere. Your class origins."

"Aren't strictly kosher," said Glenn angrily.

"That sort of remark, verging on antisemitism, proves my point . . . it's a remark no true worker . . ."

"Mrs. Gulick," Elmer Weeks interrupted soothingly, "inherited part of the Obadiah White fortune, if I'm not mistaken."

"She's very much interested in the Slade County situation. She's a very goodhearted intelligent woman." Glenn felt he was talking too eagerly.

"We can never transcend our class origins," said Irving in a condoling tone. "That doesn't mean that petitbourgeois radicals can't be useful to the government."

"I've done a hell of a lot more manual labor than you have," broke out Glenn.

"What's the use? Personalities," said Irving with a shrug of his shoulders.

Elmer Weeks was looking thoughtfully at the smoke of his pipe. "We mustn't let ourselves look at things from too narrow a standpoint," he began. As they talked Glenn found he had more and more trouble keeping their minds on the minefields. They talked about more money for the Party press, posters for campaign rallies, hiring halls and the chance the Party had of polling a considerable vote in the presidential elections, on account of unemployment, the disillusionment of the whitecollarworkers and intellectuals, the lack of leadership in the oldline trade unions . . . Glenn kept saying that if they could get those miners out of jail and keep the American Miners' Union together, they'd have a real mass basis for a labor movement. He still felt too weak and shaky to get any conviction into his voice. Finally, Elmer Weeks shook his pipe out in the wastebasket and got to his feet saying he had to speak up in the Bronx and must be off, anyway it wouldn't hurt letting Comrade Crockett see what he could do with a liberal committee. "Under proper direction," said Irving. "Perhaps."

As he went out the door of the office Elmer Weeks, with a gray tweed cap on his head and a briefcase under his arm, turned back and shook his empty pipe at them. "Comrades," he said in the staccato voice he used when he gave orders, "we must keep one thing in mind. Our function is to educate the American workingclass in revolutionary Marxism. We are not interested in the fates of individuals."

Glenn asked him if he thought he ought to go back to the

minefields now he was on his feet again. Elmer Weeks stepped back into the office and pulled the groundglass door to behind him, and stood there a moment stroking his mustache with the forefinger of the hand that held the pipe. "Just at present it looks to me as if you could do more for the movement right here in New York than anywhere else."

"You've been beaten up for the movement," said Irving nastily. "You oughtn't to complain of an uptown assignment." Glenn had an impulse to punch Irving on the end of his pale sharp nose. "Okay," he said. As he limped off in a hurry down the grimy hall, brushing past several comrades with briefcases who were waiting to see Comrade Weeks when he went out, he could hear Irving's voice rising in denunciation, behind the door that had closed again. That fellow doesn't like me any more, he told himself.

When he got back to Marice's house he found a childishly addressed letter for him that had been forwarded from the American Miners' office in Pittsburgh. It was a scrawl in pencil from Wheatly:

Comrad Sandy, we just got to git Pearl and them boys out. Pappy he went and talked to Caleb Blaine the black-hearted old buzzard and Caleb Blaine says those boys stays in jail juss so long as them furren rednecks keeps messin up things in the minefields and wont mind they own business and that they was all atheists so now Pappy's hellroarin around everywhere about how the reds aint our folks and our folks ought to stick together but Sandy you and me is the same kind of folks and all night I'm awishin you was hear and us ahuggin and kissin and things it aint proper to write like we did . . .

Glenn crumpled the letter up and dropped it in the wastebasket.

"What's the matter, Sandy?" Marice asked. She had just come into his room all dressed for dinner with a little shaker and two cocktailglasses on a tray. "Lost your last friend on earth?" Glenn stooped over with difficulty, as his back was still stiff from the cast, and picked Wheatley's letter out of the wastebasket and tore it into small pieces. "Marice, I got to get back there before they begin to feel I've run out on them."

"Why can't Less Minot go back?"

"He's all bunged up too . . . He's back running the Pittsburgh office."

"But, Glenn, you know perfectly well they'd shoot to kill this time."

"They did last time."

"I know how you feel . . . But everybody agrees you can do a better job for those miners outside the state than in. We need you to testify before the senate investigating committee, we need you to make speeches . . ."

"I know the arguments," said Glenn.

"But aren't we having fun together?" Marice said suddenly, stammering and casting her eyes down like a little girl. He took her by the ears and pulled her mouth to him and kissed it. "Sure thing," he said. "Suppose we get Mark Burgess and that lawyer up here tonight and see if we can get 'em to start something."

"I'll call Mark up right now . . . maybe they can come for dinner," said Marice, running out to the hall to the phone, suddenly all excitement. Glenn was rubbing her greasy lipstick off his lips with the corner of his handkerchief.

Mark Burgess rang the front doorbell promptly at seven looking very spruce in his lightgray suit with a blue necktie the color of his eyes. He was delighted to see Glenn again, asked about his injuries and introduced him enthusiastically to the tall man in baggy tweeds, George Hurlbut Cramm, who had come with him. Marice came swishing out from the diningroom carrying a new tray of cocktails and wearing a black spangly dress wth red slippers and a noisy red necklace. She had a great deal of rouge on her cheeks and turned her round black eyes up under Mr. Cramm's chin and sighed that now that the ablest lawyer in the New York bar was interested in taking the cases she knew those poor boys would get out of jail.

Mr. Cramm made a deprecatory gesture with a large white hand and said dear lady, just for the present all he could afford to contribute to the good cause was advice. They had a number of cocktails and sat down at the big diningtable with its stifflycreased linen tablecloth and its glitter of cutglass and silver. While Marice carved the roastbeef, Mark Burgess brought out a looseleaf notebook and began to map out a new campaign for the miners' defense to be organized by the League: Speeches, moneyraising, legal fees, etc. They had just gotten started when the maid said somebody wanted Mr. Crockett on the phone. It was Jane Sparling, she said if they didn't mind she was coming right up, she felt the Workers' Defense should be represented.

Marice had a place set for Jane, but she said she'd eaten. Jane's voice was dry and her manner was scornful; the first thing she wanted to know was why a new committee was needed, why the old defense committee couldn't handle the new trials too. Glenn put down his napkin; in the first place they had to have a broader base and a nonpartisan group who wouldn't be immediately branded as reds. After all, this wasn't a political issue, it was a matter of civil rights, Elmer and Irving agreed with him, he'd just been talking to them this afternoon, and in the second place there was the fact that most of the miners wanted to be defended by the O.B.U. Now a liberal citizens' committee wouldn't encounter ideological difficulties. "After all the main thing is to get those boys out of jail, isn't it, Jane?"

"Of course," said Jane impatiently, getting to her feet and walking around the room, "but we don't need to break up the union to do it."

"The American Miners has a hell of a lot better chance in the coalfields if we get those boys out of jail," said Glenn, "than if we leave them there to rot. The new trials are our big chance."

"But how can there be any question?" asked Marice, leaning forward from the end of the table, her round eyes shining.

Jane pushed the untidy gray hair off her square face and said, "It's no use arguing with people who don't understand what we're talking about."

"Now, Jane dear," said Mark Burgess with mock humility, "we are ideologically uninformed little liberals from the outer darkness, but we want to learn . . . we're listening to teacher."

Jane couldn't help joining in the laugh, but Glenn noticed that she and Marice were giving each other sharp looks. It was a relief when Mark Burgess said in his smooth pulpit manner: "Now I think there's a way out of this little difficulty. My old friend George here hasn't admitted it yet but I know what he is going to do."

"Gosh, Mark, I don't see how I can afford the time at this

moment . . . I have the traction company case pending and
I may have to argue a brief before the Supreme Court in
January."

"George," said Mark Burgess gently, "you know you will
. . . You always come through. The head says one thing
but the heart says another."

"I wish you could see those miners," said Glenn. "Honestly, they are wonderful guys. The state superior court has
granted new trials . . . It's our great chance."

"Well," said George Hurlbut Cramm, "I suppose we can
get some of the youngsters in my office to prepare a brief
amicus curiae if nothing else . . ."

"As for expenses," said Marice, who had been paying attention to mixing the salad in the big wooden salad bowl,
"Mark and I can put our heads together. We can get things
started anyway."

"Attagirl," said Burgess. "Now we are doing business."

George Hurlbut Cramm leaned across the table. "Mr.
Crockett," he said, "I hear that you can testify on the alibi of
two of the miners . . ."

"That's one reason they tried to rub me out of the picture," said Glenn, laughing.

"Well, they won't try anything like that this time.
There'll be too much publicity."

"Well, I can't be here all night . . . I've got to go back
to the office," said Jane suddenly. "Comrade Crockett, I
hope you won't forget you are dealing with political irre-
sponsibles." "Who, us, Jane?" asked Mark Burgess, rolling
his eyes up. "No, of course not," she said crossly, "I mean
those O.B.U. miners," and went out.

That night the phone rang just as Glenn and Marice were
climbing into bed. Yawning he shuffled into the hall in his
bare feet. It was Elmer Weeks telling him that the Central
Committee had just thrashed the matter out and decided
that the thing to do was to concentrate on getting out the
two American Miners' boys; outside of that the trial was an
educational demonstration and to be treated as such by the
liberal lawyers: and as for cooperating with the O.B.U. he
had every reason to believe it would be a mistake, after all
we knew none of our boys had shot those deputies, no use
trying to defend irresponsible elements, no time for Quixotic
gestures. Comrade Crockett's business was to go to Blue-

grass and convince Napier and Davis that their cases were separate. "But it won't be any use," Glenn found himself yelling into the phone. Elmer Weeks's voice became very dry and crisp. That was the decision, he said. Of course, he'd have a right to take the general principle up before the plenum, if he thought the movement had anything to gain from that sort of discussion.

"What on earth are you talking about so long?" said Marice who had followed Glenn out into the hall with her quilted red Chinese robe thrown over her shoulders. "Well, goodnight," said Glenn hurriedly and hung up. "Headquarters," he added to Marice, with a tart laugh, "telling us where to get off."

It was a sparkling blue November morning when Glenn and Marice drove up in front of the rambling mansarded frame building of the Bluegrass Hotel. In the back seat of Marice's Chrysler Imperial, wrapped in a plaid blanket and hemmed in by suitcases, was the lumpy redfaced figure of Dr. Blumenthal, who had come with them to study a labor situation from the psychoanalytic point of view, and also, as Marice whispered to Glenn when they were leaving New York, to act as a sort of chaperon, Glenn knew how unimaginative people were in the sticks.

Driving down the main street, between two lines of parked mudflecked cars, Glenn had hardly recognized Bluegrass. There were old cars of every model, weathered to colors like bluebottle flies, teams of mules drawing big wagons with oldfashioned round covers over them; there was even a yoke of oxen. The streets were full of miners and countrypeople in their best clothes. Lanky men with black felt hats on the backs of their heads were standing along the curbs chewing and spitting and passing the time of day. A colored man in a white jacket was selling hot dogs and pop at a little stand on the courthouse lawn. There was a fairground feeling in the air as if a calliope might start playing at any minute.

The hotel lobby was full of talk and cigarsmoke and the smell of fried ham from the diningroom where the outoftown newspapermen were eating breakfast. Glenn pointed out County Prosecutor Herb Prout to Marice as they were walking over to the desk to register. He was leaning back with his thumbs in his vestpockets looking the crowd over with the appraising air of a theatre manager watching a line waiting for tickets at the boxoffice. While the bellboy was bringing in their bags they stood a moment talking in singsong ceremonial voices to George Hurlbut Cramm and Colonel Ferris, the local attorney for the American Miners.

Harve Farrell was standing in the diningroom door; he beckoned Glenn over and introduced a skinny young man with coarse black hair as the Honorable Jim Ellis who was taking the O.B.U. cases. Harve looked the same as ever and still wore the same creased suit that didn't meet in the middle. "Well," he said, "you birds are puttin on a big show, but what do those big boys care about the workin class . . . They care about words . . . that's what you'll get, a big talkfest and the boys'll stay in Jail." "How else can you educate people, Harve?" "We'll eddicate 'em by gettin our boys out of jail."

Glenn walked back over to where Marice and Dr. Blumenthal were talking to Prosecutor Prout and Judge Crawford from Sladetown. Marice was making a great hit with the local boys. Everybody was elaborately polite and full of old southern hospitality. Everybody seemed to be having a wonderful time. A funny feeling like seasickness began to take hold of Glenn. He stood there with his ears ringing, looking at the people and the cigarsmoke and the crowds passing in the street beyond the broad dusty window of the hotel lobby, that was flanked on either side by rubberplants and flowering begonias, and that had a row of brass spittoons along the bottom of it, as if he were looking at it all from a dark quiet room through a keyhole. Among the faces outside the window he found himself looking at old man Napier's white mustaches and his broadbrimmed felt hat, and Jessie and Wheatly in new blue and pink gauze hats that were very unbecoming to them, standing kneedeep in all the little towheaded Napiers; or was it just another mountain family that looked like them?

It was a relief when Cramm put his big soft hand on Glenn's shoulder and said what about talking to their clients. They walked down the street to the jail without meeting any miners Glenn knew. One big fellow in khaki, who looked like one of the Sladetown gunthugs, had been standing in the hotel entry; he gave them a dirty look and started slouching after them through the crowd.

The old warden was very polite and greeted the lawyers warmly and even offered them cigars. He and George Hurlbut Cramm had a little chat about racehorses and whiskey and the fine fall weather. Then he called to the lame turnkey, who gave Glenn a great friendly wink, to bring down Napier and Davis and politely left them alone in his office to talk.

Glenn felt a second's embarrassment on account of his new suit when Pearl came in, but Pearl and Hank strode over to him and pumped his arms and said he looked right pale and must have been powerful poorly and he sure must have been light on his feet to dodge them bullets. That made him feel better. Their faces looked paler than when Glenn had seen them last, and they were beginning to get a bluish bloat under the eyes. He introduced them to George Hurlbut Cramm who said that the procedure was going to be to try the boys separately and not together like at the last trial that was what the superior court had ordered and they were going to take full advantage of it to bring out every bit of evidence there was.

Pearl mumbled that whatever the Union thought was all right, was all right by him, he didn't care no more. Glenn told him to cheer up, but Pearl shook his head and pulled him into a corner and whispered in his ear that they had brung in Jessie to see him that morning and he was all broke up, he could take it for himself but it sure was hard on the women and the children. Them operators had gotten in a mountain preacher who sure had been working on the poor people up above Muddy Fork about the sinfulness of the rednecks and infidels and now they had Pappy all worked up agin the Union and going around saying it had been the ruination of the Napier connection. Pearl said Pappy never did have a bit of sense, but now it looked like old age had done dried up his brains, and like as not he'd testify and there was no telling what he'd say. "But, Christ, he can't testify you were in on that shooting because you weren't." Pearl's brows stiffened into a frown. "Pappy won't be fixin to do us no harm," he said.

The warden came back and said Judge Purdy was just entering the courtroom and that he thought the Napier case was third on the docket. They shook hands all around, and

Glenn and the lawyers walked out through the courthouse into the bright sunlight outside.

On the steps they found Jane Sparling bustling around in a great stew, saying she was being followed everywhere she went, and that gunthugs from Sladetown were intimidating witnesses. The rest of the day, while the jury was being chosen in the courtroom, Glenn spent driving Jane around in Marice's car to round up defense witnesses. Jane was full of dark forebodings about a sellout. She said Harve Farrell and his lawyer were in cahoots with Prout to pin the red flag on Napier and Davis and to convict them, and then to get the O.B.U. boys off. She said Glenn's idea of trying to cooperate with the O.B.U. was criminal. He'd see when it was too late that he'd been conniving in a sellout.

Glenn asked her what she'd do if they got her on the stand and asked her if she were a radical. "I'd give 'em an earful about conditions in Slade County, that's what I'd do; flux, starvation, terror . . . If that's radicalism let 'em make the best of it."

"You and Patrick Henry."

"Sure thing." Jane laughed and brushed her stringy gray hair off her forehead. They were just climbing out of the car after their last trip. Marice came out of the hotel to meet them. She said the jury was picked and she thought they looked splendid, all honest farmers. Jane stopped in her tracks, looking Marice up and down with her sour angry stare. "I suppose you know," she said, "farmers are the worst thing you can have in a labor case."

Maybe it was the concussion had made his head funny, but all next day sitting in the stuffy courtroom, listening to droning voices, Glenn kept having the feeling that it was all happening somewhere far away. It was all happening so fast. He couldn't seem to catch up with the way things were happening.

The small colonialstyle courtroom was packed with lank, intent faces of country people and mountain people. Judge Purdy sat up in the center of everything, with ample gray hair drooping off his head, and with big jowls and mouth, drooping at the corners, like a cartoon of a judge drawn to look like a bloodhound in a radical paper. Lawyer Cramm was urbane and Lawyer Ferris was full of fair play and old-fashioned kindly southern cheer and Prosecutor Prout strode back and forth across the floor and pointed the accusing finger.

Glenn didn't like to look at Pearl Napier's furrowed brow as he tried to follow what was going on. Glenn could see that Pearl had the same feeling of not being able to catch up that he had, of not being there at all, maybe.

County Prosecutor Prout was doing a good job; hour by hour Glenn watched him building up a story, in spite of the objections and the sarcasms and the scholarly exceptions and big city ways of George Hurlbut Cramm. Glenn could see the jurymen eagerly following the story that came out as clear and simple as if Prosecutor Prout were writing it up on a blackboard in a large round hand. At the meeting at Bull Creek the American Miners' leaders had been infuriated because the sheriff's deputies were taking down their seditious speeches for evidence in criminal syndicalism indictments, and planned to ambush them after the speaking and so destroy the evidence; that was why several of the miners, including the chairman of the meeting, Pearl Napier, had left in the middle of it with anger in their hearts. Many witnesses testified to that. Witnesses testified that it was late at night when Pearl Napier and the other three men in the car with him reached his home at Muddy Fork. Everything linked up. Where had Napier been all afternoon? Lying in wait with a gun with anger in his heart and murder in his brain, lying in ambush waiting to maim and kill High Sheriff Caleb Blaine and his deputies who were proceeding on a lawful errand, doing their duty to protect the homes and the property of the citizens of Slade County in accordance to the oath they had sworn before God.

That part brought a chorus of exceptions from the lawyers and a burst of clapping from one corner of the room that made Judge Purdy threaten to clear the court.

The defense began parading its witnesses. Before he was ready Glenn found himself changed to an actor in the play. He was on the witness stand. All the pairs of eyes were turned on him. His head ached and his forehead was dripping with sweat. He still had the illusion that he was looking out at it all from out of a black humming room. He wiped his face with his handkerchief. Gradually the mist of faces cleared round him. He could see Cramm distinctly. They were talking in a friendly leisurely way. Cramm was asking him about his health. Glenn said he'd just recovered from a severe beating at the hands of . . . Prout was on his feet howling for an exception.

Cramm went back genially to the story of Glenn's activities in the minefields and especially to the drive home with Pearl Napier the Sunday of the speaking at Bull Creek, how they'd left the speaking in fear of their lives, how they'd had a flat tire, their late supper at Pearl's house with his wife and children. The story that had seemed so plausible when they'd rehearsed it with the lawyers, began suddenly to sound hollow and false in Glenn's own ears. He began to wonder if he could be lying.

He looked in the two rows of quiet attentive hick faces in the jurybox; it was so simple, they must believe it. They were kindly hardworking outofdoor men, the kind of people he got along with. Suddenly he felt at ease in the courtroom, for the first time everything seemed gentle, cheerful, almost jolly.

Prosecutor Prout was asking him questions now.

"Do you believe in God, Mr. Crockett?"

Glenn felt himself getting red. The lawyers were on their feet waving their arms. The Judge waved them back into their seats with his limp hand. Glenn was looking in Cramm's face.

"That's a complicated question."

"Answer me, yes or no."

"No."

"Do you believe in the future life promised us by the Good Book in which we shall be punished for sins committed in this world?"

"No."

The lawyers were seething. Judge Purdy consented to listen to their arguments. The jury was sent out. The Judge held that the Prosecutor was in his rights asking questions to establish the credibility of the witness. When the jury came back their faces were grim and their jaws were set. All the time Glenn had stood there with empty, aching head. Nothing to do now but go on and give them the works.

Prosecutor Prout started up just where he'd left off. "Then it's not the fear of God that makes you tell the truth?"

Glenn felt blind anger rising in him. "I tell the truth because I don't believe in lying . . . because I believe in the dignity of man," he shouted.

"Do you believe the present socalled capitalistic order of society is right and just?"

"No."

"Do you consider the Russian system of communism as practiced in red Moscow more conducive to the dignity of man as you call it than belief in the Gospel, the sacredness of the home and private property and the Constitution of the United States?"

"Yes."

"Then you prefer the red flag of anarchy to Old Glory?"

"That's not a fair question."

The lawyers were on their feet again. The jury was sent out again. Cramm asked for a mistrial. It was denied. Glenn stood leaning on the bar of the witness stand feeling sick and shaky like he'd felt as a little boy the first day in a new school when he didn't know the lesson. Judge Purdy announced the court was in recess and went into chambers with the lawyers. That was all that day. When Glenn walked over to the hotel people made a lane for him to pass through as if he had a contagious disease. Nobody looked him in the face but he could feel black looks piling up behind him. He went up to his room and lay down on the bed.

Dr. Blumenthal, with whom he shared the room, came in rubbing his hands and saying it had been most interesting to observe the purely automatic reactions of the jurors to ritualistic words and phrases. Glenn sat up on the edge of the bed and said well, he supposed it was just as well in the long run, you had to tell the masses the truth. Blumenthal took a little comb and combed his silky white wisps of mustache in front of the glass, then he turned to Glenn with his silly English giggle and said, "Quite the contrary. I never believe in telling anybody the truth, least of all the mahsses."

"But you can't build a great political movement on lies."

"You can't build it on anything else if you ahsk me," Dr. Blumenthal said, jauntily walking back and forth on his bandy legs.

Glenn was kneading his aching head in his fingers. "It's not fair," he said. "We've got to smash it, by God, we've got to smash it."

"What?"

"The whole hideous system."

"I'm very much afraid, my young friend . . ." Dr. Blumenthal's accent, that often had a slight cockney twang, became very Oxonian, "that this time it is the system that will do the smashing."

"Oh, Sandy, you were magnificent . . . it was the greatest emotional experience of my life," said Marice, sticking her head in the door. "How about a little teeny drink? Poor boy, you need it. Mamma's got a flask in her handbag."

"Splendid, my dear," said Dr. Blumenthal, rubbing his hands. "This trial is most interesting."

"Marice, for chrissake this isn't a picnic," said Glenn, brushing past her out the door.

It was dark. He walked out the rolled country road back of the hotel. Behind a hedge he saw sparks going up in the starry fall sky. Mountain people were sitting around a little fire at the rear end of a wagon. Pink light followed the curve of the canvas cover on the cart and splashed on faces and shirts and cotton dresses. Glenn leaned over the rails of a gate watching them for a while before he recognized who it was he was looking at. Then he whistled and called, "Wheatly, come here a minute." She left the others and came walking across the field with her long stride, her face stuck forward to peer into the darkness. Before she got to the fence she stopped in her tracks. "That's who it is," she said. "Hain't none of us talkin to you, but if they send that boy to the chair I'll git me a gun and blow the top of your head off an watch you squirm till you die."

"Honest, Wheatly, we're doing our best, all of us."

She had already turned her back and walked away toward the fire. Glenn went back to the hotel. In the lobby he found Jane sitting coolly reading the New York papers while two big huskies in khaki sat chewing tobacco and scowling at her from the opposite side of the lobby. "Things may look bad here, Sandy," she said cheerfully, "but from the national angle we couldn't do better."

"The trials are cooked," muttered Glenn, dropping into the chair beside her and staring into the palms of his hands that had lost all the calluses they used to have.

"I talked to Comrade Weeks over the long distance," whispered Jane. "He pointed out that this was a war. No army can expect to win a battle without losing some effectives. He says we got to get you out of here before they re-

arrest you for something. He wants to save you for speaking
. . . Say, let's go upstairs to the lovenest and talk to the fair
Marice . . . Those bozos are getting my goat."

"Jane," said Glenn, "I don't care what happens . . . I
feel that everything I've ever tried to do was a flop . . ."

"Petitbourgeois defeatism, my dear," said Jane airily.

Next morning Dr. Blumenthal, saying that after all he
had a duty to his patients, left on the early train for New York.
The jury had been out an hour, when Colonel Ferris came
over to the hotel shaking all over, to tell Glenn he didn't
think he and Cramm would be safe in Bluegrass another
minute. There'd be nothing gained by staying and getting a
bullet in them. They'd better pull out right away.

Marice was great. Her round eyes were shining and her
cheeks were pink without any rouge. She said she'd stay as
long as they liked, but Cramm started muttering about char-
tering a plane because he needed to be in his office that afternoon; so they packed their bags and were off, leaving Jane
Sparling to handle the defense. Marice drove the Chrysler.
She hit sixty as soon as she got out on the highroad. "My,
this is exciting," she kept saying. "Sandy, sign me up in your
revolution. I think it's great . . . Why, even that cat Jane
Sparling . . . I know she hates me . . . but think of her
nerve. We go in and out but she stays there in the minefields all the time."

When they stopped at a crossroads gasstation, a big touringcar full of deputies, with gun barrels sticking out in all
directions, whizzed past down the highway going hellbent
for election. Marice asked the attendant for a map and
plotted out a route, following the roadlines with the sharp
point of a glossy pink manicured fingernail. Then she
started out due west along the highroad. George Hurlbut
Cramm sat all huddled up holding on to his knees in the
back of the car, now and then casting a look backward and
giving a low groan, but nobody caught up with them.
Marice never let the car below seventy. When at last a motorcycle cop crowded them to the side of the road, they were
all puffing with relief. They could tell by his uniform that
they'd crossed the state line. Marice kidded him so coyly
and was so cucumber cool that he let her off with a repri-
mand.

They drove into Pittsburgh in the late afternoon and,

while Marice was driving George Hurlbut Cramm to the station, Glenn went over to the office of the American Miners to get in touch with Less Minot. There was nobody in the office but a little Jewish girl all smudged and inky to the armpits from trying to mend a brokendown multigraphing machine. She shook her head sadly and said he was at home ill, but the minute Glenn told her his name she said, "Comrade, go over to Donovan's Saloon on Monocacy Street. You'll find him in the back room; maybe you can straighten him out." "Will they let me in?" "Sure," she said, "this is a wideopen town."

Less did look terrible. He was slumped over a glass of beer at a small wooden table, wet with spillings, in the corner of the back room, with his hair over his face, that was swollen and grimed with dirt. He mumbled, "Hello, Sandy, old cock, have a drink." He was tapering off on beer, been tapering off for a week.

Glenn asked what the hell was the matter. Less said everything was the matter, American Miners was fucked to hell and back, the boys in Slade County was fucked and now here was this christbitten hellbound party line fucking them proper. No more dual unions. What the hell had we been getting our blocks knocked off for, and letting the boys get their blocks knocked off for, but our own party union. Now the story was go back and be good little boys and bore from within the good old Mineworkers . . . No, Mr. Conolly wasn't a crook or a socialfascist labor faker any more, he was a noble progressive fellow traveler, and we were going to work to bore from within him. Give him the order of Lenin. "Kerist, I won't dare show my face in any coalcamp in the Alleghenies."

"I'm just about through," said Glenn.

"No, you're not," said Less and started to get to his feet. "Give a hand, legs not good, wanna wash my face." Glenn grabbed one of his arms and yanked it across his shoulders and pulled him, swaying and lurching, through a passage that stank of stale beer, into a toilet where there was a tap of cold water dripping into a scaly red sink. Less stuck his head under the tap and held it there for a long time. Then he sent Glenn out to get a towel from Angelo the barkeep. After a few minutes Less had pulled himself together enough to walk back one step at a time to his table and to sit up and drink his beer. He pushed his wet hair back with his black stubby fingers and screwed his face up in a knot in an effort to look Glenn in the eye.

"No, you're not through, Sandy . . . you won't give up the fight . . . Party does some things right, some things wrong . . . Ain't nuttin else strong enough to lead the workin class outa captivity. The bosses can beat us up, shoot us, jail us, do anythin they damn please, only the Party says no . . . mass pressure . . ."

"Suppose the Party gets separated from the masses?"

"It can't while they got me . . . I'm the masses . . . Kerist, I've had every raw deal since I was that high . . . I been jailed an beat up an rolled an gypped an deported an sandbagged an shot at. They ain't hung me yet but they will . . . Hey, Angelo, another whiskey . . . Say, Sandy, got any dough? My credit's low."

"I got ten bucks."

"Jesus Christ. Angelo, make it a quart and put the rest down on account."

"Say, Less, don't you think you ought to lay off?"

"Shut up, Sandy, before I spread you out over the pavement." Less's voice was getting thick again. "When a guy's been fucked he's been fucked, ain't he? What you want me to do, go down to headquarters and bust up the office furniture?" He shook his head hard, and started off again in a singsong tone. "No, I don't do things like that . . . Less Minot was regular when your mammy was still wiping the snot off your nose . . . You be regular, Sandy, or by God I'll knock your goddam block off."

It took Glenn a couple of hours to get away from Less. Then he left him sitting there staring with eyes that had a blue glaze on them at the halfdrunk quart. It was a relief to get out in the air. He jumped on a streetcar to the hotel where he'd told Marice he'd meet her. She was all settled in a room, but Glenn asked her would she mind his driving her into New York tonight, there was something he had to attend to at the office. She yawned. Sure, she said, she was game but he'd have to drive because she was too sleepy. Coming out of the hotel they went by the newsstand. The papers all had the verdict in headlines.

MINERS GUILTY   Jury recommends mercy   Miners

get twenty years in slaying of deputies   Farmers' jury finds
all miners guilty   UNIONISTS CONVICTED

The Bitter Drink

Veblen,
a grayfaced shambling man lolling resentful at his desk
with his cheek on his hand, in a low sarcastic mumble of in-
tricate phrases subtly paying out the logical inescapable rope
of matter-of-fact for a society to hang itself by,

dissecting out the century with a scalpel so keen, so
comical, so exact that the professors and students ninetenths
of the time didn't know it was there, and the magnates and
the respected windbags and the applauded loudspeakers
never knew it was there.

Veblen
asked too many questions, suffered from a constitutional
inability to say yes.

Socrates asked questions, drank down the bitter drink
one night when the first cock crowed,
but Veblen

drank it in little sips through a long life in the stuffi-
ness of classrooms, the dust of libraries, the staleness of
cheap flats such a poor instructor can afford. He fought
the boyg all right, pedantry, routine, timeservers at office
desks, trustees, collegepresidents, the plump flunkies of the
ruling businessmen, all the good jobs kept for yesmen, never
enough money, every broadening hope thwarted. Veblen
drank the bitter drink all right.

The Veblens were a family of freeholding farmers.
The freeholders of the narrow Norwegian valleys were a
stubborn hardworking people, farmers, dairymen, fishermen, rooted in their fathers' stony fields, in their old tim-

bered farmsteads with carved gables they took their names from, in the upland pastures where they grazed the stock in summer.

During the early nineteenth century the towns grew; Norway filled up with landless men, storekeepers, sheriffs, moneylenders, bailiffs, notaries in black with stiff collars and briefcases full of foreclosures under their arms. Industries were coming in. The townsmen were beginning to get profits out of the country and to finagle the farmers out of the freedom of their narrow farms.

The meanspirited submitted as tenants, daylaborers; but the strong men went out of the country

as their fathers had gone out of the country centuries before when Harald the Fairhaired and Saint Olaf hacked to pieces the liberties of the Northern men, who had been each man lord of his own creek, to make Christians and serfs of them,

only in the old days it was Iceland, Greenland, Vineland the Northmen had sailed west to; now it was America.

Both Thorstein Veblen's father's people and his mother's people had lost their farmsteads and with them the names that denoted them free men.

Thomas Anderson for a while tried to make his living as a traveling carpenter and cabinetmaker, but in 1847 he and his wife, Kari Thorsteinsdatter, crossed in a whalingship from Bremen and went out to join friends in the Scandihoovian colonies round Milwaukee.

Next year his brother Haldor joined him.

They were hard workers; in another year they had saved up money to pre-empt a claim on a hundred and sixty acres of uncleared land in Sheboygan County, Wisconsin; when they'd gotten that land part cleared they sold it and moved to an all-Norway colony in Manitowoc County, near Cato, and a place named Valders after the valley they had all come from in the old country;

there in the house Thomas Anderson built with his own tools, the sixth of twelve children, Thorstein Veblen was born.

When Thorstein was eight years old, Thomas Anderson moved west again into the blacksoil prairies of Minnesota that the Sioux and the buffalo had only been driven off from a few years before. In the deed to the new farm Thomas

Anderson took back the old farmstead name of Veblen.

He was a solid farmer, builder, a clever carpenter, the first man to import merino sheep and a mechanical reaper and binder; he was a man of standing in the group of Norway people farming the edge of the prairie, who kept their dialects, the manner of life in their narrow Norway valleys, their Lutheran pastors, their homemade clothes and cheese and bread, their suspicion and stubborn dislike of townsmen's ways.

The townspeople were Yankees mostly, smart to make two dollars grow where a dollar grew before, storekeepers, middlemen, speculators, moneylenders, with long heads for politics and mortgages; they despised the Scandihoovian dirtfarmers they lived off, whose daughters did their wives' kitchenwork.

The Norway people believed as their fathers had believed that there were only two callings for an honest man, farming or preaching.

Thorstein grew up a hulking lad with a reputation for laziness and wit. He hated the irk of everrepeated backbreaking chores round the farm. Reading he was happy. Carpentering he liked or running farmmachinery. The Lutheran pastors who came to the house noticed that his supple mind slid easily round the corners of their theology. It was hard to get farmwork out of him; he had a stinging tongue and was famous for the funny names he called people; his father decided to make a preacher out of him.

When he was seventeen he was sent for out of the field where he was working. His bag was already packed. The horses were hitched up. He was being sent to Carleton Academy in Northfield, to prepare for Carleton College.

As there were several young Veblens to be educated, their father built them a house on a lot near the campus. Their food and clothes were sent to them from the farm. Cash money was something they never saw.

Thorstein spoke English with an accent. He had a constitutional inability to say yes. His mind was formed on the Norse sagas and on the matter-of-fact sense of his father's farming and the exact needs of carpenterwork and threshing machines.

He could never take much interest in the theology, sociology, economics of Carleton College where they were busy trimming down the jagged dogmas of the old New England Bibletaught traders to make stencils to hang on the walls of commissionmerchants' offices.

Veblen's collegeyears were the years when Darwin's assertions of growth and becoming were breaking the set molds of the Noah's Ark world,

when Ibsen's women were tearing down the portières of the Victorian parlors,

and Marx's mighty machine was rigging the counting house's own logic to destroy the countinghouse.

When Veblen went home to the farm, he talked about these things with his father, following him up and down at his plowing, starting an argument while they were waiting for a new load for the wheatthresher. Thomas Anderson had seen Norway and America; he had the squarebuilt mind of a carpenter and builder, and an understanding of tools and the treasured elaborated builtupseasonbyseason knowledge of a careful farmer,

a tough whetstone for the sharpening steel of young Thorstein's wits.

At Carleton College young Veblen was considered a brilliant unsound eccentric; nobody could understand why a boy of such attainments wouldn't settle down to the business of the day, which was to buttress property and profits with anything usable. in the débris of Christian ethics and eighteenthcentury economics that cluttered the minds of collegeprofessors; and to reinforce this sacred, already shaky edifice with the new strong girderwork of science Herbert Spencer was throwing up.

People complained they never knew whether Veblen was joking or serious.

In 1880 Thorstein Veblen started to try to make his living by teaching. A year in an academy at Madison, Wisconsin, wasn't much of a success. Next year he and his brother Andrew started graduate work at Johns Hopkins. Johns Hopkins didn't suit, but boarding in an old Baltimore house with some ruined gentlewomen gave him a disdaining glimpse of an etiquette, motheaten now, but handed down through the lavish leisure of the slaveowning planters' mansions, straight from the merrie England of the landlord cavaliers.

(The valleyfarmers had always been scornful of outlanders' ways.)

He was more at home at Yale, where in Noah Porter he found a New England roundhead granite against which his Norway granite rang in clear dissent. He took his Ph.D. there. But there was still some question as to what department of the academic world he could best make a living in.

He read Kant and wrote prize essays. But he couldn't get a job. Try as he would he couldn't get his mouth round the essential yes.

He went back to Minnesota with a certain intolerant knowledge of the amenities of the higher learning. To his slight Norwegian accent he'd added the broad "a."

At home he loafed about the farm and tinkered with inventions of new machinery and read and talked theology and philosophy with his father. In the Scandihoovian colonies the price of wheat and the belief in God and Saint Olaf were going down together. The farmers of the Northwest were starting their long losing fight against the parasite businessmen who were sucking them dry. There was a mortgage on the farm, interest on debts to pay, always fertilizer, new machines to buy, to speed production, to pump in a half-century the wealth out of the soil laid down in a million years of buffalograss. His brothers kept grumbling about this sardonic loafer who wouldn't earn his keep.

Back home he met again his college sweetheart, Ellen Rolfe, the niece of the president of Carleton College, a girl who had railroadmagnates and money in the family. People in Northfield were shocked when it came out that she was going to marry the drawling pernickety bookish badly-dressed Norwegian ne'erdowell.

Her family hatched a plan to get him a job as economist for the Santa Fe Railroad, but at the wrong moment Ellen Rolfe's uncle lost control of the line. The young couple went to live at Stacyville where they did everything but earn a living. They read Latin and Greek and botanized in the woods and along the fences and in the roadside scrub. They boated on the river and Veblen started his translation of the *Laxdaelasaga*. They read *Looking Backward* and articles by

Henry George. They looked at their world from the outside.

In '91 Veblen got together some money to go to Cornell to do postgraduate work. He turned up there in the office of the head of the economics department wearing a coonskin cap and gray corduroy trousers and said in his low sarcastic drawl, "I am Thorstein Veblen,"

but it was not until several years later, after he was established at the new University of Chicago that had grown up next to the World's Fair, and had published *The Theory of the Leisure Class*, put on the map by Howells's famous review, that the world of the higher learning knew who Thorstein Veblen was.

Even in Chicago as the brilliant young economist he lived pioneerfashion. (The valleyfarmers had always been scornful of outlanders' ways.) He kept his books in packingcases laid on their sides along the walls. His only extravagances were the Russian cigarettes he smoked and the red sash he sometimes sported. He was a man without smalltalk. When he lectured he put his cheek on his hand and mumbled out his long spiral sentences, reiterative like the eddas. His language was a mixture of mechanics' terms, scientific latinity, slang, and Roget's *Thesaurus*. The other profs couldn't imagine why the girls fell for him so.

The girls fell for him so that Ellen Rolfe kept leaving him. He'd take summer trips abroad without his wife. There was a scandal about a girl on an ocean liner.

Tongues wagged so (Veblen was a man who never explained, who never could get his tongue around the essential yes; the valleyfarmers had always been scornful of the outlanders' ways, and their opinions) that his wife left him and went off to live alone on a timberclaim in Idaho and the president asked for his resignation.

Veblen went out to Idaho to get Ellen Rolfe to go with him to California when he succeeded in getting a job at a better salary at Leland Stanford, but in Palo Alto it was the same story as in Chicago. He suffered from woman trouble and the constitutional inability to say yes and an unnatural tendency to feel with the workingclass instead of with the profittakers. There were the same complaints that his courses were not constructive or attractive to bigmoney bequests and didn't help his students to butter their bread, make Phi Beta Kappa, pick plums off the hierarchies of the academic grove. His wife left him for good. He wrote to a friend: "The president doesn't approve of my domestic arrangements; nor do I."

Talking about it he once said, "What is one to do if the woman moves in on you?"

He went back up to the shack in the Idaho woods.

Friends tried to get him an appointment to make studies in Crete, a chair at the University of Pekin, but always the boyg: routine, businessmen's flunkies in all the university offices . . . for the questioner the bitter drink.

His friend Davenport got him an appointment at the University of Missouri. At Columbia he lived like a hermit in the basement of the Davenports's house, helped with the work around the place, carpentered himself a table and chairs. He was already a bitter elderly man with a gray face covered with a net of fine wrinkles, a Vandyke beard and yellow teeth. Few students could follow his courses. The college authorities were often surprised and somewhat chagrined that when visitors came from Europe, it was always Veblen they wanted to meet.

These were the years he did most of his writing, trying out his ideas on his students, writing slowly at night in violet ink with a pen of his own designing. Whenever he published a book, he had to put up a guarantee with the publishers. In *The Theory of Business Enterprise, The Instinct of Workmanship, The Vested Interests and the Common Man*,

he established a new diagram of a society dominated by monopoly capital,

etched in irony

the sabotage of production by business,

the sabotage of life by blind need for money profits,

pointed out the alternatives: a warlike society strangled by the bureaucracies,

or a new matter-of-fact commonsense society dominated by the needs of the men and women who did the work and the incredibly vast possibilities for peace and plenty offered by the progress of technology.

These were the years of Debs's speeches, growing labor-unions, the I.W.W. talk about industrial democracy: these years Veblen still held to the hope that the workingclass would take over the machine of production before bureaucracy had pushed the western nations down into the dark again.

War cut across all that: under the cover of the bunting of Woodrow Wilson's phrases American democracy began to crack.

The war at least offered Veblen an opportunity to break out of the airless greenhouse of academic life. He was offered a job with the Food Adminstration, he sent the Navy Department a device for catching submarines by trailing lengths of stout bindingwire.

Meanwhile the government found his books somewhat confusing. The postoffice was forbidding the mails to *Imperial Germany and the Industrial Revolution* while propaganda agencies were sending it out to make people hate the Huns. Educators were denouncing *The Nature of Peace* while Washington experts were clipping phrases out of it to add to the Wilsonian smokescreen.

For the Food Administration Thorstein Veblen wrote two reports: in one he advocated granting the demands of the I.W.W. as a wartime measure and conciliating the workingclass instead of beating up and jailing their leaders; in the other he pointed out that the Food Administration was a businessman's racket and was not aiming for the most efficient organization of the country as a producing machine. He suggested that, in the interests of the efficient prosecution of the war, the government step into the place of the middleman and furnish necessities to the farmers direct in return for raw materials;

but cutting out business was not at all the Administration's idea of making the world safe for democracy,

so Veblen had to resign from the Food Administration.

He signed the protests against the trial of the hundred and one wobblies in Chicago.

After the armistice he went to New York. In spite of all the oppression of the war years, the air was freshening. In Russia the great storm of revolt had broken, seemed to be sweeping west; in the strong gusts from the new world in the east the warsodden multitudes began to see hope again. At Versailles allies and enemies, magnates, generals, flunkey politicians were slamming the shutters against the storm, against the new, against hope.

In America, in Europe, the old men won. The bankers in their offices took a deep breath, the bediamonded old ladies of the leisure class went back to clipping their coupons in the refined quiet of their safedeposit vaults,

the last puffs of the ozone of revolt went stale

in the whisper of speakeasy arguments.

Veblen wrote for the *Dial*,

lectured at the New School for Social Research.

He still had a hope that the engineers, the technicians, the nonprofiteers whose hands were on the switchboard might take up the fight where the workingclass had failed. He helped form the Technical Alliance. His last hope was the British general strike.

Was there no group of men bold enough to take charge of the magnificent machine before the pigeyed speculators and the yesmen at office desks irrevocably ruined it

and with it the hopes of four hundred years?

No one went to Veblen's lectures at the New School. With every article he wrote in the *Dial* the circulation dropped.

Harding's normalcy, the new era was beginning;

even Veblen made a small killing on the stockmarket.

He was an old man and lonely.

His second wife had gone to a sanitarium suffering from delusions of persecution.

There seemed no place for a masterless man.

Veblen went back out to Palo Alto

to live in his shack in the tawny hills and observe from outside the last grabbing urges of the profit system taking on, as he put it, the systematized delusions of dementia praecox.

There he finished his translation of the *Laxdaelasaga*.

He was an old man. He was much alone. He let the woodrats take what they wanted from his larder. A skunk that hung 'round the shack was so tame he'd rub up against Veblen's leg like a cat.

He told a friend he'd sometimes hear in the stillness about him the voices of his boyhood talking Norwegian as clear as on the farm in Minnesota where he was raised. His friends found him harder than ever to talk to, harder than ever to interest in anything. He was running down. The last sips of the bitter drink.

He died on August 3, 1929.

Among his papers a penciled note was found:

It is also my wish, in case of death, to be cremated if it can conveniently be done, as expeditiously and inexpensively as may be, without ritual or ceremony of any kind; that my ashes be thrown loose into the sea or into some sizeable stream running into the sea; that no tombstone, slab, epitaph, effigy, tablet, inscription or monument of any name or nature, be set up to my memory or name in any place or at any time; that no obituary, memorial, portrait or biography of me, nor any letters written to or by me be printed or published, or in any way reproduced, copied or circulated;

but his memorial remains
riveted into the language:
the sharp clear prism of his mind.

GROUP IV

From the Days
of the Caesars

Quiet Portico

March fourth dawned dark that year. The smudged sky hung low over streets of budding trees and lawns and colonnades that echoed Rome, Attic pediments, forensic domes, porticos

built proudly and long ago to frame the tall new men of the republic.

We stood in throngs along the Avenue waiting.

We stood all morning on old newspapers to keep the cold of the pavement out of our feet, waiting to see the discredited President whose term had expired ride by in a silk hat beside the President newly elected. We sat in jerrybuilt stands thumping our feet on the boards to keep warm. We stood on chairs and teetered on stepladders in empty lots.

We dreaded the rain to come, but there was only the raw gusty wind that tugged at the red white and blue bunting and heckled the flags

and snatched the newspapers out from under our feet and drove the torn grimy sheets out across asphalt lanes police and guardsmen cleared:

sheets that told

of panic at the locked doors of banks,

of stalled factories

and foreclosures and sheriff's sales and dispossess notices and outofwork gangs threatening state legislatures and bitter throngs round courthouses

and wheat and corn burned in the stove.

Between the Capitol and the Library of Congress we sat closepacked and shivering in windswept stands watching with anxious eyes the halfmast flags flap and tug at their poles above the watchers on the roofs of the office buildings

and the frockcoated throng of official persons crowding out from under the dome and the smooth broadshouldered figure confident and tall of the President newly elected who strode out on the arm of his son erect almost jaunty in his legbraces (in spite of paralysis) onto the rostrum above the goldspread eagle holding thunderbolts

to lay his hand on the Bible.

His voice after a moment's hoarseness was confident and full, carefully turned to the microphones, the patroon voice, the headmaster's admonishing voice, the bedside doctor's voice that spoke to each man and to all of us:

. . . a leadership of frankness and vigor and support of the people themselves which is essential to victory . . . leadership in these critical days . . .

(At the wheatfarmer's home on the plains the sheriff has driven up to go through with the sale. All around grayfaced men in overalls are scrambling out of splattered jalopies. We form a line silent with tight mouths in front of the farmhouse's rickety stoop. Five of us have guns. A cow lows from the barn. Fowls scatter cackling. The auctioneer has borrowed a table from the farmer's wife. Her face peers out a white blur in the kitchen window. We keep our mouths tight. The auctioneer's face is pale as milk. Nervously he raps on the table with his hammer. We listen silent to the lawyer's jargon. His voice is husky and he stumbles over words. There's a click as a shell slides into place in a rifle. "Four cents," a neighbor says. His voice is sharp and dry. No sound. The sheriff shuffles with his feet. "Four cents." No word. We let the auctioneer hurry through his rigamarole. His hammer drops weakly on the table. "Sold for four cents."

"All right neighbor, here's your farm back".)

The voice resounded in our ears, the pervasive confident voice:

. . . social values more noble than mere monetary profit . . .

(All morning we sit fiddling at our desks in the broker's office. No business. The ticker idles. Card indexes are *pulled open along the wall, ledgers piled over all the desks. In the senior partner's sanctum the accountants are at work. Every few minutes a curlyheaded man in his shirtsleeves with a pencil on his ear comes in to check over a column of figures on the adding machine. The senior partner walks out of his sanctum and breathes hard when he looks down at the paper strip full of figures. Stealthily he goes out the door into the washroom. He pulls a new revolver out of his trousers' pocket, bites down on the bright muzzle with closed eyes, and squeezes the trigger.)*

. . . the falsity of material wealth . . . the abandonment of the false belief that public office and high political position are to be valued only by the standards of pride of place and personal profit . . . a conduct in banking and business which too often has given to a sacred trust the likeness of callow and selfish wrongdoing . . .

The voice was confident, exultant. There was a smile on his lips. He talked with shoulders thrown back. We squinted to try clearly to see his face. We strained our ears to listen.

(Not Hiring reads the hastily scrawled card set in the window of the little green shack marked PERSONNEL at the gate of the great plant but the men still stand in line. We stand with limp empty hands staring with appraising eyes at the tall lit windows, black stacks and railroad tracks and slagpiles beyond, listening to the light throb and hiss of steam and the machinery's clank. Our hands slack at our knees we stand in line because we dread. We dread to go home. We dread to meet the women's eyes. We dread the kids' smeary faces when they cry: "Daddy's home, we'll eat now.")

This was where we cheered:

. . . I shall ask the Congress for broad executive power . . .

This was where we broke out and cheered:

. . . as great as the power that would be given to me if we were in fact invaded by a foreign foe . . .

We clapped cold hands together. We clapped and hoarsely cheered and the new President sharply tossed his chin and looked down in our faces and smiled.

Blackie Bowman Speaking

(Scene: a bed in a Veterans' Hospital)

Now that Joe Mangeone has stopped telling me his troubles maybe I can collect my thoughts again. That fellow's a menace to the peace of mind of the whole entire ward. He knows a man can't get away from him. He sneaks up behind you in his wheel chair and there he is mumbling his troubles through his mustache before you've seen him coming. Troubles hell. He's going to be discharged in two weeks and he's got a nice home to go to with his married daughter out in Hicksville and total disability. I got total disability too but the only pleasure I get out of it is being able to spend a little money on my nieces and nephews. Joe'll have to wear an aluminum foot but he'll be able to walk around with a cane not like me glued to this bed. The man don't know when he's well off. Talks like being discharged from the hospital was being thrown out to starve. He don't know what it is to starve.

Me, I've starved plenty. The time I came nearest to really truly starving was somewhere about the time Franklin D. Roosevelt was being sworn in as President of the United States. That was a winter.

There are times in a man's life when everything seems to come to an end. The Great Depression was one of those times. For me at least. Don't get me wrong. I wasn't worrying about black Friday on the stock exchange. It was deeper than that. I was on the beach high and dry way down inside. No job no money no wife no hope.

I was used to the outcast life. I was always more the hobo than the home guard. It was the degradation of the wobblies that was tearing me down. Ever since the old days of the Bridgemen and Structural Iron Workers I'd believed in myself because I was a wobbly. I'd believed in myself because I thought I was doing my little bit towards forming the structure of the new society in the shell of the old, the way it said in the grand old preamble. I was an I Won't Work, a wobbly, an IWW and I was proud of it. Just as much as any goddam cocksure Communist I thought I had history on my side. I was helping bring on the revolution, only the right way, the rank and file way, the American way.

We had a wobbly hall for the unemployed way west on Fourteenth Street. I put in a lot of time there. I didn't have a damn thing to do but tighten my belt. It wasn't the starving I minded. I've starved before and I've starved since. A certain amount of starving's good for a man, stimulates thinking. It's that kind of sharp thinking that divides the men from the scissorbills.

All those hall cats and spittoon philosophers over on Fourteenth Street were starving too. We were all in it together, share and share alike in good Wobbly style. What began to eat into me was that no thinking came out of it. Turn the bread lines into picket lines was the only slogan we could think up. What the hell did that mean?

From organizing the whole cockeyed industrial system we'd fallen to organizing a bunch of dead beats. We had the psychology of mission stiffs. Mister can you spare a dime?

We didn't do too bad that way once we got the hall organized. We sent out details of panhandlers to work the sidewalks. Another detail brought in old packing cases and stuff like that for firewood, or scrounged around the markets for soup bones and baskets of discarded vegetables. Our cook was a sawedoff little Romanian who'd been chef in a plush restaurant down in the financial district. Constantine something: we called him Con for short. Give Con a bone and a few old frozen carrots and spuds and a withered onion, and he'd cut out the spoiled parts and make you as fine a soup as you would want to eat. Not a man ever got sick off the slumgullion old Con cooked.

We lived off the waste of the city. The waste in the markets and restaurants of any big city is enough to make you sick, but in that depression time it broke your heart. The stuff was going to waste because nobody had any money to buy it.

We kept the hall clean and warm. We managed to provide the fellow workers with one decent meal a day. Half the time we even had coffee: don't ask me how we got it. Fellow workers hell, for the first time in my life I realized a man's worth comes from the work he does. It's not inherent in the animal if you get what I mean. That was why the better I ate the worse I felt. I wasn't no better than a goddam social worker.

I got so discouraged I kept haunting those coal wharves over on the East River trying to figure out what the best time would be to jump off so that the tiderip would sweep you up towards Hellgate and you'd be sure not to be able to make it to shore if you changed your mind. I'd have ended up unidentified on a slab in the morgue if it hadn't been for a woman. Every time it's been a woman that saved my life when it wasn't one that was driving me crazy.

Thelma Ulrich wasn't too goodlooking. She had a kind of wholesomelooking spudshaped face like she'd come right off the milking stool. She did come off a farm in Nebraska but that was many a weary year ago. Why she wanted to be a dancer I never could imagine.

We met up down in Macdougal Street in the Village.

It was a springlike late winter evening, just coming on to rain. I was squdging along with holes in my shoes, not looking to the right or left, just thinking about jumping in that cold East River when I bumped into a girl in a slicker. She stopped in front of me suddenly to look down an areaway where there was one of those basement coffee shops with checked curtains they used to have in the Village in those days. I backed off and said I was sorry and she gave me a nice straight friendly desperate look. The two of us just stood there. She kept staring down into that window with the checked curtains. I said, kinda low and sympathetic: "It looks like you couldn't make up your mind."

"Well I can't," she said.

"Why not?"

"I got my reasons."

She was holding me off, but she gave me the friendliest grin. She had a nice quiet voice. I was beginning to warm up to her.

She was saying it looked bad for a girl to be always going into places like that all alone. I told her I wished I could be her escort but they tended to like to see a man's money in those joints and money was just exactly what I didn't have.

Ten years before when I was living with Eileen I'd have had credit and welcome in any dump in Greenwich Village. But now all I saw was unfamiliar faces.

She seemed to like something about the way I told her about not having any dough, because she looked me right in the face and laughed. "That's my trouble stranger."

We couldn't stand there in the rain all day staring at each other. All at once she made up her mind. "Come along," she said without looking at me and started off down the street. I had to stretch my legs to catch up to her. She put her feet down neat and quick like a cat. From the way she moved her hips I guessed right away she was some kind of a dancer. She had me puffing before we reached one of those cold water tenements down on Fourth Street and then it was six flights up. "At least we can get out of the rain," she said as she trotted on ahead up the stairs. As she was scratching in her bag for her latchkey I told her it was supposed to be good for your wind to lose weight but I swore it hadn't been good for mine.

"I can make you some hot tea." She opened the door to let me in. Still she wouldn't look up at me. When she took off her wet kinda bucketshaped hat I could see her hair was dyed, auburn I guess you'd call it. I wasn't much over forty then but my hair had streaks of gray in it too. She took my coat and hat. She kept darting back and forth in the room with that little cat tread. It was a tiny room with an iron bed and a sink and gasburner behind a screen.

A pair of wardrobe trunks took up most of it. Theatrical trunks. You could read her whole career in the tags and labels and stickers. Vaudeville acts, names of theatrical companies on tour. None of them was very recent.

She made me sit in the battered pink easy chair, apologizing all the while that she hadn't time to mend a rip in the slipcover. Then she laid out two nice clean white cups and saucers and a loaf of rye bread and a little piece of cheese about as big as a minute. That was all she had for her supper. I could see right away that she wasn't no whore, just a theatre worker down on her uppers. Not that I'd have minded if she'd been a whore. I've known some whores who were pure gold, not many of 'em but one or two. What I mean is that right from the beginning we talked straight, like one fellow worker to another.

I nibbled slowly on those slices of bread and cheese. I desperately wanted to stay there as long as I could. The room was shabby and untidy but everything was clean and respectable. There was a nice homey smell about Thelma and her clothes and her things that you didn't expect in the Village. If Eileen had been housekeeping there the place would have been filthy.

Thelma noticed how slow I was eating and asked why. I told her right out that I was eating slow because I wanted that bread to last. The cheese was gone the first bite. I wanted it all to last. It was the first happy moment, sitting in that chair and drinking that tea and eating that bread, and talking to her; it was the first happy moment, sober that is, since I'd broken up with Eileen, and I wanted it to last. I didn't care if it lasted forever.

"I can't let you eat it all," she said. "I've got to save some for breakfast."

Did I feel like a piker?

Who was Eileen she asked abruptly. Eileen was my wife, I said. She flushed at that. I went on in a hurry to explain that we'd been separated for years now. I didn't even know where she was. One thing led to another and before I knew what had happened there I was telling her the story of my life like any old stumblebum hitting the sawdust trail for a plate of hash in a Bowery Mission.

Thelma got real excited when I told her about knowing Freddie Davis and Jack Reed and Eugene O'Neill and Art Young and fellows like that in the old days when Eileen and I lived in the Village. Her eyes got real big. It was that hick streak in her. "And here I've lived in New York fifteen years and never met a celebrity." She let out her breath in an amazed kind of way.

"Why celebrities were a dime a dozen in those days," I said. "I guess you were too young to remember the Paterson strike."

"What was that?"

I got to my feet.

"I'll tell you about that next time." And there I was scraping my wet dogs on the floor and looking at the window, and hoping she'd ask me to stay, but she didn't.

"Come and see me again Blackie," she said. "Tomorrow's the day I make the round of the agencies. An old trouper never gives up hope. Call me about six" — her gray eyes were right in mine — "if you feel like it."

She scribbled a number on a slip of paper. "It's the Italian grocery on the corner. They got a little boy named Tony. He's a friend of mine. Tony'll run upstairs and get me." "Sure," I said trying to sound bright and confident. I held her hand a little when I shook it.

As I went down the stairs I suddenly got mad. No damn woman was going to throw me out of doors like a cur dog into the rain. I crunched up the slip of paper that had the phone number on it into a pellet and let it drop down the stairwell. Thank God I found it again when I got to the ground floor because I hadn't gone a flight before I'd forgotten all about being mad and could only think of how wonderful it would be to see her again. I remembered what the number was anyway.

The northeaster was blowing rain in sheets over streets all shining with headlights and the red and green of the stop and go signs. I'd forgotten all about the East River and the riptide and my wet feet and the water running down my back through that threadbare overcoat. It was like being a kid again hitting the big city for the first time, the flicker and the crowds and the cars and the rain and the feeling of life and light spilling out of the big buildings.

After Thelma's nice cozy room it sure was a letdown to roll up wet and stinking in my blanket on the floor of that wobbly hall. It wasn't the hard floor I minded. A man can sleep right good on the floor if he takes the spot next the wall. It was the crowding, the guys laid out in rows like sardines in a box cursing and snoring and honking. These last weeks I'd been too hungry and miserable to worry about that sort of thing but now I couldn't sleep all night for wanting a woman.

Next morning I woke up coughing and feverish. All I could think of was how the hell could I raise a couple of dollars to take Thelma out to supper. I never did like to beg, but that day I worked the sidewalks clear up Broadway to 42nd Street and across to the Grand Central station and down Fifth Avenue and then back west to the garment district.

I sure did compete with the phony doughboys selling apples that day.

I hated myself for doing it but once you get started there's a technique to begging like everything else. You have to size up the guy you're touching. Some you plead with and some you have to bully just a bit. What I told 'em was I was coming down with the flu and had to get me a room and some victuals. It was God's truth, and it wasn't the usual line. People were conscious of flu that winter.

The nicest one was a bigshouldered black boy unloading cases from a truck on one of those cross streets.

"Mister you ought to check in at a hospital," he said with a roll of his big white eyeballs. I could see he was flattered because a white man had asked him for a dime. "I ain't got no cash," he said, "but I'll write an I O U," he said in his musical proud voice and he took me into a little lunchroom right there and made the counterman give me a doughnut and a cup of coffee. He signed on the check. It did me good to see the way he wrote his name on the back. He wrote real good. Marcus Jones, I've always remembered the name.

"He's good for it," said the little old counterman giving me a wink when Marcus Jones swaggered back to his truck. "That boy's a prince, a black prince."

I tried to cadge another cup of coffee off the counterman but nothing doing.

By the time it was six o'clock I was a mess. My clothes were soaked. It had been raining all day. I had a fever and a cough loud enough to rouse every undertaker in downtown Manhattan. But I had two dollars and fiftysix cents.

At six o'clock sharp I went into a booth to call Thelma. I got Tony all right and he said in his piping little voice he'd run and get her. Then I stood there with the receiver in my ear listening to my heart pounding in that goddam phone booth. I was in a sweat. I didn't believe she'd come. I couldn't have been more nervous if I'd been a sixteenyearold trying to make his first date. My heart was pumping so hard I could hardly hold the receiver.

God it took long. I was just about ready to hang up when there was that nice fellow worker voice right in my ear. I was hoarse as a crow by that time. I croaked something about setting her up for a feed. "Come on down, Blackie," she said. "I'll be waiting for you."

By that time I could just barely walk. When I finally made it up all those stairs to that cold water flat I was cough-

ing like I'd tear my lungs out. She must have heard me
through the door because she opened it before I had a
chance to knock. "Blackie, you're soaked," she said.

When I took off my coat she could see my clothes were all
wet underneath.

"I oughtn't to have turned you out . . . I almost cried
my eyes out after you'd left and now you've gone and caught
your death."

"Death hell," I said. "I've gone and caught enough jack
for two spaghetti dinners and a glass of red ink."

She never asked how I got it. Afterwards she told me she
thought I'd gone out and robbed some guy in the park.

Right away I told her I oughtn't to have come. I hadn't
planned to be infectious. I'd go along right after supper so
that she wouldn't catch my flu. Of course I didn't mean a
word of it.

She said not to be silly I'd brought her luck. She had a
promise of a job teaching ballet for the WPA. WPA what
the hell was that? That was the first time I'd heard of
WPA. Us old time radicals made a point of not reading the
capitalist press and the wobbly papers tended to run behind
on the news. WPA. Those letters got to sound wonderful
to us. I know a lot of it was just boondoggling and votebuy-
ing by the politicians but it sure was a godsend to a pair of
derelicts like Thelma and me. And we weren't the only
ones. For many a young fellow WPA was the Promised
Land.

Her job began Monday she said, all excited, she'd tell me
about it while we were eating our supper. It was then I noticed the change in the woman. It wasn't that she was better
looking. Her best friend wouldn't call Thelma a good-
looker. But her happiness was shining inside her like a candle in a jackolantern.

She decided I was too sick to go out. She'd take the
money and buy some groceries and cook them up there, in
her room. She put on a slicker and that funny hat and out
she went leaving me with a clean bath towel to rub myself
down with and an old ulster coat of hers to put on while my
clothes dried. I felt terrible taking off those clothes in her
nice room. They were stinking and my shorts were filthy
and all in rags. I must have been delirious, with the fever
and the flu coming on because what I did when she'd gone

was to roll them up in a ball and open the window and pitch them out into the alley. Except for the shoes. The shoes would do even if they did have holes in them.

Now she couldn't throw me out.

When she came back with a big bag of groceries all splattered with the rain she was too busy cooking spaghetti and meatballs to notice about my clothes. Sick as I was the smell of tomatopaste and garlic sizzling in olive oil sure made my mouth water.

As she worked she talked over her shoulder telling me about how her grandmother never would turn away a tramp. "The stranger may be God," was what her grandmother used to say.

And besides I'd brought her luck. This WPA job was going to pay twentyfive dollars a week. Nine months she'd been at liberty, that's what theatre people call it when they're out of work. She was down to her last dime. Well that was over. Water over the dam.

She gave me a look out of her big gray eyes that almost scared me, a look that bored right through into the back of my head. "Blackie, didn't you tell me you were a structural iron worker?"

"What's the matter don't you believe it?"

"Sure I believe it. All I was going to say was I saw something like that on the list of WPA job opportunities."

There was a knock on the door. She pushed me behind the screen. I didn't blame her. I must have been a sight with that towel around my neck and my long hairy legs coming out from under that old ulster of hers.

It was Tony bringing up a bottle of dago red. She was telling him she'd pay his father for it the first of the week and he was piping up that that wasn't going to worry them, the old man would be on easy street if everybody paid their bills like Miss Ulrich did. Tony was a nosy little squirt and Thelma had to give him a big sugar bun she'd bought for our dessert to get rid of him. He must have seen my bare feet under the screen but he didn't let on. Slum kids like that are wise beyond their years.

When I came out from behind the screen she asked me right out: "Blackie what on earth happened to your clothes?"

I didn't know what to say. I lied and said they were so

foul I'd put them out on the fire escape but I couldn't help blushing. I'm funny that way. I blush like a girl at the slightest thing.

She was craning her neck out of the window. "Well they are not there now." She began to laugh. I was red as a beet. Thank God she took it funny. "Wind musta taken 'em," I gasped. I was beginning to laugh myself. We were both laughing like fools. "Now you can't throw me out." I figured that was about the time I ought to put my arms around her.

She pushed me away. That girl really had muscles. "First things first," she said and brought out a bottle of aspirin tablets and made me take three of them. Then she poured us each a glass of wine.

She looked me straight in the eye. "Blackie," she said in that matter of fact way she had, "it looks like I was going to take up with you but you've got to let me do it in my own way. It's being in too much of a hurry that ruined my marriage and every affair I've tried to have."

I was so weak and feverish I didn't have the gumption anyway. I let her push me into a chair and sat there shoveling in the spaghetti and meatballs as fast as Thelma piled up my plate.

There weren't many things Thelma knew how to cook but she sure did know how to cook Italian food. She told me later her husband had been a singer at the Met, one of those wops in the chorus I guess, and he'd taught her.

I was sick as a dog but I was happy. That was one of the happiest meals I ever ate.

The damn wine and the aspirin and all that unaccustomed grub made me sleepy. Couldn't keep my eyes open. That feeling that a woman is really going to take care of you. There's nothing like it in the world. Thelma made me a pallet out of blankets on the floor and before I knew it I was as dead as a drunken Dutchman.

She nursed me like a baby for three days.

Saturday morning I woke up feeling a whole lot better, but weak as a kitten. The place was all tidied up. The bed was made but no Thelma. I got to my feet and looked for her. I thought she'd gone to the john down the hall but when I put on my shoes and went to look, still no Thelma. Back in the room no Thelma.

"You damn fool she's walked out on you," I told myself. What if she didn't come back. What the hell was I going to do stark naked in a strange woman's apartment?

I did have the sense to shave with a safety razor I found on her bureau. It always surprises me that women have razors too. A lot of them shave their legs and their armpits and all sorts of odd places.

I must have still been a little lightheaded from the flu because I couldn't help chortling at my own predicament. Then I felt so weak I had to lay down in my blankets. I drifted off to sleep again.

When I opened my eyes there Thelma was bustling round the room fresh and rosy as a May morning. What she'd done was go out and hock her last bits of jewelry, her wedding ring and all, and bought me some clothes. I ought to have known she was up to something when she took my measurements with a tape the day before. The suit was secondhand but it was clean and neat. She buttoned up my new shirt and helped me tie my necktie.

Then she stood me up against the wall and took a look at me. "Now you look more like somebody I could learn to love," she said.

This time she let me hug her and love her up a little but she wouldn't let me kiss her on the mouth, not till I'd gotten that flu out of my system, she whispered with her mouth against my ear. I could feel her heart beating behind her little flat breasts. Mine was pounding for sure. There was something about that woman made me shy as a lad.

That was when I told her it was on purpose I'd thrown away my clothes. "You've thrown away your old life," she cried out in her theatre voice, "and I'm going to throw away mine."

All that afternoon we just sat there side by side on the little iron bed, drinking tea and telling each other about things that had happened to us. Usually I'm pretty impatient in a situation like that but for once I kept telling myself: Fellow you go slow.

The next day was Sunday. It was sunny outside. My strength was coming back and I woke up horny as a goat. I wanted to go out and walk around the block to cool off but she said that was how folks got pneumonia going out too soon after the flu. So I just sat there bolting down the bacon and eggs.

After breakfast I helped her wash the crockery. When we'd set the last plate on the rack I pulled her to me and said it was now or never. I had to be a little teeny bit rough with her and she whimpered I was hurting her but she didn't seem to take it too hard. She made me tell her about what it had been like loving other women and that set me to spinning yarns. To tell the truth I made up most of it. I never did like to tell about my private life — not till I got old and the whole thing was over.

When You Try to Find the People

When you try to find the people, always in the end it comes down to somebody,
somebody working, maybe:
a man alone on an old disk harrow yelling his songs out at a team of mean mules (it's the off mules gives the trouble, breaking and skittish, pulling black lips back of yellow teeth to nip at the near mule's dusty neck);
it's March and the wind sears the chapped knuckles of the hand that clamps the reins; levers rattle; there's a bolt loose under the seat somewhere; it's hard to keep straight in the furrows as the pile of junk laced together with bindingwire lurches over the tough clods;
it's March and the sun is hot and the dry wind rasps the skin and ruffles the robinsegg tatters of sky in the puddles along the lane that cuts straight from the mailbox under the roadside wires up to the house with blank windows that stands half tilted back on its haunches like a mule balking:
a man in his twenties, maybe, scrawny neck red and creased from the weather sticking out of the raveled sweater, brows bent under the bluevisored cap, riding the jangle of castiron and steel over the caked clods (it's clayey land an

a rainy spell come on before he got shet of his winter plowin):

a man alone with a team of mean mules and the furrowed field hemmed in on three sides with scrub and the sky full of blackbirds that wheel and scatter and light behind him to peck hurriedly among the new small furrows; when yelling he yanks on the reins to turn in a sweep by the fence trampling the brown silverpodded stalks of last year's weeds, the blackbirds take fright and soar in circling flight, specks that swirl black against snowtopped lumps of cloud drifting like ice through the blue windy rapids of the sky;

each time he passes his kitchen door there are more clothes out to dry on the line; sometimes he sees his wife with clothespins in her mouth wrestling with a flapping wet sheet or hears the whooping of the twoyearold or the weak squall of the new baby;

harrowing towards the road he faces the wires looping from pole to pole and the shambling trucks and the shining fast cars and the old jalopies creeping like bluebottle flies cold on a windowsill;

each time he passes his kitchen door the radio fills his ears, voices bawling the price of fat stock in Kansas City, grains in Chicago, basketball scores, news of the fighting, smoothly a clause out of a government speech, swing moaning smokily from a late floorshow someplace where it's still night,

the voice direct from me to you of a candidate who wants to be nominated,

voices talking bargains, threatening sickness, offering opportunities, wheedling chances,

voices from the gargled throats of announcers in glassedin studios beyond the sky and the clouds and the blackbirds and the wind,

that beat in the ears and fade into the forgetful coils of the mind

intent on the edge of the furrow and the mean team of mules and the wife hanging out the week's wash and the kid with the whooping cough

and the weak squall of the new baby lying wet in its crib.

The Working Farmer

Paul was standing in the doorway of the bank. He raised his hand and waved her towards him with a confidential mysterious sort of gesture. "We're not getting anywhere," he said. "I thought we'd let the boys thrash out their paperwork this afternoon and take a look at the farms. I'm borrowing Petersen's car. I'll need you to come along. I've got a list of the places. Warren wants us to be back in time to go to his local of the Farmer's Union."

"George Dilling's going to speak," said Georgia.

Paul made a face at that. "I've already heard him speak."

"But Warren wants us to come," Georgia said pleadingly, and told Paul about the taxidriver and added that she thought Warren was a pretty wonderful fellow. "Imagine the struggle that boy has to put up every minute," she said. "I find life quite hard enough as it is."

Paul grunted absentmindedly. They were driving out of town through a patch of badlands. Small buttes and pinnacles of mustardyellow clay stood up into the wan sky. Sagebrush grew in the gullies between, where occasionally they saw prairiedogs at the edge of their burrows sitting up on their haunches and looking at them out of tiny glass eyes as they drove past. A little puff of dust would rise when one of them took fright and dove down his hole.

At the top of a hill the country opened up into farmland again. They drove along a straight highway over a plain bounded by low eroded hills streaked with chalky pinks and whites and ochres. A couple of times they turned off at letterboxes and drove out muddy roads to the farms. Georgia would sit in the car while Paul got out to talk to the farmer. She hunched drowsily in the front seat watching Paul's tall figure all briskness and life again now, gesticulating with odd short gestures as he strode around with the tenant asking questions. At one place he was evidently getting directions because there was a great deal of pointing over towards a gap in the hills.

"This is going to be a tough one to find," Paul said slipping in behind the wheel, "but we'll find it."

He drove back to the highway and followed it up to a place where the cement road made a rightangle turn. There he took one of the dirt roads branching off. For a long time he drove along it between waving tracts of wheat dappled pale yellow and palegreen. The car slewed a little in the ruts because the clay was still sticky underneath from last night's rain. The road narrowed and cut through a patch of badlands, grooved bleached skeletons of hills, and came out into another prairie brimful of wheat. They drove across it for miles without seeing a house. Georgia was beginning to mutter that they'd better turn back if they were to get to Meridian in time for Warren Dodd's meeting, but Paul drove on obstinately. At last they saw slam at the end of the road an unpainted twostory house with the door in the middle and a red tin roof and two chimneys like ears. When they came up to it the road ended in a sharp rightangle turn. Paul skidded in a deep pool of muck as he slammed on his brakes and just missed the gatepost by a hair. He turned to Georgia with a foolish grin. "That wasn't what I'd planned," he said.

Paul got out of the car and hopped carefully along the grassy edge of the road to keep out of the mud. When he reached the brown grassplot in front of the house he took three long strides to the front door and disappeared inside. Georgia sat looking at the unpainted weatherboarding and the broken boards of the stoop and the pile of rusty cans and bleachedout cartons out front where a few fowls picked disconsolately among the hogweed. Behind the house the windmill rattled as if every metal part were shaking itself loose. The sun was beginning to get low in the sky. When Paul came back his thick brows were knotted in a frown.

"This isn't the place but I got to stop and help the man out. His cow's having a calf and the little girl's sick."

He climbed back in the car and managed to slew it up out of the mud onto the grass. As soon as he opened the front door for her Georgia noticed mingled with the staleness of coaloil lamps a choking sweaty smell. A tall man in overalls and a blue shirt was standing in the open back door with his arms folded and his feet apart. The skin of his face and of his hairy forearms was tanned a dark tobacco hue but his neck was red and wattled. "This is Miss Washburn my assistant," said Paul.

"John Hick is the name," the man said in a hollow voice. "You see I ain't got nobody to help me."

"Mrs. Hick is in here," said Paul opening one of the doors. "We've got to see what we can do about this calf. It's a difficult delivery."

"I'll get a rope," said John Hick.

Georgia went into the parlor that had heavy oldfashioned curtains of a greenish hue looped over the windows. In the middle of the floor was a cot where lay a little grayeyed girl swathed in blankets. Beside her in a rocker sat a puffy little woman with her dress all fluffed out around her like a setting hen. She was fanning the child with a palmleaf fan. Sweat poured off the child's little sallow face all twisted up with pain. It was from her that the oppressive stuffy smell came.

Without stopping her fanning the woman started to talk in a low unaccented voice: "It's my little girl. She's been like this for twentyone days. The doctor came an said it was rheumatic fever but the medicine he gave us didn't help none an now it's all gone an the liniment too an the doctor don't come no more. We live out of the way here an there's just Mr. Hick and me now the boy's joined the Navy an she won't let me leave her a minute an poor Mr. Hick has had to do everythin. My poor little angel. She's so good, it breaks your heart. Her joints are all swole up so she can't move. She's so little. It's too much for a little girl like that an all her life shes been so good and never any trouble to anybody."

Georgia was thrashing around in her head for the right thing to say. At last she asked in a falsely professional tone as if she were a nurse, "How much fever has she got?"

"I dunno. It was real bad when the doctor came."

Suddenly Georgia thought of something and felt better: "Have you any aspirin? I know they give that."

Mrs. Hick shook her head uncomprehendingly.

"Here I've got some out in the car." It was a relief to do something. Georgia ran out and found the bottle of aspirin tablets she carried in her briefcase. Mrs. Hick shook a couple of the little white tablets out in the palm of her hand and looked at them for a moment with a fixed suspicious stare and then dropped them back in the bottle.

"I'll wait till Mr. Hick comes," she said. Then she went back to her low rapid talking not pausing between the words: "It was real fortunate you an your husband come along when you did because I don't know what's going to happen to us if we lose that calf. That was just goin to be a little cash to tide us along until we sold our wheat. Well I guess we can ship the fowls, poor scrawny things they won't bring much. Your husband being from the Department in Washington he must know somethin though he don't talk like he was no veterinarian . . ."

"Shouldn't you get the little girl to a hospital?" Georgia asked gently.

She'd hardly said it before she knew she'd said the wrong thing. The child's eyes widened with terror. She let out a little tired scream. Mrs. Hick didn't seem to notice but went on talking in her even voice. As she talked she fanned.

"There's a hospital in Meridian but how are we goin to afford it? If we can pinch through this summer an if we save the wheat crop it won't be so bad but if there's hail an we lose this crop we'll lose the farm an then what'll we do with little Margie sick an all? Here we've been fightin a mortgage — that's what Mr. Hick calls it — for nine years now an it looks like everythin we made went into it an Jackie leavin us and joinin the Navy. I hope you an your husband never get in the grip of no mortgage."

Georgia felt her face getting red but it was too late to try to explain. She wasn't doing anything very helpful, she thought to herself as she walked out of the back door to see where Paul was. Outside the last sunset light stained the barn and the outhouses and the stanchions of the windmill and the posts of the hoglot a bright liquid red. The wind had gone down and the great expanse of wheat that stretched to the horizon was still. A few birds flew over it.

She heard voices coming from one of the stalls in the barn and ran over and peeped in. On the threshold she stopped short. They were working over the cow. Paul had taken off his shirt. The two of them worked grunting and cursing as they tugged at something bloody that protruded from the hind quarters of the cow. Blood streamed from Paul's naked elbows. Neither of them saw her or looked up.

She felt her face go pale. She walked with tottery steps back to the house. She didn't want to go back to talk to the old woman. Maybe she could find something useful to do. She didn't want to think about the cow.

She peeped in the kitchen. A kettle of water was humming on the oil stove. In the ancient slate sink stood a great stack of dirty dishes and old dented pots and pans. She found a dishpan and some soap and began to wash the dishes. For the first time that day she felt lighthearted.

She'd almost finished the dishes when John Hick, his hands bloody, his head drooping in a discouraged way over his chest came shambling into the kitchen.

"Where's my hot water?" he asked.

"I used it to wash the dishes," Georgia said. He didn't answer but just stood staring at her wearily shaking his head. Then he reached for the kettle, filled it up from the bucket and set it on the stove again.

Georgia went on working. It was nearly dark by the time she'd finished the pans and left them to drain in the sink. She looked around the kitchen for a match and lit a lamp and then lit another one and took it into the parlor. Mrs. Hick thanked her quite politely but when Georgia asked her if there was anything more she could do she just started her even flow of talk again. The little girl was keeping up a low continuous whimper. Georgia sat down but she got right up. She went out and began to pace restlessly up and down the hall. She didn't want to think about the cow. At last she got up her nerve to open the back door. It was thoroughly dark now, though from the back stoop she could still see a saffron glow in the west. There was a chink of light in the barn. After hesitating a long while she went towards it and pulled open the big double doors. Under a lantern that hung on a bulky piece of machinery that might have been a combine Paul and John Hick sat at a deal table. Their shirts were off and their hair was rumpled and they were covered with sweat and flecks of blood and they looked wild as Indians. Their elbows were on the table and their hands were clasped and they were looking each other in the eyes as each one tried to bend the other's hand down onto the table. A bottle stood within reach.

Georgia stood watching them with her mouth open. The men were both breathing hard. Their muscles bulged on their upper arms and stood out sharp from the shoulder to the neck. Their fingers were white with tension. The sweat glistened on them. She had opened her mouth to speak but she couldn't seem to think of what to say so she just stood silently watching them until they suddenly both relaxed and let go hands and burst out laughing.

"Paul you're all right," said John Hick in his deep rattling tones way down his throat.

Paul caught sight of Georgia. "Sit down Facts and Figures and have a drink of John's White Lightning."

"But we ought to get back to town? How about Warren Dodd's meeting?"

"I'm having a meeting with John Hick that's enough for one evening . . . Sit down Facts and Figures."

Georgia let herself drop on an upturned nailkeg just out of the circle of light. She felt frightened. She'd never seen Paul drinking before.

"What about the calf?" she asked timidly.

Neither of them answered.

John Hick took a swig out of the bottle and cleared his throat. "Paul I've always been a gamblin man" . . . He picked up as if continuing a narrative where he'd been interrupted. "Always been a gamblin man . . . Out in this country a wheat farmer's got to be a gamblin man. We're just goddam . . ." suddenly he looked over to where Georgia sat feeling pale and mousy on her nail keg . . . "beggin your pardon, miss . . . Well . . . speculators. A wheat farmer's just as much a speculator as a johnny in a silk hat at his desk in the New York Stock Exchange only he works harder and he stands to lose more. But I'm no bellyacher . . . beggin' your pardon, miss . . . there ain't never been a Hick was a bellyacher. I ain't runnin to no government with my troubles. This here wheat crop's just as much a gamble as those faro games they set up at Reno Nevada."

Georgia got to her feet and started to tiptoe out of the barn.

"Paul take a drink," John Hick was roaring. He'd evi-

dently forgotten all about Georgia . . . "the first goddam
government man I ever seen do a neighborly thing. If
you'd been a little better veterinary we'd a saved that calf
but it looks like we saved the cow an if you hadn't a come
around we wouldn't a saved nothing . . . Paul take your
shoes off . . . You look like a barefoot kinda man to me
in spite of all that college eddication . . . I like a barefoot
kinda man."

Paul threw back his head and roared and kicked off his
shoes.

Georgia had been lingering just outside the barn door.
She felt little and lonely and sorry for herself. She turned
and walked out round the house to where the car was. For
a while she sat on the front seat and tried to catnap. Then
after a while she got out of the car and sat on the steps of
the house looking up at the stars. The inky blue night was
very clear. Overhead she could see the whole arch of the
Milky Way. She picked out Cassiopeia's chair and the
crowded brilliants of Job's Coffin. From out back of the
house she could hear Paul's and John Hick's voices pitched
high as they called to each other. What could they be doing
out in the yard? Georgia was beginning to get hungry.
She sat on the steps and whimpered a little to herself, she
felt so lonely and abused. Then she thought of poor Mrs.
Hick and her little girl and told herself to stop that foolish-
ness. After what seemed an hour she heard rapid footsteps
coming around the end of the house and made out Paul's
tall figure in the starlight. He had his shoes and socks in
his hand. Without a word he sat down beside her on the
steps to put them on his feet.

"Will the cow be all right?" she asked. She had that
tremulous feeling again of a little girl who is afraid the
boys won't let her play with them.

"I had to stay to help him do his chores . . . John Hick
. . . he's quite a feller. He wanted to rustle us up some
supper but I wouldn't let him. Well we better push along
. . . You're driving, Facts and Figures . . . Let's push
along." He sat on the step looking up at the sky with his
hands clasped over his knees. "My what a night of stars,"
he said quietly.

"I've been looking at them such a long time," Georgia
said.

It was a relief Paul wasn't drunk. The liquor seemed to have just thrown him into a slow meditative way of behaving. He was drawling out his words with more of a tarheel accent than usual.

"You must have had a time with that calf Paul," she said in her tiniest little voice.

"Too damned ignorant . . . the calf was coming out the wrong way. There's something you can do to turn it around but I didn't know what . . ." He got up stretching to his feet. "I don't know about you Facts and Figures but I got to get some food in me. John Hick says to take the dirt road to the left and that'll bring us out on the highway."

Nervously Georgia got into the driver's seat.

She managed to get the car through the mudhole all right and found the turning but there must have been some mistake because she drove on endlessly along a muddy straight road. She had to drive very slowly to avoid sliding off into the ditch. At last they picked up a row of telephone poles and after another halfhour came out on macadam. There were no signs so there was no way of telling which way they ought to turn towards Meridian. She was going to ask Paul but when she turned to him she saw he was asleep. At random she turned to the left and drove and drove. The road didn't seem to be much of a highway. It turned and twisted through a country of nibbled hills and gullies that rose up to take jagged bites out of the starry sky first on one side and then on the other. At last she caught a glimpse of a little string of electric lights flickering far away across the badlands. Several times she lost them behind small corrugated hills with crazy pinnacles but at last she saw them dead ahead and drove up to a small fillingstation and restaurant ornamented with a sign made out of rustic logs on a white ground: PHEASANT HILLS CABINS.

Paul woke up with a start when the car stopped. "I smell steak," he said. He strode ahead of her into the little whitepainted restaurant. The squarefaced man in a white jacket behind the counter had just finished wiping off the oilcloth with a rag. "Pardner I'm closin up," he said in a drowsy voice.

"Oh come now brother, it won't take you a minute to fix us a T-bone steak for two," Paul pleaded. "And a glass of milk . . . two glasses of milk."

Georgia could see that the man was weakening. "How about some French fries?" he asked in a friendly brisker tone.

"Brother," Paul said in a way that made them all laugh, "we'll eat anything you've got and more."

"How far is it to Meridian?" Georgia asked when they were settled at a table and she was sipping a glass of milk.

"Meridian? Why that's in another part of the state altogether. I'll have to look at a highway map," the man said.

"You look at that steak first," roared Paul laughing. "Well Facts and Figures we lost our way."

"What a day," sighed Georgia.

"Never felt more discouraged in my life . . . except for old John Hick. I kinda liked my bout with old John Hick."

"You sure were going native Paul," said Georgia beginning to laugh again. "I can laugh about it now," she said cosily, "but you scared me."

"First thing tomorrow we got to do something about getting that little girl in the hospital."

Smiling broadly the man brought a big untidily cut T-bone on a sizzling metal platter and set it before them.

"My this is good," said Paul with his mouth full. "A good meal's a mighty good cure for discouragement sometimes. There are times," he added forking fried potatoes into his mouth, "when I just feel like a phony, a miserable chairwarmer. I can talk about it now that I don't feel so bad . . . My you're a help Facts and Figures . . . you and this steak . . . when it seems absolutely impossible to arrange all these divergent human relations in any kind of way that makes sense. I told you how I felt about it that night at Meridian Park. Funny, Meridian seems to be our key word. Your relationship with people changes when you try to organize them into doing things. You have to kind of lower their consequence. First thing you know it's your career instead of the work gets to be the important thing. I suppose that's how politicians are made. Oh God don't let me turn into a politician . . . What's the use of talking about it?"

"Talk about it Paul."

"I get to wondering if all this social service work . . . that's what it is . . . is just dogooding . . . isn't just putting up a front for the politicians even if you don't get to be one yourself . . . I'm out of my depth. I want to be home on a nice experimental farm with a laboratory. Let somebody else save the country . . . I get so horribly depressed . . . I wish I could go back fifteen years and start over . . ."

"Maybe," said Georgia, "the country can't be saved unless it's born again."

They'd finished eating. They sat in silence for a long time looking at each other. The man in the white coat was beginning to put out the lights. "If you folks don't mind," he said in a cozening voice, "I have to open early for the truckdrivers."

Paul was yawning. "I'm all in," he said. "Brother have you got any cabins?"

"I got right nice cabins all fresh done over last winter."

"Suppose we take a look at one."

Georgia started to tremble. She let the men walk ahead. Her hands were icy. She was trembling. The stars were so bright the liquid darkness was all aflame with them.

Paul met her at the door of a glowing yellow varnished box. The man had gone.

"I took it," Paul said in a gentle apologetic tone. He took her hand and looked down at it meditatively. Then he drew her gently towards him into the cabin, closed the door behind her and kissed her. She felt herself falling. The hard knots of muscle of his arms held her from falling. The ten fingers of his hands were holding up her back. "I guess this just had to be," he said breathless when he took his lips away from hers. "I guess it just had to be." They sat down side by side on the edge of the double bed. She let her head drop against his shoulder.

"Do you want anything particular out of the car?" She'd never heard his voice so gently concerned with her. She shook her head. "I'll lock it up and fetch our bags."

She grabbed his arm tight. "Let's go together. You mustn't leave me alone. I'd get to thinking. Oh Paul we shouldn't . . ."

"Too late now," said Paul gruffly and strode off to the car. She watched him helplessly while he hauled the two bags out of the trunk. "Oh God Petersen's bag's in there. Poor devil I forgot about him," said Paul.

"Paul," she grabbed his hands. "Hadn't we better drive right back to Meridian?"

"Can't be helped now," Paul said. He picked up the bags and strode back fast with them to the cabin. By the time she caught up with him he was coming out the door again.

"But Paul," she started.

He reached over and caught her by the shoulder and drew her roughly to him. "Hush," he whispered. I thought I heard something . . . Listen." They stared out over the windworn dark shapes of the badlands. The night was growing cold. She gave a little shiver and snuggled closer to him. Then she heard away far off a thin wailing doglike sound that rose and trailed off into the starpacked sky. "Facts and Figures I think that's a coyote," whispered Paul.

"It's the West," Georgia whispered back. "Oh Paul we've rolled off the edge of the cornbelt into the West."

"You funny romantic little kid," he said kissing her all over her face. Their ankles touching, their thighs touching, their arms interlocked, they squeezed together back into the cabin. She was melting inside. She was going to faint. She clung to him. The cheap bedsprings clanked as she let him stretch her out gently on the bed. "No no no, Paul, no . . ." she kept saying in a tiny voice until his lips clamped down on hers again.

Rover

On September 11 1884 there was born in a tall brownstone house in a fashionable section of New York,

with a silver spoon in her mouth and all the aristocracy the Empire State could afford in those great days of the high bourgeoisie,

a little girl. Eleanor was a Roosevelt, an Oyster Bay Roosevelt. Her father was T.R.'s kid brother Elliott. Her mother was Anna Hall of a rich upstate family of Halls.

Except for T.R.'s roughhousing affection for his homely

little niece (she had the same buck teeth he had) her childhood was miserable.

Her father shared T.R.'s cult of the outdoors, loved
dogs and horses and back country travel, but Daddy was a
ne'erdowell and mostly he drank. He was a handsome man,
debonair. The little girl loved him but hardly ever saw him
because he was always off taking the cure in some sanitarium. Finally he retired to the Valley of Virginia where
drunkenness was still considered a rather gentlemanly pro-
fession.

Her mother was a tense nagging woman with a taste for
amateur theatricals. She called little Nell "Granny" the child
was so glum. She suffered from headaches.

Both parents died by the time Eleanor was ten.

She was raised by a succession of German and English
governesses at her grandmother Hall's place at Tivoli up the
Hudson. Mrs. Hall didn't believe in sending girls away to
school. The only outings in Eleanor's life were in connection
with the doing of good. The Hudson River aristocrats never
forgot their duty to those less fortunate than they.

Charity was fun. The Hall girls, Eleanor's aunts, properly chaperoned and at suitable times and seasons, sang
hymns in Bowery missions or dressed Christmas trees in
Hell's Kitchen. As a special treat little Eleanor would be
taken along to visit a children's hospital.

How the other half lived: there was a smell of sweat
and grime and adventure about poor people's kids. What
daydreams would be touched off by a greedy glance from a
sullenfaced Jewish boy, or the grin of some ruddy little Irish
mick. Their morals were deplorable. The aim of charity was
to reform the morals of the poor. Their deplorable morals,
said Grandmother Hall, was why they were poor.

Grandmother Hall hated Roosevelts. She wasn't too
fond of shy gangling Eleanor. She discouraged her visits to
her rambunctious uncle's house at Oyster Bay. Eleanor bit
her nails and yearned, cooped among maids and governesses
in the big old bracketed mansion at Tivoli. She read and
reread her dear dead father's admonishing letters, and books
with titles that seemed to apply: *Misunderstood, Sans
Famille, The Man Without a Country.*

When she was fifteen there was a break in the clouds.

She was sent to boarding school in England.

Allenwood, near Wimbledon Common on the outskirts of London, was, around the turn of the century, in charge of a remarkably intelligent French spinster. Mlle. Souvestre was a woman of letters, an agnostic (atheist, hissed her enemies) of the Voltairian school now exemplified by the gentle Renan, an anticlerical Dreyfusard, a pacifist, a feminist: give women votes and they'd see about man's perfectibility or know the reason why. Just the woman to stuff the head of a yearning young girl from Tivoli up the Hudson with all the glowing nineteenth century notions of the good the beautiful and the true.

A Miss Strachey, of the literary Stracheys, taught literature. This was no ordinary school. Eleanor Roosevelt was happy for the first time in her life.

Mlle. Souvestre liked Americans. She liked Eleanor and took her along on summer tours of the artgalleries of Europe. The story goes that Eleanor was still so shy and bucktoothed and gangling that Mlle. Souvestre had no qualms about letting her run around Florence all alone (no danger of her being picked up by a gay deceiver); but in the school she was a leader. She had found her place in the world.

It was real heartbreak when at eighteen the family brought her home. She wanted to go to college but her grandmother insisted on her coming out instead.

She took refuge in the Junior League and teaching calisthenics and dancing at the Rivington Street Settlement. Uplift. She became interested in sweatshops. She never forgot her duty to those less fortunate than she.

On the train back and forth between New York and Tivoli she began occasionally to meet another Roosevelt, a cousin, who got off at Hyde Park.

If Eleanor had a formidable grandmother, her cousin Franklin, an only child, had a mother who was allconsuming. At Groton she appeared almost weekly to heckle Dr. Peabody. When Franklin went to Harvard she rented a house at the edge of the Yard. When he took up law at Columbia there she was making a home for him on Madison Avenue. Maybe it was parental tyranny that brought Franklin and Eleanor together.

When she discovered the cousins were "interested"

Sara Roosevelt promptly took her boy Franklin off on a Caribbean cruise to break it up. After that she dragged him to Washington, but who should she find, when she took her boy to the White House for a cousinly visit, but Eleanor eating lunch with her Uncle Ted.

In spite of Mama they became engaged. Maybe it was Eleanor's influence that caused Franklin D, brought up as proper gold Democrat at Hyde Park, to vote Republican for her Uncle Ted in 1904.

Their wedding on March 17th 1905 was the social event of that New York spring. The newly inaugurated President was there, bubbling with "Bully" and grinning his bucktoothed grin. Vanderbilts, Sloans, Belmonts, Riggses, Van Rensselaers, Mortimers represented the 400. A rowdy mob of T.R.'s political supporters cheered in the street outside.

Hyde Park was an anticlimax. Franklin's mother took charge of everything, hired nurses for the numerous babies that appeared promptly in order, decorated their rooms, and ordered their servants around. It wasn't much fun. Franklin D was bored to death with the law. His pleasure was sailing his schooner yacht which, like a good Hudson River man, he named *Halfmoon*. At Hyde Park he served in the vestry, joined the volunteer Hook and Ladder, was director of the bank. In the same spirit he let himself be elected to the legislature.

Eleanor Roosevelt was developing a ferocious energy equal to the energy of her Uncle T.R. No outlet for it at Hyde Park where her motherinlaw wouldn't even let her boil an egg. Her real life lay in the settlement houses; uplift, the wrongs of the working girl. Conditions: the horrible Triangle fire kindled a torch.

At Albany in 1911, though his mother tried to take over Franklin's political career as she had everything else, Eleanor had her first taste of politics. There was a smell of sweat and grime and adventure about politicians. They hadn't had the advantages. She took to them. Politics like settlement work was dealing with those less fortunate than she.

Reform was in the air. The better element was going in for public service. Wasn't Uncle Ted in the White House? Professor Woodrow Wilson, late president of Princeton, was Governor of New Jersey.

Sara Roosevelt, an old lady and behind the times, still felt it was infradig. Her boy Franklin was developing a knack for dealing with people who weren't the kind of people she would want to invite into her home. Eleanor was all for it: it was the duty of the better element to improve conditions.

In Albany Franklin D acquired a familiar. An odd uncouth individual, an oldtime newspaperman named Louis Howe decided he'd dedicate his life to building a political career for Franklin Delano Roosevelt. When Representative Roosevelt came down with typhoid while running for the state senate, Eleanor had to do the campaigning. Louis Howe coached her. Eleanor learned to make speeches. They were halting but they were sincere. People responded. She loved it.

When Franklin D still showed, at that stage in his career, some difficulty in disguising his feeling that the plain people existed mostly as convenient steppingstones on which young Hudson River magnates,

educated at Groton and Harvard,

could climb to high office,

his wife Eleanor just loved them. She wanted to be folks. She'd never heard of fatigue. She poured all the capabilities that her motherinlaw frustrated at home into doing her duty towards those less fortunate than she,

and pushing her husband's career.

Louis Howe saw that as a team the young Roosevelts would go far. Already he dreamed of the presidency for Franklin D. Woodrow Wilson, the first Democrat since Grover Cleveland, had just been elected by a good majority of electoral votes. He was combing the better element (among Democrats) for deserving civil servants. After considerable backing and filling it was arranged that Josephus Daniels should offer

to Franklin D. Roosevelt of New York

the post of Assistant Secretary of the Navy. It fitted Franklin D to a T. The man was crazy about ships and the sea. Eleanor and Louis Howe couldn't help having it in the back of their minds that this was the post from which her Uncle Ted had embarked on a triumphant career.

The story is told that it was the seventeen gun salute, given her son when the warship *North Dakota* put in to

Eastport, across the bay from their summer home at Campobello Island, that finally convinced Sara Roosevelt that politics might become a gentleman's career. She hurried off to
Washington, where the young people were setting up housekeeping in a house lent them by one of Eleanor's aunts, to
boss the household as usual.

Young Roosevelt impressed official Washington. Tall
and slender, with a hearty laugh and a clear profile that
might have been drawn by Charles Dana Gibson, he was so
handsome people called him "The Gibson Man." Already
he was developing the subtly condescending smile that was
later to sweep all hearts.

With the declaration of war against the Central Powers
on April 2 1917 Franklin D's post in the Navy Department
became a cornerstone of the war effort. Eleanor's Uncle Ted
kept teasing him to resign and enlist for front line service,
but he was doing a good efficient job where he was and he
intended to stick. It broke Uncle Ted's heart when Wilson's
administration, suspecting that he wanted to steal the front
line limelight from the Democrats, refused to let him raise a
division of new Rough Riders to lead overseas.

In the winter of 1919 Uncle Ted died a frustrated disappointed man. Eleanor and Franklin were touring pros-
trate Europe at the time, liquidating navy hardware and sur-
plus stocks. They came home with the presidential party on
the *George Washington* with the glamour of victory about
them.

Louis Howe was busy. Berty McCormick in the *Chicago
Tribune* was already promoting Franklin D for the presidency. He was nominated for Vice-President and cam-
paigned with a forgotten gentleman named James M. Cox
who was soundly trounced by Harding in the election of
1920.

It was a discouraging campaign. The following summer
Franklin D suffered a crippling attack of poliomyelitis at
Campobello Island. His mother's attitude seems to have
been that now at last she had her baby back, a lifetime invalid. Everybody thought he was done except his wife Eleanor
and his friend Louis Howe. Never say die. Eleanor had
some of her Uncle Ted's ferocious spirit. Louis Howe was a

man dedicated to the point of mania. Franklin D would be President all the same.

The man's affliction transformed his public presence. Overcoming paralysis took an enormous effort of the will. Fortunatus was laid low. Misery may ennoble but it also levels. The raggedest streetcleaner out of work had not had to endure the misery Franklin D. Roosevelt endured and overcame in the four years before his return to politics. To go from room to room without his braces he had to drag himself along the floor. He ended by pretending he wasn't a cripple at all. The reporters favored him. Even the hard-boiled press photographers tacitly agreed not to photograph him in an embarrassing position.

No more private life for the Roosevelts. Louis Howe arranged every detail with an eye to the presidency.

Her husband's affliction put work on Eleanor Roosevelt's shoulders, speeches, meetings, decisions that affected the welfare of those less fortunate than she. She loved it. For the first time she had a cottage of her own at Hyde Park where she could entertain her dogooder friends. As depression threatened she fought local unemployment by starting a furniture factory to give winter work to the Dutchess County agricultural laborers.

The last of her brood was in college. Now she could devote her whole day to movements, to uplift, to improving conditions. She was a force in the Women's Trade Union League. She'd always wanted to teach. She owned an interest in the Todhunter school in New York. She began teaching classes there three times a week. Maybe she was still modeling herself a little on Mlle. Souvestre.

With the Al Smith campaign Eleanor began to sense the first intimations of New Deal politics. She and Louis Howe convinced Franklin D that in spite of his braces he must act as Al Smith's floor manager at the Houston convention. They induced him to run for Governor of New York and succeeded beyond their wildest dreams. While Al Smith lost his home state by a hundred thousand votes, Franklin D carried it by twentyfive thousand.

Eleanor had her own office now in the General Motors Building, her own staff of secretaries to handle her burgeoning mail. It was Eleanor who put Frances Perkins in the state labor department. In American politics the day of the social worker had come.

When Franklin D was nominated for the presidency in 1932 in Chicago Eleanor celebrated the occasion by performing one of her few recorded acts of domesticity. She herself personally cooked ham and eggs for the assembled company at the governor's mansion in Albany before flying to Chicago with her husband for his speech of acceptance.

When Franklin D was inaugurated as 32nd President of the United States it was his mother he gave his arm to when they went in to their first lunch at the White House. Eleanor trotted along behind.

But soon she was being described as "the woman who in all American history has played the biggest part in public affairs."

The hundred days. Social workers, bright young men, youth leaders, the brain trust. It was Eleanor who uncovered that astute uplifter Harry Hopkins from among her social worker friends. Figures from every movement for social betterment in the country crisscrossed on Mrs. Roosevelt's White House calendar: folkdancers, arts and crafters, Communist organizers, campfire girls, Negro waitresses, delinquent boys, unmarried mothers, young peoples leagues for this and that. She found time for them all. She encouraged them all. She was a pushover for the word youth.

Politics costs money. Being President is an expensive business. Like many of the congenitally rich the Roosevelts counted themselves poor if they had to dip into their principal. Franklin D was always fuming about how broke they were. Eleanor went to work to make money.

She wrote articles, she lectured, she became editor of a Bernarr McFadden magazine: *Babies, just Babies.* Radio programs. She went on the air to advertise Sweetheart soap. An endless stream of words poured out to secretaries, into dictaphones, was scribbled on scratchpads on planes or railroad trains or in the back seats of automobiles. In "If you ask me" she answered questions monthly for the readers of the *Ladies' Home Journal.* In "My Day" she prattled about her doings for all the world to read.

She was for uplifting everybody everywhere, right

away, now: working girls, bonus marchers, sharecroppers, unemployed veterans, Negroes, delinquents . . . if only they said the right word.

(A word is a package. Packaging is the national obsession. No need to look inside if you say the right word.)

As First Lady she was the supreme right thinker of the age.

In the wartime hierarchy Mrs. R became the global VIP.

Like royalty she hurried through the daily tour, the endless inspecting, of hospitals, jails, insane asylums, nursery schools, kindergartens, training camps, housing developments. The laying of cornerstones, the commemoration of events: Mrs. Roosevelt was always so interested. Always she found a way to blurt out a few words straight from the heart. In England during the bombings she walked Mrs. Winston Churchill into a collapse. People fainted in hospital corridors trying to keep up with her. Her code name was Rover.

Twenty appointments a day. Always on the move. In the hurry of secretaries and the babel of visitors and the bustle to reach the next appointment on time there was never a moment to distinguish between a good cause and a shady one. The way some people reach blindly into the medicine cabinet. Any medicine will do. Mrs. R was for youth or labor or working women or the underprivileged, for people discriminated against, come hell or high water. Sometimes there's rat poison in the medicine cabinet. It never occurred to the right thinkers that the resentments they fanned up among the underprivileged might become the sinew of new oppressions.

At that there were moments when the old humanitarian impulse rang true. Mrs. R did her best to oppose the brutal measures against American citizens of Japanese ancestry the winter of Pearl Harbor. When President Truman appointed her, after her husband's death (of course she was off lecturing when he suffered his fatal stroke), to the delegation that went to London to set up the United Nations she gave the terrible prosecutor Vishinsky a piece of her mind when he tried to get his hands on the refugees who had fled to the West from the Soviet police.

First Lady of the United Nations; uplift became global.

*

A tall spare blue-eyed woman, living in a second
floor apartment in a brownstone house in the East 60's in
New York . . . At seven sharp she got out of bed, turned
her own mattress, did calisthenics. She never smoked or
drank. Her diet was spare. By eight when her secretary
came in with the mail Mrs. R was ready to begin her eighteen hour day
     of dedication
     to the word with the welfare label.

     At seventyfive she was knocked down by a car on
the street. She was on her feet in a jiffy. Before anyone
could help her, she brushed herself off and went on to deliver three speeches that morning without losing her breath.

The Power
and the Glory

*When the President assembles his press conference he
sits at his desk with a great globe the world in the window
behind his head. In his topsecret staffroom the walls are
brightly lit maps where attachés mark out the positions of
the armies . . .*

*here ten thousand men have died on the steppe, this
river is swollen with the rotting dead . . . the position of
convoys, packs of submarines, magnetic mines: here a hundred drowned last night.*

*The President knows geography; he is interested in his-
tory.*

*Fourmotor planes arrive secretly at dusk, depart at
dawn, Very Important Personages are hurried in long limousines to the White House.*

(Like as not it's only a light thud amidships instead of

the explosion you expected. Sometimes you don't know when the torpedo strikes. The blackedout ship, shambling easily through the slow swells on the zigzag course in a sighing surge of broken water through the night of faint moonlight smudged with soft low clouds, begins all of a sudden to lose steerageway, to wallow gently in the trough, the wind is silent in the rigging. Abandon ship. The tilting deck is quiet. Nobody loses his head. It's so like lifeboat drill

except that there's something jammed in the davits and the lifeboat hangs white in the pale night nosedown in the water. Skillfully we cut the lashings of the liferaft. Where it smashes the surface a fringe of phosphorescent flecks lightens the black swell. We go through the motions of abandon ship so like lifeboat drill . . .

but then it's a man alone thrashing in wreckage, hands failing to tear loose, legs kicking into vacant cold that drags him down into black oil, swallowing, strangling . . .)

In Argentia Bay under the chill slate sky the British sailors in their funny caps
piped the presidential party
up the gangway of the doomed ship:
gold braid, aiguillettes, ribbons on the breast, all the old pomp of empire. The Heads of States attended services on the battleship's quarterdeck according to the rites of the Church of England and sang Onward Christian Soldiers; at lunch they toasted Gentlemen the King and the old scepter of the waves slipped from the hand of the Prime Minister even as he was proclaiming that it was not his intention to preside over the liquidation of an empire.

"After the war one of the preconditions of a lasting peace will be the greatest possible freedom of trade," said our President. It was a time of Caesars: the Heads of States declared a few new freedoms to order the tortured world;
the battlefield was the whole blue globe.

We Learned. There Were Things
We Learned to Do

We learned. There were things we learned to do.

We learned to redesign war's equipment; to the aircraft carrier, the battleship, the cruiser, the troop transport we added

the duck, the weasel, the landing ship tanks, the host of motorboats and flats and barges in ingenious shapes and the floating piers that carried the amphibious landings.

We learned to roll out an airfield in a week, to push the jungle aside with bulldozers, to keep our rifles dry wading at night through surf over the shoals of pitted slippery coral.

We learned to lie on the beach beyond the surge of the breakers and there in complete silence

to bite the marl and die.

We learned to palletize supplies, to keep the tankers moving in a steady flow; officers in control rooms plotted the position of freighters, refrigerator ships, floating drydocks, repairships; on squaredoff maps they played a grim parcheesi with the rule of the geometrical rise in the difficulty of supply in proportion to the distance.

We learned to refuel at sea, in the air for that matter, to transfer anything from one moving ship to another from a sixteeninch shell to an icecream freezer.

We invented the floating base.

By reorganizing the notion of the bridge of ships — keep the supplyline dense; an army travels on its transports — we changed the rules of war.

Sea war was the engagement of carrierbased planes. Capital ships hid behind the bulge of the globe. In the Coral Sea the issue was doubtful but by the time of the great three-day battle off Midway Island our torpedo planes and dive-bombers were ready to inflict on the Japs a decisive defeat.

At home we organized bloodbanks and civilian defense and imitated the rest of the world by setting up concentration camps (only we called them relocation centers) and stuffing into them

American citizens of Japanese ancestry (Pearl Harbor the date that will live in infamy) without benefit of habeas corpus:

I swear loyalty to the United States and enlist in the War Relocation Work Corps for the duration of the war and 14 days thereafter . . . I accept whatever pay, unspecified at the present time, the War Relocation Authority determines . . . I shall be financially responsible for any government property I use while in the work corps: and that the infraction of any regulations of the War Relocation Authority will render me liable to trial and suitable punishment. So help me God.

The President of the United States

talked the sincere democrat and so did the members of Congress. In the Administration there were devout believers in civil liberty. "Now we're busy fighting a war; we'll deploy all four freedoms later on," they said.

At the desk in the White House in front of the brightlit globe

sat an aging man, an ill man, a cripple who had no time to ponder history or to find the Danube or the Baltic or Vienna on the map: so many documents to sign, so many interviews with Very Important Personages, such gloss on the young men: "Yes Mr. President," "No Mr. President." The decisions were his. He could play on a man like on a violin. Virtuoso. By the modulations of his voice into the microphone he played on the American People. We danced to his tune. Third Term. Fourth Term. Indispensable.

War is a time of Caesars.

The President of the United States

was a man of great personal courage and supreme confidence in his powers of persuasion. He never spared himself a moment, flew to Brazil and Casablanca, Cairo

to negotiate at the level of the leaders;

  at Teheran the triumvirate
  without asking anybody's leave got to meddling with
history; without consulting their constituents, revamped ge-
ography;
  divided up the bloody globe and left the freedoms out.
  And the American People were supposed to say thank
you for the century of the Common Man turned over for re-
location behind barbed wire so help him God.

  We learned. There were things we learned to do
  but we have not learned, in spite of the Constitution and
the Declaration of Independence and the great debates at
Richmond and Philadelphia
  how to put power over the lives of men into the hands
of one man
  and to make him use it wisely.

A Great American

As MILLARD walked down the long hotel corridor he took off
the alternate delegate's badge he found still hanging from
his lapel and poked it in his pocket. He knocked on the
door of Walker Watson's suite. There was no answer so he
went on down the hall to his own room. He let himself
drop into the chair at the desk and took out his fountainpen
to write a letter to Lucile. Dear Lou, he started but he
couldn't phrase an opening sentence. His head was hollow.
His head reverberated hollowly like the great cave of the
Stadium with words bawled over the public address system
with bands playing Hail to the Chief and Happy Days Are
Here Again and For He's a Jolly Good Fellow and the jazzing
organ coming in to top the cheers and the bellow of applause.
His hand was sore from handshaking. He'd had too many
drinks. His nose reeked of cigarsmoke and cigarettesmoke

and of the sweat of packedin delegates. There were motes before his eyes from the dazzle of spots and Klieg lights and the flashlight bulbs of photographers. He could still feel the nudging of elbows in his ribs and the slap of broad hands on his back. He sat nodding over the piece of hotel writing paper. Dear Lou he wrote again. Dear Lou was all he could write. He needed Lou's sharp neat little phrases to cut the fog in his head. He'd call her long distance. He gave the operator the number and went into the bathroom to take a shower.

He'd barely slipped out of his clothes and stepped under the cold water before the call came through. With a towel round him he ran dripping across the room. Lucile's voice was precise but far away at the end of a humming tunnel. "Hello Oz. Holding up?" "Oh Lou I wish you were here. No it's not much fun. I never have a minute to myself but I'm damn lonely, never felt lonelier in my life. I guess it's all the doubletalk that gets me down . . . You probably know more about what's happened than I do just from listening to the radio. Mr. Big was renominated sometime in the small hours. You know he released all his delegates. So far as I could make out it was a real draft. A great spontaneous demonstration. That was a moment I wouldn't have missed. And now if they can settle up the vice-presidency we can all go home and start acting like grownup people again . . . Maybe we can use all this war production to accomplish something useful . . . Boys all right? That's good . . ."

All at once the connection cleared and it was almost as if she were in the room with him . . . "Oz come on down for a weekend before going back to Washington. You can do it if you try. We'll go take the boys fishing at Port Isabel." "It would have to be nearer than that. I can't tell yet. I'll call up when this madhouse is over. It'll take me a month to get the agency running again. They're all loco with the big balloons now . . . Lou I wish you were here . . . Goodnight honeybug sleep tight. I'll be thinking of you."

After he'd hung up he sat there at the desk looking tenderly down on the piece of writing paper with a picture of the hotel on it where he'd written Dear Lou Dear Lou Dear Lou.

"Mugs Allen's the name." Millard started at the big sidewalk voice behind him that bit off each word and spat it out. He got to his feet with the towel held tight round his middle. "Mugs for Mulligan."

A squarish young man with a crew cut and a pinkstriped silk shirt over which gushed a blue necktie ornamented with the signs of the zodiac was standing in the middle of the room. He wore a big red badge. He grinned confidentially into Millard's face and, talking strictly out of the corner of his mouth, repeated his name. "Mugs Allen of the James P. Toohey Democratic Club on the Sout' Side . . . Put it dere Mr. Carroll."

Millard shook a beefy hand. "Excuse me a second. I was in the middle of taking a shower when I was called to the phone."

"Take yer time. I got all night. Chimmy sent some o' de boys over to help you gents out."

Millard went back into the bathroom to finish up his shower. Then he slipped on a bathrobe to go to his suitcase to fetch a clean shirt. Mugs was all primed for him. "How did yer like de spontaneous demonstration Mr. Carroll?" he started as soon as Millard stuck his head out of the bathroom door. "Chimmy, he calls de boys together an he says boys de mayor says dis gotto be de biggest spontaneous demonstration ever was. Chi's de convention city an we gotto make it stick . . . It was Chimmy's idear. Boys he says if you don't lift dat Stadium roof ten feet off its hinges it's no dice" . . . Millard slipped on the clean shirt and went to the mirror to tie his necktie . . . "So dey rigged up some highpowered mikes for de guys down in de basement. Dey had claxons an cowbells an every goddam ting. De girlfrien she told me it sounded real natural. She was tuned in all night."

"What can I do for you Mr. Allen?" Millard asked coldly as he straightened his necktie.

"De Honorable Walker Watson wants you to step over to his suite. Dere's sumpem he don't dare discuss over de phone."

"Thanks. I'll be right over."

"Got any hot tips on de VP Mr. Carroll?"

"Not the least idea," Millard said. "Don't look like I knew anything about what was going on around here," he added inaudibly to himself as he pulled on his jacket.

"De gang's gettin up a pool . . . I got my idears but I ain't tellin."

"Well good night Mr. Allen." Millard rattled his key nervously.

"Mugs' de name." The sidewalk voice trailed off as Millard hurried down the corridor.

The parlor door of Walker Watson's suite was open this time. Inside the rooms were full of bustle as a railroad-station. A secretary sat typing something at a desk. Two large rednecked men in pongee suits stood whispering together in a corner. In the center of the parlor waiters were setting a round table for dinner. Jo Powers in a long black and gold evening dress was trailing back and forth in front of the windows taking quick anxious puffs on a cigarette while she listened to Marice Gulick who was expanding in an overstuffed chair over a cocktail. Beyond them through the windows stretched the hazy expanse of the lake blue as a robin's egg. Mike Gulick, pale, his face beaded with sweat in spite of the air conditioning, sat hunched at the phone near the door: "In a rapid poll of a number of delegations during the recess we find Walker Watson sentiment definitely growing . . . He's a Westerner, at least a middle Westerner. He comes of sturdy farming and missionary stock, born in a log cabin and educated in the little red schoolhouse, you know what I mean? He's a staunch New Dealer and a true liberal but he has not been associated with the lunatic fringe of radical experimentation. He had the confidence of all groups of organized labor. He appeals to small business. He's a man of the people who can talk to the common man in his own language. He's very much the cracker barrel philosopher . . . his brilliant personality will add earthiness and color to the ticket . . . He's a great American."

Jo Powers caught Millard's eye while he was still standing just inside the door without knowing exactly what to do with himself and hurried over to him. She stared solemnly into his face.

"Millard we're expecting you to dine with us," she said in her throaty voice . . . "This is a very wonderful experience . . . The great spontaneous demonstration when the President was nominated. It was the most wonderful moment of my life."

"Where is Walker?"

She tilted her head gravely. "In through that door," she whispered in a voice droning with portent.

"How is he?"

"Millard, he's not a well man . . . Please go to him." *

As Millard went through the door that led into the other rooms of the suite he caught sight of Mugs Allen sidling into the parlor behind him with the reverential look on his face of a man about to take communion. It was quiet between the double doors after the hubbub of the parlor. He had no sooner closed one door behind him than Mugs opened it to follow him. He walked faster.

He found Walker sitting in his underclothes on one of the beds in a large double bedroom. An electric pad lay on the counterpane beside him. With an air of great concentration he was dropping some yellow liquid with a medicine dropper into a glass on the bedside table. His long face was yellow and bloodless but his eyes swam feverishly bright under his pale brows. Immediately he started talking low and fast. "Millard I've got a favor to ask you. I want to use your room for a few minutes while I interview a certain person . . . I want you to be present at the interview if you don't mind . . . I know I don't have to explain myself to you and I know that you are not a man who goes blabbing around . . . This is a personal matter between ourselves. There are things going on, dirty sinister things that might do us all a great deal of harm, might even harm the President. The people have spoken. We must all stand behind the President."

"Sure Walker," said Millard. "You can count on me. What's the trouble?"

"First tell me the number of your room . . . No you better . . . Please call the desk and tell them to send Madame Arno up to your room. She is waiting in the lobby. We'll go and meet her there. You'll be interested . . . You are interested in human psychology."

While Millard was at the phone Walker got slowly into his clothes. "Want a drink?" he asked reaching for a flask in the bureau drawer. Millard shook his head. "You know I'm not a drinking man. In fact I hate the taste of the stuff . . . But tonight I'm taking a good stiff one, the doctor recommends it in a glass of milk." He showed Millard the silver flask. "Jo gave me this. Wasn't it sweet of her? You see, it's got my initials on it, W.W."

When they went out the side door into the hall they found Mugs Allen waiting for them still wearing his churchgoing expression. "You know Mugs," said Walker cheerfully. "He's going to see that no one interrupts our little conference."

"Yessir," said Mugs with a confidential grin and doubled up his left fist.

Back in Millard's room Walker sat down glumly to wait, Millard hurried the soiled clothes trailing on the bed out of sight.

The door opened and a stumpy woman in a dull maroon cape walked in without a word. Her black hair was slicked back off a bulbous forehead. Her face was red and her breath came very short. Her eyes looked as if she had been crying. The heavy lids trembled as if she were still holding back the tears. All of a sudden she plunked down on her knees on the carpet in front of Walker. He gave an astonished start but sat with his face to the window without looking at her.

"Master," she said, "it was a terrible misunderstanding. Forgive the mistake of a lonely woman ignorant of the world or the evil motives of men. How could I imagine that the publication of those beautiful letters could do you harm?" She spoke with a slight European accent pronouncing her words with drama school unction. "Oh my injured friend, they are full of truth and inner wisdom. How could I know that our researches into the sublime mathematics of the universe could bring you anything but credit in the world of men. We learn from suffering . . . Here they are every one. They have been safe in my bosom. I swear to you I have allowed no copies to be taken . . . Forgive me, Master. I allowed myself to be deceived." Still on her knees she reached down between her broad breasts incased in black silk and produced a packet tied with red ribbon.

Walker snatched at it. After he had counted over the letters, he gave a deep sigh. "Well that's that," he`said and walked over to the window. Madame Arno started to follow him across the room on her knees. He stood without looking at her studying the bright triangles of the sailboats on the lake all lit up with the sunset. A tanker left a long chocolate smudge of smoke along the horizon. Millard walked over to her.

"You'll tear your stockings that way," he said. He gave her a hand to help her to her feet.

She stood beside him short broad and panting.

"Before I go I must speak two words to my injured friend. What I have to say is for his ears alone."

"I haven't time tonight," said Walker without turning around.

"It is about tonight. There has been no change in the stars . . . I swear it to you."

Walker turned and made a gesture with his hand towards the door. Flushing with vexation Millard went out and stood in the hall outside. Mugs Allen greeted him like an old friend.

"Some dame," he said making a clucking noise with his tongue. "Where did he dream her up? Now if any of you gents want to meet real classy dames, you know entertainers, after de convention recesses tonight just say de woid. Chimmy he says, 'Boys de best ain't none too good for dem delegates. You watch over 'em boys like dey was your own daddies, an see dey don't get no bum steer' . . . Don't you go wid no dames widout clearin 'em wid Mugs."

Millard didn't answer. He felt the blood rising to his head. In another minute he was going to sock somebody in the jaw. The door opened and Madame Arno, her face set in a look of exultation, the corner of her cape pulled tight across her bulging chins, stalked out into the hall. "Peace," she whispered and moved slowly towards the elevators. A moment later Walker Watson followed. His face wore the same set look. His chin was thrust out. "It's time we were back," he muttered fretfully to Millard as if it had been Millard who had kept them waiting. Millard found himself keeping step with Mugs forming a sort of bodyguard after Walker Watson down the corridor.

At the door of the suite Mike Gulick met them with two big rednecked delegates in pongee suits. Mugs stayed outside to hold back a cameraman and some skinny young reporters.

"Walker, meet Alderman Pasternak and Alderman Sullivan," said Mike.

"We just came in to greet . . ." began Alderman

Pasternak . . . "A great big man," took up Alderman Sullivan.

Walker held out both hands to them. While they were pumping each of his hands holding them encased in their great paws, Walker Watson looked back over his shoulder at the reporters' faces peering across Mugs' thick arm. "Come in gentlemen, come in," he called.

"How does it feel," asked Alderman Sullivan who seemed to have had a couple of drinks, "to be in line for the greatest office . . ."

". . . within the gift of the 'merican people," took up Alderman Pasternak . . . "Or any other people," said Alderman Sullivan in his deep whiskey baritone.

The bulb on the photographer's camera flashed.

"Boys," Mike cried nervously, "this is strictly off the record."

Walker cleared his throat. "If, I say, if the party should honor me with the nomination . . . my fervent prayer . . . my dearest hope . . . would be . . . that I should never be called . . . to exercise that office."

"You know just as well as I do," said Alderman Sullivan, "that the Boss'll never live through another term."

"B-boys I don't n-n-need to remind you," Mike stuttered shrilly, "that every bit of this is off the record."

"We are one big happy family," said Alderman Pasternak and turned towards the reporters a jowly smile.

Walker Watson bowed his head. "The Lord giveth and the Lord taketh away. Blessed be the name of the Lord," he said.

"If we are going to get a bite to eat, we had better eat," Mike rattled excitedly. "Boys you'll excuse us, won't you? We've none of us had a bite all day." He started crowding the reporters towards the door. Mugs took up the position of a professional bouncer beside him.

"Just one more shot as he sits down to eat," pleaded a second photographer who had just come in.

Walker had hurried over to the window and was whispering into Jo Powers's pink ear. As Walker talked, though Millard couldn't hear what he was saying, he could see Jo Powers drawing herself up to her full height and filling her lungs like a contralto about to launch into an aria.

Both cameras pointed towards the window.

"No, no . . . At the table," Mike shouted. "You boys are covering the convention not the society column . . . At the table . . . that's it." Mugs balancing on his toes stepped in front of the cameras. Marice was bustling about with her competent laughing hostess manner getting people seated. The waiters were advancing from the serving table with their bright-covered dishes. Walker strode over from the window rubbing his hands together gently with an abstracted look on his face as if he were alone in the room. As he sat down the waiter snatched the whitemetal covers off his plate to disclose two pieces of buttered toast. Walker sat stooping over the plate with his eyes halfclosed. Then he solemnly poured a little hot milk out of a pitcher over his toast and started to eat. The flashlight bulbs flickered. "All right boys, that's enough . . . Thank you very much," said Walker gently and yawned. Mugs skillfully herded the newspapermen out into the hall and closed the door behind them.

As Millard slipped into a chair beside Marice a string of sentences was running through his head like the illuminated letters spelling out the news in front of a newspaper office: Millard O. Carroll Secretary . . . The Carroll Plan Adopted to Save the Familysized Farm . . . The Carroll Plan for Migratory Labor . . . the Carroll Plan for Industrial Peace . . ."

Marice was talking to him . . . "I wonder how many years it's been since we've had a First Lady who was really young and pretty," she was saying.

Jo Powers had been sitting next to Walker with her eyes fixed on his face while he ate his milk toast. All at once she turned towards Marice and Millard a smile so radiant her gums showed. "How do you address the Vice-President's wife?" she asked. "I never met her."

Marice threw back her head and laughed until tears came to her eyes. "My dear like anybody else."

"My poor little mother," Walker's voice had started its deepdrawn . . . "My poor little mother used to say . . ." As people stopped talking and turned towards him Walker looked around the table with his slow lopsided smile. Millard looked up from his broiled chicken and watched Alderman Pasternak's suety countenance crinkle into grins as Walker looked at him. Next him Mike's worried frown had turned into a showman's possessive proud smile. "My poor little old mother out in Nebraska had a saying," Walker went on, "that a cat may look at a king."

The phone rang. Frowning again Mike jumped up. In a second he tapped Millard on the shoulder.

"It's Judge Oppenheim, Millard. He wants to talk to you."

Millard excused himself and wiping his mouth with the napkin went to the phone at the desk. "Millard how are you? Is Chicago pretty hot? I thought . . ." The meticulous voice was quietly sarcastic . . . "I thought I'd tantalize you a little by describing the fresh Atlantic breezes. I never saw Penobscot Bay more beautiful than it is tonight. It's been a warm day. Nell and I both wish we had you and Lucile here to eat some lobster with us. Is she with you in Chicago?"

"No Lou went home with the boys for the summer."

"Well how are things? Are you pretty much worn out?"

"I've never been so confused in my life. I guess conventions aren't my dish. Lord Judge I'll be glad to get back to work I understand."

The Judge's laugh came softly over the wire. "How's Walker holding out?"

"Very well I'd say. Do you want to speak to him? He's right here. We're all of us eating a bite of supper before going back for the rest of the show."

"No no I don't want to bother him now. I just wanted you and Mike to know I was thinking about you and commiserating with you. Of course you know the European news couldn't possibly be worse. Massacre and dictatorship advancing unchecked . . . Britain knocked out, kept alive only by the mighty spirit of one man . . . I just want you to remind our friend a little of this situation. No matter how the events of this evening come out the man in the White House has got to have an administration that works together like a welltrained team. Whether a man is in one position or another doesn't really matter so long as he gives his best. I'm telling you this Millard because I know that you aren't subject to the frenzies that seize some of us when we are confronted with the possibility of high office. Your influence can be very stabilizing . . ."

"I get your drift Judge, but I'm sure enough in a daze."

"Well I wouldn't worry Millard. You have nothing at stake in this situation personally. Your good honest spadework is very highly appreciated . . . where it needs to be appreciated . . . you know that. Well I shan't keep you. Give our love to Lucile when you see her and goodnight. Get a nice long rest when this is over."

Millard hated to have the Judge hang up. The distant amused dispassionate voice gave him back the feeling of aloof selfconfidence he had been losing all afternoon. He was still smiling when he went back to the table. Nobody was talking. Everybody had stopped eating. "Where's Walker?" he asked.

Mike looked up at him, his face worried as a monkey's.

"He's on the phone. It's the White House. He's taking it in the bedroom . . . This is it." His voice came in a breathless rasp.

Marice was making up her lips looking intently down into the little mirror in her handbag and now and then giving Mike an anxious protective glance across the table. Alderman Pasternak was eating peach melba and seemed sunk in his own thoughts. With a silent and catlike tread Jo Powers walked up and down in front of the window where the dusk over the lake had deepened to violet.

Millard started to hack at the broiled chicken that had grown cold on his plate. He put a piece in his mouth but it had a rubbery taste. Everybody was smoking with fury. Alderman Sullivan handed him a cigar and, although he didn't usually smoke cigars, he accepted it. He heard a step behind him and found himself looking up into Bruce Slater's black eyes. He got to his feet.

"Why Bruce," he said. "Where on earth have you been?"

Bruce didn't answer but gave him a slow ponderous wink. Then he pulled a small pad out of his pocket and wrote a name on it and showed it to Millard.

"Well I'll be God dammed . . . begging your pardon, Marice."

Marice was on her feet. Her handbag closed with a sharp click. "It's time we left you gentlemen to your smokefilled room," she was saying. She walked over to Jo Powers and put her arm around her waist. "Well dear let's go to my room and tidy up and then we'll take a cab to the Stadium."

Mike's hand was shaking when he stepped over to take the piece of paper out of Millard's hand. He gave it a glance and handed it to Alderman Sullivan.

The alderman let out a loud whistle. "Well gentlemen," he said, "we live and learn." He walked around and whispered a name loudly in Alderman Pasternak's ear.

"Well thank God it ain't the incumbent," said Alderman Pasternak.

Mugs had come forward from his place by the door. "Well there goes my twentyfive bucks," he said.

Jo Powers's face had knitted up like the face of a little girl who'd been scolded. "I must go to him," she almost sobbed. She pulled away from Marice and with her eyes on the floor made for the door into the bedroom. As she brushed past Millard he heard her muttering low to herself, "I'll marry him anyway . . . I'll marry him anyway."

Bruce walked up to Millard with that solemn birddog look of a man who knows much more than he's able to tell, opened his mouth as if to say something but changed his mind and merely shrugged his shoulders heavily. Alderman Sullivan and Alderman Pasternak were already out the door. "See you over to the Stadium," they called back as they left. Bruce slipped away after them. Mike had dropped into the chair at the desk and sat with his head bowed making doodles on the blotter. Marice stood beside him stroking the sparse hair off his forehead with little pats of her hand.

When Walker Watson came back into the parlor he was breathing heavily as if winded from a long climb. Jo Powers had hold of him under the arms and seemed to be propping him up on his feet.

His voice had a weak spiteful sound.

"Mike," he said, "you'd better get busy while there's still time . . . I shall not allow my name to be put before the convention. It is my irrevocable decision."

We Learned; But Not Enough

We learned; but not enough; there is more to learn.

The American People
entered our years of defeat with so little preparation
we have not learned how deep the disaster. We had
leaders but like Moses they led us into the wilderness and
like Moses
died;
and I am left leaderless
in wild darkness and the terror of death. (Death is not
terrible;
but the misgiving of our light, the little light that gave
hope's inkling flicker to the toilsome piecing of torn deceits
into a fresh, hazardous, already perhaps threadbare, so
sought for
phrase, that may perhaps with luck hold true;
the fear
that our drudgery, the urging of mind and muscle to
hard work, laughter and the sick surprise of pain, our com-
mon comfort
in the sayings our fathers said,
in the grimy comicalness of everyday,
might not,
as I believed,
be the beating out of a link, however flawed, however
badly made, in the chain of lives, linked by danger and
miseries and splendor and crime through suffering genera-
tions, proceeding, blunderingly and illadvised, to some
better, though hardly explainable, destination;

that fear is very terrible.)

As an American I believe:

always in the beginning long ago way down, beneath
my father's doubts and the fears his father felt,
    there was belief that stood them in good stead:
    in the anguish of departure and the queasy ships,
    in the quick heartbeat of arrival in sight of the low
gray land afloat on bays and inlets, the lowering forests
inland, (everpresent the threat of fires, the smokepall over
the jerrybuilt settlement); there was belief that flared against
fear under the bright sky,
    the newworld wind northwest;
    in the sight of fish in unimaginable millions churning
the estuaries in their spring rush upriver to spawn, in the
green corn's quick sprouting, and the abundance of peaches;
and in the pack of furs the trapper brings in on his back,
    promise of independences: — the hut of sods
will next year be a cabin, the muddaubed log house
will next year be tight clapboard or a mansion of brick;
exultation
    in the windy freedom of a continent, the singing birds,
plentiful shots along the woods' edge at game for the pot:
    in the jostle of immigrants in the seaport slums,
    busy to forget the old world, to learn the new, to make
    money make money, to turn an honest dollar, busy to
cheat,
    to be cheated, to invest, to get plenty for nothing,
busy to
enjoy opportunity, to exercise independence.
        Always in the beginning long ago,
        way down, there was belief that next year:
"Me I'm not much but my boy:
        he'll go to school and learn American."

In our years of defeat
in our century of power we have forgotten
our American:
    the harangue delivered from a stump at the edge of
town, the affirmation penned by candlelight in a Spencerian
hand, the protests of delegates in convention assembled,
the congregations sitting silent with furrowed brows search-

ing for the light within, the blankfaced obstinacy of town-
meeting, the brawling, hot with torchlight and whisky, of
mobs for independence, the battering down of obstacles,
the opening of wagonroads, canals along the rivers;

 the fury of secession; the Union made irrevocable

 in massacre and in sorrow and in murder

 and by the sacrifice of righteous men; the founding of
states out among the sagehens on the prairie, railroads advancing rail by rail with clamor of hammers through the
West. My father knew

 that language; those things his father learned; but
there is more to learn. Shall I sicken for the lack of will

 to blazen in words my belief

 against the driving sky that rains disaster? Our century
of

 power to ruin has wrought no answering power to
build,

 to establish, to plant securely on foundations.

 Do we lack the penmanship to declare again the independence that lived in the flourish of my father's signature,
in Mother's homilies: "An American is as good as any man,
he must behave better," to a naughty small boy made to
stand in the corner; in the needlepoint (the careful jams
and jellies, the meticulous rinsing of china, the affirmation
of old prints, The Peaceable Kingdom stored in dust in the
attic, pride of ancestry in the notes in the family bible, shade
trees planted with posterity in the mind), of Grandmother's
domestic economy?

 It was how they behaved: my father's goodhumor with
darkskinned diggers of ditches, the enquiry after the health
of the waiter, his daily joshing with the officer fresh from
County Cork full of sweat under his high blue helmet at
the Avenue crossing, the way his deference brings out the
innate gentle manners of the bushy old barefoot man

 who shows us the spring on the mountainside

 who can't read and write but no matter in a land
where there is plenty

 of freedom

 a man's worth his weight; a man free from hate or
suspicion or envy will recognize kinship in other men for
no other reason than that they are men; a free man has a
splendor about him,

moving easily joshingly courteously among a variety
of equal citizens, varying in antecedents, in ancestry in
honesty, in schooling, in attainments, each smirched with
the common (in which I share by inheritance, by education,
by preference) degradation of the shoddy mean,
 but sharing an infinitesimal, always near extinction but
never extinguishable, inkling of splendor.

My father, my grandfathers living out their lives, in
some things fortunate, in some things unfortunate, Americans varying in antecedents,
 assumed without thinking, taking it for granted, often
denying it,
 their belief in the precarious splendor
 a man's life assumes when he is for a moment free
 from tyranny and taskmasters and the cramping cage
of enslaving institutions. The words
 are tired and old: "democratic," "republican," a coin-
age worn senseless in the market's transactions, the birth-
right's daily sale, but they ring. (There is so much evil in
the life of man that a tiny good, a moment's opportunity,
a breath of independence, produces us immediately abundance of lesser goods so readily mortgaged and sold that
we forget
 the price our fathers paid. That is why God's temple
is always full of moneychangers, because of the riches it
offers.) The words are slurred with too much saying but
they ring
 as loud as the meanings we endow them with.

The republic's foundations are not in the sound of
words,
 they are in the shape of our lives, fellowcitizens.
 They trace the outlines of a grand design. To achieve
 greatness a people must have a design before them
 too great for accomplishment. Some things we have
learned, but not enough; there is more to learn. Today
 we must learn
 to found again
 in freedom
 our republic.

GROUP V

A Creature That Builds

Walking the Earth
under the Stars

Walking the earth under the stars,
musing midnight in midcentury,
a man treads the road with his dog;
the dog, less timebound in her universe of stench and
shrill, trots eager ahead.

The man too senses smells:
the frosted pasture and the cold loblollies,
the warmsweet of cows, and perhaps a hint of the passing of
a skunk; hears
the hoot, hoot, hoot-hoot of the horned owl,
as full of faraway foreboding as the hoot of a
woodburning locomotive heard across the plains as a child
long ago; sees
Orion overhead sport glistening Rigel
and Betelgeuse, and the three belt buttons
that point out Sirius, and Belletrix that indicates
smoldering Aldebaran.

Eyes sweep
the bluedomed planetarium pivoting on the
polestar which the meditative Greeks and the Bedouin
dreamed
engraved with the quaint creatures of the
zodiac; the spheres spun to music
and cherubim, benign to man,
with halcyon voices chanted
glory to God.

The dog stops short, paw poised, sniffs deep
and takes off yelping after some scuttle in the under-
brush.

✿

The man walks on alone.

Thoughts swarm; braincells, as multitudinous as the
wan starpoints that merge into the Milky Way overhead,
trigger notions; tonight,
    in the century's decline,
    new fantasies prevail. Photoelectric calculators
giddy the mind with numbers mechanically multiplying
immensities by billions of lightyears.

A million hostile chinamen a month; a hundred and
thirty thousand miscellaneous manmouths a day added to
the population of the planet Earth.

But rockets successfully soar and satellites trundle
on their punctual trails above the stratosphere. Sam the
Rhesus returns in his space capsule, his little face as inscrut-
able as when he went up. An aeronaut from a twelvemile-
high balloon spies moisture in the Venustian atmosphere.
Norbert Wiener says his calculators are hep; watch out if
they get a will of their own. A certain Dr. Otto Struve has
predicated the possibility of ten million lifebreeding plan-
ets among the island galaxies, and, at Green Bank, West
Virginia

(far from the sins of the world)

they are building a radio telescope the size of a
baseballfield, tipped sixty stories up in the air, where the
physicists of project Osma plan to listen for messages
emitted with intelligent intent
    from tau *Ceti or* epsilon *Eridani.*
A million men on a million nights, heirs of a
million generations, ponder the proliferation of their
millions to the millionth power till
    multitude bursts into nothingness,
    and numbers fail.

I feel the gravel underfoot, the starlit night about
me. The nose smells, the ears hear, the eyes see. "Willfully
living?" "Why not?" Having survived up to now at least
the deathdealing hail of cosmic particles, the interpreting
mind says "I am here."

❋

*In the underbrush under the pines my dog yelps in
hot chase. Furry bodies jostle in the dark among the broken
twigs. Fangs snap, claws tear; barks, growls, snarls, panting
breath as jaws close on the soft hairs under the throat. A
shriek, not animal not human, a shriek of unembodied agony
rips the night.*

*In the silence my dog panting drags a thick carcass
through the brambles out on the road*
and places at her master's feet
in the starlight
a beautiful raccoon
that was alive and is dead.

This much is true.

Proconsul

In the unmilitary United States there flourished during
the nineteenth century a number of families who raised their
children to the sound of bugles; among the most dashing were
the MacArthurs.

The first general, Arthur MacArthur, was the son of a
Scottish lawyer who had become City Attorney in Milwaukee
and Lieutenant Governor of the state. At seventeen he joined
the 24th Wisconsin Regiment to help quench the rebellion.
He carried the regimental colors through the smoke and
slaughter of Missionary Ridge and became known as "the
Boy Colonel of the West." He continued in the army after
Appomattox, married the daughter of a North Carolina physician and went to fight Indians. It was a life of jingling
spurs and sweated saddles and trailbreaking;
reveille and taps on the parade grounds of dusty outposts.

❋

On January 26 1880 at the Little Rock Barracks there was born to the MacArthurs a son who was to fulfill their fondest hopes. "I think there is material for a soldier in the boy," said the father when he took young Douglas, wearing a mass of golden curls and bearing a toy musket over his shoulder, to be photographed in San Antonio. While his father was stationed at Fort Sam Houston, young Douglas attended the West Texas Military Academy. There he won a gold medal for "extraordinary excellence" in sports, deportment and scholarship.

While the son was astonishing the schoolmasters the father was earning a Congressional Medal and climbing promotion's ladder to Lieutenant General (American generals were scarce in those days) and Chief of Staff.

When the short summer war against Spain almost by accident catapulted the American dream into the sweltering Orient the elder MacArthur received the assignment of straightening out the Filipinos. The Insurrectos had been all for American help to throw out the Spaniards, but when the Americans decided to stay they turned recalcitrant. The five-year pacification proved an ugly business.

> Underneath the starry flag
> Civilize them with a Krag

went the soldier's song. (There was more to it than that: with the rifle and the flag went the old copybook maxims; life, liberty and the pursuit of happiness; devoted missionaries and teachers, effective administrators and the new science of sanitation. For better or worse after Aguinaldo's surrender the conglomerate populations of those distant scattered islands began to see their future as American.) Arthur MacArthur was our first proconsul.

He looked the part. He acted the part. His arbitrary behavior caused misgivings among the Washington civilians. When a civilian commissioner arrived to install due process he was treated with scant respect. In 1901 General Arthur MacArthur was summarily relieved of his command.

Meanwhile young Douglas, with his mother in Milwaukee, was tutoring for the West Point examinations. A brother was already at Annapolis. Needless to say Douglas

MacArthur passed with an extraordinary score. A tall handsome deadly serious young man with impeccable manners, in spite of a little rougher than the usual hazing by upperclassmen, in spite of the indefatigable supervision of a ubiquitous mother who insisted on renting a house near the Military Academy to be near him, he broke all records of scholastic and military deportment. He made the baseball team. As senior he was First Captain. He graduated at the top of his class.

He chose the unpopular Corps of Engineers because advancement was rapidest there.

He saw his first field service in the Philippines but soon he was detailed to Tokyo as his father's aide on a spit and polish mission to the Orient. He accompanied General Arthur MacArthur as an observer during the Russo-Japanese War.

When in 1912 the father died suddenly of a heart attack at a Grand Army reunion of his old Wisconsin regiment the son was already well on his way to succeed him. He held various staff jobs in Washington. When Woodrow Wilson began to apply the Big Stick to the tumultuous Mexicans, the youthful Captain MacArthur in the company of a young German observer named Fritz von Papen scouted hostile positions outside of Veracruz, disguised, his biographers tell us, as "a Mexican bum."

World War I found him in France as chief of General Menoker's staff. It was MacArthur's idea to assemble a Rainbow Division made up from units of twentyseven different state militias. He believed in the citizen soldier.

Preux chevalier san peur et sans reproche, already he had a reputation for never perspiring. His uniform didn't wilt in the hottest weather. He seemed without fear. He went into combat without sidearms or gasmask or helmet. He'd taken to pulling the wire lining out of the stiff uniform cap and wearing it at a rakish angle. Newspapermen called him d'Artagnan of the AEF.

He won his promotion to colonel on the battlefield. He was gassed, twice wounded, decorated thirteen times, cited seven times for extreme bravery under fire. Pershing promoted him to Brigadier General and put him in command of the Rainbow Division he had helped create.

After the war he was for three years Superintendent at West Point. It was MacArthur who first gave the cadets a complete college curriculum and introduced compulsory athletics. Of course he was the youngest superintendent on record, as he'd been the youngest brigadier general, and the youngest divisional commander.

He married late (assuredly the dowager Mrs. MacArthur had kept the girls at bay); even then it seemed more an affair of the Social Register than of the heart. Louise Cromwell Brooks was a rich grass widow who had queened it over the social doings of the higher echelons of the AEF in Paris after the armistice. General Pershing, himself a widower, is said to have suffered from her charms. The society columns hailed the affair as *The Marriage of Mars and Millions*.

The union was shortlived. After the splendors of New York and Paris the lady is said to have found Manila, where MacArthur was appointed to his father's old post as American commander, quite unamusing. It is admitted that the general lacked humor.

These were trying years. When General MacArthur became Chief of Staff in 1930 the army was unpopular. Disarmament was the obsession. Because MacArthur saw dangers ahead from the rising dictatorships of Germany and Japan he was labeled a warmonger. His trips abroad were described as medal hunts.

MacArthur had a bad press.

When President Hoover ordered him to disperse the bonus marchers the Communists were stirring up to sedition in their poor Hooverville on Anacostia Flats, he superintended the job — which he could well have foisted off on a subordinate — himself, and saw that it was done efficiently and with a minimum of bloodletting. For that public service he was denounced as a "man on a white horse" by the weteyed journalists who were heralding the New Deal revolution.

It was noised against him that seven years before he'd sat on the courtmartial that dismissed his friend Billy Mitchell from the service for expressing too soon his conviction of the wartime ascendancy of the airplane. The vote was secret. Not till years later did the story leak out that MacArthur had voted for acquittal.

All the same Franklin Roosevelt put through his appointment as Chief of Staff for an unheard of second term. What little combat readiness there was in the army the day of Pearl Harbor was largely due to McArthur's interest in motorized warfare.

In 1935 Manuel Quezon, who as a boy Insurrecto had surrendered to MacArthur's father, became the President of the independent Philippine Commonwealth. Alarmed by the advance of the Japanese Co-prosperity Sphere, he asked Washington for the loan of the American general best versed in Far Eastern affairs to help plan the island's defense.

At the age of fiftyseven Douglas MacArthur retired from the United States Army to become Field Marshall in the Army of the Philippines.

In the course of the long steamship trips between the West coast and Manila he met, besieged and soon married an agreeable young woman from Tennessee.

This time it was for keeps. The dowager Mrs. MacArthur, now a very old lady indomitably bent on following her son's career, reached Manila only in time to take to her bed and die.

The MacArthurs were raising their small son at their penthouse on the roof of the Manila Hotel when they had the news of Pearl Harbor.

MacArthur had been twentythree years a general officer. According to the hymenopterous punctilio of military stratification the general officer lives in a sealed world. A proper brass hat doesn't know whether it's raining or sunshine until he's briefed by his staff. Like the queen been he's fed on royal jelly.

MacArthur in the Philippines was the brass hat of brass hats. A man of brilliant intelligence with the real strategic bent, he must have been strangely cut off from the real world to allow his Flying Fortresses, after eight hours warning, to be smashed in rows on Clark Field by Japanese planes flying all the way from Formosa. He hadn't enough planes or PT boats to begin with. Now he had nothing.

He declared Manila an open city to save the lives of the puzzled Filipinos who had trusted him as they would trust the Virgin Mary.

The retreat to Bataan was a routine performance plotted

long ahead. It certainly was not lack of physical courage that kept him so long in the tunnel under Corregidor. The doomed troops never saw hide nor hair of him. "Dugout Doug" they shouted after him when he fled (under direct orders from Washington) by PT boat, through infested seas to Mindanao. He took his wife and the little boy and the little boy's Chinese nurse along with him. There was just time to snatch them in a fourmotor plane off the Del Monte strip just before the Japs closed in.

It was the old MacArthur who stepped out of the plane on his first Australian airstrip. The American collapse, Rommel in Africa, the loss of the British battleships off Singapore had scared the Australians out of a year's growth. Their military men were talking grimly of holding the Brisbane line. MacArthur showed no interest at all in the Brisbane line. He talked of invading the Philippines. He would only plan for victory.

Fresh from humiliations and defeats that would have ruined any lesser general's career, the Aussies saw MacArthur sit cool and unwilted in his headquarters in Brisbane smoking his corncob pipe — a folksy touch that gave an edge to his starched uniform and punctilious manner — plotting the strategy of victory. "I came through and I shall return," he broadcast to the Filipinos to let them know he'd escaped through the Japanese lines. The Aussies caught fire from MacArthur.

He couldn't have done it without the navy, or the marines who squandered their lives on forgotten reefs and coral-strewn beaches. He couldn't have done it without the Aussie prospectors' early knowledge of the Owen Stanley Mountains and the stinking Kokoda trail in New Guinea; or without the amphibian techniques developed in the Central Pacific or the erosion of the Japanese airforce or the floating bases and the incredible supplylines that girdled the globe;

but he knew how to seize the right moment,

he knew that attack was defense;

with a chessplayer's skill he kept four moves ahead of the Japs; where they were he wasn't. Where their defense was spread thin he was landing in force;

until, leaving wellarmed Japanese troops frustrate and starving on a score of islands,

MacArthur, having darkened the sky over the Philippines
with little books of matches bearing his picture "Rely on me:
I shall return,"
    waded nonchalantly ashore
    amid the whirring of motion picture cameras
    on Lingayen Beach.
"I have returned. Rally to me. Let no heart be faint."

"Boldness and disdain of the enemy" he explained to the
correspondents at his headquarters at San Miguel the day his
troops got their first toehold in the suburbs of Manila. He
was proclaiming the city's capture . . .
    (Press releases. Army and Navy and Marines; their brass
fought the Japs allright, but they fought each other for headlines in the stateside press. MacArthur's PRO beat everything. God and the General were so often linked in the news
people could hardly tell which was which.)
    . . . there was mighty little left of Manila when after
weeks of block by block fighting the last Jap threw up his
hands. "Boldness and disdain of the enemy":

    The Manhattan Project. Iwo Jima. Okinawa. The
mushroomshaped cloud over cities become heaps. In spite
of pulling and hauling in Washington by adherents of the
various services it was to MacArthur that Harry Truman
awarded the palm of victory. As General of the Army he took
the Japanese surrender in Tokyo Bay.

    Supreme Ruler of Japan,
    Douglas MacArthur was as inaccessible as he'd been in
that desperate tunnel under Corregidor, but somehow he
managed, decking them out in terms of the hour, to promul-
gate the old copybook maxims that had Americanized the
Filipinos in his father's time:
    civil liberties,
        freedom of the press,
            land ownership for the peasants who worked the soil,
unhampered trade unions, the rules of fair play. He kept the
Communists off base and foiled the best spy-diplomats that
Moscow could train.
    When the Emperor Hirohito renounced his divinity, the
displaced godhead seemed to hover for a while over the GHQ

of the Supreme Commander, Allied Powers; Commander in Chief, United Nations Command; Commander in Chief, Far East; and Commanding General U.S. Army, Far East.

A movement to nominate him for the Presidency in 1948 seemed an anticlimax. No American before him had ever occupied such a pinnacle of power.

In spite of the five stars and the gold braided caps and the chest banded with rainbow after rainbow of ribbons

Douglas MacArthur, as an old man at seventyone, was to look once more

into the grinning skull of defeat.

When through a series of wrong moves, so maladroit that historians will be puzzling over them for a hundred years, the managers of America's destiny managed to leave the friendly republic they'd been fostering south of the 38th parallel in Korea

wide open to attack by the vigorous army the Russians trained in the north,

war broke out overnight.

Again as in Manila, it was MacArthur the unready. (All the brass hat knows is his briefing from his staff.) Early reverses were wiped out by a skillful amphibious landing at Inchon. MacArthur ordered the advance to the Yalu. In spite of the fact that the first Chinese thrust had been with difficulty repulsed, MacArthur's PRO's were filling the press with accounts of his troops eating Thanksgiving Dinner, victorious,

in sight of the Yalu River.

The mighty MacArthur would clear the peninsula and get the boys home by Christmas. A few days later the boys were on the run, or dead, or prisoners dripping with dysentery in stinking stockades.

"Boldness and disdain of the enemy." Every reader of the *New York Times* knew that the Chinese were massing an army on the Yalu; they announced it themselves. (A brass hat lives like a queen bee, sealed off from the world, dependent on his staff to feed him the royal jelly.)

In spite of the retreat conducted in the best War College style by the troops in the northern mountains (flying boxcars

flew in a whole suspensionbridge for a rivercrossing by the
First Marine Division)
    the Chinese inflicted a smashing defeat
    on the forces under MacArthur's command.

    The rest was the facesaving diplomacy of failure.
    When Douglas MacArthur was, like his father before him,
summarily relieved of his proconsular post, the little ward-
heeler from Independence Missouri who occupied the White
House
    made the dismissal as curt as he could,
    but somehow managed to give the impression that the gen-
eral's crime had not been his defeat
    but his insistence on planning to win;
    "There is no substitute for victory."

    Win or lose MacArthur had grandeur. Perhaps most
Americans agreed with Harry Truman that grandeur was for
the birds,
    all the same they greeted him as no defeated general has
ever been greeted before. In New York City the streetclean-
ers figured that sixteen million tons of paper and ticker tape
were dumped out of office windows by the frenzied inhabitants during the MacArthur parade. Clearly a record. In
Washington the members of both houses of Congress listened
in awe
    as the old general offered his ritual submission to the civil
government, and pulled about him the nostalgic toga of the
old soldiers of the Republic (Washington too made his farewell):

        I am closing my fifty-two years of military service.
    When I joined the army, even before the turn of the
    century it was the fulfilment of all my boyish hopes and
    dreams . . .
        . . . The world has turned over many times since I
    took the oath on the plain at West Point and the hopes
    and dreams have long since vanished . . . 'Old soldiers
    never die, they just fade away.'

He set the whole nation to humming the old song.

When You Try to Find the People

When you try to find the people,
it comes down maybe to a boy seventeen who's worked
all day in a chainstore; at last he's home (his old man's a
rummy, his folks don't understand him, his hours are too
long and his pay too short, he needs a new pair of shoes, he's
scared to pick up girls; he wants a sports model car, to own
a messjacket, to be manager and sit at a broad slick desk,
somewhere dimly sometime to be President); he's nuts
about radio;
he runs up four flights of stairs (it's an old dwelling
converted to flats), he keeps his ears closed to neighbors'
voices, phonographs, favorite programs, girlie doing the
scales on the piano, somebody's steak frying, unlocks the
attic door, slams it behind him, breathes happily the hot
close air of old chests full of mothballs and dry dusty lumber
and glue from busted tables and chairs;
under the dormer on a threelegged table securely
propped by a packingcase nailed to the floor so that it can't
jiggle stands his two-way set:
sending and receiving:
short wave; when he pulls the earphones over his un-
combed hair that he ought to get cut (his pimples are terri-
ble, he forgot to write for that cure for acne, nights in bed an
agony of woman dreams): the switch is right, he's plugged
in; his ears glow with the hum from the warming tubes:
he's on the air, resounding immensity, concave with
voices, dotted with signals,
limitless sphere: his ears are everywhere, his tongue,
trigger of wisecracks (Have you heard this one?), talks to
everybody, to unseen hams,
to unknown stations that fade roaring

on the horizons (last night he tinkered with that con-
denser until he fell asleep in his chair) of the power of his
homemade set:

the policecars are talking, heavy cops' voices: three-
alarm fire on Conduit Road, man abusing woman at Locust
and State, fight in bowling alley back of Freeland Street
. . . it's George on Catalina Island, talks like a guy knows a
lot . . . our little yawl . . . the race . . . she jibed . . . I
cracked her over and she held . . . before we knew what it
was all about she turned on a dime and we had about thirtyfive cents left . . . okeydoke on Long Point . . . had us a
time . . . Joe (he sounds like a heel), he's going to a dance
tonight, went downtown and hired him a soup and fish . . .
that crazy galoot that won't stop talking he's a vegetarian,
worked all week on his crystal set to tell the world about
carrots, ain't hep to a thing . . . Fred picked up Melbourne
last night, now he's shooting for Bombay. How's for some
swing? . . .

ears throb to a rumba band and a woman's small voice
whining tangos in Havana:

up in the attic the window's dark, must be late; supper;
when he pulls off his earphones

it's the universe gone

and left only the cramped restriction of every day, the
worn soles of his shoes, the frayed trouser cuff, the spots on
his only good necktie,

the crazy need for change.

The Sinister Adolescents

James Dean the motion picture actor was no relation to
William Frishe Dean the general. About all the two had in
common was that they both came from the Middle West.
They represented different generations. Very.

There is nothing much deader than a dead motion picture
actor,
　　　and yet,
　　even after James Dean had been some years dead,
　　when they filed out of the close darkness and the breathed-
out air of the second and third and fourth run motion picture
theatres where they'd been seeing James Dean's old films,
they still lined up:
　　the boys in the jackboots and the leather jackets, the boys
in the skintight jeans, the boys in broad motorbike belts,
　　before the mirrors in the restroom
　　to look at themselves
　　and see
　　James Dean;
　　the resentful hair,
　　the deep eyes floating in lonesomeness,
　　the bitter beat look,
　　the scorn on the lips.

　　Their pocket combs were out; they tousled up their hair
and patted it down just so;
　　made big eyes at their eyes in the mirror
　　pouted their lips in a sneer,
　　the lost cats in love with themselves,
　　just like James Dean.

　　The girls flocked out dizzy with wanting
　　to run their fingers through his hair, to feel that thwarted
maleness; girl-boy almost, but he needs a shave . . . "Just
him and me in the back seat of a car."
　　Their fathers snort, but sometimes they remember: "Nobody understood me either. I might have amounted to something if the folks had understood." The older women struggle
from their seats weteyed
　　with wanting to cuddle to mother (it's lack of motherlove
makes delinquents) to smother with little attentions the poor
orphan youngster,
　　the motherless, brotherless, sisterless lone wolf brat strayed
from the pack,
　　the poor mixed up kid.

　　The pressagents told us James Dean lacked parental
love, that he was an orphan, a farmboy who couldn't get

along at school, a poor mixed up kid from the blacksoil belt in Indiana. (He never could quite get rid of that Hoosier twang.)

. . . Hoosier ghosts of forgotten Penrods, crackerbarrel reveries . . . *the thoughts of youth are long long thoughts . . . for I was once a barefoot boy . . . Life on the Mississippi . . . The Arkansas Traveller* . . . Hundredyearold Huck Finn drifting with runaway Jim downriver on their eternal raft . . . The young used to be comical in America . . .

"I'm a serious minded and intense little devil," the movie magazines quoted James Dean as saying, "terribly gauche and so tense I don't see how people stay in the same room with me. I know I wouldn't tolerate myself."

The teenagers approved: "Everything he said was cool."

In midcentury America the barefoot boys are all shod in loafers.

The Hoosier farmboys have no cows to milk before day, no wood to chop, no horses to currycomb or oats to measure out into the manger, no coaloil lamps to fill, no chores: "If it's housework let Mother do it"; no chapter of the Bible to read every day,

no roaring preachers to remind them from the pulpit every Sunday that good is Heaven and bad is Hell,

no examiners to ask hard questions;

only perhaps an occasional package to carry out from the A&P, or maybe the family car to wash

before driving down to the drugstore for a coke and a cigarette of some advertised brand, and a comic book; (nothing in midcentury America is less comical than a comic) diagramming murder and mayhem and rape, tirelessly strumming on the raw nerves

for kicks.

Kicks are big business: the sallow hucksters needle the nerves. Through radios drumming rock and roll and blurred girls crooning on TV

they hammer on the wracked nerves:

buy,

buy speed, buy horsepower, buy chromium, buy happiness in a splitlevel ranchhouse, elegance in shocking pink lipstick, passion in a jar of Parisian perfume,

or that portable transistor set
you can take along on your vacations
so that even beside the thunderous ocean, or camping out
in some hidden intervale green in a notch of the hills, you'll
never be free
from the clamor of salesmen.

Why not resentful? There's more to life; the kids knew
it. Their fathers won a war but weren't men enough to keep
the peace, they let the pundits and the politicians wheedle
them into defeat; they let the goons pilfer their paychecks,
too busy watching TV to resent oppression . . . (Freedom
what good is it? Let's have social security
and welfare and tailfins on our cars
and packaging)
There's no cellophane can protect the glory of life when
you've lost it; the kids knew it.

Even in success James Dean was resentful. This kid had
talent. That's how he differed from the general run of drugstore cowboys. The critics said he had the makings of a great
film actor. He won awards. Even after he was dead the audiences voted him the best actor of the year. James Dean was
resentful, we were told,
because he came from a broken home. "My mother died
on me when I was nine years old. What does she expect me
to do? Do it all myself."
His father married again. An aunt and uncle raised him on
their neat farm in Fairmount, Indiana. He was a moody boy.
He was terribly nearsighted: he did poorly in his studies,
but in highschool he played baseball, basketball, led the
track team and excelled in dramatics. They gave him a medal
for the best all around athlete senior year.
His elocution teacher took a fancy to him. She spotted the
talent. She coached him in parts in school plays and had him
win a statewide contest in public speaking
reading THE MADMAN, by Dickens.
When she induced him to enter a national contest held out
in Colorado, the judges passed him over. He resented that.
He never forgave that poor teacher.

*

His father went to work as a dental technician in L. A. After young Dean graduated he went out to stay with his father and stepmother. Farmwork wasn't his idea. A boy with talent is too sensitive to work on the farm. His father set him up to a course in physical education at a junior college. Then he switched to pre-law courses at the U of C. His schoolmates didn't appreciate him. He got into a fight with his fraternity brothers and dropped out of college in a huff. He didn't take to that kind of schooling;

but when a fellow he knew started to study acting with a retired motion picture performer, James Dean tagged along; he panicked the class acting the part of a pinetree in a storm. Now he knew he wanted to be an actor.

He hung around LA, broke most of the time, working as an usher in movie theatres, getting an occasional part as an extra on the lots, or a bit on TV,

dreaming and yearning and hungry,

eating cold spaghetti out of the can.

Dirty shirt, never a haircut, needed a shave, the grubbiest guy in town. Sometimes he got a job parking cars in a parking lot to earn the two bits he needed for a hamburger and a cup of coffee.

At last he made a break for New York, rode East all the way on the bus. He had a friend with TV connections. For a year he hung around Broadway with the outofwork actors.

"New York is vital, above all fertile," he told the reporters later. "I fit to cadence and pace better here." He developed a lingo

out of tearoom talk about bebop and Bach,

and stale shards of Freud, sex treatises in paperback, captions dubbed in on Cocteau's films, explanations tacked on the wall beside the paintings of Miro at the Modern Museum,

existentialism,

and scraps out of French translations sold under the counter:

"Include me out"; selfexpression.

In the drab summer desert of New York, James Dean lacked friends; he lacked girls, he lacked dough;

but when the chance came he knew how to grab it: a

young director took an interest, invited him out sailing on a sloop on the Sound — farmboy turned deckhand — gave him a part in a show which immediately flopped;

but he'd been seen on the stage. Next he played the black-mailing Arab in a dramatization of André Gide's *Immoraliste* He walked out on the part, the play closed, but he'd been seen by people who knew show business: rave writeups: he was an actor.

They took him on to study at the Actor's Studio. The Actor's Studio was celebrity's lobby in those days. That year Marlon Brando was the artistic idol of the screen. Directors saw a young Brando in Dean (the hepcat school, sideburns and a rat's nest for hair, leather jackets, jackboots and a motorcycle at the curb. These are tough guys, delinquents; but sensitive: Great God how they're sensitive). Elia Kazan hired him to play a sinister adolescent: "Live the part," Stanislavski told his actors.

Dean did just that. He was obstreperous as hell. "I can't divert into being a social human being," he snarled at the reporters through the butt that dangled from his lip, "when I'm working on a hero who's essentially demonic."

Demonic, but lovable under it all.

The sinister adolescent was box office. Long before the picture was released he was besieged by Hollywood agents, promoters, feature writers, photographers.

He wanted to have it known that he was crazy about racing cars. Speed was how to die. Artistic. He made up his own mobiles, was planning to be a bullfighter: *Death in the Afternoon.* "Cool," echoed the teenagers. "Everything he said was cool."

In Hollywood he went on playing the parts he played on the screen: He would keep Hedda Hopper, the Eleanor Roosevelt of the motion picture press, waiting two hours for an interview,

then he would turn up in a torn dirty sweater and riding breeches out at the knees. He quarreled with his friends. He walked out on dates. He drove his directors crazy by being late on the lot. Wouldn't rehearse. He pouted and sulked. Sometimes they couldn't get a word out of him — "A wary suspicious loner," one director called him. Another was more forgiving: "Just a boy on the rise."

He was always nice to his fans though, the teenage crowd. He was just one of the gang with the night watch; the young wouldbe actors who hung around the early morning hamburger joints on Sunset Boulevard. Three glasses of beer made him woozy, he never cared to drink liquor; so he chainsmoked cigarettes and drank cup after cup of coffee right through till it was day. No wonder he couldn't sleep and turned up late and blearyeyed at the studio. *Rebel Without a Cause.*

The teenagers saw themselves in James Dean. Everything he said was cool.

Already he was beginning not to like it much if people didn't look up when he slouched into the Italian restaurant where he ate his meals. Wasn't he James Dean?

He was handy with the mambo drum. His bachelor actor's home was loud with hi-fi. He had to pick an isolated location so that the neighbors wouldn't complain about the rock and roll. In quiet moods he liked to be seen at night spots with another celebrity. He played around with the girl who'd made a name for herself up and down the Coast playing Vampira on TV, the ghoul who gave people right in their own homes their daily creeps,

like a Charles Addams cartoon. (No romance, said their friends,

and how she was real warmhearted underneath and understood his resentments.) He told her everything.

A few days before he died she sent him a postcard picture of herself posed beside an open grave. "Come join me," it said.

An actor had to have a hobby to satisfy the public relations staff. Dean owned a horse but racing cars was his personal bid for publicity. He'd won a race for novices at some meet. His racing, the public was told, gave the producers fits. He was quoted as telling them that speeding was a glorious way to die. (Life couldn't be all social security and safety first. The kids knew that. It was glory a man had to have.) Some friend furnished him with a St. Christopher medal, but the studio, so it was said, had written it into his contract that he wasn't to race a car until the picture he was working on was ready for release.

❖

The last day of September he was free from that clause. There was to be a meet at Salinas. Instead of taking his white Porsche-Spyder with the 130 painted on its side over to the track on a truck like most of the contestants he had to drive it over himself. His German mechanic went along.

A photographer followed in a stationwagon.

He wanted to feel her speed.

Already at Bakersfield a traffic cop gave him a ticket for doing sixty through a forty mile zone.

The sun was setting. It was nearly dusk. He wanted to feel her speed. He was making seventyfive, eighty, a hundred — accounts differ — when near Paso Robles on the empty highway he collided head on with a car turning in from an intersection,

a Ford driven by a young man named Donald Turnupseed.

James Dean was killed. The steering wheel went right through him; Turnupseed and the mechanic were hurt but recovered.

Dead at twenty four:

"James Dean can't be dead," the girls told each other, "he's in hospital undergoing facial surgery." It would take a long time but some day they would see him slouching out onto the screen again.

People paid fifty cents a head to see the wreck of his car.

In LA the clairvoyants and psychics did a land office business interviewing James Dean in the spirit world. Some interviews were printed. "Everything he said was cool," the teenagers said.

At Warner Brothers the requests for photographs, which had merely been average, went up by the time he'd been dead a year to seven thousand letters a month. Everybody from his grandmother to the waiters at the Italian restaurant was interviewed by the motion picture press. The pulp-merchants sold oneshot lives of him in hundreds of thousands of copies. Bronze heads and plaster masks were marketed in bulk. One popular item was made of a plastic supposed to feel like human skin when you stroked it.

The teenagers found it hard to believe that James Dean was dead. There he was right on the screen when they saw his old pictures. The promoters had been struggling hard to blow up the story that millions wouldn't believe he was dead, but when they released a picture on his life nobody went to see it. James Dean was dead sure enough.

An Answer Simple Enough

When Major General William Frishe Dean turned up alive at Panmunjom after three years as a Communist prisoner he did his best to keep people from making a fuss over him. No man could honestly claim to be ashamed of the Congressional Medal, that he admitted, but he explained that he came close to shame when he thought of the men who had done better jobs than he had without such recognition and died doing them. He kept reminding the reporters that he was a general captured because he took a wrong road.

"I lost ground I should have not lost. I lost trained officers and fine men. I'm not proud of that record," he told William L. Worden who wrote up his story for the *Saturday Evening Post,* "and I'm under no delusions that my weeks of command constituted any masterly campaign."

It puzzled General Dean that the American people insisted on making a hero of him all the same.

He described himself, with characteristic candor, as an "inbetween curious kind of a general officer," who had never been to West Point, who hadn't seen action in World War I and who hadn't come up from the ranks.

As far back as he could remember he had wanted to be a soldier. He was the son of a rural dentist, born and raised in Carlyle, the small country seat of Clinton County, in southern Illinois. Maybe it was on account of his mother's German blood that he was so carried away by the sight of soldiers drilling when his folks took him to the St. Louis World's Fair. He had a cornbelt childhood in the public schools; sold magazines to buy himself mailorder courses in physical culture.

As a kid he was a crank about physical fitness, weight-lifting, dumbbells, pushups, chinning himself. He was an inveterate hiker.

No student, he flunked the West Point exams after graduating from highschool. The war was on in Europe but he was too young to enlist without his mother's permission.

When the family moved to California he enrolled in a pre-law course at the university. For spending money he worked as a stevedore on the San Francisco docks, as trolley conductor, washed dishes and even pounded the beat for a while as a student cop during the period when a Berkeley police chief was trying to interest college boys in the policeman's career. What he liked best about college was the students' army training corps.

He never did get a degree, but the Army had a crying need for officers: mighty few boys wanted an army career after the War to End War ended in the disillusioned peace. When Dean was twentyfour he managed to pass the examination for a commission as Second Lieutenant in the regular army.

The man was a natural born infantryman. Still a crank on physical fitness he coached athletic teams, rode, played polo. A young lady whose horse ran away when he took her out for a canter while he was stationed at Fort Douglas, Utah, ended by becoming his wife. The Canal Zone was their honeymoon. They were happy in the army life. He served as a lieutenant for twelve years, was promoted to captain at thirtyseven, to major at fortyone.

He landed in France on Omaha Beach with the 44th Infantry Division and ended the war in command of it. He liked to boast that in all the fighting up through France and across the Rhine into Germany he only lost fortyfour men captured. As a general officer he didn't believe in soldiers getting captured.

In 1947 he was military governor of South Korea, trying, through interpreters, to teach the Koreans how to run their sawedoff nation American style. Later he regretted he hadn't tried to learn more about the Koreans before he tried to do that job. At that he was known as "the walking general" because, instead of zooming about in a starspangled staffcar, he walked to his office in the morning. He was occasionally seen poking through the slums of Seoul or hiking far up into the hills to shoot pheasants. After elections, duly approved, he turned the problems of Korean self-government over to Syngman Rhee and left for a new tour of duty in Japan.

One Saturday night in June 1950 General Dean and his wife attended a fancy dress party at Headquarters of the 24th Division at Kokura. They wore Korean costumes they had brought away as souvenirs from Seoul. The costumes were admired, but the general, who was six feet two, remembered that the robes were much too short for him. He was uncomfortable in the hard stovepipe hat of a yang ban.

Next morning the North Korean army, trained by Russian instructors and armored with Russian heavy tanks, crossed the 38th Parallel. World War III, here it comes, they told each other at Headquarters in Kokura. General Dean's troops were scattered all over the southern islands of Japan. Regiments were under strength. A bare fifteen per cent had seen combat. Men were soft from occupation living, PX beer and the delicate attentions of the Jap girls they shacked up with. They didn't know where the hell Korea was and couldn't care less. While they were busy tending the refugees, military and civilian, who came out in planeloads, orders came to hold South Korea.

General Dean found himself, after a number of false starts, fumbling around in the fog on a C—45 looking for the Taejon airstrip. That highway and railroad junction in the middle of the peninsula had been picked for the hub of defense. Looked like a good place for headquarters on the map.

The fog down in Taejon was thicker than in the air above it.

Everybody was on the run. No communications. No intelligence a man could rely on. Fifth column work. At ROK headquarters sliteyed officers were yelling Communist in each other's faces. For an American who didn't know the language it was hard to tell friend from foe.

Before General Dean had time to set up his headquarters organization the Communists had broken through down all the arterial roads. Their heavy tanks outclassed the American light tanks that had already been nearly obsolete when the fighting stopped in Europe five years before. Ammunition was short. Nobody knew the terrain. Some outfits were putting up a scrap, a few brave men selling their lives high, but nothing was holding anywhere.

It was decided to move headquarters southeast down the railroad to Yongdong. Communications were so bad General Dean decided he'd be better able to judge what was going on if he stayed a while in Taejon.

One hot July morning the general woke to the sound of gunfire. The problem that day was how to pull out of Taejon while there was still time. He spoke afterwards of the "sombre poetry" of combat. "The phrase 'fight and fall back' has a brave sound," he told Worden; and about the smells of the Korean summer morning, of ricepaddy muck and human excrement and the punky reek of smoldering thatch, laced now and then with the sharp sea of cordite. "Bone wearying" was how he described the fighting that day and the days before it.

Communist tanks were already in town.

A general's business is to give orders. Although he still had one telephone line open to the rear General Dean and his aide and a Korean interpreter were so thoroughly cut off there were no orders left to give. He decided that if he couldn't give orders he could at least give an example.

Taejon was full of infiltrators wearing the white clothes of the country people, turncoats sniping out of windows. Dean got the clerks and cooks and messengers of the regimental command together into a party to stalk tanks. Fight and fall back. In covering the retreat they accounted for a number of snipers, made unsuccessful attacks on a couple of Communist tanks they found waddling about without infantry support. The last many of the retreating troops saw of General Dean he was blazing away with his fortyfive at a tank that rumbled unconcernedly by. "Dean losing his temper" was how he explained it.

At last he got hold of a man with a bazooka who still had ammo for a wonder and crawled with him up into a plastered room overlooking a narrow shopping street. They found themselves looking down the muzzle of the cannon of a Communist tank. The general indicated a spot at the base of the cannon. The bazooka fired pointblank. A horrible screaming came from inside. Two more rounds. The tank was out of commission and the street was quiet.

The general was keeping a list that day of men he intended to decorate for bravery. (He'd been feeling a little guilty, so he said, about skimping on decorations in the European Theatre.) He even had a dozen or more medals in his jeep all ready to pin on.

Dean's brave men never did get their decorations. Things moved too fast. Already it was dusk and time to evacuate what was left of the regimental post. Some light tanks sent up to relieve them were having a hard time holding their own in a firefight with the Communist armor. His troops were clumsy about taking cover, Dean reminisced sadly, hadn't played enough cops and robbers when they were kids.

The main road out was jammed with jackknifed trucks and burning halftracks. The road was under fire as far as you could see. In a squall of bullets the general's jeep roared through an intersection into a wrong road. No way to turn back.

They came on a bunch of men talking surrender under a wrecked truck. Some were wounded. Dean filled his two jeeps with the wounded and as many others as could climbed aboard. They drove careening into a Communist roadblock. Nothing to it but to take to the ditches.

Dean's aide was wounded. Afterwards Dean told of how proud he was of this Lieutenant Clarke for the way he kept the seventeen men together as they crawled through the muck of a beanfield. One of their Koreans, a welldressed one, fell into a "honey pit." Later Dean remembered waiting for dark on a riverbank and delivering a lecture about putting halizone tablets into your canteen before you drank the water.

Carrying one man too badly hurt to walk, they crossed the river at dark and climbed a steep mountain spur hoping to cut back to the road beyond the Communist roadblock. The wounded man was delirious. He drank up all the water they had and kept calling for more. At a point on the mountain, while Lieutenant Clarke was giving his little outfit a rest, Dean thought he heard water in a gully. He slipped away from the group and started to climb down. He never knew how he came to trip and plunge headfirst down the hill. He blacked out.

He must have rolled a hundred yards at least because when he came to he was lying alone on the hillside in the black night. His shoulder seemed to be broken. He was bleeding from a gash in the head. No sign of the other men.

About daybreak a Communist patrol almost stumbled over his carcass. Dean was conscious enough to hear the goatlike scamper of their feet up the stony slope. When they had gone he dragged himself into a clump of bushes where he lay all day groggy with pain.

By night he had himself in hand. His legs were all right. His head was clear. By favoring his shoulder he found that in spite of the pain he could crawl. By the time he reached the top of the ridge he was walking. All the boyish physical culture was standing by him now. He'd walk to the American lines.

He found himself, like in a nightmare, climbing handhold to handhold down a perpendicular cliff in a downpour of rain. He joined company with a young lieutenant, lost him again in a haze of weariness escaping from some Korean riflemen across a paddyfield. Day followed day. He lost track of time.

For thirtyfive days, hiding out by day in the rocky ridges and traveling at night, blarneying the country people out of a little rice now and then in the villages, he managed to escape capture. Gradually he made his way south towards the shrinking perimeter of the Pusan beachhead. He could already hear the distant rumble of American guns when his luck failed.

A pair of Koreans, named Han and Choi, whom he thought he'd secured as guides through to the American lines, led him into an ambush.

His shoulder was still agony. He was too weak from undernourishment and scurvy and dysentery to put up much resistance when fifteen home guards jumped him on a moonlit road and trussed him up like a calf and dragged him off to the Communist police in the nearest town. Still he tried to fight so hard they would shoot him: he wanted his children to know he had put up a fight to the end.

On account of the language difficulty he never really knew

whether his guides had intended to betray him all along or whether they couldn't help themselves. They are said to have been paid five dollars for his hide.

Anyway there he was, an American major general locked in an L shaped cage in which he could neither stand up or lie down in a smalltown police station, a prisoner of war of the Communist Koreans.

Defeat. Captivity. This was like no other war in the nation's history. No more could any American general boast about how few men he'd had captured. All over Korea Americans were surrendering.

These were the kids who'd been soaked in wartime prosperity while their elder brothers manned the amphibious landings and the desperate beachheads and the floating bases and the great airstrikes of World War II;

raised on the gibblegabble of the radio between the family car and the corner drugstore and the Five and Ten.

Nobody had ever told them anything
except to get more and do less.

Nobody had ever told them that to be an American meant anything more than to look at the comics and to drive around the roads in a new automobile
obtained on easy monthly payments
and to reach for packaged foods out of the frigidaire;

and particularly the army hadn't explained to them what they were doing in this lousy country that was all steep hills and muddy fields
that smelt of shit,

helping one bunch of gooks fight another bunch of gooks that had a hellofalot better tanks
and seemed to know what they were doing. (United Nations; what the hell was the United Nations? Wasn't that a building in New York?)

General Dean had been proud of how few of his men surrendered in the European Theatre. He felt ashamed enough squatting in that little cage, a prisoner: he'd have felt worse if he'd known that four days after the fighting started
a captured officer
of his own 24th Infantry Division

was broadcasting enemy propaganda over the Communist radio.

After the stalemate and the exchange of prisoners across the 38th Parallel, army authorities went to consider-able trouble — statistics were collected, reports compiled, books written — to discover
why,
out of seven thousand one hundred and ninety army men captured,
thirteen percent became out and out creatures of the Com-munists and roughly one third collaborated in some way or other with the enemy. They were the "progressives."

There were so many informers that not one single man made good his escape from a prisoner of war camp (and you ask why the prestige of our nation has sunk so low in the world).

They'd all had some schooling but no one had taught those poor kids that spirit, the little spark of God in every man, is what keeps man alive in adversity. The Communist indoctrinators were able to appeal to a sort of ignorant idealism that is the dead shell of the protestant ethics our fathers lived by. Idealism without ethics is no compass.

"One of the most difficult problems for a prisoner is main-taining his judgment," General Dean told Worden.

For judgment read sense of right and wrong.

No one had told those kids that right and wrong was the inner compass that points true north. When army discipline broke down they fell to pieces, each poor devil by himself. They didn't help each other the way the Turks did or the Marines. They didn't take care of themselves. If you can't help yourself you can't help the next man. They wouldn't eat the gook chow. Two thousand seven hundred and thirty let themselves die in captivity. Of the survivors two thirds confessed to the army investigators they had "played it cool."

Thirteen percent told the enemy nothing, wrote no con-fessions, joined no study classes, memorized no Marxist lita-nies. They were the "reactionaries." They had tough sled-ding but they came out best in the end,
and with honor.

☼

Fiftyyearold General Dean with a broken shoulder and an infected foot, suffering from dysentery and every disease that fatigue and underfeeding brought in their train, would definitely have been described as a "reactionary." Dean had spirit enough and to spare.

For thirty years Communism had been building a technique, using everything from the thumbscrew and the rack to the latest psychological methods of the scientific laboratories,

and dark and cold and solitude and starvation

to kill God's spirit in man. They tried threats and misery on Dean; they tried rational argument; they tried luxury;

but still Dean talked back.

Torture? No they didn't torture him, not a bit.

He was taken first to a modern sort of penitentiary (he'd inspected it himself as military governor). The commandant suggested kindly that he must go on the air to explain to his family and friends that he was safe, that they were treating him with the deference his rank deserved, and incidentally that the Communists were being welcomed as brothers by the Koreans of the south.

No. Dean wouldn't go on any radio.

The commandant asked him whether if they turned him loose he would continue to fight.

Dean said that if his country gave him a chance after the mess he'd made of his command he'd try to do better next time and kill a lot more Communists.

Torture? No they didn't torture him, not a bit.

He was taken north and put in the hands of a certain Colonel Kim who was learned in the techniques.

It was Kim's business to try to make Dean sign a propaganda petition. At first Kim tried good food and pleasantries. He even sent in a doctor to attend to Dean's dysentery. He offered him a pleasant country house and all the whiskey he wanted to drink and the assurance that he wouldn't be tortured.

Dean said he didn't drink whiskey.

Colonel Kim's geniality faded. He took to waking Dean up in the middle of the night.

About the time of the Inchon landing there was a break.

Dean was hurried into Pyongyang the Communist capital and interrogated by the Chief of Security about the American plan of maneuver. He insisted on a written answer. Dean wrote it out with stiff fingers:

Fortunately I do not have the information you seek. But even if I did I wouldn't give it to you, because by so doing I would be a traitor to my country. So help me God, William F. Dean.

He was sent back to Colonel Kim. The real interrogation began. It was winter by that time. Day after day and night after night they made Dean sit on a hard chair in the light summer suit they'd given him when they took away his uniform. His infected left foot had swelled so he couldn't bear a shoe. He had lost so much weight that sitting on the hard straight chair was agony. He had to sit on his hands. Sitting on his hands made them swell up almost as much as his foot. The interrogations seemed to be heading towards his trial as a war criminal. Colonel Kim and another Kim and a Ph.D. worked in shifts.

The room was cold. The temperature about 33°. Colonel Kim complained because Dean's teeth chattered. Colonel Kim who wore a heavy overcoat said it wasn't cold at all. To prove it he made Dean strip down to his shorts. Day after day they went on keeping him awake, starving him, freezing him, using oldfashioned third degree methods. The only breaks were when Dean had to go running to the latrine.

No they didn't torture him. Not a bit. Colonel Kim interspersed his interrogation with references to the torture to come. At last Dean could stand it no more. Afraid he might tell something under torture in his wornout state he managed to steal the revolver off a sleeping guard. When the Koreans jumped on him from all sides he couldn't get the revolver to fire. Dean was sorry for the poor guard, a simple fellow who had been nice to him. He was led away and probably shot for falling asleep on duty.

Somehow the desperation of Dean's act impressed his captors. Colonel Kim was seen no more. There was no more talk of torture. Doctors visited him. He was kept warm. His food became fairly decent.

By that time MacArthur's army was sweeping north. Ill as he was Dean was hurried in trucks and jeeps up to the Yalu and across into Manchuria for safekeeping as the Korean Communist army broke in pieces.

On that trip Dean could relax a little. Everybody was too busy to interrogate him. He wasn't treated too badly, now that the Americans seemed to be winning.

Dean began to make observations. Already he had observed with some interest that sitting motionless stripped to the skin in extreme cold, his body, even in its weakened condition, somehow managed to retain a little warmth.

His guards were enemies but they were sometimes friends. He became interested in what he described to Worden as "the manysided, kind and cruel, inventive, clever, stupid, resilient unpredictable Korean character." Maybe getting to know these people was worth what he was going through. It would never have happened to an uncaptured general.

After the Chinese victories rolled back MacArthur's advance he was spirited from place to place. He had an idea the Korean Communists were trying to keep him out of the hands of the Chinese. He wasn't mistreated but he was never allowed out of doors. Months passed cooped in tiny rooms. He had no reading matter. They wouldn't let him play the local form of chess his guards played. To keep from losing his mind he squared numbers and did square roots and kept track of the flies he killed. His biggest day he killed 522.

He began to be cozy with the Communist Koreans. A number of his guards were training to be officers. He became interested in their careers and helped them with their homework. He learned all he could about their Communist theory and practice.

"The most important discovery to me," he told Worden, "was that the ordinary Communists who guarded me and lived with me really believed that they were following a route that would lead to a better life for themselves and their children . . . It was easy for us to say they were mistaken but not so easy to explain to these men of limited experience just why their ideology must fail . . . We can't convince them with fine words. We've got to show them something better. We must have an answer simple enough for the dullest to understand."

At last after three years Dean was exchanged with the

rest at Panmunjom. The first Americans he saw were gaunt
prisoners in a column of trucks. "Hi General Dean!" they
yelled. "Hi General! We didn't know we were waiting for
you." The Yankee voices sounded wonderful to him.

Soon afterwards with unaffected dignity, with perfect candor, he was telling his story to the world's press assembled
at Freedom Village. Somehow in everything Dean said, in
everything he did while he was a prisoner there had appeared that answer simple enough for the dullest to understand.

The American people were right to make a hero of him.

Man Is a Creature That Builds

Man is a creature that builds
institutions
    out of abnegation of lives linked for a purpose
    the way the flowerlike polyps, the coralmakers of the
warm salt seas
    build
    from incrusted layers of discarded careers:
    niggerheads, atolls, great barrier reefs
    and coquina benches forming the limestone basements
of peninsulas where civilizations flourish and flower and fall
frazzled to seed.

    Man's institutions fashion his destiny,
    as the hive, the nest, the hill, the sixsided cellular comb
of the honeybee, serried, tiered,
    grouped according to impulses
    inherent in the genes,
    fashion the social insect, his castes and functional
diversities:
    the winged males and females, the blind workers, the
soldiers, the nasuti, the alternates of the "fourth caste"

of the pale termites,
dwellers in dark,
whose complex society has so astonished the
naturalists.

Institutions, so the sociologists tell us,
shape man's course,
as the comings and goings of the hardshelled ants —
their diligence since the dawn of philosophy has delighted
the makers of fables and the pointers of morals — are
predetermined by instinct.

Institutional man,
like the termites and the social insects among the hymenop-
tera, must, we are told, sacrifice individual diversity for
diversity of caste. (Already in his bureaucratic form, with
a diligence which would astonish any uncommitted natural-
ist, institutional man accumulates
in vaults and cabinets and files —
paper,
the same paper the polistes wasp builds his
house of
and the termites of the tropical uplands
their towering castles.)

Lecturing on "Social Insects" the late Professor
Wheeler of Harvard used to point out with some malice to
his students
that the ants,
too,
in spite of the predestined perfection
of their institutions,
suffered what he called "perversions of
appetite."
Their underground galleries and storied
domes
are infested by an array of lethal creatures, thieves and
predators, scavenger crickets, greedy roaches and rove beetles, and one particular peculiarly plumed little bug
which secretes in its hairs an elixir so
delectable to antkind
that the ants lose all sense of self, or species, preservation
and seek death in its embrace.

Tomorrow the Moon

IF HE didn't mean for me to pick 'em up why did he have to leave his credit cards laying around on the bathroom floor? I certainly didn't mean to take 'em. I meant to give 'em back all the while but they never gave me a chance. "Here are your credit cards, Uncle Jap," I was planning to say, "you dropped 'em on the bathroom floor," and to give him a dirty look and a sneer.

It's his own damn fault. Why did he have to leave 'em laying around if he didn't expect me to pick 'em up? Or did he do it on purpose just to see what I'd do?

No he didn't. Drunk that's why. He let 'em fall out of the inside pocket of his jacket because he was drunk, the cards and a small wad of bills. He was good and drunk. Gets drunk every night, the old soak, and if I get so much as enthusiastic over a can of beer, he lectures me on the evils. He must have wanted a son awful bad and it's too late now, so the crazy clod takes it out on me with his little peptalks.

I meant to show all that in my tone of voice and the way I looked him in the eye when I gave him back the credit cards. I'm Stan Goodspeed and I'm not taking a thing, I meant my look to say. But they never gave me a chance to slide in one word. Too damn busy listening to themselves gibblegabble about how they were going to blow up the world with their nuclear friction, or whatever the screwy name is they have for it.

They say teenagers are screwy but it's the adults who are really nuts. At teenage parties we have a happy violent time getting rid of our frustrations. We have fun. But these damned adults, all the poor clods do is sit there beating their brains out over their liquor. It was that egghead way they just sat there, drinking sips out of their drinks with their little fingers crooked, smiling like it was all just too cute to blow up the whole entire goddam human race, that got me started. That's nothing to smile about.

I know I'm emotional. Maybe I ought to take tranquilizers. I've been going slowly crazy ever since I came home from that lousy school. They had it in for me at that school right from the beginning. That housemaster hated my guts from the time he first set eyes on me.

I don't blame Aunty she's just so soft on him she does anything he says. Imagine sending Stan Goodspeed to a dump where they won't let you go out for a little relaxation Saturday nights. The nerve of them to expect a kid to go to bed at half past ten. I'd just have laid there getting more and more frustrated. They must think I'm chicken. One thing I sure showed those masters I wasn't. They acted all the time like they thought a guy ought to be scared pissless of them. Not Stan Goodspeed. Not while there is a taxicab left in the world.

Now to be real truthful — a kid oughtn't to lie to himself — I didn't exactly mean to give the bills back. Uncle Jap never would miss a couple of skins. Let him worry about where he dropped them. Shit I don't know what I meant. It all just got under my hair. That's what. Sanctimonious talk about how blowing up the human race was the love of God. Why can't they say what they mean?

And soninlaw sitting there with his eyes on that old square's face like he was in church listening to the Lord's Prayer. That old square thinks he's God Almightly. I used to think Will Jenks was the greatest man in the world, a singlehanded superman fighting the gangsters for everything that was on the level. If he told me to stick my hand in the fire I'd a done it. I went down on my knees to beg him to let me drive a cab for him. I'd have given my life for him like that crazy clod Terry Bryant. If he'd let me fake my age and drive a cab for him I wouldn't be all frustrated and disturbed like I am. A kid gets to the point where he has to have action.

Maybe I'm neurotic but it gave me the cold creeps to sit there and see Will Jenks sucking up to that old square just because he needs money to put in his screwy taxicabs. It's crazy. Will Jenks a brownnose. Made me ashamed of myself for belonging to the human race. If I hadn't walked out on 'em I'd have puked, I'd have thrown up all over Aunty's silver lamé tablecloth or whatever screwy material it's made of. What did they expect me to do? Take it till I upchucked over the table and that girl staring at me with the come hither eyes, she was a dog if I ever saw one.

When I ran off down that hill I was all excited. I didn't know what I was going to do. I just ran on down, tripping and stumbling through the bushes till I got a stitch in my side. What was the use of getting all out of breath and sweaty? What was there to get chicken about? None of 'em was going to come after me. All too wrapped up listening to Money Bags.

They couldn't care less. Except Aunty. I'll write Aunty saying not to worry.

So I started to walk on quietly down the road into Providence Forge. I had to play this one cool. Here's where I'd begin to live it up. So I walked along through the misty mild moonlight night listening to those screwy whipporwills and smelling the sexy sweet honeysuckle that made me want a playmate real bad. Take it easy. Playmate coming up. Play this one cool. "Stan, don't you do anything foolish," I kept telling myself.

As luck would have it there was a bus marked Philadelphia standing right in the busstation. I hopped right in. The bus was full of kids coming home from some screwy picnic. The girls were all dogs so far as I could see. They looked up at me as if to say "Now what's his racket?" But I didn't mess with them. My racket was to get far away fast. So I just sat there with my eyelashes over my eyes looking over the literature that came with Uncle Jap's credit cards. That's how I got my big idea.

When the busdriver asked for my ticket before he started I tried to get away with a hardluck story about how I'd lost it down a drain in the busstation but he wouldn't fall for that one so I had to use some of Uncle Jap's hardearned folding money to pay my fare into town. That left me fourteen dollars and a quarter. May sound like a lot of dough but it was just peanuts for what I was planning.

As the bus went zooming along through the moony summer night I sat there studying Uncle Jap's signature on the credit cards. He had his Jasper Milliron written in kind of a shaky immature round hand. Isn't it a sign of immaturity for an old clod like that to sign his name like a kid? Maybe that's what's wrong with Uncle Jap. Maybe that's what attracted Aunty. Aunty's too full of mother-love for her own good. If he weren't immature he never would have stuck his neck out and got all messed up trying to tangle with one of the biggest milling concerns in the country over some kind of screwy new machinery. Why can't he get help? Aunty always said that if he'd kept his mouth shut and let things ride, he'd a been chairman of the board to this day. Of course Aunty thinks he's wonderful, always was crazy about dead cats. It's immaturity accounts for his drinking.

Copying Uncle Jap's signature wouldn't be forgery, indeed it wouldn't. Didn't he tell me once he wanted to adopt me as a son? I had a time shaking that one off. "Let's let it ride," I said. "That's OK Uncle Jap," I said.

So I sat there reading about how to charge services including *food, drink and room accommodations at the finest restaurants, night clubs and hotels* (I was getting hungry and sleepy just reading it) *in major cities and resort areas throughout the country* (and I sure won't be alone), *auto rentals* (safety fast, that's what the ads say) *through the world's leading auto rental agencies; motel accommodations, interstate liquor package* (yeah man!) *and retail liquor charging where the state law permits* (I'll buy me a case. Won't make me mad), *gasoline and repair services at more than three thousand affiliated stations from coast to coast, gift and florist shops in major cities throughout the world; air, sea and rail transportation and other travel facilities and men's* (just watch for that bleeding madras jacket) *and women's clothing stores* (women's! Wait till the chicks see what I can buy 'em on credit) *and much more.*

What do they mean by "much more"?

Did I need a tranquilizer? Just play it cool, Stan Goodspeed, I kept telling myself. And I sat there in the bus telling myself that if I didn't do anything foolish and kept moving fast enough the bills would never catch up. Maybe they would blow the screwy world up before the bills came in at that.

If the worst came to the worst I'd just explain to Uncle Jap that I wasn't costing him any more this way than if I'd stayed home and gotten all frustrated and disturbed so he'd have to take me to a psychist or whatever the screwy name is of those nut doctors they take disturbed kids to. Why there was a kid in school whose parents paid some analyzer twentyfive dollars an hour for years and years to have him analyzed, and they still do.

Then the bus stopped and all the kids got out and right away everybody was gone. I almost chickened out all by myself walking around in the empty lonesome glare of the downtown streets. I knew I couldn't get me a real plush pad without luggage at that time of night so I just walked down to the Thirtieth Street station and just sat there in the waitingroom. I sat there all night reading the ads out of a wad of slick paper magazines and smoking pack after pack of cigarettes. I guess I musta smoked four packs. The more I smoked the more I thought. "Play it cool Stan Good-speed," I kept telling myself.

First I had to have my story in case they questioned how come I had this credit card. I'd say I really was Jasper Milliron Jr. and the crazy clods had left off the junior, but it was all in the family and Dad would be good for it anyway. Then I had a kinder second string yarn about how my dear Uncle Ben had died and left me all this jack, his entire fortune to think of it, but I couldn't get my hands on any cash, natch, and had to live off my credit cards till the estate was settled. I wasn't going to do like that kid I read about in the paper who did great on his credit cards but got snagged by the cops because he cashed a check and it bounced.

So there I sat hazily dreamily thinking about how I'd find me a playmate with kinda sultry blond hair and beautiful big bubs all a lovely even tan in a cabaña built for two on some beach on the Coast. Or why not Lake Tahoe on the way? And then Honolulu? Honolulu was the place to go, but not alone. A girl on a beach. A girl. A girl.

It would have almost turned into a wet dream if a big cop hadn't scared me out of a year's growth. When I looked up from my glossy paper mag with my eyes batting, there he was standing over me and saying this was a waiting-room, it wasn't no dormitory for runaway teens. I opened my eyes wide. Just to show I was in the groove ("Keep your shirt on my good man," was in my tone of voice) I told

him I'd gotten in late on the bus from school and was waiting for a morning train to New York. I gave him Merman,
Milliron Associates as my dad's address and all that. And
then I showed him all this rich identification and told him
I didn't get me a pad at the Bellevue because I was so late
it didn't seem worth while to blow in all that dough for
such a short time because I was saving my pennies to buy
me a Grumman Gulfstream for a private plane. The crazy
clod just about took off his hat. He called me Sir. Can
you beat it?

Stan Goodspeed, this is going to be cool.

First thing a kid needs is to be nicely dressed, not too
snazzy but casual, like the beachnik togs and wash and wear
nantril fiber slacks they advertise in the slick paper mags,
and airplane luggage to go with it. If I get past the first
couple stores the way I wowed that flatfoot bugeyed, I'll be
all set. Then I buy my airplane tickets and drive me a U-
Drive It car from one of the world's leading auto agencies.
Jeez how I love the kinda sweet sharp rubber varnish
leather smell of a new car. Why don't some of those perfume companies put out a perfume smelling of Chrysler
Imperial right off the floor? You could sprinkle it over
some playmate before you worked her. Say why not hire
me a car and pick up some chick on the way to the airport?
Yeah man.

By that time it was daylight. With my mags in a bundle
under my arm I walked around outside the station. A beautiful pink early light made everything look out of this world.
My tongue was black from smoking all those cigarettes but
I couldn't care less. This was going to be Stan Goodspeed
day.

All I had to do now was wait for the stores to open strolling around in the lovely sunshine. I didn't want to spend
any more hard money than I had to but I did have to go
to the terminal drugstore and buy me a safetyrazor. Cash
was going to be my toughest problem. I knew that the sky
was the limit on credit but if I got snagged it would be for
lack of two bits to slip to a bellhop. Still I had to wear a
shining face. I went to the men's room moving fast and
keeping my eyes to myself to keep out of the way of the
lurking homosexuals and shaved and patted down my hair
and cleaned up good.

At nine thirty I tried my first store. I'd already spotted it an hour before by a little sign, "Credit Cards Honored."

The crazy clod was so anxious to make his first sale he didn't check on a thing. Was I tense? While he was writing up the bill for me to sign the guy noticed I was all of a sweat. I told him it had been the night before the morning after but he wasn't trying to pin anything on me. All the crazy clod was trying to do was sell me some screwy new deodorant to stop tension odor. Can you beat that?

The man in the luggage shop was wackier yet. I thought he'd kiss me when he figured out the amount of the bill. Couldn't he send the suitcases around to the hotel? No I'd pick 'em up on the way to the airport. I was catching a jet to the Coast. I talked big but he sure ate it up.

I was just walking into the U-Drive It place when I stopped dead in my tracks. I remembered my driving license. Sure as hell they'd want to see it and it read Stan Goodspeed. Thinking ahead like that showed I was in the groove. Nothing to it but to spend cash money on a taxi. I never did mind spending money on taxis. Meanwhile I had to waste two nickels on the phone to make me a plane reservation. The clod at the other end of the wire was apologetic as hell because he couldn't put me on a jet right there. I'd have to fly to Washington and change. Nonstop to San Francisco. This was the life. I hopped into a cab. Restaurants, nightclubs, hotels in the major cities and resort areas, affiliated stations from coast to coast, men's and women's clothing stores, gift and florist shops throughout the world, here I come.

And much more?

A handsome outboard cruiser sleeping two with the famous fiberglas hull that never needs scraping, sanding, calking or painting; a sports compact deluxe convertible featuring nimbler handling, that easyriding zoom; a pad for indoor-outdoor living, airconditioned, soundconditioned with builtin appliances and luminous ceilings; an easy to operate aerodynamically advanced private plane for fast cool clean direct nonstop travel, a cosmic butterfly powered by parabolic mirrors, a spin out beyond the stratosphere in a supersonic spaceliner. Why not?

And much more . . .

Stan Goodspeed's throwing a ball . . . Yeah man.

Oh My America My New Found Land

THAT NIGHT Jay had hardly got to bed it seemed before he was dreaming that he was in court and it was the most important case he'd ever had, but he'd lost his glasses and whenever he lifted the typewritten foolscap to his eyes to see the little letters the little letters squirmed like worms . . . worms on a corpse a voice said in his ear, the corpse of a dying society, and the voice had an Italian accent and when he looked up the judge was old Mat Sabatini who kept twisting the ends of his white soupstrainers and saying, "Young man, why has the defense presented no brief?" He was winking one eye in a lewd and lascivious manner and Jay turned round to see who he was winking at and it was Hedda Gelber doing a hootchykootchy in red flannel tights and Jay was horribly affected and he kept trying to press it down with his hands because he knew he was in danger of death, he was not the attorney he was the defense; he was not on trial he was convicted. If he could only remember the words he could go free. If they would only let him look for the brief. But already the girls in the chorus were tying the hangman's noose round his neck tying it in pretty bows and furbelows and standing back with appraising smiles and fluffing it up with their pink hands round his neck. It's all in the brief. My secretary is bringing the brief. "And what is her name?" asked Leo Sabatini's pale twisted face rolling out like a severed head on the judge's rack. "I can't remember. I can't remember." Jay's eyes rolled back into his brain he tried so hard to remember. But everything he had written there was white and squirming worms and he'd forgotten her name and as the executioners raised their rifles in a nightmare shriek he woke.

Ben was looking at him from the other bed. Jay put his

glasses on to see his face. "Sorry," he said, "I dreamed I was in court."

"Must have been a courtmartial," said Ben and rolled over to go back to sleep. Jay hurried into the bathroom and shaved and splashed in a cold tub and came out in his shorts feeling bright and alive as the bright early day outside and humming:

> *One more river to Jordan*
> *One more river to cross.*

Lulie, too, woke up early that morning and ran to the window and looked out into the slanting sunlight and called to Garde, "Hark hark the lark."

"At heaven's gate sings," echoed Garde sleepily with her dark hair streaming over her face. "But why on earth so early? I could sleep for weeks."

"Let's not stop in Montreal," said Lulie.

"I wanted to go down the Lachine Rapids on the excursion boat like Mother and Dad did when they went to Niagara Falls on their honeymoon," said Hildegarde getting to her feet and walking with drowsy dignity into the bathroom, "but no matter."

"I've had enough city in Chicago to last me for years," Lulie called after her. "Jay and I aren't going to live in cities ever."

"So you really are going to marry him," came Garde's voice amid the tumbling of water from the bathroom. "You know I never thought you would."

"Garde don't be horrid."

Lulie started yanking savagely at her hair with a comb in front of the mirror. "I've said it, I've said it." Her nose was windburned and looked, she told herself, like the beak of a confederate ram. She was whimpering into the mirror when Hildegarde came up behind her all dressed in white piqué and gave her shoulders a hug and said, "I'm so glad . . . You know I want your happiness. But isn't he an odd kind of fish?"

"He's not so odd as me," said Lulie beginning to laugh through her tears. "Aunt Lyde said all the Harringtons were odd."

Once they'd had breakfast and started out in the car Lulie couldn't think of anything but what fun it was to be entering the Province of Quebec. She cried out that it was her first glimpse of the old world. Now she felt travelled like *The Beloved Vagabond* or the people in those books by the Williamsons Aunt Lyde used to love so. The grim gray pointed churches and the low stone farms and the mansard roofs and the people and the carts and the horses and especially the dogs began to look French. After skirting the tiresome outskirts of Montreal and deciding to leave for another time Quebec City and gallant Montcalm slain on the Plains of Abraham and Wolfe reciting

> *The lowing herd winds slowly o'er the lea . . .*
> *And leaves the world to darkness and to me*

to the men in his boat on the flooding tide the night before the assault, they crossed the St. Lawrence and found a road which according to the map would lead them straight into the State of Maine. "But the trip's coming to an end too soon," Hildegarde complained as they studied the signposts at the crossroads. "Thalassa, Thalassa," chanted Lulie. "I want to see the sea."

Late that afternoon with Ben at the wheel they were winding up a road along a narrow darkgreen river between lightgreen fields full of cattle while blackbirds circled overhead against ranks of fluffedup summer clouds and Lulie was sitting in the back seat with the suitcases piled high between her and Jay, but his hand had found its way across the suitcases and had hold of hers. She sat there looking out in a trance at each bend of the road like a little girl turning the pages of a picturebook. She came to with a start when the car slid gently to a stop at the brow of a little rise in the road and Ben grumbled that his brakes were gone. They all got out and studied the wheels and Don Modesto who had neatly tucked a stone under the rear wheel was saying, well of course a car didn't really need brakes. They'd driven Fiats during the late unpleasantness and they had hardly ever had any brakes.

They were at the entrance of a lonesomelooking little town of gray stucco houses with slate roofs. The whitewash on the trunks of the little trees along the street gave them a chilly look. Facing them was a stiff iron statue of the Virgin Mary painted gray and, beyond, steep graystone steps rose to a graystone church with twin steeples. "Brother Ben why not run into that garage?" She pointed to a blue sign peeping out at a street corner ahead. "Garage in French I take it means garage . . . We'll look for a restaurant . . . that's French too. Don Modesto can tell the good ones by sniffing in the door. I send him in like a bird dog . . ." She grabbed Jay's hand. "Come on let's explore."

Beside the grassplot under the statue they stopped in their tracks. Shepherded by nuns in whitewinged headdresses a troop of little girls in darkblue uniforms with round unbecoming darkblue hats on their poor little heads, two by two, the smallest first, then the next smallest, then quite big ones gawky in the shrunken uniforms, trailed up the steps. The fat nun was in the lead and two thin ones brought up the rear. A yellow door opened in the wall beside the church and the little troop filed in. Then the door closed behind them and at the same moment the churchbell began to ring in cold cracked complaining tones, and a sprinkling of old people in black baggy clothes appeared on the steps suddenly, as if they had come out of the cracks in the old stones, and crawled like wounded beetles up the hill and vanished into the black of the church door.

Lulie grabbed Jay's arm and held it tight. "I feel as if somebody was walking over my grave," she said. "Come on let's explore."

The street was very short. In a twinkling they were out on the other side of town looking through apple orchards up the hill in the high white clouds. "Don Modesto," said Lulie when they stopped breathless to turn back to find the others, "don't let them send me to a nunnery."

When they hurried back to report that there was only one hotel and that they found it shuttered and grim and to suggest they'd better push on, they found the Buick standing pathetically on three legs in an alley beside a little shack that looked remarkably like an oldfashioned blacksmith shop lorded over by a broadbearded man in greasy dungarees who spoke not one word of English. Hildegarde, a desperate expression on her face, kept repeating in her finishing school French: "Les freins ne fonctionnent pas," while the village smithy and his wartyfaced assistant pointed black accusing fingers at the brakeband. Don Modesto immediately began to rattle off the French, and began to look exactly

like a Frenchman as he did so, but they didn't seem to understand him any better than they did Garde or Ben's dialect out of aboriginal Evanston. It came out eventually
through a welter of misunderstood words and much shrug-
ging and pointing that the blacksmith would have to drive
his own char into Mon'rayal to purchase new drums from
the agence Buique. "I'm sure," Lulie said as they straggled
off towards the hotel with their bags, "that when we come
back in the morning we'll find they've put horseshoes on the
Buick."

The hotel spoke English and looked clean but it smelt
dreadfully of vinegar. Lulie and Garde were ushered into a
room that had the chill of the tomb and blue and amber
glass in the windows. The halls and floors and even the
walls were plastered with gingercolored oilcloth in a variety
of dreadful patterns. Lulie gave her hair a couple of per-
functory pats in front of the spotted mirror and, as Garde
had disappeared in search of a bathroom, flashed downstairs
to find Don Modesto. The intelligent animal was waiting
for her studying the patterns in the lower hall. "It's the
linoleum museum," he said cheerfully and led her out the
back door into a little yard flagged with square gray stones
where an agreeable sheepdog wagged his tail for them and
cringed politely at their feet when she said "Bon chien."

"See he speaks much better French than the people do,"
said Lulie.

"It would be interesting to study Canuck," Jay was re-
marking in a serious tone that reminded Lulie of her father.
"It's amazing how fast languages change when people can't
read and write. It must be based on some Normandy dialect."

As if he'd known the way all along he led her through a
gate and down a path across a clear brown brook, that
looked as if it might have trout in it, into a little pocket in
an overgrown thicket of raspberry bushes under an appletree. She snatched at an apple. "Lulie they are too green
. . . collywobbles," he said smiling down at her fatherly-
indulgently. She took a small defiant bite and tossed the
apple into a crack in the wall. "Oh Lulie let's hurry," he
said reaching his arms out towards her. "I've been waiting
so long."

She pushed him away. "Don Modesto has it occurred to
you that I hardly know you?"

He looked baffled for a moment. Then he said, "But what about our trip on the Rideau Canal . . . and our travels in the Orient?"

"True true," she answered. Before she knew what she was doing she had tilted her mouth towards his and whispered, "Have you got a kiss on your face? Just a little one? . . . We are being observed," she said as she pulled herself out of his arms.

A white rooster with a very red comb was cocking an enamelled eye at them from the top of the wall. Jay shook his head ruefully. "There's very little privacy in the world," he muttered and suddenly made a boo at the rooster. The rooster flapped his wings and was gone into a great clucking of invisible hens on the other side of the wall.

"Talk to me Don Modesto . . . Don't let me go. Talk to me."

Jay started talking at random: "I'll tell you a story about Jake and his dory and now my story's begun . . . it used to make me so mad when my mother used to start that one when I was little because there really isn't any story only I did want to explain . . ." and then he began to tell her about his notion that practicing law might be made, instead of a sort of racket, a form of citizenship, like under the Roman republic, but for him — he started kicking nervously into the sod with his heel — but for him it wasn't an end but a means, a clumsy procrastinating deceitful old means of exploring the country and the people . . . the world in fact . . . Hell, part of the time I always wanted to be an explorer . . . He laughed. "And now my story's done."

"Why Jay I thought you were going to tell me about your prospects," she said teasingly. "I thought it was right formal of you. I thought it was the Frenchman coming out."

"Two thousand dollars in the bank and a vague future with a firm of Jewish attorneys in New York who want a gentile name on their letterhead even if it is wop. I don't say that meanly because Larry Raisen is a hell of a nice fellow and I'm very fond of him. Gosh Lulie the honest truth is that I've been singularly successful at arranging myself an unprofitable career . . . and I can't get away with a goddamn thing. Everything I do or say gets people

sore . . . I have friends who do and say much more unpopular things and everybody thinks they are wonderful
. . . A mighty poor match for the season's petite débutante
if you ask me."

"I can't get away with anything either . . . Isn't it awful? But I've got a little nestegg saved up from the great
Hugh Swanson's and I'm like a dog Jay . . . I don't care
where my next meal's coming from . . . Maybe it's because we're such awful orphans."

"An awful pair of orphans."

When he bent over to kiss her again and she felt his
thighs hard against her thighs and his tongue groping between her lips she felt as if she were going to faint and
broke away roughly and ran back to the hotel and up to
her dim room and lay down on the lumpy bed and told
Garde, whom she found ruining her eyes reading a book
in the weird light that came through the colored glass, that
she had a headache and didn't want any supper and that
maybe she was getting the curse.

Next morning pacing up and down the street without
Lulie Jay thought he would lose his mind waiting. The
blacksmith had come back with the parts but he was slow
as cold molasses at his work. At breakfast Garde said Lulie
had stayed in bed reading. Afterwards Jay roamed around
the little town with Hildegarde, reading the signs and the
notices at the post office and looking in the grocerystore
window, and exchanging curious glances for the curious
glances of the inhabitants.

"I feel as if we'd lived here a year," Jay was saying to
Garde when they caught sight of Ben doing semaphore signals, which of course they didn't understand, from the end
of the alley. They started off at a run and found that the
car was ready and that the brakes worked and Lulie was
up and dressed. Without stopping for the picnic lunch
they'd been planning to order at the hotel they went off
up the road, happy to be rolling again, with Ben at the
wheel driving smoothly and fast. Lulie sat back in her
corner looking pale and quiet and after a while went to
sleep. The road climbed out of the broad green valley and
hills began to swell up ahead of them under a bristle of
woodlands and there were more elms along the fences and

Garde said the country was beginning to get that Vermont look and Lulie woke up and began to chirp and squeak about the scenery.

In the last large town before the border there was some argument about whether to try to smuggle in any whisky. Jay kept his mouth shut. Ben was against it but the girls won the day saying they'd look too silly arriving at the Brooks's emptyhanded. They bought four pints of aged old bourbon and Lulie and Garde took the bag along when they disappeared to find a lady's room and when they came back they had various packages from the drugstore but the four pints were nowhere to be seen.

"You boys just act like the three monkeys," Lulie said as they drove out of town.

"See no evil, hear no evil, speak no evil," added Garde in a schoolteachery tone.

When they reached the border station and a squarefaced young customs officer began rummaging in the car, Jay got in such a cold sweat he felt everybody would notice and had to do a lot of studying of the road map to keep from fidgeting. It would be just his luck to be caught and probably jailed and while he was in jail Lulie would take up with somebody else and then oh God he really wouldn't have anything to live for. Meanwhile inside the customs office Lulie and Garde were cheerfully pulling out their purchases and asking the customs people if they really thought that woolen material was worth what they'd paid for it and by the time they drove away the old customs man and the young customs man were grinning and kidding and couldn't look at anything but Lulie.

"Weren't they nice?" she said when they stopped at a fork and chose the road through the lakes. "My it's nice to get home again after our travels in the old world. Things look more exciting on our side of the border. Even the trees look fresher."

"Maybe it's that they are nearer the sea," hazarded Jay.

"I know everything's perfectly awful in this country, with prohibition and Teapot Dome and everything," said Lulie, "but it's more fun."

That last day's ride was a long day's ride. There were stretches of gravelled road where they had to go slow. They had a flat tire and at noon they couldn't find any place to eat. They lost the road a couple of times and in the after-

noon it came on to rain and then towards evening they hit
fog. "We'll run into the ocean and get drowned and I'll
never see it," Lulie started pretending to whimper. At the
turn of the road where the dim blurred shapes of firtrees
loomed through the headlights Jay, who was driving at
the time, pulled to the side and stopped the car suddenly.
"A thousand pardons," he said when there was a shriek
of brakes from the car behind and two muffled headlights
veered past them and blundered off up the road. "Smell
it?" asked Jay. They all leaned out of the windows and
sniffed.

"Of course," cried Lulie. "I never smelt it but I know
what it is."

"It's saltmarshes and mudflats and seaweed on rocks and
salt water."

"He's descended from Christopher Columbus. Of course
he can smell it, but I can smell it too."

"Not that I know of," said Jay, "but there is a streak
of the salt in the rascally Genoese."

"That's what I'm telling everybody," cried Lulie. "The
fog is saturated with Atlantic Ocean . . . Oh Lord, we're
far from Woodlawn Park."

"This is the place to have a drink," said Garde, "or
maybe we shouldn't."

"Of course we should," said Lulie. "That's what Xeno-
phon did when he saw the sea. He had a drink of fine
old smugglers' whiskey."

She was fumbling in a square parcel on the floor at her
feet.

"Where did you hide it Loo?" asked Ben.

"That would be telling," said Lulie and Garde in chorus.
"When the young nicelooking one looked in the package
he blushed," said Lulie. They passed the pint around and
each took a swig. "Thalassa," cried Lulie for a toast.
"Here's to Aphrodite's girdle," muttered Jay not very loud
and started the car with a grinding of the gears back into
the road. After that they took turns every half hour picking their way down winding roads in the fog until from
the top of a hill they heard a foghorn in the distance. The
wind in their faces was wet off the sea. It was late and
they were very hungry and their eyes were popping out of
their heads from staring through the fog by the time they
entered the hilly town full of dripping elms and tall stately

houses barely visible behind the haloes of the streetlamps.

They cruised sleepily up and down blurred streets and asked the way to the Brooks's house in a drugstore and at last at a corner under elms Garde climbed out and crossed a wet lawn. They could see her tapping on a lighted window. Josie and Dabney and a great group of people young and old in flannels and summer dresses streamed out of a handsome white doorway framed with Ionic columns and ushered them into the whitepanelled drawingroom and Dabney poured them drinks and it was all awfully pleasant. Everybody was talking at once making plans for the wedding that Jay had thought was a secret, and there was a telegram on the tiptop table from the elder Willards saying they were arriving tomorrow on the Bar Harbor express and that they felt Lulie was like their own daughter and the elder Brookses and the younger Brookses were all gabbling happily about flowers and wedding dresses and decorations and arguing about whether they'd have the ceremony in the drawingroom or the garden and who ought to be best man and who was going to give the bride away and it was midnight before Dabney Brooks escorted Jay and his suitcase around to the inn where they'd engaged him a room. All evening he hadn't had a chance to say two words to Lulie.

Jay was still dazed from meeting all these new people and redeyed from the long drive through the fog when he woke up in the chintzhung white inn room. The first thing he noticed was the salt breeze off the sea flapping the curtains in the window. While he was shaving he found himself humming

> One more river to Jordan,
> Just one more river to cross.

It cheered him up but not enough. Eating breakfast by himself in the dispiriting inn diningroom he felt like crying from disappointment. Too keep the top of his head from blowing off entirely he made a list in his notebook of the things he had to do.

> Town Hall: Marriage license
> Used car dealer; buy car
> Clergyman?

> *Introduction to bank.*
> *Cottage somewhere. Swimming, boat, canoe?*
> *Rent typewriter*
> *Driver's license*
> *Suit. White flannel pants?*

The gray coffee had a strange flavor that he imagined must be of Old Dutch Cleanser. The idea amused him sufficiently so that he was able to down one more swallow of it just to see before going out to explore the town. The fog had lifted but the sky was gray and a chill easterly wind was blowing. Out of the corner of his eye he caught sight of the Brooks house under the elms with its small white columns and its green shutters and of garden hats and light summer dresses stirring behind the lilac hedge but he shied off from it and headed down the street to the harbor. It was the prettiest little seacaptain's town imaginable with white Eighteen Twelve houses and immense elms and old wharves and sailboats on the bay which, between the greenpointed islands was ruffled into scalloped waves like in the picture of the Florentine Aphrodite rising shellborne from the sea. When he finally screwed himself up to the pitch of presenting himself at the Brooks house he approached it by a side street from the rear. Hildegarde, coming down the brick path with a teasing smile on her face and a cup of coffee in her hand, found him skulking among the phlox at the end of the garden. "Why Jay what on earth's the matter?"

"Hildegarde please send Lulie out. I've got to talk to her."

"Why don't you come in and have a cup of coffee? The Brookses all think you're wonderful."

"There are all these damn details we have to thrash out," Jay muttered sulkily.

"Anyway you're coming to lunch, Mother and Dad'll be here by then."

Lulie in a yellow dress he hadn't seen before came towards him down the garden path. Her face looked small and thin and worried under a broadbrimmed straw hat.

"Don't tell me, don't tell me," she called. "Garde said you looked grim. It's the real Mrs. Pignatelli has turned up with the children to forbid the banns."

Jay burst out laughing. "You're the real one Lulie."

"Then let's go swimming."

"Water looks kind of cold."

"Of course it will turn us to stone but no matter . . . Get your suit. I've got the key to the bathhouse."

"But Lulie first I've got to find the town clerk. I went just now but he wasn't in his office, and then we ought to buy a car, and I've got to get me a decent suit."

They were walking in step down the street towards the courthouse. They were slipping gently down the hill in the sunlight. Suddenly it all seemed so easy.

"If I act a little crazy it's just to keep from going crazy," explained Lulie in a low practical voice. "We didn't plan the excursion but now that it's started we might as well enjoy the hayride," she went on recklessly. She gave one of her little shrieks. "Neither one of us can back out now, Mrs. Adams is baking the cake and the Brookses have rented us the cutest little red house at thirty a month. Josie and Garde drove me out there before breakfast. It hasn't any plumbing, but it's on a little point of land that's almost an island and we heard a seal bark in the cove."

"It's not too near?"

"No, it's twenty miles away, across the bay."

She went on chattering all the time they were walking up the steps to the town clerk's office. Jay made his application and it cost him two dollars. At the garage the Brookses had recommended they found an old Chrysler roadster and Jay said let's take it, like he was buying a toothbrush. While they trotted around checking off the items the silvery sun was very gradually breaking through the clouds. "The Brookses say it's a dry easterly," Lulie explained. "Isn't New England lovely," she said breathless when they were walking back up the hill for their suits. "It's all like pictures. Where I come from people haven't lived there long enough to make it up into pictures yet . . . Where do you come from Jay?"

"God I wish I knew . . . I start from right here. I feel like my grandfather the first day he landed."

"Where did he land?"

"I don't know; Charleston I think."

"Bet it seemed a wilderness, an untidy wilderness."

"Still is. But of this wilderness we must carve our home."

"Sounds like a sampler," she panted as she shot away from him, through the Ionic doorway into the house.

Thank God nobody at the Brooks's wanted to go swimming; too freezing cold, they said. As he tore off his clothes Jay suddenly felt he was his own self again instead of the grim automaton who had waked up in that room at the inn. The weathered boards of the dock of the little ramshackle yacht club were warm under his bare feet, the water was green over brown. They both plunged in helter-skelter. "I've been in colder at the lake," Lulie gasped in a strangling voice. "I dare you to swim around that stake." As they swam icy collars formed round their necks. Their fingers turned to glass. When they climbed out the blood was boiling under the icy skins. "Wasn't it inconsiderate of nature not to give us fur?" Lulie panted as she jumped up and down on the end of the wharf. There was nobody in sight except a few men in dories and a motorboat far out in the harbor. "I like you this way." Jay grabbed her all cold and wet into his arms. Her mouth tasted salty. She let him kiss her and kiss her. At last she ducked out from under his arm. "Let's get dressed now," she said. "Don Modesto, at our house in the wilderness this morning, I really did hear a seal bark."

> *One more river to Jordan*
> *One more river to cross,*

he kept humming inside his head during the cocktails and the chatter and Mrs. Willard's stale lavender sweetness and Jeff Willard's smokingcar kidding and the lobsters for lunch and the uproar and the laughter over coffeecups in the garden, and somehow he got through the afternoon and the dinner the Willards gave them in a restaurant overlooking the river's mouth, and the sailing party next day and the picnic under a canopy of hovering gulls on the rocks rough as elephants' hide of the island where the old lighthouse was, and teaparties, and cocktailparties arranged by pleasantvoiced ladies in pleasant parlors of old sea-captains' houses, and the next day and the next. Then Ben appeared that morning while Jay was eating his glum breakfast at the inn over a copy of yesterday's *New York Times*. "As the bride's only male relative, Zeke being non compos due to absence, I feel it my duty Mr. Pignatelli to ask you, have you provided yourself with a ring?" Jay got red in the face and they both laughed like they'd burst. "Lord I never thought of it . . . In fact we neglected to get engaged."

"Too late now," said Ben keeping up his mockserious manner. "Let bygones be bygones but the ring is . . ."

"Of the essence as the lawyers say," Jay finished the sentence.

They snatched up Lulie with the roadster all flustered and protesting that she wouldn't have time to dress and rushed her downtown to the jeweller's to pick out a ring and Jay went back to the inn to get into his white flannel pants and to check and recheck on the license and the envelope containing the ten dollar gold certificate for the minister which he'd put in the inside pocket of his blue serge jacket. Finally he borrowed a safety pin from the chirping so excited gray spinster at the desk and pinned them in. When he started up the street he missed the ring. He searched in every pocket, broke out in a sweat and at last found it hung on his watch chain.

The Unitarian minister with the white scraggly vandyke was already there and everything went off faster than anyone could have expected. The minister didn't read the words as well as Jay had hoped and he hardly dared look at Lulie, but right away it was over and Jeff Willard was making a champagne cork pop and roaring, "A royal salute!" and Mrs. Willard was crying and Hildegarde's and even Ben's eyes looked very wet, and everybody was kissing Lulie and Dabney was slapping him on the back.

The champagne helped them through the breakfast that lasted much too long. Jay never knew what he ate.

The afternoon turned hot and Jay and Ben got horribly sweaty fitting the awkward assortment of suitcases into the rumbleseat of the battered green roadster.

Then all at once there was a silence around them and he was rolling slowly along the road above the blue bay so full of islands with blunt spruces and pointed firs, looking at the dark line of the ocean beyond, and Lulie was beside him. They were sitting in the sun. There weren't any other cars on the road. They were alone in the green world.

"Thank God that's over . . . Pleasure can be a nightmare sometimes," Jay said.

"I just love them all and they loved doing it for us but they don't know about us." She let her head drop against his shoulder.

"What about us?" Jay said. He pulled over and stopped the car at the edge of the road.

"Let's not hurry," Lulie said.

He put his arm round her and she snuggled up against him and they sat sniffing the warm smell of sweetfern, looking out over the shining blueberries through spruces and firs and balsams at the sea. She yawned. "I'm sleepy," she whispered. "Have you ever thought you'd like to live forever?"

"I can't say that I have."

"Let's," she whispered.

When he walked out of the house on the first morning the sky was already glowing. The grass drenched his feet. A cricket chirped among the logs under the woodshed when he leaned to gather an armful of sticks. He lit a strip of birchbark with a match and started a fire in the old cast-iron range. He stood in his bare feet on the old oak boards of the kitchen listening to the growing crackle of the kindling and fed on wood till the stovepipe roared just a little. When he partclosed the damper the heat warmed him. When he walked again through the long wet grass to the well the light was brighter. Birds stirred in the appletree. He drew a bucket of water and carried it back into the kitchen. He put on the coffeepot, filled the kettle for hot water, squeezed out two oranges and set some slices of bread to toast on the hot iron. Brightness was filling the little hall when she came out of the bedroom. They stood side by side on the granite step in the soaring brightness. In front of them were the seaweedy rocks of the cove and the spruces and the pointed firs and the dark bay and islands and the line of the ocean heaving with light. The waves breathed in the cove. "Husband," she said "Wife," he said. The words made them bashful. They clung together against their bashfulness. "Today we begin," he said, "to make . . ." "This wilderness our home," she said. The risen sun over the ocean shone in their faces.

Sendoff

Musing midnight and the century's decline
man walks with dog,
shuffling the roadside gravel where sometimes we used
to find among the quartzy riverpebbles,
spent arrowheads of the Powhatans.

Overcast blots the stars. Not even a glimpse of
impudent Echo, America's toy balloon the radio man said
go out and see. The fall's too late for lightningbugs, only
a chill hint here and there of a glowworm in the wet grass.
The dog trots eager, sniffing the night, proud of her
man's steps behind. The man,
shamed drags beaten strides, drained of every thought
but hatred
of the tinpot pharaohs whose coarse imprecations
the impartial transistors have been dinning in his ears.
Evil is indivisible. By hate they rose to flashbulb glory and
the roar of cowed multitudes, police sirens shrieking how
great the leader, how little the led: the abject mike ever
waiting to receive
the foul discharge of their power to kill. The lie
squared, the lie cubed, the lie to the power of x deals death
like a tornado. By hate they live. By hate we'll see them
die. We've seen them die before. The hate remains
to choke out good, to strangle the still small private
voice that is God's spark in man. Man drowns in his own
scum.
These nights are dark.

In the light of the carriagelamps on the brick steps
of the sleeping house back home the man pauses for a last

breath of the outdoor air; the dog's nose nuzzles his hand.
She bows, wriggles, cavorts, goes belly up, eyes rolling in
frantic appreciation:

walker on hindlegs, hurler of sticks, foodgiver, builder
of shelter, toolmaker, creation's lord, initiator, master of
Yes and No;

wagging dog-Shakespeare her tail declaims:
Oh paragon of animals.